Fluff 2

Fluff 2

RavensDagger

Podium

Podium

Fluff 2

Stress

Part of being a good mother was dealing with the constant concern that her child wasn't as safe, comfortable, and happy as she could be.

Claire hoped that she was a good mother. Emily, her only daughter, was a strange but kind girl. She had her share of issues, her nearly crippling social anxiety the foremost of those, but she was still a good girl, and Claire was so proud of her daughter.

When Emily had, with all the meekness of a mouse facing a cat, declared that she would attend college and move out of the house, Claire had never been prouder.

Proud, but worried.

Emily was a wonderful girl, but she had a lot of difficulty with more . . . social things. She stuttered, she had a hard time meeting people's eyes when she spoke, and before every interaction she needed to psych herself up. Her Emily wasn't as ready to face the world as some other young ladies her age.

Claire gave even odds that college would either teach Emily to open up a little, or her poor daughter would rush back home. She was hoping for the best. Emily needed to spread her wings, to grow up into the beautiful young woman she was.

The past weeks, with Emily at school, had been awful. Claire waited for the phone to ring, for the bad news to come pouring in. As time went on and no call came, she started to hope and fear in equal measure.

In the end, it was her husband who practically kicked her out of the house and told her to go check on Emily. The big softy was just as worried as she was, though he wouldn't ever say so aloud.

She arrived at her daughter's room. The dormitory building was nice and clean, with decent security. It was about as safe as a place filled with young adults could be. Claire adjusted her blouse and skirt, then straightened her back and knocked. It was no mystery where her daughter got some of her shyness; Claire had had to work hard to overcome some of her own anxiety.

There was a shuffle on the other side of the door, and Claire thought she heard voices. Was Emily watching something?

The door opened a crack, and Claire felt some of the tension lifting from her shoulders. Emily was there, safe and sound, and . . . with very obvious panic on her face.

The door slammed shut.

"Emily, sweetie?" Claire asked. Was something wrong? Claire listened, but the chatter on the other side died down. Not a show then. Was Emily entertaining guests? Claire felt some blood rushing to her cheeks. Oh my. "Um . . . if you're really busy, I can come back? Give you time to clean up or . . . sweetie, are you with a boy? I hope you're wearing protection."

More mutters. Definitely more than one person. They sounded feminine.

Claire swallowed, uncertain what to think anymore.

She decided not to jump to any more conclusions. That sort of thing only led to silly misunderstandings and fights. She would wait until Emily explained things and then she'd figure things out from there.

On that note, she reached up and knocked on the door again. "Sweetie? I'm sorry, but I did call. You haven't been answering your phone."

There was a long moment of silence, then the door opened. Emily looked at Claire, failed to meet her eyes, then spoke quickly. "Mom. Give me two minutes."

"Sweetie?"

Her daughter's mouth opened and shut as she searched for words. "I'm naked," she settled on.

Claire looked down. Emily was in a nice sweater-vest over a blouse, and she wore a skirt that Claire would have found far too long back when she was Emily's own age. "Okay?"

This time the door didn't slam shut.

Claire leaned closer and tried to listen in on what was happening on the other side. She couldn't make out much, just indistinct voices murmuring to each other. The soundproofing was pretty decent.

The door opened yet again, and Emily's hand shot out to grab her mom's. Claire was gently tugged into the room and the door was pressed closed behind her. "Emily?" Claire asked.

Emily pressed into her, arms wrapping around Claire's waist and her head coming down to nestle on her shoulders. Claire sighed. This was a little more familiar. Emily was never the most touchy-feely girl, but she didn't refuse hugs from her parents. Not unless they were in public, of course.

Claire hugged back as best she could. She wanted to enjoy the hug, but she couldn't help but notice that her daughter's room currently looked like a day care. "It's good to see you, sweetie," she said as she dropped her purse. "But who are all these girls?"

She felt Emily tensing up. "Mom, we need to talk."

"I can imagine," Claire said as Emily broke the hug. She decided to start with things that were a little bit easier. "You need to tell me how you've been? How are classes? Did you make any friends? Why do you have five children in your room? That last one especially."

"Right, right. You might want to sit down for this," Emily said.

Claire placed a hand on her hip and raised an eyebrow as she looked up to Emily . . . since when was her daughter taller than her? Probably she had been for a while, but Emily's constant hunch hid some of her height. "I might not be a spring chicken, but I can still take a surprise or two."

Emily licked her lips. "Right," she repeated again. "Like ripping a Band-Aid then. I'm . . . a Hero. More or less."

A million confused thoughts raced across Claire's mind. She wasn't sure what to expect, but that wasn't it. "Pardon?"

Emily laced her fingers over her stomach and focused on the ground. "You remember Power Day, uh, about a week ago?"

"Yes?" Claire said. It was hard to forget. It was shortly after Emily had arrived at the college, and the news was rattling on about the big day while Claire and her husband worried about Emily.

"Well, I got a power. I can make, um, little sisters for myself. Sorta." Emily gestured to the girls, who were all smiling. "These are my summons? I can't unsummon them or anything. They all have their own powers too."

Claire looked at the girls. They were cute, in a sort of rascally pest way. They were also very obviously trying to be on their best behavior. They were her daughter's . . . her superpowered daughter's power.

"Can I sit on the bed?" Claire asked. She stumbled toward the bed, then paused. "Or would you rather I use the chair?" Technically this was Emily's place, so it was only polite to ask.

One of the girls, the shorter one, with the chubby cheeks and a shirt that read BEAR in large blocky letters, raced over to Emily's chair and rolled it closer. "There you go, uh—" She glanced over to Emily. "Hey, Boss, what do we call the old lady?"

Claire wasn't sure how to feel. Insulted? At the same time, the girl was kind of endearing, in a clumsy way.

"Anything but 'old lady,' you dumb bear," another one of the girls said. She was the tallest of the lot, though not by much. A lankier, skinny girl, with sharp features and a pair of large glasses perched on the tip of her nose. Her eyes were large and very serious as she turned to Claire. "Hello, Grandmother," she said.

Claire looked up to Emily. "Emily, you know how I always wanted to have grandkids one day? I was expecting maybe one. Two at most. This is considerably more than that."

"It's okay," three of the girls said at exactly the same time. The strange stereo effect sent a shiver down Claire's spine. The girls were all entirely identical, now that she looked. It wasn't just their clothes, their faces were all the same. "You can count all three of me as one."

Emily rubbed her face, and for a moment Claire almost didn't recognize her daughter. The shyness was gone, the insecurity was buried. Instead, there was just frustration, embarrassment, and another emotion that Claire couldn't quite pin down.

"So I should probably introduce everyone. Mom, this is Teddy." Emily gestured to the girl with the bear shirt. "She can turn into a bear. She won't demonstrate that here because it's against the rules."

"I'm real soft," Teddy said. "Way more soft than any of the others when I'm a bear. I bet you'd like petting me just as much as the Boss does."

"The Boss?" Claire asked. She decided that just sitting back and asking questions was probably the best thing to do.

"That's Big Sister Emily's Hero-slash-Villain name," the taller, more serious girl said.

"Villain?" Claire asked.

She hadn't really noticed that sinking feeling in her gut before. It was too confusing and mixed in with a host of other feelings. Now the sinking was replaced by a sheer drop.

"Don't worry, Best Mom," the three girls said at the same time. "We wouldn't Villain you."

"Emily?" Claire tried to smile, but it felt brittle at the edges.

"Hey, Boss," Teddy asked, "does your mom need to poop?"

"No, Teddy, my mom doesn't need to poop," Emily said. She patted Teddy's head absently. It was a strange gesture. "Okay, Mom, where do you want me to start?"

"I think that maybe you should start from the top?"

Emily nodded. "So, it all began on my first day here . . ."

CHAPTER ONE

The Talk

There were very, very few things Emily wanted to do less than explain to her mom how she had—through no fault of her own—become a Villain.

Worse still, she then had to explain how she had acted and possibly earned just a little bit of that title.

The problem was, of course, that Emily wasn't in the habit of lying to her parents, and even if she was, she had five little sets of eyes paying attention to her as she related an abridged version of the adventures she'd had over the past couple of weeks. Teaching her little sisters that it was okay to lie would be . . . a catastrophically bad idea.

Her mom sat in Emily's chair, hands on the armrests and purse on her lap. She was staring somewhere past Emily's shoulder, deep in thought. She had been listening, making all the right sounds, and even asking for some clarification, but so far she hadn't really said much.

It was somewhat comforting. When Emily had a rough day at school, she had often returned home to rant to her mom about it. Her reaction had often been similar then, too. "So?" Emily asked.

"Give me a moment, sweetie, I'm processing." Her mom took a deep breath, then let it all out in a long whoosh. "You know, when I came here, I was making up all sorts of terrible scenarios in my head. Oh, and some not-so-terrible ones too. But this? This is all rather unexpected."

Emily twiddled her fingers together. She wanted to sit down and maybe hide under her blankets, but that would have been far too awkward. So, instead, she just stood in the middle of her room while her little sisters watched from her bed and from where they sat on the floor. "I'm sorry."

Her mom bent down, placed her purse on the floor, then stood up and pulled Emily into a tight hug. "Don't be sorry," she whispered. "In fact, you have nothing to apologize for. You did your best with a situation that you were very much not ready for."

"Thanks, Mom," Emily said.

"Mom's right," Athena said. "You did good work, Big Sis."

Emily felt her mother stiffening just a smidge as Athena spoke up.

They broke the hug—after her mom gave her a final reassuring squeeze—then it was time to address the elephants in the room. "Okay. Clearly, things have been difficult, but you've made the best of it. Now . . . well, now the question remains: what do you intend to do?"

"I was hoping not much," Emily said. "I have those files from Cement, I'll look over them and see if there's anything urgent there, but if there isn't, then I think the best thing to do now would be to lie low and try not to attract any attention."

A slow nod was her mother's reply. "That's a nice plan, sweetie. How realistic is it?"

"Realistic?" Emily asked.

She got a gesture to her sisters in response. "These five seem quite active, more so than you were at their age, I think, and even if you were quiet, you were a handful sometimes. Not to mention this place is far too small for six people to be living in it. Then there's the money issue. Food and clothes aren't free. And they need an education."

"Right," Emily said past the sinking feeling in her gut. "I can find work, maybe?"

"I think you're going to need more than just a part-time job, sweetie. Kids are expensive."

"We could brainstorm ideas on how to make more money," Athena suggested.

Emily spun around, but she was too slow to put the idea down; the others were already tossing out ideas.

"Getting enough money to live a comfortable life should be every-one's responsibility," Teddy said. "So we'll just take everyone's money, then redistribute it evenly."

"We can steal stuff," Trinity said. Three racoon-eared heads nodded all at once. "Break into people's homes, like that one time, and just take all their stuff."

"I bet I could make someone so afraid of money that they'd just give all of theirs to us," Athena said.

"No," Emily said. "Just . . . no. We'll find a more honest way to make money." She ignored the pouting in favor of keeping her sanity.

"Money would be a solution, yes, but it's not the biggest concern." Emily's mom started to pace the room. It was a familiar mannerism, but her mother had a way to make it look far more graceful. "We need to find proper lodging, and a secure source of income, then we can take care of the rest. How are your classes going?"

"Ah, well so far? I've been doing all my homework, and the tests aren't for a while. We're still doing introductory things," Emily said.

"Good, good. I know how excited you were to start learning, I wouldn't want that dream to fall apart over this."

"Thanks, Mom."

Emily's mom smiled. "No problem. Now, since I didn't expect to drive all the way back home tonight, I booked a place at a B and B. I can do a little bit of babysitting for the next couple of days."

"That's . . . nice," Emily said. "But two days isn't a very long time to figure things out."

"It's enough time to make an educated choice," Claire replied. "You don't have to face all this alone. Didn't you mention doing a training thing with the Heroes? I'm certain they would listen to your story and that they could help."

Emily cringed in response.

In reality, it was a logical and even smart choice to make. The Heroes were, ostensibly, good guys. They'd offer Emily some help if she approached them. She wasn't sure, but she had the impression that her power was very strong. Or at least very versatile. She basically had five weaker powers in the form of her sisters. The PR potential there was also noteworthy. Her sisters might have been little brats, but they were cute brats.

There were a lot of Hero-themed products out there. Emily could just imagine someone putting Teddy's face on something like dog-grooming products, or using Athena to sell glasses or Trinity to sell . . . trash bags? She shook her head.

The problem was that she didn't trust the Heroes. That, and for all the help they'd offer her, they'd ask things in return.

"I'll figure something out," Emily said.

She wasn't entirely out of resources herself. She had her sisters, she had information of questionable value from the town's last resident Villain, she had a few contacts in the world of Supers and Masks.

Better yet, she felt increasingly confident in her own ability to figure things out. That wasn't to say she was that confident, but it was a lot more than when she'd started out.

"If you can babysit them all for just a day or two," Emily said, "then I'll do my best to find a way to take care of everything, I promise."

Her mom eyed her carefully, then the woman's eyes watered and she pulled Emily into yet another hug. "Oh, my baby's growing up so fast."

"Hey!" Teddy said. "The Boss ain't a baby."

"She said 'my baby,' you idiot," Athena said.

"Yeah, so? Boss don't belong to her, neither."

Emily sighed. "Girls, please don't insult my mom. In fact, just listen to her as if she was me, okay?"

It took a bit, but she got three (technically five) affirmatives from the girls. "So what do we call the Boss's mom?" Teddy asked.

"Grandmom?" Athena asked.

"You're not my daughters," Emily pointed out as quickly as she could.

Her mom chuckled. "No, I don't think I'm quite old enough to be a grandma, not yet. Please."

"Uh, how about the GrandBoss, then?" Athena asked.

"That's a good Villain name," Trinity said.

"Let's not give my mom a Villain name, please," Emily said.

Teddy shook her head and pointed—rather rudely—right at Emily's mom. "She's your mom, which makes her important, and you're, like, the best Villain around, so she has to be at least a bit secretly Villainous."

"Teddy, my mom's not Villainous," Emily said.

"Well, I have had a few less-than-charitable thoughts before."

"Mom!"

"If the Boss is our sister," Athena said. "Then that makes the Boss's mom our mom, too."

"I . . . I don't know how I feel about that," Emily said.

Teddy eyed her. "But you said that sharing between sisters was important."

"I don't think this is entirely the same."

Her mom chuckled, then patted Teddy on the head. The bear girl leaned into the touch. "I don't mind being called Mom. I have been called worse before. Besides, they aren't entirely wrong. If they are your sisters, then I suppose I'd be something like a stepmom, at most."

"Step-Boss," Teddy said. There was a definitive note in the word, as if she'd just given the answer to an obvious question.

Emily closed her eyes. The day had far, far too many ups and downs for her to deal with, and it was far from over.

CHAPTER TWO

A Much Needed Break

"Are you sure?" Emily asked.

It wasn't the first time she asked.

In fact, she was quite certain it wasn't going to be the last time she asked the same question.

Her mom rolled her eyes. "Emily, I know you. I think in some ways, I might know you better than you yourself do. I can tell when you're fraying at the edges. You have that same look in your eyes as when your father and I drag you to a party and you've been forced to socialize for more than an hour."

Emily frowned. "I'm fine."

She received another hug. It felt a little condescending, but she accepted it all the same. "Sure you are, sweetie. And you'll be a lot more fine with a couple of hours of time spent alone to think and decompress."

Emily fidgeted. "You'll keep in touch?"

Her mom nodded. "I have my phone, you know my number. I'll send you a picture once we've arrived."

Emily nodded, then she turned to her sisters and tried to adopt as serious a look as she could manage. "And you three will behave?" she asked.

Five heads nodded. "We'll be good," Teddy said. "We're not gonna mess with Step-Boss. We'll do exactly as she says."

"Please, sweetie, just call me Claire."

"Sure thing, Step-Boss," Teddy said.

Emily pointed to Teddy. "No turning into a bear unless it's super-superurgent and you'd best believe that you'll have to explain it to me if you do."

Teddy's head bobbed up and down.

Emily turned her finger toward Athena. "No making people paranoid for fun. And don't tease your sisters too much. Just because you're the most well-behaved doesn't mean you can get away with more."

"Yes, Big Sis," Athena said.

Emily pointed to Trinity, to all three of her bodies. "And you. No dumpster diving."

Trinity squawked in protest from three mouths at once.

"None," Emily said. "Not even a trash bin on the way over."

Her mom's laughter cut her off short. "I never thought I'd see you being so bossy," she said. "It suits you. Now, don't worry, I can manage a few kids. It's just a quick run for ice cream. I'm sure we'll be fine."

"Please, stop jinxing it," Emily said.

She got another hug, then five more as she knelt down and hugged each sister as they moved out of her room.

The door closed with a click, and suddenly Emily found herself in her room, alone.

She turned, taking in the room. It was a little messy. Something impossible to remedy when there were so many little mess-makers stuffed in such a small place, but otherwise it was the same room she'd started her school year in. It was just . . . quieter.

Emily frowned, then crossed her arms. She refused to miss her sisters after less than a minute had passed. Not after an entire life of trying to avoid people wherever she could.

Instead of wallowing in contrarian and bizarre feelings, she moved over to her desk and pulled it open. The papers they had acquired from Cement were all there, in a neat stack under a few crayon drawings on looseleaf. She didn't bother hiding the papers, not when she couldn't think of a good place to hide anything.

She pulled her chair closer to her desk, fished out a fresh notebook from her backpack, clicked the tip of a pen out, then leaned forward to study.

In reality, she figured that the likelihood of the papers having an answer to her problems was slim, but that didn't mean chances for that were nonexistent. Besides, she could let her problems percolate in the back of her mind as she studied.

The papers, unfortunately, weren't designed by a teacher who intended to teach anyone. They weren't extracted from a textbook, either. They were a semiorganized pile of reports, maps, printouts from various websites, and printed pages.

She gave up on reading them all of five pages in, then started to work on cataloging them instead.

Her pen flew across her notebook as she started to break everything down into smaller chunks. First, she put a number on the top of each page. That would be their name. Once she had an idea of the broad category they fit in, she could add a letter designation to that.

Her desk was soon split into two dozen little piles, with a few more on the floor next to her when she ran out of space.

"This is a mess," Emily concluded. But it was becoming a comprehensible sort of mess.

There wasn't a manifesto in the papers, nor an easy explanation for what she had. Instead, it was the disjointed evidence of the creation of . . . of what she was realizing was a criminal organization.

Some of the papers were blackmail material. Evidence that different people had committed a crime of some sort or had cheated on a spouse. Most of the evidence of that nature was found in accounting reports with highlighted sections. They were from a few companies set in the city.

Most of the website pages were listings for buildings that were for sale. One of them was the place she had raided with her sisters. Hideouts? Safe houses? She flipped her notebook forward and made a list of the addresses. She could visit them, see if any were lived in.

The reports she had almost all ended with an H at the very bottom, one that looked a little bit like a crude drawing of a house.

Homie. The Villain that she and Teddy had captured with Melaton's help.

She skimmed through the reports. Mostly they named shops and stores across the city that had had issues with smaller gangs, then they detailed how those gangs had been pushed away. There were also "collection" reports, with donation sums next to them. They didn't amount to too much individually, but altogether was another story. Cement had been raking in tens of thousands of dollars a month in protection money.

He also ran a pair of little businesses. Entirely innocent, from what she could tell. Innocent except for the way they turned those donations into taxed revenue.

All in all, the collection racket was barely any more than what they were making from selling cheap pizza to hungry college kids.

Emily was only halfway through the pages and her hand was already cramping up.

She leaned back in her chair and folded up her legs under her. It was a lot of disjointed information to try to piece together.

To be fair, it wouldn't have made sense for Cement to have everything labeled clearly. It was his business, and these were his notes. He didn't need to explain his operations to himself.

She was struck by how small it all was. Complicated, certainly, but still very small. A few tiny scuffles with other gangs, a few reports of known thieves getting bruised up. A few little rackets run by a few little groups. The city probably never noticed any of it.

Emily had to reconsider what she knew about Cement. She had originally assessed the older Villain to be little more than a passing threat, but now she started to see that she had been underestimating him.

It was a scary thought to have.

Her phone buzzed, and Emily almost jumped out of her skin.

She was getting too used to constant noise, so that now she was spooked by silence.

Grabbing her phone, she opened it to find a few messages from her mom. Pictures of the girls all sitting around a table, with ice cream cones in their hands, and plenty of ice cream on their faces and clothes, too.

It looked like they were having fun.

She smiled, then sent a quick reply to her mom before glancing back at all the papers. If she didn't figure something out, that fun might soon evaporate.

Feeling a little more resolute than usual, Emily picked up her notebook and flipped back a few pages. Cement ran a couple of businesses. Honest ones, as far as she could tell, at least when it came to anything but their accounting.

With him gone, who was running those?

And then the people paying into the protection racket he had going, how would they react to Cement being gone? Would it be favorable?

Two leads to follow.

Emily nodded to herself as she made note of some addresses.

She had classes tomorrow afternoon, but the morning was free. That would give her plenty of time to investigate.

If the people who were now freed of Cement's protection racket were generous, maybe that would be the first honest bit of money she'd make in a while. And if the businesses could use some help, maybe that could be a good source of income too.

It was something.

CHAPTER THREE

Hyperactivity

And then we asked if we could have those sprinkles, and Step-Boss said yes, so we all got sprinkles, and they were so good!" Teddy said.

Athena was nodding next to her. "And Step-Boss asked me how I was doing, and I said okay, and she said that if I ever had trouble I could tell her, and she was really nice."

"Best Step-Boss gave me three cones. Three!" Trinity said.

Emily stared at her sisters with mounting horror as they prattled on and on. Teddy, usually the most placid of the bunch, was bouncing on the bed; Athena was pacing in little circles in the center of the room; and Trinity wasn't even trying to hide how hyper she was feeling. The girl was, quite literally, all over the place, running around and bumping off herself. She'd crash to the ground, then spring back up and keep going.

"W-what did you do to them?" Emily asked.

Her mom looked far, far too satisfied with herself. "I did what I would do to any child I was only temporarily responsible for. I gave them sweets, loaded them up with nice things, and gave them all the attention they could want. Now they're your problem."

"Mom!" Emily hissed.

"Oh, don't be that way. They're going to crash any minute now." She glanced at the sisters, who were clearly not crashing. "Any minute now." She cleared her throat. "Anyway, I need to head back. I took the bus over from a stop close to the B and B I'm staying at. I don't want to have to walk all the way back. I've done my share of walking today, I think."

"We can walk you back to the bus stop," Emily said.

"I can take care of myself that far, sweetie," she said.

Emily shook her head. "It's not a problem. And besides, I want these three to bleed off more energy. A lot more."

Her mom hesitated, then nodded. "Sure, why not? They're all still dressed up for it, anyway."

"It's not too cold out, is it?" Emily asked. It was starting to get cooler out, but winters had been getting milder, and they were starting later in the year besides.

"Oh, just you wait. Getting five little bodies into winter gear is going to be something else."

Emily guided her little sisters out of the room, then to the elevator where her mom was waiting. Athena started talking to her mom while they waited for the elevator to reach their floor. When it did, a surprised Sam exited, pressing herself to the side of the corridor so that all the little sisters could get by. Emily shot her an apologetic look. The girl from the room across from hers was nice, but Emily wasn't sure if she could convince her not to tattle to the housing director about all her little sisters.

Another reason to find a better place to stay in a hurry.

They exited the dormitory and started down one of the college's quieter roads. A few students were out still, but they were subdued, heading back home after a long day. Maybe if it had been the weekend, or Friday night, there would have been a more festive air outside, but as it was, the campus was cool and quiet.

"Did you find anything while we were out?" Emily's mom asked.

Emily breathed into her hands to warm them up. When she lowered them, they were both grabbed by Teddy on one side and Trinity on the other. She smiled. "Yeah, I got to dig into some things. I think I have . . . something of a plan."

"That's good. How much is something?"

"It's not much, honestly, but it's a start? I'll know more tomorrow. I plan on heading out and looking into a few things in person. It might be nothing."

"You'll be fine, I'm certain. And if you're not, then your father and I will do what we can to help you out. You're not in this alone, Emily."

"Yeah, Boss, you've got me," Teddy said.

"And the rest of us," Athena said. She shot a glare at Teddy.

"Thanks, all of you," Emily said before that could devolve into an argument about who was the most useful.

The bus stop wasn't as far as Emily remembered it being. Then again, she had mostly been walking all over the city. They had to wait for a few minutes for the bus to arrive, a few minutes that Emily's mom filled with inconsequential chatter and gossip about work and the neighborhood and even a few old classmates of Emily's. Athena stayed close and listened while Emily's other sisters fooled around nearby, always close enough that Emily could keep an eye on them.

The bus pulled in with a squeal, and Emily gave her mom a tight hug. That meant that all her little sisters had to give her hugs too. The older woman ended up running into the bus while the driver looked on, unamused at the delay.

The bus moved on, and Emily let out a long breath that came out as a plume of steam. "Okay, let's get back home," she said.

"Dibs on the bathroom," Teddy said.

"You can't dibs the bathroom!" Trinity said. "I need it too."

"I need it more," Teddy said.

"I have three times more pee than you!" Trinity said.

Emily rubbed at the bridge of her nose. "Trinity, Teddy, keep your voices down, please. We'll . . . figure things out once we're back home."

The walk back didn't give her that much time to think, not when she had to wrangle her sisters. Her plan was still to head out in the morning and talk to the businesses that Cement had been involved with. Securing any sort of income would make everything else significantly easier.

They arrived back at the dorm, moved up to the fifth floor, and were on their way to her room when Emily noticed the door to Sam's room open and the girl stuck her head out. She saw Emily and grinned. "Hey, neighbor," she said. "Can I, ah, have a word?"

"Um," Emily said. "Sure, just give me, ah, a minute?" She unlocked her room's door and let her sisters in. They started arguing over bathrooms and other stuff, so she figured they'd stay distracted for a few minutes. "Okay, what's up?"

Sam chewed on her lower lip, then glanced up and down the corridor. "Want to talk in my room? It's a little more private."

Emily hesitated, but then Sam moved back and she didn't have anyone to argue with, and the mounting awkwardness had her following the girl into her room.

The room was a mirror of Emily's own. At least, the floor plan was. The decorations couldn't have been any more different. Sam had awards on a shelf over her bed, soccer trophies in a neat, glittering row. There were posters for obscure bands on the walls, and a big desktop computer next to a desk much larger than Emily's own. There were also a lot of clothes on the floor and half piled into a basket next to the bathroom.

Somehow, Emily's room was cleaner, despite having her sisters occupying it. "S-so, ah, what did you want to talk about?" Emily asked.

Sam moved around her and closed the door. "Right, so this is a bit strange," she said as she moved over to her bed and sat on the edge of it. She was still nearly as tall as Emily sitting down. "So, you're a Villain, right?"

Emily's heart skipped a beat, then a second. "No," she squeaked after too long a pause.

"Hey, hey, don't freak out," Sam said. "Look, we haven't talked much, but you seem pretty cool. So, you probably don't know this, but I'm majoring in psych. It's been pretty easy so far, but I'm an ambitious sort of girl, you know? I don't want to just be some two-bit small-town therapist."

"W-what?" Emily asked.

"I want to discover stuff. I want my name to be, like, mentioned in some textbooks," Sam continued. "So when I discovered that the girl across from me was a Villain, I told myself that it was an opportunity."

Emily shook her head and tried to regain her wits. She had a skill that would allow her to teleport a sister to her side, which would definitely alert the others. She had to pick which to bring over, though. Athena was the cleverest, so she'd figure that something was wrong fastest when one of the others disappeared. Maybe Teddy? Trinity would run back to the room to get the others while also helping Emily, though.

"That's when I came upon this great idea," Sam said. "I want to be your minion."

Emily blinked. "Huh?"

"Yeah, see, I get to chronicle and test aspects of the psychology of an actual Villain. It's not perfectly scientific, but hell, it's better than what anyone else has. And everyone knows that the best science is criminal."

"N-no," Emily said.

Sam pouted. "Don't be that way. Come on, I'm great minion material. And I have a car!"

This was, Emily knew, an insane and terrible idea. On every level that an idea could be insane and terrible on.

CHAPTER FOUR

Doing What's Probably Right

Emily had not had the most restful sleep. There was too much weighing on her mind. Also, Teddy had started to snore right into her ear, and while Emily could sleep through her fair share of noise, the sound somehow grated on her throughout the night.

In addition, Trinity managed to have the sharpest little elbows, a fact that wasn't helped by the sheer number of elbows she had at her disposal.

So Emily woke up feeling groggy, as if she had only slept for two hours despite whatever lie her clock told.

After shuffling through the new morning routine of forcing her sisters to take quick showers one after the other, then enduring a cold shower herself, Emily got dressed, packed up all their costumes in a backpack, and then took a couple of quiet minutes in the bathroom, where she pressed her head up against the mirror and willed herself awake.

She figured that all that was just part of the college charm, though. At least, from all the testimonies she'd heard from others, that was part and parcel of being a student.

"So, Boss, what's going on this morning?" Teddy asked.

"We haven't done anything Villainlike in a while," Athena said.

Emily frowned. "We broke into someone's home and beat up a Hero yesterday."

"Feels like it was a long time ago," Trinity said. She stared off into the distance in three different directions. "Do I feel time three times more than other people?"

Athena shrugged. "Maybe having three bodies and therefore three sources of living experience is changing your perception of time?"

"That makes sense," Trinity said.

"Did you even understand what I said?" Athena asked.

"No, but it had lots of big words, so it's probably right."

Emily had to hold back a chuckle. At least her sisters could be kind of funny. Not on purpose, which was both a shame and terrifying, but still funny. "Come on, we're going to meet someone."

"The new minion?" Teddy asked.

Emily wanted to protest, but that was exactly what Sam had called herself. "Yeah, we're going to meet the new minion."

They left the room, then made their way downstairs. Emily didn't pause to see if Sam was still in her room or not. They had set a meeting spot the night before, and Emily had to hope that Sam was the sort to be punctual when it came to meetings and the like.

Emily had never visited the student parking area, but it wasn't too difficult to find; it was a multistory building, with most of it tucked underground and out of sight. The gate at the front had a fancy reader system that would open if a student presented their ID. Basically, it gave students a place to park without having to deal with parking on the roadsides.

Emily was the one to set the location of their meeting after Sam had revealed that she had a car, so Emily figured it was a fairly safe spot to meet. Somewhat quiet, somewhat secluded, and if things devolved into a fight, there was room to move and plenty of cover around.

She wished she didn't have to start thinking so strategically about things as simple as morning meetings with other students.

She guided her gaggle of sisters down a flight of stairs and to the bottom level of the parking garage. It was strange going from the bright light of the early morning to a place that was nothing but gray on gray illuminated by sterile neon white, the only splash of color coming from the few cars that dared to be something other than white, black, or gray.

"Where're we going now?" Teddy asked.

There wasn't much to see or do in the spot, though one of Trinity immediately moved over to a mysterious door with some warning signs screwed into it and started poking around.

"Now we wait," Emily said. "Don't wander too far. I don't want any of you to get hit if a car pulls in." She'd seen some of her fellow students driving. It was pretty obvious that they weren't all that experienced.

She found a large pillar to lean against and pressed her head back against the cool stone. After half a minute of nothing, she glanced at her phone. She was maybe a bit too early. Sam had another five minutes to arrive on time.

Five minutes with nothing to do while her sisters played patty-cake to one side or argued over what was cooler, Emily's mom or the concept of communism.

It was enough time to look into some things that she hadn't had time to tackle in a while.

Emily focused for just a moment, then blinked her eyes open. "Status," she muttered.

Name: Emily Wright		
Alignment: Villain		
Alias: The Boss		
Level: 1		
Powers		
Sister Summoning		
Create Sister	Rank 5	
Sisterportation	Level 1	
Double Trouble	Level Max	
Healpats	Level 4	
Triple Threat	Level Max	
Points		
Power Slots: 0	Skill Upgrades: 5	Skill Slots: 0

Sometime yesterday she'd gained a Skill Upgrade point. As it was, the only skills she could use that on were Sisterportation—the skill that allowed her to teleport a sister to her side—or Healpats—her on-touch sister-healing skill. Neither was exceptionally useful just yet. She'd consider putting a point or two into them if her next skill wasn't as useful.

If the pattern held, her next skill would be a utility skill, not another little sister. That was probably excellent news.

Emily glanced over to Teddy. She was Emily's first sister, and probably the one she understood the most. Which was strange, considering that Teddy was a girl Emily had only known for a few days.

"Status, Teddy," Emily said. She wondered if she'd need to use Teddy's full name for the skill to work, but a screen appeared before her, hovering next to her own status page.

Name: Teddy Wright		
Alignment: Villain, Little Sister		
Alias: None		
Level: 1		
Powers		
WereBear		
Rip and Bear	Rank 2	
Iron Bear	Level 1	
Points		
Power Slots: 0	Skill Upgrades: 3	Skill Slots: 0

Teddy had also gotten a Skill Upgrade point. Was it taking down Black Shield? That . . . was probably the case.

"Status Athena." Her owly sister was the most mature and quietest of the lot, and the one Emily secretly worried about the most. Of all her sisters, Athena had inherited the most from Emily, including some of her more negative social traits.

Name: Athena Wright		
Alignment: Villain, Little Sister		
Alias: None		
Level: 1		
Powers		
Owl Seeing Eye		
Owl Alone	Rank 1	
Points		
Power Slots: 0	Skill Upgrades: 1	Skill Slots: 0

She hadn't had much chance to unlock more Skill Slots. If ever Emily decided to take things more seriously, then they'd all need to work on getting more of those. They seemed to be the fastest way to grow stronger.

"Status Trinity," Emily muttered.

Name: Trinity Wright		
Alignment: Villain, Little Sister		
Alias: None		
Level: 1		
Powers		
Eternal Racoon Hurricane		
Three's Company	Rank 1	
Points		
Power Slots: 0	Skill Upgrades: 1	Skill Slots: 0

Emily stared at the name of Trinity's power. Eternal Racoon Hurricane? "What does that even mean?" she muttered.

"Heya!"

Emily swiped her hand before her, and all four panels disappeared with a blink. She stood up straighter and glanced over to the stairwell where Sam was exiting. The girl looked a little scruffy, her tightly curled hair still wet.

"Hey, Boss, this the new minion?" Teddy asked.

Emily rolled her eyes. "Everyone, this is Sam, our neighbor from across the corridor. Sam, these are my little sisters. That's Teddy, that's Athena, and the other three are Trinity."

"They have the same name?" Sam asked.

"Three bodies, one sister," Trinity said from three spots at once.

Emily nodded. "She's one person with three bodies. It's . . . weird."

"Power weirdness," Sam said. She grinned from ear to ear. "That's really cool."

Trinity puffed out all her chests. "You hear that? I'm cool!"

"I saw you eating trash before, you're not cool," Athena said.

"Eating trash is supercool," Trinity said.

Emily sighed. "Trinity, don't eat trash, it's not . . . cool. If you eat trash, you'll never be cool."

It was hard to place the confused and conflicted expressions crossing Trinity's face. One part hopeful, one part disappointed, one part bewildered.

"Oh, this is going to be great," Sam said.

Teddy spoke up next to Sam. "So, just so you know, the order of minion-ness is me, then Athena, then Trinity, then Trinity two more times, then you and other minions like Alea Iacta."

"Wait, you have other minions?" Sam asked.

Emily hesitated, considered what to say, dismissed it, then finally settled on something that explained everything as succinctly as possible. "It's complicated."

CHAPTER FIVE

Thesis

So, just the one other minion, right?" Sam asked.

"Yes. Technically," Emily said.

"And he's got powers?"

Emily nodded. "Some strange sort of luck manipulation. It's a bit complicated."

"And he works for you?"

"Well, he owes me, a bit. And I think he might be a little afraid of me?"

Teddy piped up at that. "Boss is scary."

"Right, right, cool," Sam said. She flicked a thumb over her shoulder. "This way then."

Emily glanced at her gaggle of sisters, then made sure they were all following behind her as she kept up with Sam. The girl had longer legs, and she didn't seem to put much thought into her stride as she moved.

"So I get that you need my car," Sam said as she started to walk down the parking garage. "But you haven't told me where you need to go."

Emily frowned. "You're right, sorry. It's just . . . I don't know how to say this. I guess it's only fair that I fill you in a little."

"That'd be nice, but we can wait until I can take proper notes," Sam said.

"Notes?" Emily repeated.

"For my thesis paper."

Emily just shook her head. "All right then. Well, we'll be heading to a few places. None of them are too far from here. Is that okay?"

"I guess, yeah. Any interesting places?" Sam asked. She fished into her purse and pulled out a key chain.

"Not really, no," Emily said. She glanced over to a little car as its lights flashed and its doors unlocked. It was a dull gray car that looked . . . like any other car on the road. Emily didn't know cars well, but even she could tell that it was about the safest, least offensive car around. Maybe six or seven years old, with a tiny bump on one side of its rear bumper hastily covered by a college sticker.

"This is my ride," Sam said. "Uh, we might have to shove aside a few things to make space. Are all the kids coming?"

Emily glanced in the car. There were three spaces in the back, two in the front. She didn't need to count to know that they'd be two shy. "I guess the girls can squeeze into the back."

"Two of me could stay here," Trinity said. "I could go back home, and if you need me, I could take a bath with Mister Toaster."

"I . . . would rather not have to resort to that," Emily said. "Although keeping one of you home to watch over things isn't a terrible idea. A bit late now."

"What did she mean about the bath and the toaster?" Sam asked with obvious concern.

Emily thought too long about how to explain that. It gave Trinity plenty of time to reply. "Me and Mister Toaster took a bath the other day, then there was a big tingle-snap and one of my bodies died," Trinity said. At Sam's confused look, she explained some more. "I get better when I die."

"Trinity has an . . . interesting relationship with death," Emily said. "It's complicated, but because she's one person with multiple bodies, ah, dying isn't a problem for her. She just sort of reappears next to herself."

"Wow," Sam said. "Hey, Trinity, can I interview you later? I'll give you, like, chocolate or something."

"Really?" Emily asked.

"Look, at first I was just aiming for some great grades and maybe a publication in a few of the more fun psych mags, but this is starting to smell like a Nobel."

"There . . . isn't a Nobel for psychology," Emily said.

Sam shrugged. "Then whatever's right under that."

Emily decided that maybe Sam wasn't entirely sane, not that Emily had missed all the earlier hints. "Okay, everyone in the back. Trinity, you're the smallest, so how about you sit in the middle and on the edges."

"We're probably supposed to use kid seats," Sam said.

"I don't know what that is, but I refuse to sit in one," Teddy said.

"It's like a chair for babies so they don't hurt themselves," Athena said. "You'd definitely need one."

"Girls," Emily said. She opened the back door and gestured into the car with her head. The sisters piled in, then she shut the door and waited for Sam to clear some space on the passenger seat before sitting herself. The car smelled like energy drinks, coffee, and pine freshener. Emily sat with her bag on her lap, so it wasn't hard to reach in and find her notebook. "Do you have a GPS?" Emily asked.

"I do, yeah," Sam said. "But I'm from here, I know my way around the city."

"Oh, that's useful," Emily said. "I'm, uh, from nearby. Anyway, this is the first address." She tilted her notebook toward Sam and tapped the address in question.

Sam scanned the address, then blinked. "Azzip's Pizza?"

"You know where it is?" Emily asked.

Sam nodded with a chuckle. "Of course, I've ordered from there my whole life. They have this special Upside-Down pizza, it's great. You've got to try it."

"Uh, I'll take your word for it."

"We're . . . not going to rob them, right?" Sam asked.

Emily shook her head. "No, we're not doing anything like that. The place was paying protection money to another Villain. He was called Cement."

"The one who was arrested?" Sam asked. She put the car in reverse and soon they were navigating their way out of the parking garage.

"That's him, yeah," Emily said. "He fought some Heroes, but I don't think they were proper Heroes. There's a . . . I don't know how much I should say."

"Oh, conspiracies," Sam chortled.

Emily shook her head. "It's not like that. It's another thing I'll have to talk to you about later, I guess. When we have more time."

"All right, all right," Sam said. She drummed her fingers on the wheel as they arrived at a red light. "So, you haven't told me why we're going to Azzip's. We're taking them over? Doing some racketeering? Getting some protection money?"

"No, the opposite. We're, uh, freeing them," Emily said. She still had a lot of doubts about . . . everything. Things could go very wrong, but at the same time, she wasn't seeing many other options.

That, and there was a sort of pressure to keep moving. It was a weird balancing act. More time to think would be great, but it would maybe mean less time to act, and more opportunities outright missed.

They made it off the roads around the college and Sam started to navigate her way through the city the way only someone really familiar with the area would. That meant turning into gas station parking lots to exit out behind them onto quieter streets and cutting through small alleys as they beelined for the pizza place.

"We're just visiting the one place?" Sam asked.

"No," Emily said. "We have a dozen places to look into. But it'll all depend on how long they each take."

"So, your plan's to walk in and be like 'hey, you're free now' and then hope for the best?" Sam asked.

Emily felt her cheeks warming. "Uh. Well, maybe?"

"Wow," Sam said. "You really haven't figured this all out, have you?"

"I haven't had time to figure most of it out," Emily said. "It's not like Villainy comes with a manual."

"I mean, it doesn't, but there are literally hundreds of books and movies and shows that show you how it all works," Sam said.

"I don't think those are an accurate portrayal of things," Emily said. "Besides, I, ah, don't really care for superhero fiction. I always found it a bit silly."

Sam just gave her a *look*. "Anyone ever tell you you're a bit strange?"

Emily pressed herself into her seat. "I guess."

"Hey, the Boss ain't strange. She's great," Teddy said. "She's been working hard to be a better Villain, too. She used to be all shy and stuff, now she's just scary."

Emily glanced back at Teddy. She wanted to deny the girl but . . . but Teddy was probably not entirely wrong. Some of that fear she felt when dealing with people had faded. Not entirely . . . or maybe not at all. In fact, it was definitely still there, but it was now buried under other, bigger fears.

None of the therapists she'd ever spoken to had suggested being too busy to be shy before.

"I'm working on it," Emily said. "But, uh, do you have a better idea?"

"For getting protection money?" Sam asked. "Yeah, of course." She pulled up along the side of the road, glanced around, then put the car in park. They were right behind the entrance to an alleyway, in front of a closed restaurant on one of the older streets of the city. "Tell you what, I'll come with you, like a proper minion should, and we'll work this out together."

"Uh," Emily said.

"Yeah, I've always wanted to bully people into giving me stuff," Sam said. "But, like, being a bully's kind of frowned upon, you know? Now I get to let loose!"

"Wait, what?" Emily asked.

It was too late—Sam was already stepping out of the car, and her little sisters were rushing out of the back as well.

Emily groaned. What had she gotten herself into?

CHAPTER SIX

Definitely Not Extortion

Azzip's Pizza wasn't what Emily was expecting.

For some reason, she had a mental image of the kind of grungy, dirty pizza place that would give a health inspector literal and metaphorical hives.

Instead, the place was a clean, if modest, little shop. Some chairs and tables were placed in a small area out front, with a bench next to the doorway, and enough parking space for two and a half cars next to the building.

Emily, Sam, and her gaggle of sisters could see the building across the street from the tight little alley they were in.

"So, you going to go in the front door in costume and ask to talk to the boss?" Sam asked.

Emily knew that she had failed to plan this well, but it still made her cringe inside to have her terrible planning rubbed in her face. "Yes," she said.

"With all the little ones?" Sam asked. She glanced back at the sisters.

Emily shook her head. "No, that would be . . . frankly, kind of terrible. I don't even know if we'd all fit. I'll take . . . Athena? She's the most, ah, socially mature."

"Hey, what's that mean?" Teddy asked while Athena smugged next to her.

"It means that I'd rather you stay and watch over Trinity and Sam while I'm away," Emily said.

Teddy crossed her arms, but she didn't protest.

"You sure you can manage that, Boss?" Sam asked.

Emily stared at the young woman. "What do you mean?"

Sam's smile didn't diminish at all. "Emily, you're kind of, like, . . . the most socially awkward girl I've ever met. You're sweet, I think, and mean well, probably, but I have the impression that social stuff's not your forte. Meeting a stranger and telling them you're there to extort money out of them while making it seem like you're telling them that you're helping them is, like, way above your skill level."

"That's not what I'm doing," Emily said.

"Sure it isn't," Sam said with the tone of someone who was just humoring someone else.

"Fine then," Emily said. She gestured to Sam. "You'll do the talking."

"Me?" Sam asked.

"You're my minion, aren't you?"

Sam shrugged. "All right." She casually reached into her purse and pulled out a domino mask. She pushed her curly hair back to hook it onto her ears, then grinned at Emily. "How do I look?"

"Did you have that mask with you this whole time?" Emily asked.

"I don't normally carry a mask around," Sam said. "But I figured it might come in handy."

"And you just had that lying around?" Emily asked.

Sam shook her head. "It's a blindfold, for sleeping. I cut some holes into it." She tugged at the edge of the eye mask to demonstrate.

Emily didn't know if she should be impressed or disturbed. She settled on neither and gestured across the street. "We don't want to be out in costume too much. Someone might see us. Then they'll post it on some site, and the next thing you know we'll be followed all over." She shuddered at the thought of people asking her for autographs, or worse, asking any sort of probing question of her sisters.

Fortunately, finding a place to change wasn't as tricky as convincing all her sisters to look twice before crossing the road.

They took turns getting dressed behind a dumpster in a dead-end alley. That took longer than Emily would have wanted, but it was soon over and she looked onto five costumed-up sisters, proud that they'd all managed to get dressed without lighting a building on fire or mugging someone while her head was turned.

Trinity was dressed as the tiniest little bandit. Black-and-white-striped shirt, and bags with big dollar signs and all. It was the most outright Villainous of their costumes, but judging by how Sam couldn't resist cooing at them, it came out as more innocently roguish than intimidating.

If Emily planned on appearing like a Hero, that would be important.

Athena's costume was a little less thematic. She had her leather jacket on and an owl-shaped face mask. Otherwise, she might have been able to just blend into a crowd as another kid, or a short teenager. That could come in handy too.

Teddy's costume wasn't complicated either. A pale-yellow sundress, her slightly oversize boots, and a plastic bear mask. It was simple, but Emily thought it was cute. Besides, Teddy's power turned her into a bear.

"Oh, all three of you are so cute!" Sam said. "Can I take a picture?"

"Uh," Emily said.

"I won't post it anywhere, I swear," Sam said.

"Fine, I guess?" Emily said. "Just watch over them while I get changed too."

Her own costume was a little strange. A pin-striped suit, a clean button-up shirt, and a small tie. All that coupled with a domino mask and a black fedora. She looked like a gangster from the late fifties. Maybe it was too much of a hint at her power's Villainous nature, but it looked all right, and it was all she had.

If she ever started making proper money, she'd find a way to get better costumes. Though nothing like spandex. She couldn't live with herself if someone saw her wearing something skintight.

Maybe some sort of armor? Very thick, very imposing armor that would keep her nice and safe so that she'd never have to meet people face-to-face while doing Heroic things.

Emily returned to her sisters and minion while adjusting her hat. Sam looked her up and down, then gave her a thumbs-up. "Not bad. Got to say, your whole group has nailed the discount Hero look."

"Is that good?" Emily said.

"Well, considering that I suspect you are operating under a tight budget, it's pretty good, yeah," Sam said. "It sends a message, you know? 'We're a group of Masks who put some time and effort into our gear, but we're still small-scale and probably not superscary yet.'"

"I guess that's not the worst impression to give people," Emily said.

"A lot of Masks go out with normal clothes and, like, a balaclava with swimming goggles on. It's not a great look. Also, if I get a minion uniform, should I go all fifties gangster too? Not like you, though, but something obviously a rung or two below? Maybe slacks and suspenders?"

"Uh," Emily said. "Let's just go to the pizza place, please."

"Yeah, I want some pizza," Teddy said. "You guys haven't had any yet, but it's the third-best thing."

"What's the first-best thing?" Trinity asked.

"The first-best thing is the Boss," Teddy said with unwavering certainty. "The second-best thing is the warmth you get from being with comrades"—Emily felt moved for a moment—"and kicking the shit out of capitalists." Just a moment.

They arrived at Azzip's and Emily glanced at her sisters. "Athena, you're with me. Teddy, stay in that alley there. Trinity, watch us near the entrance and have one of you near the back end too."

Her sisters scampered to obey, and Emily turned toward the shop again. She stared at it.

"So . . . you going to walk in or are we just going to stand out here all day?" Sam asked. "I didn't say anything, but I have classes this evening."

Emily shook her head. "We're going in, I was just, ah, seeing if there was anything to notice."

"Right," Sam said.

Emily felt a hand grabbing hers, and she looked down to meet Athena's smile. "It'll be fine, Big Sis."

She nodded. Failing on her own was one thing, failing after getting such an expectant look from her sister was another. Emily started to the pizza place, and the others followed.

They stepped into the restaurant to the jingle of a bell over the doorway. The place was empty save for a girl maybe a year or two Emily's senior behind the counter. She looked up, saw the three with their masks on, then swore. "Uh, are you here to rob us?"

"No," Emily said. "We're, uh, Heroes?"

"Oh," the young woman said, her shoulders loosened, tension bleeding out of her. "Then . . . did you want to try our daily special? It's two subs for the price of one?"

"Not that, either," Emily said. She was glad she left Teddy outside. "We were hoping to talk to your boss? Or the owner?"

"Oh, right, I can do that," the cashier said. She half turned. "Rose! People for you! Heroes!"

Emily winced at the volume, but she didn't comment. Soon enough an older woman showed up. She reminded Emily a bit of her mom, if her mom wore a hairnet and spent too much time around fatty foods.

Rose took in the room. "Hey there. Is this going to be one of those conversations best handled in private?" Emily nodded, so the woman flicked a thumb over her shoulder toward the back, past the fryers and all the cooking equipment. "Best follow me then."

"Gladly," Emily said.

Maybe things would work out in her favor after all.

CHAPTER SEVEN

Racket

Rose took Emily, Athena, and Sam to the back of the restaurant. The air was filled with the smell of grease and cheese and tomato sauce. Emily expected to find a few people in the kitchens but they were empty. Was it only Rose and the girl at the counter?

"We'll have to make it quick," Rose said. "It's only me on the floor until just before noon. We don't usually have much business in the morning, but I need time to cook and prep things for the rest of the day."

"We'll try not to take too much of your time," Emily said. "This isn't anything too urgent."

"Hmm," was Rose's only reply.

She ushered them into a small office that was little more than a desk covered in paperwork and a computer that looked like it was old when Emily was starting school for the first time. The office was too small for them to sit, so Emily pushed the one seat on their side of the desk aside, then she folded her hands at the small of her back. It was less awkward than not knowing what to do with them.

"All right," Rose said. The woman fell onto her office chair, the seat squeaking in protest. "What's all this about?"

Emily licked her lips. It was now or never.

Which is why it was terribly inconvenient of her mind to just empty itself of all thoughts all at once.

The silence stretched out for a few seconds past awkward when Sam jumped in. "You know the Villain Cement?"

Rose's eyes narrowed. "No. No, I don't."

Sam nodded. "Good. Makes sense that someone sensible wouldn't know him. Not that it matters. He was taken out by some Heroes recently. No one's left from his organization. Not that a small fry like him has an organization of any sort, of course."

Rose nodded slowly. "I don't suppose he would. Not that it's any business of mine."

"'Course not," Sam said. "Now, the Boss here decided, out of the kindness of her heart, to make the rounds of all the places that she felt might . . . ah, be aware that Cement's fall was none of their business and make sure that everything was good with them."

Rose sniffed. "Subtle," she said. The woman pulled a drawer of her desk open, and Emily tensed. Was she going to pull a gun out? Instead, a letter envelope hit the table with the dull *thwap*. "This is for the month."

"Um," Emily said.

Sam stepped up and took the envelope. She opened it, and Emily saw the flash of green in it. Money?

"We appreciate it," Sam said. "Is there anything we can do to help? We love donations from the community, but it's only fair that we give back, right?"

Rose nodded. "Damn right. Cement had a soft touch to him, kept things nice and smooth. Not that I'd know, of course. Now, if you are . . . collecting community donations in his place, then you'll have to smooth things out in the community the same as he did, right?"

"That sounds very fair," Sam said.

"Good. I've had two delivery drivers waylaid near the industrial park. You know the place. Group of punks calling themselves the Chains or something. I think the leader is called Iron Chains. Took our goods and emptied my driver's pockets too."

"What sort of goods were your drivers carrying?" Sam asked.

Rose stared at her. "Pizza. We only deal in pizza. Sometimes subs. Often fries. But mostly pizza. I don't do business with anything more complicated than that. Margins are tight, but I can live with them. What I can't have is more drivers quitting because they're getting stuck up by some punks, and I can't just stop delivering in a part of the city, not when a quarter of my customers come from there. If you want next month's donation, you take care of that. Fair?"

"You're, um, very open about this," Emily said.

The woman sniffed. "Girl, I've been running this place since I was younger than you are. It was my dad's place, and his father's before him. I know how the world works. Cement did right by us, but your sort never lasts forever. Do good by us, too, and things will keep on keeping on."

"Sounds good to me," Sam said. She tucked the envelope into her purse as casually as if it had been a pamphlet, then she gave Rose a quick nod. "We'll get out of your hair, let you get back to work."

"Sure thing," Rose said. "Let me get you some fries on the way out."

The three of them were shown out of the restaurant by means of a back door leading to an alley that smelled keenly of trash. At least Emily had a large bag full of nearly expired fries that Rose had shoved into her arms to keep the odor at bay.

"That went well," Sam said. "Who knew that extorting money from people was so easy?"

"That . . . was easy, yeah," Emily said.

"Well, easyish," Sam said. "At a guess you have, like, three hundred bucks here. It's not a ton, and it's not what I'd want as payment to have to deal with an entire gang."

"What?" Emily asked.

"Those Chains she mentioned," Sam said. "The ones messing with her drivers. You have to take care of them now. That's the whole gimmick with protection money, right? You get the money, but you kinda have to offer protection, too; otherwise, the business might start looking for someone else who'll accept their money to get rid of you."

"Oh, right," Emily said.

Sam pulled the envelope out and smacked it into Emily's hand. "There ya go. I'd tuck that away. Don't want it to be too obvious that you've committed some crime."

"Uh," Emily said. She looked at the envelope for a moment, then folded it and stuffed it in a pocket. It almost felt warm against her side, like something she wasn't supposed to have.

Sam stretched. "Right, next place? Or did you want to send a message first?"

"Send a message?" Emily asked.

"You know, beat the snot out of that Chains gang before the Heroes get to them. Then when you come to others for protection stuff they'll know you mean business."

"Sounds logical to me," Athena said.

Emily shifted the bag of fries around, then rubbed at her eyes. "There's a few places I wanted to visit. One of them might be closer to the industrial area. I left my notebook in your car."

"Brilliant!" Sam said. "In that case, masks off and let's head back."

They met with Teddy and Trinity on the way back; the two were excited to hear Athena's exaggerated recounting of the events—which painted Rose as a scary monster of a woman—and were even more excited about the fries.

"Sho wherhre whe going nhow?"

"Don't talk with your mouth full," Emily chided.

Teddy swallowed, barely chewing the fistful of fries she'd shoved into her maw. "Where are we going now?" she asked.

Emily didn't answer until they were back at Sam's car and everyone was stuffed into place. She pulled out her notebook and shuffled the pages to the list of addresses she had to visit. "I don't know if any of these are close to the industrial area," she said. She didn't have a mental map of the city that included all the street names she was looking at.

"Let me see," Sam asked. She leaned over and read the addresses until pointing to one. "That's close. Just a block over. Man, these addresses are all over the city."

"Cement must have taken a while to set this up."

"Most of them are mom-and-pop kind of places, too," Sam said.

"Huh?" Emily asked.

"No franchises. Just family-owned sorts of places," Sam explained.

Emily frowned, but it didn't take much thought for it to make sense. The owner of a franchise was likely too far away to care about protection money, and their store was an investment, not something they needed to live. That kind of detachment would make it hard for them to really care.

"I guess that makes sense," she settled on. "So this place next?"

"It's a barbershop," Sam said. "Been there forever. I went with my dad once or twice. Not for my own hair, mind. Lots of old guys who just sit around and chat about nothing all day, usually complaining about how things used to be in their day. You know the sort."

Emily nodded. She'd accompanied her father to a place or two like that. The men there always strained her social nerves. "Well then, let's head over. Hopefully we can get this all over with before noon."

"Yeah, we wanna finish before lunch," Teddy said from the back.

"Can't be Villains while hungry," Trinity said. One of her currently had the fry bag tipped upside down over her head and was licking the greasy insides of the empty bag.

Emily rolled her eyes. "I'm sure you're right," she said.

CHAPTER EIGHT

Sisterly Love

Athena was riding a pretty great high. Sure, she was squeezed in between two of Trinity's bodies in the back seat of a car that smelled like Im Orton's coffee and wet socks, but none of that mattered. The happy in her heart warmed her enough that no amount of stinkiness could subdue her good mood.

Emily had picked Athena over the others, and everything had worked out for the best.

That, on top of a whole morning entirely dedicated to doing Villainy? It was gearing up to be the best day ever.

The new minion parked the car along a quiet road, and then they all piled out. Athena shot Trinity a glare as she tried to scramble over Athena (who had decided to use the seat belt because safety was important). She got out soon enough, and as usual they all took their places around the Boss.

This was something they had discussed between themselves. The more sisters Emily had, the less time she'd have to spend with all of them, which was awful and no good. No self-respecting Villain would allow someone else to just take what was theirs, but at the same time, sisters were important. They were the friends you didn't get to choose.

So, the sisters (mostly Athena) had devised a cunning system where they'd all have their own positions and important jobs to do. That way, when the Boss inevitably grew much stronger and had a whole army of sisters to rule the world with, they would all have important places right next to her.

Teddy was the muscle, Trinity the disposable fodder, and Athena was the one who looked around and made sure that no one was pulling a fast one on the Boss. It was the most important position of them all, not that she'd said as much to her sisters.

She carefully turned her head around, scanning the neighborhood for problems.

It wasn't the nicest neighborhood. The cars weren't as new-looking as some she'd seen, the houses were older and some obviously needed a bit of cleaning up. There was a corner store at the end of the street that had a peeling sign that said it sold cigars and alcohol and other boring adult stuff, and about halfway between that and where they parked was a barbershop.

Athena paid particular attention to that since that's where the Boss said they'd be going.

"Are we going to hide in an alley again?" Trinity asked.

"Uh, I don't think so, no," Emily said. "Not here at least; there aren't any alleys to hide in."

"Aww, that sucks," Trinity said.

"Why do you want to hide in an alleyway so much?" the Boss asked.

Trinity grinned three times over. "There was a neat dumpster in the last one that smelled funny. I found a dead rat! And then we got fries."

"The . . . the first had nothing to do with you hiding in an alley. And did you wash your hands? Did you touch the rat?"

"Yeah, it was real hard."

The Boss reached up and rubbed at her face while the new minion reached into her purse and fished out a bottle of something that she insisted they all rub on their hands.

Athena didn't complain; the stuff was cold and smelled like a sting to the brain. Trinity fussed and tried to only wash one set of hands, but the new minion insisted and the Boss didn't tell her off for it.

"All right," the Boss said. "I think this one will just be me and Sam. Can you girls, uh, act nonsuspiciously out here for a little bit?"

"No problem, Big Sister," Athena said. She gave the Boss a good, non-suspicious wink to assure her of her seriousness.

The Boss looked at her strangely for a bit before shaking her head and moving toward that barber's shop.

On arriving near the front of it, Emily gestured at a bench sitting under a streetlamp. "Just sit around there and try not to make too much trouble, please."

"Yeah, I'll watch over them," Teddy said, as if she was the boss of them.

Athena stepped on Teddy's foot. "We'll be fine, Boss," she replied with a confident smile.

The Boss and Sam stepped up and into the barbershop, only pausing to let some old guy pass as he left. Athena didn't think he was a customer, not with the big shiny spot on his head where hair should have been. Or maybe the barber was really bad at his job?

"What was that for?" Teddy asked as she rounded on Athena.

"What was what for?" Athena asked.

Teddy gestured to her boot. "You stepped on me."

Athena sniffed and crossed her arms. "Only because you were being brutish."

"That's not even a word," Teddy said.

"Yeah, it is, and you'd know it if you weren't so brutish."

Teddy growled. "I'll brutish you all across the sidewalk," she said, one fist rising.

Athena grinned. Teddy was being annoying because Teddy was jealous that Athena was proving to be a better sister. It was the best kind of jealous, because it came from Athena being better than someone.

"The Boss told us not to," Athena countered.

Teddy's eyes narrowed, then she lowered her fist, though her scowl stayed in place. "Yeah, well, whatever. I'd kick your butt anyway. You don't even have any cool secondary powers."

"I will, eventually," Athena said. "I'm just waiting for the optimal time to do some Villainy."

"Bet you're too afraid," Teddy taunted.

Athena glared back. "Am not," she retorted.

"If you're so not afraid, why don't you, uh . . ." Teddy glanced around, then grinned and pointed to a group of guys walking just a couple of dozen yards away. "Mug those guys."

Athena rolled her eyes. "I'm not going to mug strangers just like that. The Boss told us not to make trouble. Besides, they're just normal people, they probably don't have anything worth mugging."

The guys were now closer, and one of them snickered and smacked his buddy against the side. "You hear that? We're not worth mugging," he said.

The guy in the lead laughed. He was a big, muscular sort of guy, with a leather jacket—not as cool as Athena's—over a tank top. Strangely enough, he had a bunch of chains wrapped around his middle, and he jangled a bit as he walked.

Weirdo.

"So you girls don't think we're scary, huh?" he asked.

"I'm not afraid of anything," Teddy lied, like the lying liar she was. Athena knew that Teddy was afraid of all sorts of things. "But Athena's probably peeing herself right now."

"I am not!" Athena gasped. "I've never peed myself before! And I'm not going to because of some ugly boys."

"Ouch," one of the boys said. He looked at his two friends and shook his head. "I've been ditched and rejected before, but somehow this hurts more."

"Hey, girl, how about you apologize, huh?" the guy with the chains asked. "Insulting people's not nice, now is it?"

His friends chuckled, as if that was somehow funny.

"I'm not a nice person," Athena said.

Teddy sighed. "If you guys aren't going to help me insult Athena, then just keep going, yeah?"

Athena stiffened. "So you'd rather spend time with these ugly guys than us as long as they'll say what you want them to say?"

"I'm not a capitalist, I don't care to make people say what I want them to say," Teddy shot back.

"That didn't even make sense," Athena said.

"It totally did, you're just too much of a good girl to understand," Teddy said.

Athena and all three of Trinity gasped.

It was obvious that Teddy caught on to what her mouth said a moment later. Her eyes widened and she looked at Athena. "Ah, shit, I'm sorry. I shouldn't call you good."

"I should tell the Boss," Athena said.

"What? No!" Teddy said. "Nah, don't do that. I'll make it up to you."

"Oh yeah, how?'"

"Uh," Teddy said. "Wait, we're here to beat up some gang, yeah?"

"Yeah," Athena said. She was a little curious to know where Teddy was going with that.

The bear girl nodded. "Then I'll let you beat up the leader."

"Wait, what're you girls talking about?" the guy with the chains asked.

"Shut up, comrade," Teddy said.

"Fine then," Athena said. She extended a hand to Teddy. If they were gonna do this, they'd do it properly. "When we meet that Iron Chains guy, I get to kick his butt for the Boss."

"Wait," the guy with the chains said. "What was that?"

Teddy shook. "Deal."

"No, really, what did you just say?" the guy added.

"We're busy, old guys." Athena said. "And we're not supposed to talk to strangers. Go do boring old people stuff elsewhere. Sheesh."

The guy looked at his friends. One looked worried, the other just shrugged. "Yeah, all right," he said. Athena watched them walking off for a bit before turning toward the barbershop. The Boss was exiting, and she looked . . . pretty fine. Things had probably gone well then.

CHAPTER NINE

The Simplest Plans

Emily was feeling pretty good about her prospects as she left the barbershop. The owner was a kindly old guy who had talked to her while snipping away at the hair of an equally old man. The youngest person in the room was a few years her father's senior.

The owner had been receptive to her questions . . . well, all right, Emily wasn't going to lie to herself. Sam had been the one doing most of the talking on her behalf. The girl was a lot more personable and friendly than Emily could ever manage, and somehow that charisma made everything so much easier.

As it turned out, there had been some trouble lately. A group of what the barber and his clients called ruffians were going about, kicking over trash cans, playing music at impolite volumes, and most important of all—at least to Emily—they'd been extorting money away from some shops. It hadn't turned into outright muggings yet, but the clients were worried that the young folk making a mess of their little corner of the world wouldn't take long to progress toward that kind of violence.

In the end, it only took Sam asking them where the ruffians hung out to give Emily everything she needed to know.

"The old maple depot, next to Roson's garage," one of the old men said. He raised his cane and pointed in the rough direction he was talking about. "Old rusty place, a street over from the old main road from back before they tore down the bridge."

Emily nodded. "And, ah, did you happen to see how many there are? Maybe? It's all right if you didn't notice."

"Just a few of them," another man said. "You're not planning to head over there on your own, are you?" he asked.

Sam grinned, big and proud. "The Boss here's a big damn Hero, and she's hardly alone. We'll have those kids behind bars before you know it."

"Could be dangerous," the barber said. He shifted around to his client's other side and continued to snip away at stray hairs.

"We'll handle it, don't worry on our account," Sam said. "We're just doing our part to help the community. You know how the big-name Heroes are. Always chasing after the big scores and the big Villains. The Boss here is a lot more of a street-level sort of Hero. We're just doing what needs to be done. Others have done the same, like Cement. He cared for the community the same way we intend to."

Emily stared at the back of Sam's head. The girl was just so damned subtle about things. Or at least, more subtle than Emily imagined she could ever manage. If the customers didn't know Cement, they'd assume he was some other Hero. It was unlikely they'd look him up, either, if they even remembered the name by the time they could. But the way the barber's shoulders tensed up . . .

"Tell you what," he said. "You girls take care of our ruffian problem for us, and I think I could make a small donation to your cause. Just being a fair neighbor, right?"

A few of the clients seemed pretty proud with the move, and Emily nodded along. "Th-thank you, sir, that would be very appreciated."

It didn't take much after that for them to say their goodbyes and leave.

Emily eyed her sisters and counted heads. One, two, three, four . . . she glanced around and found one of Trinity's rear ends sticking out from under a bush. That was five.

"Hey, girls," Emily said. "So, I think we know where to find that Iron Chains guy."

"Cool," Athena said. "I can't wait to put the fear of spankings into him." She grinned up at Emily, surprisingly feral.

"Right," Emily said. "Sam, do you know if it's a long walk from here?"

"Roson's, huh? We got our tires changed there a few times. That's, like, two blocks over that way," Emily's new . . . friend said. She pointed and Emily followed with her gaze. She looked down a mostly empty street with a few older bungalows along it and a trio of guys halfway down the road.

"All right then, I guess it's far enough that we should get back in the car. I wouldn't want to have to run only to find that the car's a few blocks off."

"Why would we have to run?" Teddy asked.

"I'm hoping we don't run into anything that bad," Emily said. "But if we do, I want the option to run to be available."

Teddy nodded sagely. "That's some good Villain thinking there. Only Heroes and idiots stick around when running's smarter."

"Aren't they the same thing?" Trinity asked.

"Nah, Heroes are more dumb than idiots," Teddy said.

"Yes, I'm sure they're very dumb compared to my wonderful sisters," Emily said. "Come on, back to the car. Trinity, why are you still under that bush?"

"There's wrappers," she said.

"Leave them there," Emily ordered.

The raccoon girl looked disappointed for a moment, all three sets of her shoulders slumping, but it only took all of a minute until she was distracted by something else and was running down the road to be the first back into Sam's car.

Once everyone was piled in, they pulled out onto the road and Sam navigated around the city. The older parts of the city so close to the industrial area were mostly made up of narrow roads and one-ways, which made crossing a few blocks a surprisingly time-consuming affair.

At least Emily had time to take in the area and make sure it was moderately quiet.

They parked not too far from the maple depot. It was an older building, with a tin roof and siding stained by water and rust.

A few interesting cars were parked by the front, low-riding sports cars with very obvious modifications, some of them painted in bright colors, others with parts of their body not matching the rest.

Emily eyed the place for a bit before shifting in her seat. "All right, we might want to come up with a plan here."

"There's going to be a fight, right?" Sam asked.

"Maybe," Emily said. "I hope not, but I . . . I guess there might be." She should have felt a lot more worried about it than she did. Was she getting used to the idea of fighting people? That was strange; she was still anxious about talking to people, but getting into a fight didn't make her nervous? It wasn't just strange, it was downright nonsensical.

She didn't have time to really examine herself, though.

"I think one Trinity will go in first. We can wait outside. Teddy, you'll be at the front. Sam and I can wait a bit to the side with Athena and another Trinity or two. If the area is clear, then we'll go in and snoop around."

"Pretty simple plan," Sam said.

"We'll figure it out as we go," Emily said. "Hopefully that Iron Chains guy will be willing to surrender peacefully. Then we'll just need to hold him until the police arrive."

"Not gonna call the Heroic Response Force?" Sam asked.

Athena scoffed. "They work with Heroes," she said.

That was the same reason Emily was worried about calling them. The HRF probably still thought she was a Hero, too, but she was certain they had ties with the Cabal.

"Before we head out . . ." Emily said. "If you have any quests that apply here, uh, like taking out a powered person, or something like that, then maybe now would be a good time to accept them." She didn't like the quest system that came with powers, but it was a path to becoming stronger. Teddy's last upgrade made her tougher. Emily liked the idea of her sisters being that much harder to hurt.

She had her own options to pick from.

Quest!

The Queen with the Silken Sword, Continued

Become an outstanding member of your community!

Reward: +1 Skill Upgrade point per 10 people who recognize you as "good." Scoundrel +1 per 10 people who recognize you as "good."

Accept? Refuse?

That seemed like it was a recurring quest. She accepted it easily enough. Any path toward something other than Villainy was welcome.

She scrolled through all the other quests she had, outright ignoring any of those that would push her deeper into Villainy.

New Quest!

Breaking the Chains

Take apart a local gang before it becomes a problem!

Reward: +1 Skill Upgrade point per adversarial gangster eliminated.

Accept? Refuse?

That was an easy one to accept.

New Quest!

Queen takes Knight

Defeat Iron Chains

Reward: +1 Skill Slot for defeating, capturing, or killing a powered adversary. + Villainy for properly securing your territory.

Accept? Refuse?

Emily chewed on her lower lip. That Villainy was awful. But . . . and it was a big but, that Skill Slot was invaluable. Skill Upgrade points would allow her to improve an existing skill, but a Skill Slot? That was a whole new facet to her power unlocked.

"Boss, you coming?" Sam asked.

She glanced around, realized she was the last one left in the car, then with a flush, tapped the button to accept the quest. She hoped it would be worth it.

CHAPTER TEN

Rattle

The old maple depot looked like the best and worst place for a hangout. It was in a rough state, the tin walls and cement base in dire need of some attention, but it was still a big building in a quiet little area, with a few windows on the second floor looking down onto the street and big sliding doors at the front allowing people entry.

Or they would have if they weren't chained up at the moment.

"I can bust those down," Teddy said.

"Best not to," Emily said. "Trinity, can you run around the back? Just go check if there's a second entrance."

"Yup, I can do that!" Trinity said. She ran off with a pitter-patter of little feet.

"So does this place count as a base or is it a lair?" Sam asked.

Emily replied, "Does it matter?"

"Boss!" Teddy said.

Athena shook her head. "Big Sis, you're being silly," she said. "Of course it matters."

Emily flinched back a little. "What's the difference then? Between a lair and a base."

"There's more than just the two," Teddy said. "But yeah, a base is a place where people go to do stuff between doing things, and a lair is a place where people go to do stuff between doing things, but it's cooler."

Sam snorted. "Bases are for, like, organizations. Lairs are for Villains. I think the Villainy matters more than the level of organization though.

Like, if a person is a solo Villain and they have a hideout, then that place is a lair. And if the Villain has an organization, then it's a lair, too."

"All right," Emily said. "What's a hideout then?"

"That's just a base that's hidden," Teddy said. "It's better than a base, but not as cool as a lair."

"They could be both," Athena said. "Your lair can be a hideout as long as you're doing Villain stuff in it."

Emily raised a hand. "Wait, so if you're not doing Villain stuff, then it's not a lair?"

"I think that's because part of a place being a lair is about the aesthetic," Athena said.

"Yeah, those are important," Teddy said. "Gotta be real fancy or scary to be a proper Villain."

Emily glanced up at Sam, who was very obviously hiding a grin. "Thanks, girls, I'm glad we've cleared that up," Emily said. "I'll keep it in mind if we ever get a lair."

"We totally should," Teddy said.

Trinity tugged on Emily's jacket, and she looked down at her smallest sister. "Hey, there's a door at the back. It's not locked. Oh, and there's, like, snacks and stuff inside. They have a TV, and a fridge, and a bunch of neat things."

"You went inside?" Emily asked.

Trinity looked at her innocently. "No one's there."

Emily considered what to do for a moment, then with a decisive nod she started toward the back of the depot. "All right, Teddy, stay on the ground floor near the doors; Trinity, one of you will stay with me, too; the other two and Athena, look around for anything suspicious. Athena, you're in charge of the looting. Don't take things we don't need. We're mostly trying to learn about the people we're dealing with here. Sam, stay close too."

It felt . . . interesting to take charge. At least when it was just her sisters who didn't question her orders.

One of Trinity's bodies charged ahead, arms raised in a cheer as she screamed, "Loot!"

The back of the old maple depot had a single door with a rickety staircase leading to it. Emily paused by the door and retouched the latch. "Trinity, was this open?"

"Nah," Trinity said. "I used that bar there to wiggle the door open." She pointed to a flat metal bar casually discarded on a pile of dead leaves and trash pressed up against the edge of the building.

That was . . . clever of Trinity, Emily admitted to herself. She patted the girl on the head, which set Trinity's ears to wiggling and had the girl looking unreasonably smug for a moment.

The interior of the depot showed some pretty obvious signs of having been lived in recently. The floor was all old beams, and there was a loft on the level above, reachable via a spiral staircase tucked in the corner.

A few old crates were shoved up against the walls, but others were stacked up to divide the floor up. Someone had dragged in a big blue chemical toilet booth and tucked it away in one corner.

A beat-up old couch took up the middle of the room, with a TV sitting on a table in front of it. Athena walked over to the TV, found the remote, and clicked it on. She started channel surfing while the others spread out a little. Trinity found a minifridge at the back and was tossing out beer cans on a quest to grab all the junk food inside and stuff it into one of her dollar-sign bags.

"This place is, uh," Emily began. She wasn't sure how to describe it.

"It looks like a bachelor pad, but worse somehow," Sam said. "Bet it's supercold in here when winter comes around for real."

"Somehow I don't think the people who spend their days here are all that concerned about that kind of thing," Emily said. She grimaced at some of the junk left on the tables. Fortunately, there didn't seem to be any drug-related stuff beyond an old glass bong with a burned bottom. "I guess we should try to learn more about this gang while we're in their, uh, lair."

"I'm not sure if this is a lair," Athena said. She paused her channel surfing on a cartoon channel that was currently playing some loud and colorful ads for Hero plushies. "This is barely even a hangout."

"It's a dump," Teddy said.

Emily had to agree. "I don't think we'll be finding much of worth here," she said.

"What?" Trinity asked. "That's not true, look at all the stuff I've found!" One of Trinity ran over and opened her bag to reveal a lot of junk food, some toys, and a few bits of trash all stuffed into the bottom.

"That's . . . nice," Emily said.

She was about to try to convince Trinity to dump all that stuff somewhere when they heard a heavy rattle.

Metal clinked against metal, and Emily stared at the front door as the chains holding it in place unwound themselves. She couldn't see much through the growing crack in the door, but it was clear that more than one person was on the other side.

"Uh, do we run, or . . . ?" Sam asked.

Emily hesitated, and that cost her. The chain finished coming undone and the door was shoved aside by the single heavy-muscled arm of a young man. He was far taller than Emily, with roughly chiseled features and a thick leather coat on.

Worse, chains were hovering around him like coiling snakes, ready to strike.

"I guess we fight," Sam muttered. She ducked down next to the couch and came up with an aluminum baseball bat.

Emily took a small step back, then she settled herself. "Teddy, get ready. Athena, do your thing if he turns hostile. Trinity, make sure at least one of you stays back at all times."

"I'm gonna guess that you're not fans," the guy said as he stepped in. He stood tall, eyes narrowed as he scanned the room. He even glanced up to the Trinity on the second floor. "Care to tell me what you're doing in my base?"

"It's not a base, you idiot, it's a lair," Teddy said.

"It's not even that, it's too poopy to be a proper lair," Athena said.

"Is this some sort of prank?" the guy asked.

Emily licked her lips and glanced at Sam. The girl gave her a thumbs-up, which was very much not what Emily wanted from her. Seeing as no one else was going to speak in her place, Emily shifted her shoulders and stood up taller. "I'm the Boss, these are my teammates. You're Iron Chains?"

"Yeah," he said. "I thought that'd be obvious." He jerked a thumb to the chains hanging in the air around him.

"It's nice to be sure," Emily said. "Now, we can do this the hard way, or the easy way. Please surrender."

"Yeah, sure," he said.

Emily blinked. "Oh, that's really appreciated. While I'm sure we'd win a fight, I'd really rather not."

He shook his head, frowning now. "No, you're supposed to say 'really?' then I'm supposed to say 'no' in a really sarcastic tone."

"I, uh, what?" Emily asked.

"You're going off script," Iron Chains said.

There was a script? Emily was just growing more confused by the minute.

"You know what, never mind. I'm not going to surrender, all right? How about you and your toddler squad piss off instead, huh?"

Emily sighed; that was better. "No," she said.

CHAPTER ELEVEN

Iron Chains

Luis wasn't sure what he was supposed to be feeling.

He'd had an all right morning, joking with the guys, playing games, chatting up Tim's babe of a sister. Just a nice day.

His life had taken a turn for the better after Power Day. No more taking anything from his jerk of a stepfather, no more being pushed around. Having powers was nice. It was more than nice, it was intoxicating.

He was a big guy, tall enough, wide at the shoulders. He worked out. Figured he'd end up in some job that had a lot of labor, something honest but simple. Now he wasn't so sure on that account.

So he was having a nice day. Maybe later he'd have to be a little more responsible with his powers or whatever, but for now the money was just rolling in. He was making new friends and remaking old ones. Girls who hadn't given him a second look in high school were chatting him up, and when he wanted something, he got it.

Yes, he was being a bit of an ass. But that was fine; who wouldn't be after getting a power? He could be a Goody Two-shoes later.

He was a Hero, after all.

Name: Luis Laurent	
Alignment: Hero	
Alias: Iron Chains	

Level: 1		
Powers		
Chain Snake		
Chain Dance	Rank 3	
Bind	Level Max	
Chain Drain	Level 1	
Points		
Power Slots: 0	Skill Upgrades: 1	Skill Slots: 0

So that begged the question. Why in the world was his new hangout spot filled with random girls and children?

The one he was talking to, the one in the suit, she had to be a Mask. No sign over her head, but that was fine. He kept his hidden too. Smarter that way.

He'd been in a scuffle or two, in and out of school, so he knew how to hold his own in a brawl. Didn't have much time for martial arts or anything like that, but he knew how to read someone well enough. The girl was standing there, completely flat-footed. It was almost like she was taunting him to come and knock her around.

Who did she take herself for?

"No," the Boss said bluntly to his request for her to piss off.

Luis licked his lips and hesitated for a moment. There were a lot of them. The kids had masks on, too. Those were some bad odds, but they were kids. And besides, he was a *Hero*. Heroes did not get pushed around like this. They were the ones in charge.

What was it the TV had called those dogs in charge of the others? Alphas? That's what he was.

His chains shifted, and he could feel a few more left here and there across the room. They uncoiled themselves and rose out of the nooks and crannies he'd left them in.

Thing with chains was that they hurt when they hit. They had the flexibility of ropes, but the weight of a hammer. He tilted his head left and right, neck popping. "Fine then," he said.

Luis took a step forward.

Then the girl right in front of him growled.

It was weird, just some kiddy noise. "Get out of here," he said.

She growled louder, then she turned into a bear.

"Ah, no man, I'm not doing this," Jean said. "I'mma peace out back to my car, bro, you, uh, take care of this bunch, yeah?"

The coward. Luis didn't bother to swear at him as he ran off.

"You think I'm going to be scared just 'cause you're a bear?" he asked.

"That would be the smart thing to do," the girl in the suit said.

"I didn't ever let myself be stopped from doing something just because it was smart," he shot back.

He wasn't entirely sure that meant what he wanted it to, but it was the tone that counted.

The bear roared again, then it charged.

Bears, he discovered, were pretty fast.

Chains were faster.

Jumping into a roll, Luis dodged out of the bear's path, but not without leaving a trap behind. The bear's roar turned into a surprise . . . well, it was still a roar, but it was a choked and confused one. The large chain he usually kept wrapped around his waist spun around the bear's massive neck, then tightened, metal links clinking together in a racket that he'd come to really enjoy.

Luis came out of his roll and ducked down under something big and brown that flew over his head and crashed into the ground behind him.

A box?

He glanced up and saw one of the kids up on the second floor, grinning at him as she raised a second box over her head, then flung it right back down at him.

Luis stepped to the side and sent a smaller chain spinning up at her like a bolas. She screamed in protest as it caught her hard across the chest and wound around her arms. That was one more down.

"You shouldn't've messed with me," Luis said. "That's two of you down now."

He grinned at the girl in the old gangster outfit, then at the girl behind her, a tall, darker-skinned girl with a baseball bat who was a lot more his style.

"Sorry, but I'm going to have to chain you up," he said.

"Let Teddy go," the Boss said. Her voice was pitched low, not a growl or anything like that, just deeper than it had been. It was that kind of no-nonsense voice his mother had used on him when she was actually angry. "And I won't have to hurt you."

Luis shifted just a little bit.

"No, you're the one who picked this fight, Boss, I'm just going to put you in your place."

He started to step toward her while all around the room, chains rose out from behind boxes and crates. A few rushed to him and wrapped around his forearms and torso and partly around his head.

"Sisterportation, Teddy."

Suddenly, the bear was in front of him, and his heavy chains clanged together as they squeezed around nothing.

"Oh," he said before the bear swiped at him.

Luis was flung back, but he slowed his tumble with his chains and stayed on his feet. "All right, you want to play hard, huh?!"

The bear chuckled. "Athena, you said he was yours," it said with a voice like an old motorcycle rumbling to life.

"Yeah, he's mine."

Luis looked around. He knew there were a few other kids in the room. He'd hardly kept track of all of them, but he couldn't tell where they all were.

He glanced back and made out a girl in a white-and-black-lined shirt, with a poofy tail behind her. Wasn't she the one he'd knocked out above? But no, he could still tell his chains up there were holding on to someone, someone trying hard to get loose.

Luis whipped his head around as he caught some movement from the corner of his eye. At the same time, a chain flicked out, smashing into the thing that moved.

The old TV on the crate stand exploded apart as his chain whipped into it, the on-screen cartoon animals squealing for a second as the TV fritzed.

Luis refocused; he couldn't just fling his chains out like that, he had to be careful. A few bruises were fine, maybe a broken bone or three, but Heroes didn't kill. It's what made his power so great.

"Last chance," the Boss said.

He narrowed his eyes on her.

It felt like she was so far away, but she hadn't moved at all, had she?

He shook his head. The room was . . . no, it wasn't twisting. He didn't feel like he was drunk, or high. He wasn't imagining it though. The shadows were deepening.

He felt his heart racing, a *thump-thump* beat that he couldn't mask over with the clink of his chains.

A girl laughed. He didn't know which one. All of them? But no, it was only the one.

"Hey!"

He looked up, then flinched down as a crate came crashing down.

One of his chains caught it and shoved it aside. Then something small and fast rammed into the back of his legs and he stumbled forward . . . and right into the bear.

He'd forgotten the bear!

It smacked Luis in the chest, but his chains caught it. Then he screamed as a huge maw opened and tried to swallow his head.

The chains covering his face sprang forward and grabbed the bear's head like a net, tugging it back and away.

Another kick to the back of his legs, right in the crook of his knee this time. He caught a flash of black-and-white stripes and a smiling face as he crashed to the ground.

And then that babe with the bat was on top of him.

When did she go from cute to scary?

She grinned. "I always wanted to do this," she said before she raised the bat.

CHAPTER TWELVE

All Chained Up

"Uh, now what?" Sam asked. "Because that? The chains flying all over, the screaming, the weird crazy look in his eyes before she rammed into him"—Sam pointed to Teddy—"not to mention her turning into a *bear*, that was wonderful. Pretty sure I can write an entire paper just on my experience here."

"That's nice," Emily said absently. She was looking at the man lying flat on his back in a dusty corner of the depot. His chains had loosened and fallen onto the ground here and there, and it was pretty clear from the welt on his forehead that he wasn't about to get up.

"Boss?"

Emily looked up. Teddy was staring at her with her big bear eyes. "Huh?"

"Boss, what do we do?" Teddy grumbled.

Emily blinked. "Right, do. Uh . . . Trinity, clear out the chains, just take them all and toss them into that crate over there. Put the cover on it when you're done. Athena, I need you over here. Tell me if he's about to wake up. Teddy, you stay close too. If he wakes up, tell him not to move. Trinity, tell us if the chains move."

Trinity lifted one chain off the ground with a clink of metal on metal. During the fight, as short as it had been, the entire room was filled with a constant rattle. It was almost deafening. "It's moving," Trinity said as she wiggled it.

"No, I meant moving on its own. As if he's controlling them," Emily said.

"Oh, right, that makes sense!" Trinity said. "Good thinking, Boss!"

Emily held back a sigh. Her sisters were at least quick to move where she told them to. "Sam, can you search his pockets?"

"Hey, minions get loot last," Athena said.

"I need his phone," Emily said. "We can talk about loot . . . later. Way later."

Sam leaned down next to Iron Chains and patted his sides. She found a wallet held in place by a pocket chain—a bit late nineties but Emily figured it was a thematic thing—a pocketknife, and, finally, a smartphone with a beat-up case.

"Here you go, Boss," Sam said as she tossed the phone up.

Emily fumbled it out of the air but eventually caught it and spun it around. "Thanks," she said.

"Who're you going to call?" Sam asked.

"I'm thinking about it," Emily said. "But . . . maybe the Heroic Response Force? This is their kind of business, and I want to help us appear more, uh, you know, like good guys."

Athena's face twisted in distaste. "I get why you wanna do that, Boss, but it's still icky."

"Yeah, real nasty. I didn't take this guy down just to be called a Hero for it," Teddy said.

"What?" Athena asked. She spun around to face Teddy. "I took him out!"

"No, you didn't," Teddy said. "I did all the work."

Athena opened and closed her mouth, then she grinned. It was a very disturbing sort of smile. "So you're saying that because you did more of the work than others, you should be compensated more?"

"Uh," Teddy said.

"Despite being part of our community, you want to take the rewards for yourself?" Athena asked.

Emily sighed. "Athena, don't attack your sisters psychologically."

"Teddy started it!"

"No, I didn't!" Teddy defended herself instantly. "I don't even know what a psychologically is!"

Emily turned to Sam. "You watch over them, I'm going to make a call. I'll be right back." Sam didn't look ready to babysit a bunch of superpowered brats having a sibling argument, but then, neither was Emily and things had turned out more or less fine so far.

The number for the HRF was listed as an emergency number, which meant that she didn't need to figure out Iron Chains's password to get to it. That was probably for the best; his phone was a crusty mess and she wanted to touch it as little as possible. She dialed the three-digit number, then held the phone close to her ear without touching it.

"Heroic Response Force, what's your emergency?" a woman's smooth voice asked over the line.

Emily cleared her throat. She would have preferred to use her own phone, but last time she'd used her home computer to look things up, a clever person had tracked her down. She didn't trust the Heroes not to bug her phone somehow if it was in their best interest. It was paranoia, she knew, but she figured that knowing it was paranoia counteracted some of the insanity that came with it. "This is the Boss; uh, I'm a Hero, from Eauclaire?"

"Do you wish for me to patch you into the Recruitment Department? You can find a counselor there who will assist you with joining the good guys!"

"What?" Emily asked.

"I'll patch you in."

"No! Wait, that's not what I'm calling for," she said in a hurry. She paused, made sure she was still on the line, then continued. "I captured a, uh, Villain. I was calling to get a pickup, some police? I don't know what your, um, procedure is?"

"Oh, that's impressive work. Can you give me your location? We'll dispatch a team to assist you right away. Are you injured? Are there any injured civilians in the vicinity?"

"I'm fine," Emily said. "And no, no hurt civilians. We're at . . . uh . . ." She walked over to the front door, still ajar ever since Iron Chains made his entrance, and stuck her head out. She had to squint to make out the nearest road sign, which she read to the person on the phone. "Is that enough?"

"Certainly. A team is on its way, ETA seven minutes. How is the Villain restrained?"

Emily glanced over to Iron Chains. It looked like he was coming to, which was both good and not. "He has a bear on him."

"Pardon?"

"A grizzly," Emily elaborated.

"I . . . see," the dispatcher said. "Are you the independent Hero Boss who works with another independent called Teddy?"

"That's me, yes," Emily said. "You-you've heard of me?" Her stomach twisted at the thought.

"We have files with some details about local Heroes. Such information can be invaluable. Is the Villain in need of medical assistance? Are they breathing correctly, bleeding from any wounds? Are they coherent?"

"Yes? I mean, no, I mean, they're alive." Teddy growled in the back. "For now." Emily lowered the phone, a hand over the front of it as she turned to see what was going on.

It looked like Sam was talking to Iron Chains, her bat clinking onto the floor next to his head while Teddy leaned in over him. He looked properly cowed by it all.

"Yeah, he's fine," Emily said.

"Is he tied up?" the dispatcher asked, still in that calm tone.

"Not exactly," Emily said. "Teddy is watching over him, with . . . another independent Hero and one of my min— One of my, uh, a friend."

"All right. Please consider tying the Villain up. Ropes or chains if you lack proper restraints. Remember, Villains don't have the same sense of morality that normal people have, they won't balk at stabbing you in the back even after you've defeated them."

Emily tilted her head back from the phone. That was just rude! "All right, I don't think using chains would be a good idea. His name is Iron Chains."

"I see. While we wait for assistance to arrive, could you give us the highlights on his power? I can relay that information to the team en route."

"He controls chains," Emily said. "They can float and move around. I think he could use them as whips, too. And he can wrap people in them. It looks like they could tighten a lot." It took a lot of strength to stop Teddy from moving when she was a bear, and holding her jaw shut wasn't easy, either.

"Noted. Thank you, Boss."

"You're welcome," Emily said on reflex. "What's the, um, ETA again?"

"Four minutes now. Don't worry, the team is coming with an experienced Hero and some well-equipped troopers. They'll have everything secured within moments of arriving. But, just to confirm. The people on location are yourself, female, approximately eighteen years of age. Costume that resembles a suit. Teddy, a bear or a child of approximately twelve. Costume appears to be a sundress and a bear mask. And one civilian assistant?"

"Why do you need to know?" Emily asked, her suspicions high.

"To avoid friendly fire. Troopers arriving on the scene don't appreciate more unknowns appearing from nowhere."

"Oh," Emily said. "In that case, add four more. One looks like a biker girl, she's the same age as Teddy. Leather jacket. And the others look like burglars. They have tails."

"Um," the dispatcher said. She sounded uncertain for the first time since she called. "There are four more Heroes on location?"

"Yes," Emily said.

She pretended not to see Trinity putting loot into one of her bags, or Athena grinning as she looked at Iron Chains, who was sweating beneath her. "That's right, four more Heroes."

CHAPTER THIRTEEN

The Good Guys

The Heroic Response Force were the *good guys*. At least, that's how they appeared in all the movies and shows. Usually they weren't in the forefront, though. No, the people who really got all the attention were the Heroes, and sometimes even the more popular Villains.

Emily had seen her share of Hero movies. It wasn't her favorite genre, but she'd still seen a few. There was a sort of cultural pressure to keep up with the most popular new movie, and in all those that featured Heroes (sometimes played by the Heroes themselves, which was always cringe-worthy but fun), there were HRF agents in the background.

Emily was barely holding back the shakes as three vans and an armored truck pulled up in front of the maple depot, sirens blaring and lights flashing.

The vans opened up and five or six agents jumped out of each. Some moved out in a wide circle while others set down cones on the road or laid down big metal panels that unfolded into temporary barricades.

They were all armed, with long shotgun-looking weapons that had yellow-black barrels. Their actual guns were all by their hips.

Emily almost raised her arms when a few of them approached her. "Are you Boss?" one agent asked.

"Huh?"

"Are you the independent hero known as Boss?" he repeated.

"Oh, yes, that's me. The others are just inside. Let me go tell them to, uh, stand down." She spun on a heel and darted back into the depot. It was to tell her sisters not to cause trouble, she lied to herself while running away from the scary men and women behind her. "Girls, the Heroes are here," she said.

"We fighting?" Teddy asked.

"No!" Emily said. "We are not, because we are also Heroes, and Heroes wouldn't fight each other, right?"

Teddy—who was still a two-ton bear—looked like she was thinking real hard for a moment before she nodded. "Yeah, I got ya, Boss. We're big damn Heroes is what we are."

"Super Heroic," Athena said. She winked. With her eyes being a bit larger than average it was incredibly obvious, and Emily wanted to hide her face, but then it was too late.

The agents moved in, two on either side of the door, one kneeling, the other standing, then one of them shouted "Clear!" and a couple more moved in. And with them, a Hero.

Emily swallowed.

"Ah! It's the Boss!" Silver Fox said. The Hero walked into the place as if he came here every day. He walked with his chest out, his back straight, and his perfectly coiffed hair combed back in a neat twirl. "Good to see you again."

"Uh, hi, sir," Emily said. She wasn't starstruck, she was star-terrified. "Th-this is the Villain." She gestured to the side where Iron Chains was also staring, mouth agape.

"Wait, what?" he asked. "Hey! No, I'm not a Villain, I'm a Hero! A Hero!" Iron Chains said.

"Boss said you're a Villain," Teddy growled. "So that's what you are, all right. She'd know better than you what makes for a Villain."

"Yeah, shut up!" the nearest Trinity added.

Silver Fox looked around, took in all of Emily's sisters, then brought his attention back to her. "Quite the cadre of Heroes you've gathered. I take it you're this team's leader?"

"Uh, yeah," she said. "I'm their boss. The Boss. Um."

Silver Fox grinned, somehow both handsome and comforting. "I think I get it. You know, we have a lot of PR services that are free of charge for new and independent Heroes, if you're looking for that kind of help. In the meantime, though, do you mind if we take custody of the Villainous young man?"

"I said, I'm not a— Whoa, whoa, okay, I'm staying quiet," Iron Chains said. Emily didn't bother turning around to see whatever it was her sisters were doing.

"Yes, please take him," she said.

"Wonderful," Silver Fox said. He gestured, and the agents nearest to him darted over to Iron Chains. Teddy stepped back, letting them grab hold of Iron Chains, pull him to his feet, and secure his arms behind his back, all under the watchful eye of other agents with their Tasers trained on Iron Chains.

Emily was glad it was all over. Now all she needed . . . was to wilt as Silver Fox walked right over to her, a couple of agents in less armored uniforms in tow.

"Should we debrief here, or would you rather take care of that at the station?" Silver Fox asked.

"Um," Emily said, "debrief?"

"We need to know what happened. Both for our own investigation, and to better understand how to keep—Iron Chains, was it?—under lock and key."

"Oh, right," Emily said. "Here is better, I think. Uh, maybe outside?" It would be easier to keep an eye on her sisters that way.

"Sure thing! I was about to suggest that anyway. It's best to do these kinds of things under the light of the sun. Besides, it makes for better photographs. Have you ever been on the news, Boss?"

"N-no?"

"Well, then! First time for everything."

Emily turned toward her sisters, and Sam, and waved them over. "Okay, I'm going to talk to Mister Silver Fox. You four, uh . . . Sam, you keep them close, all right?"

"I can try," Sam said. "I'm not exactly a pro babysitter you know."

"Just do your best," Emily tried.

"Hey, wait," Teddy rumbled. "Why do we need to follow her? We're higher ranked. She's just a minion."

"Uh," Emily said. "You don't. I mean, I need you three to work hard guarding Sam. Since she's just a normal person and isn't as strong as you. Okay?"

Teddy's eyes narrowed. "Okay," she finally said. "Okay, this will be fine." Emily turned and headed out the door, squinting for just a moment as the bright sunlight hit her. She had to step to the side a moment later as a team in hazmatlike suits darted into the depot.

The vans had moved a bit, and long strands of bright yellow tape were hanging from poles across the street, behind which HRF agents were watching over everything. Beyond them, a few concerned citizens had come out to watch, and the news was there.

Emily tensed a little as she noticed two crews unloading cameras. A reporter-looking person was talking to one of the agents; she kept glancing at where Emily was standing, then pointing to where Iron Chains was being held back by two burly agents in what looked almost like plate armor, if painted all in matte black.

"Boss!" Silver Fox called out. He waved her over, and Emily dragged herself to stand next to him and the tablet-holding agent. "This is Allison, she'll be recording and taking notes."

"All right," Emily said. "What do I say? Or do?"

"Could you describe the situation leading to the fight with suspect Iron Chains?" Allison asked in a monotone.

"Uh," Emily said. "Just before or . . ."

"Usually it's best if they know how you discovered they were a Villain," Silver Fox said. He pointed to the name and title floating above his own head. "Not everyone leaves their tag blazing like this. Villains least of all."

"Right, well, we spoke to a few locals and it turns out that Iron Chains's been taking money from some local shops."

"Awful," Silver Fox said while shaking his head. "To extort money from people that way. A protection racket, I imagine?"

Emily nodded. "That's right. Him and a few others. Uh, young men. Some were with him, but they ran off."

"Too bad, that," Silver Fox said. "Could you describe them?"

Emily tried to recall what they looked like but was coming up blank. "One had a beanie? Uh, they were both white . . . young, I guess."

The Hero's face twisted into a frown. "So, this Villain not only started to extort the locals, but started his own gang. Taking the young and foolish under his wing and leading them into a life of Villainy."

"Uh," Emily said.

She turned as a siren went off.

Her sisters were all next to the big armored personnel carrier, one of the agents showing the girls, and Sam, the buttons on the dashboard. Trinity had climbed in at some point and was very obviously pressing everything to try to shut the sirens off.

"Yeah, leading children into Villainy," Emily said. "Right. A-anyway. We got here and ran into him, then we beat him. That's it."

Silver Fox looked at her, then nodded. "I suppose that might have to do. You're wise to keep your companions' powers under wraps; information like that has a tendency to leak in all the worst ways. By the way, well done, Boss. You've done the city, and the world, a service today. Now, if you don't mind, I think someone needs to address the press, unless you wish to accompany me?"

"No, please, go ahead," Emily said.

She sighed as the man left. A glance at the sky hinted that it wasn't even noon yet. She still had classes to go to, and sisters to wrangle.

Emily watched as Iron Chains was pushed into the back of a van while the cameras rolled.

Quest Complete!

Queen takes Knight

Defeat Iron Chains

Reward: +1 Skill Slot for defeating, capturing, or killing a powered adversary. + Villainy for properly securing your territory.

CHAPTER FOURTEEN

Public Relations

All right, girls," Emily said. She clapped her hands together twice, and five little heads turned her way.

Her sisters were still with Sam, though all three of them were currently hounding some HRF agents with questions, and she couldn't help but notice that Trinity had stolen one agent's unfolding baton and was stuffing it into one of her dollar-sign bags.

Sam was meant to watch over them, but the older girl looked harried. "We're heading back," Emily said. She looked past her sisters toward the line that the HRF had formed along the middle of the street. The media was still there, and it looked like everyone in the neighborhood had shown up.

She had to wonder if people were all idiots. If the HRF was here, that meant some sort of fight probably had occurred. Did they want to get caught up in a battle? The reporters and journalists she could understand, at least a little. It was their job to film things.

"They've been given permission to go," Allison said from next to Emily. The more logistics-focused agent was easy to forget, she was so quiet. "You can head out at any moment, Boss."

"Thanks," Emily said. She waved her sisters over. "Come on, we have a bunch of things to get done before the day's up." It was past eleven, she had classes starting at twelve, and the campus was a good fifteen minutes' drive away. She was pretty sure she wouldn't have time to take a shower before class.

Her sisters ran over and gathered around her. "We got to honk the sirens!" Trinity said.

"You don't honk sirens, idiot," Teddy said.

"I'll honk you!" Trinity snapped back.

"You're both making a fuss. Stop being so annoying and be better, like me," Athena added.

"Girls," Emily said, something of a warning in her tone. It worked, shutting all her sisters up long enough for her to continue. "I'm . . . I'm a little stressed, okay? Can we just go back home? I still have a lot of things to do today."

She got five nods. Smiling, Emily patted Trinity on the head, then because she noticed the jealous looks on her other sisters' faces, she gave them pats, too.

Sam gestured to the crowd gathered on the other side of the yellow tape. "Think we'll have a hard time getting by?" she asked.

"They'd have to be pretty stupid to interfere with this many Masks," Emily said.

"So is that a yes? Because I don't usually like gambling against people's stupidity."

Emily sighed, then turned toward Allison, who was still standing nearby. "I'm very sorry, but could we have a ride? Just down the street and away from all the, uh, them." Emily gestured at the crowds.

Allison adjusted her glasses, then glanced back at the vans parked nearby. "I think we can arrange something like that, sure. We have a protocol for delivering allied Heroes to locations where they can change and disguise their presence."

"It happens often enough that you have a protocol?" Sam asked.

"Some Masks take the separation between their identities very seriously," Allison said. "We make a point not to alienate the people assisting us when what they're asking for is easy to provide."

"Is, uh, hiding your identity that big of a deal?" Emily asked.

Allison nodded her head toward the crowd. "There are vans from three news stations there. Mostly they'll be focused on Silver Fox right now. There are print journalists out there too. When their ratings and sales depend on being as sensationalist as possible, you can be certain that on occasion they will twist a story in a way that will ensure more sales. That can be to the detriment of a Hero, at times."

"Yikes," Sam said. "Giving some poor chump bad PR for more views is kind of dirty."

"It's why the HRF puts so much emphasis on appearing friendly and helpful," Allison said. She tapped a few things on her tablet, then looked over to the vans. "That one right there, 35B, will be the one carrying you out of the area. You can give the driver any address in the city."

"Thank you," Emily said. "Uh, and for the information, too."

"You're welcome. If you have any questions, please call us. Or you can contact me personally here." Allison tugged a card out from a pocket on her bulletproof vest and handed it to Emily. It was just the woman's name and contact information next to the embossed logo of the HRF.

One of the agents opened the side door of the van they were to ride in, revealing an interior filled with uncomfortable benches that looked too small, somehow. There was also a cage with a bunch of equipment where the passenger seat would be on a more normal van.

"All right, everyone in," Emily directed. Her sisters scrambled into the van, then Sam hopped in and Emily followed.

The driver was already up front. He half turned to address them. "No belts, I'm afraid. We operate under the same rules as a bus. There are handrails, and unless there's an emergency, I'll be driving safer than a soccer mom being tailgated by a sheriff."

"Uh, thank you," Emily said. She settled on one of the seats and discovered that her initial assumption about its comfort was spot-on.

"So . . . that was something," Sam said.

"Yeah," Emily agreed. She leaned forward, elbows on knees in what she knew wasn't a very womanly pose, but it was just her and her sisters and Sam, and besides, she was a little too . . . not exhausted, but something close to care. "I hope that was worth it."

"Your reputation will get a boost from this," Sam said. "Think of how happy the locals will be that you took out a gang led by a Villain. This entire part of the city owes you one."

Emily nodded slowly. She could read between the lines there.

"And we got stronger," Teddy said from behind her. "Got a Skill Upgrade point for being badass."

"Don't swear, please," Emily said, mostly out of reflex. So Teddy had gotten a Skill Upgrade, too? "Did everyone get a point like that?" She looked over her shoulder at her sisters who were all nodding.

"I got one," Trinity said.

"Likewise," Athena said. "We'll all be a little bit stronger now, more fearsome!"

"We'll kick even more butt!" Teddy cheered.

Sam laughed before she leaned up behind the driver. "Can you take us next to Elm? There's that little corner store there."

"The one with the big wall full of candy?" the driver asked.

"You know it?" Sam asked.

"I live here, too, you know."

"Right, right, can you drop us off behind that?" Sam asked. "We'll make it back safe from there."

"Can do," the driver said before he turned the wheel and started moving them around the street. Emily looked out ahead, as there weren't any windows in the rear. The walls looked like they were a lot thicker than a normal car's. Were they bulletproof? She didn't put it past the HRF to have armored vans for carrying agents around.

The rest of the agents looked like they were packing up already, a few of them waiting in little groups that were clearly just loitering while nothing interesting happened.

It had been something of an overreaction to send out what felt like an entire army (though she imagined it was only maybe thirty or forty agents) to capture one Villain.

Then again, maybe it made sense to overreact. It was better than the opposite.

She leaned back into her seat and, as they drove on, Emily listened with half an ear as her sisters chattered and giggled about silly things in the back.

If she really was going to challenge the city as a sort of Villain, she might end up having to face this kind of response. Could she do anything about it?

They had guns and Tasers, they had body armor and helmets. They were incredibly well equipped. Then they had training to put that equipment to work.

Her sisters were the opposite of well trained. Though she couldn't exactly insult them by saying that aloud. They were doing their best.

The van pulled to a stop, and Emily almost jumped when Sam reached over her and tugged the door open. "Come on!" she said as she hopped out.

Emily scrambled to follow her and was soon followed by her gaggle of sisters.

"Thanks for the ride, old man!" Trinity called to the driver.

He laughed, waved, then put the van into drive again and moved on.

That left Emily and company next to the entrance of an alleyway right next to a quiet little corner store.

"My car's only a block away," Sam said. "Want to keep up the good work, or are we done for the day?"

"I think," Emily said, "that we're done for the day."

CHAPTER FIFTEEN

Maddening Skills

Going to class was always such a weird experience. For a couple of hours she was nobody, just Emily Wright, the quiet girl sitting to the side and near the front (historically, where the teacher was the least likely to notice her and ask a spontaneous question).

The transition from the Boss, fledgling Villain mastermind, to a nobody was hard. A boy had accidentally bumped into her when she entered the lecture hall and she had *glared* at him. He even backed up and apologized.

She'd spent the next ten minutes reenacting the event in her head over and over again, which was actually pretty normal for when she messed something up. Her reaction to the boy's bump, though, was just so unlike her.

Class ended before she'd really come to grips with what had happened. She made sure not to bump into anyone on the way out, and even made doubly sure to avoid the boy who'd bumped into her.

Was her power changing her? Was it just the situations she was in that were encouraging her to be more confident? After all, she'd never been in Mask fights until recently. She never had personal power before, either.

Was it a bad change?

She refocused on what she'd learned during the lecture and tried to keep her mind on task while she returned to her dorm. It was hard, but not impossible. She did intend to get good grades, Villain or no.

Maybe if her grades slipped, one of her sisters could sneak into the professor's office and . . .

Emily slapped a hand over her mouth.

Was she thinking of cheating?

No, no, there was nothing wrong with *thinking* that. She'd thought of doing all sorts of bad things before. A bad thought didn't mean that she was a bad person, as long as she never acted on her less-kind thoughts.

Emily arrived at her dorm and rode the elevator up to the fifth floor. Things were relatively quiet out in the corridor. Sam's room was closed up, but she knew that the girl had a pair of lectures to attend in the early evening, so it was unlikely they'd see each other again until the next day.

She knocked twice on her own door, heard the shuffle of a few brats on the other side, including a hushed conversation that ended in a loud "shut up!" Shaking her head, she unlocked the door and slipped in.

Athena was on the floor, both hands over two of Trinity's mouths while a third Trinity was clinging onto her back.

Teddy was on the bed, sleeping with her back curved way out because she'd seemingly been too lazy to sleep under the covers instead of in them.

"Hey, girls," Emily said. "Athena, Trinity, stop whatever that is. And no, I don't know who started it or whose fault it is, I just want it to stop."

There was a chorus of "Yes, Boss," and "Okay, Big Sis." Then Teddy joined in with a particularly loud snort.

"All right," Emily said. She set her schoolbag down next to her desk, then flopped onto her seat. She was burned right out.

"What's the plan for this afternoon?" Athena asked.

"We took down a Villain and started a protection racket," Emily said. "I think I've done enough for one day."

Athena nodded. "Yeah, we made good progress. I even got a new skill."

"Have you used the point yet?" Emily asked.

Athena shook her head. "I was waiting for you to be here."

Sitting up, Emily considered it for a moment. Having the points and not spending them wasn't going to ever help. "Well, we might as well get to that right away. You might get a skill that you'll need to practice with."

"All right!" Trinity cheered. "I'm going to be even more powerfuller!"

Emily scooted back in her seat, then folded her legs up under her after slipping her shoes off. "All right, who wants to go first?"

"I should," Athena said. "I'm the one who's oldest with the fewest powers. I need them more."

Trinity shrugged. She looked eager, but the racoon girl could, on occasion, be surprisingly patient. "All right," Emily said. "Trinity, want to wake Teddy up? Carefully. Athena, come a bit closer? We'll see what you get together, all right?"

Athena grinned, head bobbing up and down. She adjusted her glasses, then looked right at Emily. "Should I do it?"

"Go ahead."

Her eyes narrowed for a moment, then she smiled. "Done!"

"Nice," Emily said. "Status, Athena."

Name: Athena Wright		
Alignment: Villain, Little Sister		
Alias: None		
Level: 1		
Powers		
Owl Seeing Eye		
Owl Alone	Rank 1	
Who's Hoo	Level 1	
Points		
Power Slots: 0	Skill Upgrades: 1	Skill Slots: 0

"Who's Hoo," Emily repeated. "That's an interesting name." She didn't point out that it was another terrible, terrible pun. "Skill: Who's Hoo," she muttered.

Who's Hoo
Owl Seeing Eye
Level 1
Allows the user to confuse an adversary's sense of who is an ally and who is an enemy.
Activation: Thought
Cooldown: One Hour

That . . . seemed particularly cruel. And useful. It could be a skill that leveled a playing field. Though it looked like Athena could just target one person at a time with it. Would it work on powered enemies as well as normal people?

"That seems very powerful," Emily finally said.

"Yeah!" Athena agreed. "Can I use it on Teddy? She's probably too thick to figure it out, though."

Emily shook her head. "Please, don't hurt your sisters, or use your powers on them. It's not nice."

Athena pouted. "Fine. I guess she is my sister, even if she's a dumb brute."

Emily raised her arms for a hug, and Athena eagerly crashed into her. Once the hug was over, Athena rushed back to the bed and leapt up onto it.

"Hey! I warmed that spot up!" Teddy protested.

"And now you're not there, so it's mine," Athena shot back.

Emily rolled her eyes and focused on Trinity. "You're next?" she asked.

"Yeah!" Trinity said. One of her ran over to Emily and jumped backward so that she sat on Emily's lap. "Okay, so I just unlock a new power, yeah?"

"That's right," Emily said.

Trinity's faces all twisted in concentration, and Emily was worried for a moment before she grinned three times over. "Got it!"

"Status: Trinity."

Name: Trinity Wright		
Alignment: Villain, Little Sister		
Alias: None		
Level: 1		
Powers		
Eternal Racoon Hurricane		
Three's Company	Rank 1	
Sticky Fingers	Level 1	
Points		
Power Slots: 0	Skill Upgrades: 1	Skill Slots: 0

"Aww, yeah!" Trinity said. She immediately ran into a wall with one of her bodies, thumped against the drywall hard enough that Emily winced at the possibility of leaving a crack, then instead of falling back, she clung onto the wall with an open palm. She started to try to climb her way up the wall, but all she could manage was to bounce on the spot while her hands stayed stuck above her head.

"Uh," Emily said. "Skill: Sticky Fingers?"

Sticky Fingers
Eternal Racoon Hurricane
Level 1
The user's fingers are able to cling onto things with incredible force.
No Cooldown

That was a rather horrific skill. She could imagine Trinity sticking onto people, or walls, or things she wasn't supposed to touch. She closed her eyes and tried to pretend the headache away.

"Hey, is it my turn yet?" Teddy asked.

The bear girl was still bleary-eyed, her hair all mussed up and matted with drool.

"Are you ready to use your Skill Slot?" Emily asked.

"Yeah," Teddy said. She crossed her arms. "Yeah, it's done," she said.

"Let me see," Emily said. "Status: Teddy."

Name: Teddy Wright		
Alignment: Villain, Little Sister		
Alias: None		
Level: 1		
Powers		
WereBear		
Rip and Bear	Rank 2	
Iron Bear	Level 1	
Bearly Hurt	Level 1	
Points		
Power Slots: 0	Skill Upgrades: 3	Skill Slots: 0

"Bearly Hurt?" Emily asked. "Is that another ability that'll keep you safe?"

"Yeah, I need to be even harder to hurt," Teddy said. "That way I can protect people better and focus more on hurting others."

"I see," Emily said. "Skill: Bearly Hurt."

Bearly Hurt
WereBear
Level 1
Blows directed at you will be weaker, proportional to your mass.
No Cooldown

"That looks like a great skill," Emily said. She didn't know how much protection that would offer, and it seemed to give less when Teddy was in her normal, human form, but any amount of additional protection was good.

"Yeah," Teddy said with obvious confidence. "I'm gonna be so tough."

"Physically, maybe," Athena said.

"What's that supposed to mean?" Teddy asked.

"Girls," Emily warned.

She still had her own Skill Slot to use up. She hesitated for a moment, but there wasn't much to gain in not using it. Unless it gave her a fourth sister to take care of . . . then again, so far there had been a pattern, and she was pretty sure it would hold true.

Do you wish to spend a Skill Slot point on the Power: Sister Summoning?

"Yes," Emily said.

New Skill unlocked!

Menagerie Family has been added to your Power's Skills!

She frowned as she opened the skill's description.

Menagerie Family
Sister Summoning
Level 1
Allows you to temporarily copy an animal trait from one of your siblings.

Activation: Vocal Command
Cooldown: One Hour

That had some potential.
She'd have to test it all though.

CHAPTER SIXTEEN

Traits

Emily was certain that the big, proper Hero groups had entire teams dedicated to helping new Heroes learn about their own powers. She had seen a hint of that already and had to admit that it was pretty interesting.

Unfortunately, her team of power-testing assistants were currently arguing over which cartoon to watch on her laptop.

She leaned back into her seat and stared at the description for her new skill. Menagerie Family. The name wasn't terribly helpful. It was a pun, which was pretty typical of her skills. Were the skills of other Masks also all puns? Could she look that up without raising suspicions?

Something for later.

The skill would let her copy an animal trait of one sibling for an indeterminate amount of time, after which she had to wait another hour to reuse the skill.

That left a lot of questions unanswered. She opened her desk drawer and took out her notepad. It had been a day or two since she'd made a proper list.

What animal traits were copied?

Was the cooldown fixed, or was there an individual cooldown for every sister?

Did the traits appear as physical changes?

Did she need physical contact with a sister to initiate the skill?

Were there any negative consequences?

She tapped the back of her pen against her bottom lip before nodding. "Girls, I'm going to be trying out my new power now."

"Oh yeah, you got a power too," Teddy said. "What is it?"

Emily almost dismissed Teddy's question, but she stopped herself before she said anything. Teddy had once shown that she knew a lot more about the system than most, and the other girls weren't fussing over their new powers, they just accepted them as if they knew what they did right away. "It's called Menagerie Family," Emily said. "Do you know anything about it?"

"Nah," Teddy said. "What's it do?"

"One sec," Emily said. She pulled up the skill's screen, then read its description to her sisters, who were all paying attention, mostly—one of Trinity's bodies was carefully typing something on the laptop while the others were distracted. "Uh, Allows you to temporarily copy an animal trait from one of your siblings. It has a one-hour cooldown."

"Yeah, that sounds about right," Teddy said. "Gonna be one of those skills that lets you switch things around. Does it say how long you can be a bear for?"

"It doesn't say a bear, it says an animal trait," Athena said. "I hope the trait she gets from you isn't your smarts."

"It, uh, just says temporary," Emily said. "And, Athena, don't hurt Teddy's feelings."

"Eh, I'm fine," Teddy said.

Athena nodded. "Yeah, if it doesn't specify how long it takes to stop, then you can probably keep the skill going on one trait for a long time."

"So the Boss is gonna be bearlike all the time?" Teddy asked.

"Why would she want to be like a bear?" Athena asked. "Who wants to sleep around all day and be lazy?"

"Anyone sane."

Emily waved her hands to calm the two down. They'd been increasingly volatile toward each other lately, and she wasn't sure if they actually disliked each other, or if it was all some sort of weird sibling bonding thing. "Okay, so what traits would the skill copy?" Emily asked.

"Bet it won't be the same ones," Teddy said.

Emily nodded, encouraging her to go on. Teddy usually had good insights on why powers did what they did.

"That'd be too boring," the bear girl added. She started to pick her nose.

Emily stood up from her chair and walked to the middle of the room. "All right, let's try it," she said.

"Cool!" Teddy said. "What kind of bear will you get traits of? A polar bear? Those are pretty cool. Almost as cool as grizzlies."

"She should do mine first, actually," Athena said. "Bears are big and clumsy and dumb. Owls are graceful and small and awesome. So my traits will make her even better so she'll be able to get used to the skill faster."

Teddy glared at Athena, who glared right back.

"Hey! You should become a racoon," Trinity said. "Because it's not one of the other two."

"You know what, you're right, Trinity. I think these two need to cool their heads a little. So how about we start with your trait."

Trinity raised her six arms up. "That worked!" she cheered.

Emily stood tall, took a deep breath, considered whether or not power-testing in her tiny dorm in the middle of the day was a good idea or not, then let the breath she was holding out in a long exhale along with a tiny fraction of her stress.

"Okay. Menagerie Family: Trinity."

Emily felt something like a burp travel up her esophagus, but there was nothing to accompany it, and for just a moment she was hit by a wave of dizziness.

"Uh," she said.

Menagerie Family

You have obtained the traits of the Racoon!

You may now eat trash without ill effect!

"What'd it do?' Trinity asked. She hit Emily with the triple racoon eyes, all big and eager.

"I can now eat trash," Emily said.

Trinity gasped, hands rushing to cover her mouths. "It worked," she said. "You're just like me."

"Uh-huh," Emily said.

"We need to test it," Trinity said. "I've got some chocolate I found, here." She reached into her pockets and pulled out a partially wrapped candy bar. It was a little melted. There were hairs on it.

"No," Emily said. "Please put that in the trash."

"That's where I got it from."

"I . . . yes, well, put it back there, please." Emily walked over to the bathroom and looked at herself in the mirror. She couldn't see any changes, not until she opened her mouth and noticed that her canines were sharper . . . maybe. She ran her tongue over her teeth but couldn't quite tell if they were all that different or not.

"Okay, do mine next!" Teddy said.

Emily walked back to the middle of the room and nodded. "All right, fine. Do you think I can just go from one to another, or do I need to cancel things in between?"

"Should be able to just reuse the skill," Teddy said.

"I suppose we'll need to test both options out. Menagerie Family: Teddy."

The burping sensation returned, though this time reversed, which was strangely horrific. She was soon distracted by a sensation all over her body, like all her muscles twitching faintly at once.

Menagerie Family

You have obtained the traits of the Bear!

You are now stronger!

Emily glanced down at herself. No obvious change again, unless . . . she raised an arm and looked at it.

She was never *that* hairy before, was she?

"So are you cooler now?" Teddy asked.

"Stronger, apparently," Emily said. "And maybe a tiny bit warmer in winter." She felt at her teeth and was comforted to notice they weren't as sharp. So the traits faded. She wouldn't need to shave every time she used Teddy's.

"Hey, Boss, lift me up!" Teddy asked. She moved over to Emily and stood with her arms out to the side.

Shrugging, Emily leaned down, placed her hands under Teddy's armpits, and lifted.

She felt like a vein was going to pop in her forehead, and her muscles all strained, but, bit by bit, she managed to lift Teddy up.

She was maybe stronger, but it was likely that it depended on her initial strength, which was about par for a young adult woman whose main exercise was leaving the couch to grab chips.

"Okay, I'm a little stronger. That might be useful in a pinch." She didn't know how to put that strength to good use, but it was there. "Cancel Menagerie Family: Teddy," she tried.

It took a moment, but that strange feeling came over her again, and suddenly Teddy's weight felt like it was so much more than it had been a moment before. She set the girl down, then checked her arms again.

She didn't think of herself as vain, but she might have some issues with looking fuzzier than the most testosterone-heavy man ever.

"Okay, that was good. Uh, Athena's next, I guess. Maybe I'll keep yours on overnight, to see the duration? Do you think there could be side effects?"

"Only because you won't be using the coolest trait," Teddy said.

"Okay then. Menagerie Family: Athena."

This time, the strangeness was all in her eyes and head. Like getting a very enthusiastic but awful scalp massage that reached all the way down to behind her eyes.

She shivered, then blinked.

The room was so much brighter. She turned her head, and the sound of her neck brushing against her shirt almost made her jump.

"Big Sis?" Athena screamed. "Oh, your eyes are prettier!"

Emily winced. It wasn't a scream, her hearing was just a lot more acute. Her vision, too. Not just to the lighting but, well, perhaps years of staring into screens had rendered her less than twenty–twenty capable.

Menagerie Family

You have obtained the traits of the Owl!

Your perception has been sharpened!

"Huh," Emily said. "Okay, I can work with that."

CHAPTER SEVENTEEN

A Sneaky Peak

The next morning, there was a knock at the door, but for once, it didn't set Emily's heart racing or send a cold sweat down her spine.

"Athena, can you check the door, please?" Emily asked. She was at her desk, homework opened on her laptop.

"Sure thing, Big Sis!" Athena said as she hopped over to the door. "Hey, who is it?" Athena asked.

"It's Sam," came a faint reply from the other side.

"Big Sis, it's minion Sam," Athena repeated.

Emily nodded. "She sent me a text, it's okay. Let her in."

The door opened and Sam snuck into the room, a backpack thumping in next to her. "Hey, kids; hey, Boss," Sam said. "I got some stuff, but that's for later. How's everyone doing?"

"We're all right," Teddy said. She was lying on the floor, an arm wrapped around a Trinity who was currently being used as a blanket. The other two Trinity were standing next to Emily, "helping" her with her homework.

"Cool, cool," Sam said. She shuffled over to Emily's bed and sat down on it, which seemed to be what everyone was doing recently. "So what sort of nefarious deeds will we be doing today?"

"Nothing, I hope," Emily said.

Sam pouted. Actually pouted. Emily could forgive that in her sisters, they were basically preteens, but Sam was—at least according to her age—a proper adult. "That's no fun."

"Yeah, it ain't fun, Boss," Teddy said. She squeezed the Trinity she was hugging closer as if in protest.

"Hey! You're choking me," one of Trinity's other bodies said.

"Teddy, don't choke your sister," Emily said. "And, Sam, don't encourage them, please?"

Sam shrugged. "Sure. Still think that you're missing out here. Inaction's not going to help you in the long run. You're on the news right now, you know? It's time to capitalize on that. Do something to grow your empire, or maybe work on your PR."

"I thought you were trying to be a silent observer for your thesis paper," Emily said.

Sam grinned. "The nonsilent bits aren't going to go in the paper," she said.

"Isn't that . . . I don't know, lacking in academic morals?" Emily asked.

"Emily, I joined a Villain as a minion. I don't think a bit of academic dishonesty is the most morally wrong thing I've done this week." Sam bounced back to her feet. "So! If we're not going to be Villain-ing, then what should we work on?"

Emily sighed. She was about to put her elbows on her chair's arms when she bumped into Trinity, who had a head on the arm. She started running her fingers through the girl's hair, vaguely amused at the way Trinity's ears twitched whenever her fingers brushed by. "I have a few ideas, I guess. Cement's papers indicated that he has a few safe houses. Alea Iacta is in a safe house still; I don't know if he's returned to school or anything. Anyway, that's two things I want to do. Look into the other safe houses and bases, and touch base with Alea Iacta."

"Your other minion," Sam said. "All right, cool. I vote on checking out the Villain lair first.

"I vote lair," Athena said.

"Me too," Teddy said.

"Me three," Trinity replied. Then she started giggling at her own joke.

Emily reached into her desk and lazily pulled out her notebook with the addresses and locations of various safe houses. There weren't many. Three locations, two of which were apartments and one that they'd been to already and where they'd fought Black Shield. The lair locations were just below that. Two places . . . more or less. "Check this out," she said before handing the notebook to Trinity who ran it over to Sam.

"Okay," Sam said as she scanned the page. "So what am I looking for?"

"The last two. There's one lair in a place called the . . . Garter Belt. It's a little dance club-slash-bar."

"I know the place," Sam said.

Emily paused. "You've . . . been there?"

"Huh? Oh yeah, they'll let in any girl if she's hot or confident enough," Sam said. "I'm both, so free drinks, you know?"

"Uh, sure," Emily said. She dismissed the warmth trying to cling to her cheeks. There was no way in a million years she'd go to a place like that. "I think that's where Homie worked before he got arrested. The place might still be running?"

"Another protection racket to set up?" Sam asked.

"I think it might be more legitimate than that," Emily said. "More of a money laundering place, maybe? Anyway, it's the other base location that's piqued my interest."

"Yeah," Sam said. "The address isn't telling me anything."

Emily turned to her laptop, then opened a window that had been left minimized. "It's right here," she said. "I don't know what the building is, but it doesn't look big."

Sam came closer, then squinted at the screen. "Oh! I know that one."

"What is it?" Emily asked. "The street view isn't very helpful."

Sam nodded. "Yeah, okay, so history lesson time. Way way long ago, like back in the early nineties, there was this thing where they wanted to have an Eauclaire metro. It would connect over to a couple of places. The center of the city, the campus, then a few spots on the edges and maybe even to the next city over. It wasn't going to be this huge system, but, like, it was supposed to be cheaper than a bus once everything was set up."

"I don't remember there being a metro," Emily said.

"Canceled," Sam said with a dismissive shake of her head. "Like, within a year or two of it starting up. I think it was a mess of budget issues, and a gang started up with the construction crews. Then there was a bunch of corruption stuff. It was a whole thing. But long story short, nothing got done and the project died off."

"And this building was part of that," Emily said. "Maybe Cement had a base inside there?"

"Could be, yeah," Sam said. "Don't know how far along they came with the construction, but they were at it for a year or two, at least. Might be a whole bunch of old caves under there. I think some kids went exploring once and got lost. Lots of drama. Then they blocked off all the access points into the underground bits."

"Hmm. Okay. I guess there's no harm in looking into it. There might be more information about Cement's organization in there."

Sam was already halfway to the door with Emily's sisters bouncing after her. "I'll get my car warmed up!"

Emily watched them all file out of her room, then with a panicked "W-wait for me!" she rushed around to grab her shoes and ran after them.

Half of her sisters had, of course, forgotten to get dressed properly before leaving. So they rushed back in and searched for jackets and running shoes and boots they could wear while out in the city.

Once Emily made sure everyone was ready for a trip across the city, they headed down and over to the parking garage where Sam's car was tucked away and waiting for them.

"It's not too far from here," Sam said. "We could walk, even, but I'd rather ride."

They reached the car, squeezed into it, then they were off and heading across the city again.

Emily worked on her soft skills and asked Sam about her life. Fortunately, Sam was more than willing to fill the void with constant chatter about teachers, classes, and her increasingly wild plans for the near and far future.

Sam had been right when she said that the station wasn't too far from the school. It was right next to some of the older shops in what was once the middle of the city. There was a defunct mall, now filled with stores that sold luggage bags and flowers and phone cases across the street from an UrgerKing that hadn't been renovated since the early 2000s.

Sam parked at the far end of the mall's lot, then pointed across the street. "That's the one. The gray box."

The would-be metro entrance wasn't quite a gray box. It had more potential than that. But it wasn't exactly nice, either. It didn't look like the place was seeing much use.

"The door has a sign on it," Emily said. "I can't quite make it out from here, but it doesn't look good."

"It says 'Closed,'" Athena said. She squinted through her big glasses a little more. "And that trespassers aren't allowed."

"Why do you have glasses if you can see so good?" Teddy asked.

"Because I can't see so good without them, idiot," Athena said.

"Girls," Emily warned. "Calm down. Let's snoop around, maybe there's an entrance at the back or something."

"I've got a lockpicking kit," Sam said. "And, like, three hours of Outube tutorials under my belt."

". . . Great."

CHAPTER EIGHTEEN

Metro

Emily jogged up to the side of the station and poked her head around the corner. She hoped she was being fast enough that anyone looking her way wouldn't have time to spot her before she pulled back.

"Is it clear?" Sam whispered from behind her.

"Why are you two being all sneakylike?" Teddy asked at a volume that was very much not a whisper.

Emily spun toward the bear girl. "We're trying not to be noticed," she said.

Teddy just stared at her for a moment before looking up and down the street. "Yeah, there's only a few people here, Boss. No one cares. If you're gonna be sneaky out in the open, the best way to do that's not to be sneaky at all."

"Teddy's right," Athena said. "Trying to sneak while you're in public's mostly about looking as normal as possible. Just look at how good we are at looking normal." Athena gestured to herself, then to Trinity, who was picking all three of her noses, and Teddy, who had her hands stuffed in her pockets and was yawning as if it was well past her bedtime.

"I suppose," Emily said.

"Yeah, I've heard that kind of thing before," Sam said. "Feels weird, though."

Athena went on explaining. "Looking sneaky looks suspicious. You only wanna look sneaky when no one can see you looking sneaky."

"Yeah," Teddy said. "Come on, Boss, just follow me, all right?" She stomped off past Emily and around the corner.

Emily had decided that breaking in through the front of the building would be a terrible idea. It was out along the roadside, and in the open as well. Anyone would be able to see them from the street. So she decided to go around and see if there was a way in from another angle.

It turned out that there was. "That's a door," Sam said. "But, uh, I don't know if we'll be able to break into that one."

The side entrance was a flat steel door with a grated platform next to it. Just two loud metal steps led up to the door whose only real feature was a rusting plaque that read EMPLOYEES ONLY in black block letters.

Sam grabbed the handle and tugged on it. It didn't do anything.

"Do you think you can pick the lock?" Emily asked.

"I mean, I can try," Sam said. "Going to need a minute or two, I think."

Emily hesitated. She could call the whole thing off. She didn't even know what she expected to find in the old metro station. Then again, they were there already, and she didn't know how busy the coming weeks and months might become. Finding another safe house now could be a life-saver later. "Do what you can. Trinity, you go on either end of the alley, check to see if anyone's coming by. Athena, Teddy, stand around Sam. We don't want anyone seeing her work."

She received a chorus of replies from her sisters before they moved into place.

Sam opened her little lockpicking set on the ground, then pulled out her phone and looked at the lock. "What are you doing?" Emily asked.

"Looking up the lock online. There's sites that explain this kind of thing, you know?"

"Oh," Emily said. She felt a little silly for asking. Still, she installed herself behind Sam, leaning against a railing where she could see the girl at work.

It took Sam a good five minutes of fiddling and muttering the sorts of words that Emily was dearly hoping her sisters didn't pick up, but in the end, she cheered as the lock clicked and the door opened a crack. "Got it!"

"Good work," Emily said. "Really, I'm impressed." She reached out and held the door open—the last thing they needed was for it to close and lock itself up again. "Come on girls, gather up."

Teddy peeked into the room beyond the door, then came back frown-ing. "Dark in there."

"I can see in the dark well," Athena said. "I'll take the lead if you want."

Emily nodded. "You first, then Trinity, me, Trinity, Sam, Teddy, and Trinity at the rear." Emily pulled out her phone and turned on its flashlight mode. "Sam, do you have a light?"

"I have a key chain light and my phone," Sam said.

That was one more light than Emily had.

They slipped into the metro station, into what was obviously some sort of office and maintenance area away from the public-facing sections of the building. The corridor, lit only by their swaying lights, was long and narrow, with doors on either side that lead into even darker rooms.

"Menagerie Family: Athena," Emily muttered.

Her eyes and head tingled, but when she blinked again the shadows had changed. They didn't quite recede, but the fuzzy shapes in the dark were in much starker contrast. It was easier to tell what she was looking at, even without her light shining on it.

Menagerie Family

You have obtained the traits of the Owl!

Your perception has been sharpened!

"What was that?" Sam asked.

"That," Athena said with dripping smugness, "was Big Sister's newest and best skill. She can borrow our animal traits, and of course mine are the best."

Emily decided not to step into that particular puddle and delivered her own, less-biased explanation. "I can take on animal traits from my sisters," she said. "Athena's are owl-based, so better eyesight and hearing, mostly."

"Oh, that's neat," Sam said. "Doesn't sound like a superstrong power on its own."

"I don't think it's meant to be? It's more that I get a bit more versatility. My sisters are still my main power, I guess."

"Cool," Sam said.

They poked their heads into the rooms they were crossing. Mostly they were unfinished office spaces, with desks but little else. Even the light bulbs were missing from the ceilings and some rooms were left unpainted and with bare cement floors.

"This place really was never used," Emily said as she stepped out of another empty room.

"Yeah, a bunch of lost taxpayer money here," Sam said.

"We could turn this place into a lair," Athena suggested.

Emily considered it. "It's a bit too out in the open, I think. There are still windows and things, and someone might think it's suspicious if we continue to come here. Besides, I don't think there's power, and there's probably no running water."

"Right," Sam said. "That would be nice."

They continued to the end of the corridor, then down a set of stairs and through another plain metal door. This one opened onto the side of the main lobby at the front of the building. There was a large staircase going deeper down, made of plain tiles and with boards on the sides for ads that had never been placed.

The girls fanned out a little as they headed down and deeper in. A row of turnstiles greeted them, rusting and unused and covered in dust. Emily could imagine people slipping through them on the way to the next train out to wherever the station connected to.

The boarding area itself wasn't anything impressive. Just a spot with a few benches next to the trench where the train tracks were.

"It looks like it was almost ready," Emily said as she looked around. There was a stack of benches up against one wall, and a few piles of materials on wooden pallets.

"I guess they canceled it at the last minute," Sam said. "I don't remember much about it, really. Maybe they were a few weeks away from opening."

"That's a bit sad, actually," Emily said. She gravitated over to a wall that had a map on it. It was Eauclaire, though a smaller, older Eauclaire. The metro line stretched out and around the city, with two existing stops—one where she was, and one near her school. Three more stops were marked as "Coming Soon!," including one outside of the city.

"Hey, Boss!" Teddy called. Her voice bounced around the empty room.

"Yes?" Emily asked.

She found Teddy on the edge of the tracks, squinting into the dark. "I think there's something that way," she said while pointing into the dark tunnel.

"Uh," Emily said. "I don't think we're supposed to go down there."

"We're not supposed to be here, either," Sam said. She sat on the edge of the trench, then dropped down to the bottom. "Come on! Let's go check it out. It's not like there's a train that can hit us here."

Emily chewed on her lip and then winced as Trinity stepped off the edge and crashed at the bottom. "I'm good!" Trinity said.

"Fine, let's go check out . . . whatever's lurking in the dark. I'm sure this is a wonderful idea. And don't touch the middle rail!"

CHAPTER NINETEEN

Mobile Base

The tunnel went on seemingly forever, swallowing every bit of light they had and leaving the distance as nothing but shifting shadows, even through Emily's temporarily enhanced senses.

"I don't know if this is a good idea," Emily said as she stared ahead.

"Well, we're already down here," Sam said. "And it's not like we can get lost. No intersections, just a straight path, you know?"

The passage was relatively clear. A few wrappers were left next to the edges, and a coating of dust covered everything, but for the most part, there was little to see in the tunnel as they walked on and on.

In reality, Emily knew that they hadn't moved far. For all their bravado, none of her sisters were moving at more than a shuffle, and she could see how tense they were. Which was about half as tense as she was.

She kept expecting some city inspector to show up and give them an earful. Or worse, a cop.

"There's something ahead," Athena said.

"Yeah, that's what I said," Teddy replied. She was putting up a brave front, but she also bumped into Emily's side at every step because of how close she was staying. Emily let her hand fall down and Teddy instantly grabbed on to it for reassurance.

Athena turned out to be right. The large form of a train car appeared ahead of them.

"That's a weird train," Sam said as she brought her phone up in one hand.

The caboose wasn't what Emily expected from a subway car. It was a bit lower and made of what looked like riveted steel sheets with a door in its middle and steps leading down to almost ground height. There was a single round window, no bigger than her forearm, covered by a curtain within.

"Trinity, want to go around the edges?" Emily whispered.

"Got it," Trinity echoed herself before she ran to either side of the train car. It didn't take long for her to report. "There's just three of them. And the one at the front's weird."

Emily frowned, then walked over to the right so that she could see for herself. Trinity wasn't wrong. The entire train was three sections long, with the frontmost clearly some sort of engine. "Maybe it's a maintenance train?" she asked. The people working on the station needed a way to get around, too. She imagined it made sense that they would have their own little train for that.

"Maybe," Sam said. She grabbed one of the railings at the rear and pulled herself up to the back door. It clunked open at her prying. "Not locked," she said.

Emily and her sisters lined up behind Sam, one part curious, one part wanting to seek shelter within the tighter confines of the trains.

She was expecting something like a mobile workstation, maybe an empty car, or one filled with cargo. Instead . . . "This is a living space," Emily said as she inspected the car from over Sam's shoulder.

Athena reached out and flicked a switch against one wall and everyone tensed for a moment as lights along the car's ceiling came on.

The car was long and narrow, with a corridor down its middle. The entire thing was split in half, with rooms on one end that had bunk beds, and then a wide section at the other end that had a TV, a small kitchen space with a camp stove and microwave, and even a little desk to work at.

"Huh," Sam said. "Like a bigger RV."

"A what?" Trinity asked.

"An RV? Uh, a recreational vehicle? People use them to travel around and camp. It's like a bus you can live in. This looks like that, but bigger. The decor is a bit seventies, but it looks clean, at least."

Emily nodded along. The car was obviously not something new, but it had been well maintained, she suspected. No visible rust, not too much dust, no detritus or things tossed aside.

Teddy let go of her hand and moved into the kitchen area where she opened some of the cupboards. "Hey, canned stuff."

Emily followed her and took a can off a shelf. It was still well before its expiration date. "This can't have been stocked before the metro closed," Emily said.

"Maybe the city is still maintaining things?" Sam asked.

It was possible, but Emily felt like something was off. She expected a place that workers frequently used to be a bit messier, more worn out. "Let's look at the next car," she said.

The cars were connected via a set of doors lined through a grate catwalk. The next door wasn't locked, either, and it led into a vastly different room.

They saw black floors and white walls; cubicles along one side; and a large table in the center surrounded by high-back chairs. One chair, at the far end of the room, was taller than the rest by a good eight inches.

"Oh," Teddy said as she looked around. "This is a lair."

"Um," Emily said.

"Yeah," Sam said as she followed. "This is totally a Villain lair."

The room had a divider at the far end that hid the door into the next section. Other than the few cubicles near the entrance, there wasn't much in the room itself. Athena found another light switch, then a switch that lowered a projector and screen from the ceiling along one wall.

Some hardware was left in the cubicles. Internet routers and the like, but the sort that looked rather expensive. And, of course, there was a whiteboard on one wall with a map of the metro, covered in tiny notations.

"I guess this was Cement's base," Emily said as she took it all in.

Sam poked her head around the dividing wall at the far end. "A *mobile* base. There's a big engine in the next car and the controls for it, too. I think it's a diesel engine?"

"So this whole thing can move?" Teddy asked.

"That's what mobile means," Athena said. "Which you'd know if you were."

"Athena, apologize," Emily said.

Athena pouted and crossed her arms. "Sorry, Teddy," she muttered.

"I don't even know how that was an insult," Teddy said.

Emily could tell that Athena was visibly biting her tongue from flinging another insult at Teddy. Fortunately, she stayed quiet.

Crossing the room slowly, Emily inspected the simple but elegant decor while running a hand over the surface of the table. There was more dust, though it was faint. She reached the thronelike chair, then hesitated.

"Oh, the Boss is gonna sit," Trinity said.

Suddenly there was a rush as the girls found seats around the table. Teddy to the right, Athena to the left, Trinity squeezing all three of her bodies next to Teddy.

Her sisters watched Emily as she carefully slid the big chair back, then stepped into its place and pulled it up behind her.

She watched her sisters, who were all grinning ear to ear.

Somehow, it felt *right*.

"Having fun?" Sam asked.

Emily "eeped" and jumped on the spot. She was entirely spooked out of her daydream.

"Hey, minions sit at the boring end of the table," Teddy said.

"Yeah," Athena agreed. "Or you can stand at the far end and cross your arms to look intimidating. But no bothering the Boss when she's in her Villain throne."

"It's not a Villain's throne," Emily said.

Teddy reached over and patted her hand. "It can be a Super Villain throne if you want."

"I, uh, really don't."

Sam pulled out one of the seats near the far end of the table, then leaned back and set her boots onto the surface. "So what are we going to do with this place?"

"Can we do anything with it?" Emily asked.

"Yeah, we should take it over," Teddy said.

The other sisters nodded unanimously. "Teddy's right," Athena said. "Plus, look at the map on the whiteboard. There's some routes that take this place close to the school. If that Cement guy was worth anything, then there has to be a secret entrance near there."

"Oh yeah, secret tunnels under the city," Sam said. "That's kind of awesome."

"We really don't need all this," Emily said.

"We could leave the last car behind and use it as a cool place to hang out," Teddy said.

"We could use the tunnels to pop out from all over and take stuff from the streets before those no-good good-guy trash trucks take it," Trinity said.

Emily rubbed at her forehead. She had the impression she had just inherited a lot of trouble, somehow.

"We'll see," she said. "We need to find out if this thing can even move first."

"I can get on that," Sam said. "How hard can moving a train be? It's not like it can even turn."

"Right," Emily said. She was having doubts. "I feel like I should be telling my mom about this."

CHAPTER TWENTY

Putting the Super in Villain

We should probably head home," Emily said. It was going to be a decently long walk back to Sam's car.

"What?" Teddy asked.

Emily looked down the table at her little sister. "What what?" she replied.

"We can't just head back already," Teddy said. She smacked the table for emphasis. "We all sat down around the Villain table in the Villain lair. We can't leave until we've plotted."

"Yeah, we need to plot things," Trinity said from where she was squished on her seat.

Emily turned to Athena and Sam, hoping that at least one of them would be reasonable. Unfortunately, both were nodding along. "You have to," Sam said. "It's basically a requirement. Plus you look nice and intimidating in that seat. Now, imagine if you were in costume."

Fighting back a blush, Emily crossed her arms and glowered at the table.

"Yeah, exactly like that. You need a cat, though, like on your armrest," Sam said.

"I can be the cat," Trinity said. "Those are just uptight raccoons."

"I don't need a cat," Emily said. She pretended not to notice the sighs of relief from all her sisters, because frankly, she didn't know what to do about them. "And what would we even plot about?"

"Your takeover of the city?" Sam proposed.

She received unanimous nods for that.

"I'm not going to take over the city," Emily said.

"But if you were," Sam began. She quickly raised her hands in surrender. "No no, it's a hypothetical. If you were, hypothetically, going to take over the city. What would you do? Come on, no harm in answering a hypothetical."

Emily shook her head, but there was no harm that she could see. "I guess it wouldn't be all that easy. There's the Heroic Response Force to deal with, other Heroes, the police, politicians, the school administration and city, and then there's the Cabal. We have no idea what they're up to, but I imagine it's not great."

"We'll kick all their butts; just line them up and bend them over for me," Teddy said.

"Uh, no," Emily said. "Some of them . . . a lot of them . . . will definitely be stronger than us. And others can't be defeated with a fight. You need the city government on your side, at least a little, I imagine. The HRF and the Heroes can probably be cowed into stepping back if you're strong enough and aren't so evil that they'll do anything to stop you."

Sam leaned her elbows onto the table. "So how would you deal with it?"

Emily knew what the woman was trying to do. But then . . . Emily's feet ached a bit from all the walking, and a few more minutes of sitting down couldn't hurt. "I guess you'd need to tackle the problem from a, uh, different angle. Do it like a politician would."

"Whoa," Athena said. "That's superevil."

Emily frowned. "I mostly meant that if you want to take over the city, then you need to have the city want you to take over. You need to be popular or charismatic enough that the people will be happy to see you act. That's the opposite of how Villains are seen."

"I can be charismatic," Teddy said. "Real charismatic. Just watch me, I'll have the people fighting by my side in no time. The common people will know that I am a bear of the people, for the people."

"Right," Emily said. "In this hypothetical situation, I guess the most important thing would be to be seen as both more competent and friendly than the average Hero. Then, I guess you'd need to start leveraging that into actual political power of some sort. Maybe getting the police on your side by highlighting their efforts over those of the HRF, maybe . . ."

Emily squinted as she thought. How *would* she take over a city?

She'd heard of plenty of Villains who had tried before, but never successfully. She imagined that those who did succeed did so quietly and subtly.

"I guess you'd need to have a good amount of control over the city's economy. Maybe whatever the main sources of revenue in the city are all need to be under your control, or at least most of them. You'd need to start buying up businesses and homes. You could just legally own a good portion of the city if you snowball things correctly, and by then I suppose you'll rule the city by dint of the city needing you to function."

"Needing you to function?" Sam asked.

"I would make sure to own enough of the franchises and smaller businesses that ousting me would mean costing the city so many jobs that the local economy would collapse," Emily said. She cleared her throat. "Hypothetically, I mean."

"Whoa," Teddy said. "The Boss is so smart! Where do we start, though?"

"I think we've started already," Athena said.

"We just need to keep on doing as the Boss says," Trinity said.

"Wait, no," Emily said. She waved her arms side to side in denial. "I haven't been leading anyone into a life of Villainy. You're misunderstanding things."

Sam grinned. "No, I don't think anyone's misunderstanding. So I guess the next step is working hard to become staples of the community. Volunteer work, helping old ladies across the road, knocking down any criminals."

"No!" Emily said. Then what she heard caught up to her. "Wait, I mean yes."

"Yeah!" Teddy said. "Doing lame good stuff in the name of Villainy."

"I . . . okay," Emily said. She wasn't sure what she was supposed to say, but she felt like anything she did say would be twisted around regardless. She bounced to her feet. "Let's head back home."

Teddy smacked the table twice. "Meeting adjourned!" she declared.

The other girls scrambled out of their seats, and Emily noted that the dust from the seats stayed on them. She patted down her own pants, then glanced around the train car. "What are we going to do about this place?" she asked.

"Boring thing is nothing," Sam said. "Smart thing . . . probably figure out a way to get it closer to the school, then use it as a sort of mobile base?"

"That's the smart idea?" Emily asked.

Sam shrugged. "You're going to need a place to stay one day that isn't the dorm. I don't know how you're cramming this many girls in one small room as it is. I find my room a bit small, and I'm alone in there. What's going to happen when you get even more sisters?"

Emily shuddered at the thought. That was reaching a critical number of knees and elbows that would poke at her while she slept. "You're right. But I don't know if this is the best place for that."

"Well, spruce it up a bit then," Sam said.

"I don't mind cleaning if it's a Villain's lair," Athena said. "That's the cool kind of cleaning."

"There's no such thing as cool cleaning," Teddy grumped. "Just wipe the dust off the beds, it'll be fine."

"That's nasty," Athena said. "Why am I the only clean sister?"

"Come on," Emily said. "We can see about cleaning this place some other time. I think it would be nice to get back home."

"And eat," Trinity said.

"And, yeah, we need to grab something to eat, too," Emily agreed. She was a little hungry herself, now that she paid attention. Feeding all her sisters would be a further drain on her money, but maybe with her new protection racket, things would ease up.

She closed her eyes. It was hard enough to convince her sisters not to be Villainous without immediately accepting things like protection rackets as viable ways of earning money.

The group left the train the same way they entered it. Somehow, the dark, unlit tunnels weren't as scary the second time around. They had discovered what hid in the depths, and it wasn't all that bad.

Climbing back onto the platform proved more difficult.

Sam was the more athletic between herself and Emily. She leapt, grabbed the lip of the platform, and pulled herself up until she could kick a leg over the side.

Emily grabbed a Trinity and helped her up, then did the same for the next. The two helped her third body up, dirtying the front of her outfits in the process.

Then Emily found herself stuck in the pit until Teddy turned into a bear and hoisted her up by biting her belt from the back.

Once they were all up, they headed back through the station and out the side door. Being in the sun again was blinding, but also relieving. "Okay," Emily said. "Let's grab a bite, and then back home."

That, of course, was the moment where her phone decided to buzz, then start ringing.

Emily picked it up, saw the incoming call from her mom, then noticed the twenty-nine missed messages. "Ah, crud."

CHAPTER TWENTY-ONE

Busy City

Hey, Mom," Emily said. She couldn't help but sound a little sheepish as she replied. Being underground had probably cut off any phone signal she had. She had heard that in some stations and underground places there were these signal repeater things that would allow a phone to work despite the location, but she imagined that those had never been installed in the Eauclaire metro system.

"Emily," her mom said with obvious relief. "Are you okay?"

Emily glanced around. They were heading back to Sam's car, her sisters trailing out ahead except for one Trinity who was gripping onto Emily's free hand. "We're fine," she said. "We were about to head back home. A . . . well, a lot has happened, I guess."

"Okay, good, good. Did you eat lunch yet?"

She couldn't help the smile. "No, not yet."

"Then I'll pick something up and meet you at your dorm, okay?"

"That would be nice, Mom," Emily said. "I'll talk to you in person, then?"

It took a bit of back-and-forth to convince her mom to hang up, and a few embarrassing moments where Emily had to tell her mom that she loved her—with Sam giggling in the background to make everything worse—but eventually she hung up and was able to slip her phone away.

"Looks like we'll be eating back in the dorm," Emily said. "You're, um, welcome to come, too, Sam."

Sam grinned. "Making sure to feed your minions, huh? Just remember that gas isn't free, either, and I can't afford to drive you all over the place all the time."

"Right," Emily said. "I'll be sure to pay you back as soon as I can."

Sam bumped her shoulder against Emily, and she almost tripped over nothing from the contact. "Hey, don't worry about it, Boss."

Everyone piled into the car, and Emily had to tell Trinity that no, she couldn't have one of her bodies sit on Emily's lap in front, no matter how small she was. Once everyone was about as safe as they could be, they took off back toward the school and home.

"So what's the next step in your master plan?" Sam asked. "Anything I can help with?"

"I don't know," Emily said. "I think . . . I think I'm going to call Alea Iacta. See how he's doing. Then maybe we can continue to investigate Cement's organization? I don't like the risk we're taking with that, but it feels like the only way we can earn any money quickly. I'll see. I need some time to think."

"All right," Sam said. "Might want to hit while the iron's hot, though."

"What's the iron in this analogy?" Emily asked. It was a little strange how quickly she got used to talking to Sam. Maybe being in a position of relative power was making it easier to just . . . talk to someone. It was something to think about later.

Sam hummed. "I think in this case the iron is your reputation and power. You're . . . no, *we're* probably the coolest new Heroes in the city."

"Oh, eww," Athena said. "I know we're doing it 'cause the Boss said so, but that's still nasty."

"Yeah," Teddy said. "Don't say that kind of thing about us out loud, it's rude. We're Villains pretending to be Heroes. We're just real good at it."

Sam rolled her eyes. Fortunately, they were at a red light, so it wasn't a big distraction from the road. "You know what I meant. The media's gonna love you. The brats back there are like . . . a PR gold mine."

Emily half turned to see her sisters. She guessed they were kind of cute . . . maybe? Teddy and Athena were roughhousing, Trinity was picking two of her noses and licking the inside of a chocolate wrapper she'd found . . . somewhere. Emily reached back and snapped that out of Trinity's hands and shoved the wrapper into one of the cupholders in the front. "I guess they're a little cute."

"Come on, they're like, perfect for marketing," Sam said. "Just saying, there's a lot of money to be made in exploiting children."

Emily blinked. "That doesn't sound very, uh, good?"

"Yeah, I'm not liking this whole idea," Teddy said. "It's sounding awfully capitalistic of you, minion."

Sam raised her hands in surrender. "All right, all right," she said. The conversation turned to other things, mostly school stuff. It reminded Emily that she needed to find a way to get her sisters an education. The comment about child exploitation was hitting a little close to home.

They slid into the parking garage, found a spot on one of the lower floors, then they all exited, the sisters stumbling over one another to get out of the car first. They streamed back up and out of the parking garage, then over to the dorms. Emily couldn't help but notice that a lot of people were stopping and staring. Her sisters were way too young to fit in around the campus.

It was going to be a problem eventually, especially if they became even mildly popular. Someone would look at the Boss and her five Heroic companions, then spot Emily and her five sisters and put two and two together.

Emily unlocked the doors for everyone, some of the pressure leaking off her back as they finally returned to her rooms. "Home at last," she muttered.

"Yeah!" Teddy agreed. "I missed my bed."

"That's not your bed," Athena said. "It's the Boss's bed."

"Well, she ain't using it now," Teddy said as she started to climb on.

"Hey, hey," Emily said. "Go wash up first. Please. We're all dusty. We don't want to dirty the bed. Please."

She herded her sisters into the washroom, then started going through the clothes she had and looked for things for them to change into.

Another visit to the thrift shop was in her near future.

"Man, being a Villain-slash-single mom is complicated, isn't it?" Sam asked as she returned from her own room.

"Tell me about it," Emily muttered.

A knock at the door followed by a familiar voice calling out her name had Emily rushing over to the entrance.

Her mother was on the other side, her hands gripping the handles of cheap plastic bags. She smelled wonderful, like fried food and spices. "Sweetie," her mother said. She raised her arms a little. "I brought lunch."

"You're going to be really popular here," Emily said as she let her mom in.

"Step-Boss!" came the immediate cheer from her sisters before they swarmed around her mom. The looks in their eyes as her mom started placing paper boxes of Thai food on Emily's desk was just short of worshipful.

Her mom cracked the whip, though, and with a snap the sisters were off washing their hands and behaving like the most angelic little creatures ever.

"Your mom's scary," Sam muttered as she watched Emily's mom portion out some of everything onto paper plates while admonishing the girls to be careful as they ate.

"I am very scary," Emily's mom said with a nod and a knowing smile. "Now, who are you, dear?"

Sam grinned. "I'm Sam, ma'am. Pleased to meet you! I'm Emily's front-door neighbor, and I guess I'm her minion, too."

"Oh, my little Emily is making friends, that's wonderful."

"Mom," Emily said as she tried to keep the mortification down.

"Call me Claire, Sam. I'm glad Emily has friends who are closer to her own age. Though I wonder if you're a good influence if you're so quick to jump into this whole Heroing business."

"No worries, ma'am, so far we've been perfectly safe," Sam lied.

Emily's mom glanced at her, one eyebrow perked. "I do listen to the news, you know. I saw you girls stopping that Villain yesterday. Iron Chains, was it?"

"That was a bit unexpected," Emily said.

"I'm sure. Did you hear about the bank robbery this morning? Some young wannabe Villain held up the entire place and made out with several thousand dollars long before the Heroes could show up. It's normal that these kinds of things happen so soon after Power Day, but this is a lot more excitement than we usually see in Eauclaire."

"I hadn't heard of that, no," Emily said. She shifted over to the food and started grabbing some for herself. The room was hardly big enough that she couldn't continue the conversation. Plus, she was starving. "Did anyone get injured?"

"No, I don't think so," Claire said. "A clean robbery. But that does mean that the Heroes will be on their guard in the coming weeks until this Villain is caught. Eauclaire has never had this much Villainous activity all at once before."

"That is actually kind of worrying," Emily said.

Could she end up having some competition? Not that she should care. More Villains just gave her more opportunities to act the part of the Hero. It was a good thing.

At least, that's what she told herself while fiddling with some chopsticks over a bowlful of pho.

CHAPTER TWENTY-TWO

Convincing Arguments

What?" Teddy asked.

No, she *demanded*.

Teddy, her annoying sisters, and the Boss were all on a sidewalk in some lame suburb a couple days later. One of those places where all the houses looked the same because capitalism demanded that every niche in the market be filled, including the niche of boring homes that all looked the same. Step-Boss was there, too. She had brought them here, to this one random house.

The Boss licked her lips, bounced on the balls of her feet, then pressed her hands together, all without meeting their eyes. "You three will be staying here for the rest of the day. Just until this afternoon, really. And while you're here Mrs. Headerson will teach you all sorts of things."

Teddy crossed her arms, and next to her Athena did the same. It was a rare moment of solidarity between the two. "I don't like it," Teddy said.

"You're going to leave?" Trinity asked. She was behind Teddy and Athena, on both sides and between them, and all three of her faces looked like they were close to crying.

"I'm not leaving you," the Boss lied as she leaned forward. "Uh, it'll just be for a few hours, so that I can go to class and take care of things. And all three of you need an education. We can't get you to a normal school yet, so until then . . ."

"Wait, you mean you're planning to abandon us to a normal school later?" Athena asked.

"You want us to get propaganda'd over at one of those private corporate institutions?" Teddy added. "I don't want to be exposed to their trash learning and stuff."

"Schools have trash?" Trinity asked, perking up a bit.

"Girls," the Boss said. "Come on, it won't be that bad."

"You're locking us up in some lame 'Merican dream home with some wrinkly old teacher lady who will try to cram weird stuff into our heads," Teddy said.

"What kind of weird stuff?" Trinity asked.

Athena half turned. "Math and stuff."

"Oh no," Trinity said. "I only have this many fingers and that's all I need." She raised her six hands.

Step-Boss patted Boss on the back. "Let me," she muttered as she stood next to Boss. "Girls, Heather is a good old friend of mine. She used to teach at Emily's school when she was much younger, before she had Steffie. She's an excellent teacher."

"Yeah, but we don't need that," Athena said. "We know all the things we need to know already."

"We know how to beat people up," Teddy said.

"And how to break into homes," Trinity said. "And how to make the best snuggle piles."

Teddy nodded. Those were the important kinds of skills that they wouldn't learn in some lame school. Forcing them to go to one anyway was weird and stupid and bad.

Step-Boss nodded. "Yes, you're all very talented. But maybe you might learn some new things? Tell you what. If you three do a good job today, and behave and learn a bunch, then . . . we'll get pizza for supper."

Teddy paused, considering the offer. That was a pretty good deal.

"Only if we get bacon pizza," Teddy counteroffered.

Step-Boss grinned, which was basically a yes.

"But don't expect us not to go full Villain on this Heather woman if she's a pain in the butt."

Step-Boss tapped her lower lip. "Hmm. How about, if she does anything you don't like, you tell Emily or me about it, and we'll take care of it for you?"

So, if this woman disrespected them, she'd have to deal with the wrath of the Boss and Step-Boss? That was a deal as far as Teddy was concerned. "All right then," she said.

Step-Boss led the way over to the front door of the house. There was a little garden to one side, and a lawn that had been raked recently so that it wasn't all covered in dead leaves and stuff. Step-Boss knocked on the door, and it opened after half a minute to reveal an older lady in a skirt and blouse with her hair tied back.

"Claire! And you brought the children, too. You're a bit early."

Step-Boss nodded. "I thought it was best to be a little early. In case we had to convince the girls to stick around. Besides, it gives them more time for introductions."

The lady nodded, then stepped back into her home, the door wide open. "Come in, come in," she said.

The inside of the house wasn't anything special. A little living room with a couch in the middle and a TV against the wall, a small kitchen on the other side of a counter with a basket of fruit on it, and a few corridors that led off into the rest of the house.

They didn't get to explore, though, since everyone decided to stay crammed up in the entranceway for some reason that Teddy couldn't figure out.

"So, introductions?" the lady asked. "My name is Heather, but you girls should probably call me Mrs. Headerson. My daughter's called Steffie, you'll meet her soon, she's getting ready for class. So, can I have your names, and maybe a bit about yourselves, if you're not shy?"

The Boss looked at them, and Teddy got the message. "Yeah, I'm Tedd— Theodora Wright. I'm the biggest sister, and the best one too."

"Pleased to meet you, Theodora," Mrs. Headerson said. She extended a hand, and Teddy shook it seriously.

"I'm Athena, Athena Wright. The smart one."

"Shouldn't you be smart then?" Teddy asked.

Athena poked her in the short ribs, and Teddy was about to retaliate when the Boss bapped them both on the head. "Girls, please."

"Sorry, Boss," Teddy muttered.

"Sorry, Big Sister."

Mrs. Headerson giggled. "I see. A clever girl then, and what about you . . . triplets?"

"I'm Trinity," Trinity said. "And this is all of me. I like . . ." She blinked, her eyes going blank for a moment. "I like a lot of stuff, do I need to say all of them?"

The Boss cleared her throat. "Um, my mom told you about their, uh, circumstances?" she asked.

"Yes? A little," Mrs. Headerson said. "I've worked with children who needed special attention before."

"Right, that's great," Emily said.

Mrs. Headerson smiled, then turned to another Trinity. "And what's your name, dear?"

Trinity blinked again. "I just told you. It's Trinity."

"Oh? Are the triplets fond of pranks?" she asked.

"Well, yes, but she's not wrong, and she's not triplets," the Boss said. She rubbed at her nose. "Trinity is all three of these bodies. At the same time. This is all of her. It's . . . it's a power thing."

Mrs. Headerson's mouth made a little "o," which had Teddy huffing. She couldn't wait to show the lady her much more awesome power if this was how amazed she was by Trinity's lame, boring power. "Are all five . . . powered?"

"Three," Emily said. "Uh, Trinity's just one person, even if she's got three bodies."

"When I get dead, I get back," Trinity explained.

"Pardon?" Mrs. Headerson asked.

The Boss smiled; it was one of her strange smiles. "At least you won't need to worry if she chokes on something?"

"I see," Mrs. Headerson replied in a way that meant that she didn't. She turned toward the Step-Boss. "When you said this might be a bit complicated, I was thinking . . . well, my mind was very much elsewhere."

Step-Boss sighed. "I know, Heather, but you're the only one I could turn to. Besides, the girls are genuinely sweet, nice children."

Teddy puffed her chest out. Damn right she was.

"We can promise not to wreck your place, miss," Teddy said. She didn't mean it, but it earned her a pat from the Boss, so she was happy she said it.

"Yes, well," Mrs. Headerson said; she hesitated for a moment, then smiled again. "How about you girls go into my classroom? It's the playroom, just down that corridor and to the right. There's a washroom if you continue straight, in case you need to wash up or anything. And I'll be bringing snacks in a moment."

Teddy perked up. No one had mentioned there being snacks involved.

Teddy jumped when Trinity charged to the room, two of her bodies blocking Athena and Teddy's path. "No! I'm gonna be first!" Trinity protested. "Last one there's a rotten good girl!"

"Don't run, please!" the Boss said. But the Boss didn't understand how important it was that Teddy not be the last one there.

Athena slipped past Teddy in the corridor and jumped into the room right before Teddy could catch up.

"Hah! You're last!" Trinity said.

"No, you are!" Teddy said. It was true: two of Trinity were only then entering the room.

"But I was first, too."

"You were two-thirds last," Athena said.

"Um."

The sisters all paused and took in the fourth girl in the room. She was sitting at a small school desk and was staring at them all with wide eyes.

"Hi?" she said. "Who are you?"

CHAPTER TWENTY-THREE

The Little Adventures of Steffie

Steffie wasn't sure what to make of the five girls stumbling into her classroom. Her mom had said that they'd have some new friends over, and Steffie was . . . well, she wasn't sure if she was looking forward to it or not.

New people could be scary. But her mom told her that learning to make new friends was important. It was one of the most important things someone would learn at school.

Steffie couldn't go to normal school, not yet. Her mom said that maybe she could go to high school later, or middle school if she felt better by then. But then Steffie would have to live with people asking her questions about her wheelchair.

She spun the wheels of her chair around so that she was facing the girls. "Hi?" she started. "Who are you?"

Her mom had said there would be one or maybe two girls. This was . . . five. Steffie had been hyping herself up to deal with way less than that.

The girls spread out, two of them—who looked the same?—walked off to the blackboard and stared up at it while the other three formed a rough line by the door. "Question ain't who are we, it's who's you?" the shortest but stockiest of the girls asked. She was wearing shorts and a T-shirt with the word BEAR on the front.

"That," the tallest girl said, "was the worst English I've ever heard. Did you learn how to speak from that little red book of yours?"

"Hey! I speak well enough," the stocky girl defended herself.

"Hi! I'm Trinity," the other girl who hadn't spoken yet said. "Can I have your chair?"

"Um, no," Steffie said. That was a bit rude to ask.

The tall girl sniffed. She crossed her arms with a creak from her leather jacket, set her legs, and looked down at Steffie. "I'm Athena. And the idiot here is Teddy."

"I'm not an idiot," Teddy said. "You are."

"Aww, not this again," one of the girls by the blackboard said. She was holding up a chalk stick and . . .

"Hey!" Steffie said. "You're not supposed to doodle on the blackboard."

"Why not?" the girl asked. She was about halfway done with a surprisingly nice image of a raccoon. Steffie blinked. Did the girl have a tail?!

Where had her mom found these girls? They were *weird*.

"So what kinda shit do you learn here?" Teddy asked.

"That's a swear word," Steffie gasped. "You're not supposed to say those."

Teddy grinned and raised her head up as if she was proud. "I can. Wanna hear another?"

"Teddy, don't scare her. She'll tell her mom, who will tell the Boss, and then we'll all get into trouble," Athena said. She walked over to the desk next to Steffie's. Her mom had pulled a few of them over and set them down. They'd be two desks short as it was. "So you're Mrs. Headerson's daughter, right?"

Steffie felt herself sinking into her chair. Without being all angry at the girls, it was a lot harder to talk to them. "Um, yes. I'm her daughter. You're here for classes, too, right? We're doing geography today." She gestured to a world map on one wall.

"That doesn't sound fun," Teddy said. "Don't schools do, like, running around and exercising?"

Trinity whacked Teddy behind the head, then pointed to Steffie. "She can't do running around. She has wheels instead of legs."

"I didn't know that!" Teddy said while rubbing at the back of her head.

Steffie tried. She tried really hard. But there was no way she could hold it in, and the giggles came pouring out of her. They only got worse when Trinity became smug and Teddy's face fell into a big pout.

Athena grinned back at her even as Steffie worked hard to stifle her laugh. "So what's your name?"

Steffie glanced away. Her cheeks were burning already. "Ah, I'm Steffie," she said.

"This is where you learn stuff?" Teddy asked.

"Yeah. Mom was a teacher. I guess she still is. She mostly does substitution now because, ah, I need a lot of help for stuff."

"What kinda stuff?" Teddy asked.

Steffie turned to her and gave the girl a bit of stink eye. Her mom told her it wasn't very nice to look at people that way, but Teddy probably deserved it. "I need help with a bunch of things," Steffie said.

"That sucks," Teddy said. "You going to get better eventually?"

"Teddy, you're being more of an idiot than usual," Athena said.

"What?" Teddy whined.

"Stop being a jerk, or I'll tell the Boss," Athena said.

Teddy crossed her arms and glowered, but eventually she recanted and looked down at Steffie. "Yeah, I guess that was rude. Sorry. You look all right. Better than my dumb little sister, at least."

Athena sniffed, but it was obvious that she didn't put much weight in the insult.

Steffie wondered if this was how all girls were. "Apology accepted," she said. A glance at the clock above the blackboard revealed that it was actually getting to be a bit late. "Mom usually starts our lessons by now. Did you want to self-study before we begin? I-I can help you all catch up?" That would be nice. Steffie wanted to be a teacher one day.

"Sounds boring," Trinity said. Or was it one of the other girls who looked like Trinity? Steffie had lost track, and they hadn't given her their names. She wasn't going to ask now, though; what if she pointed to one and used the wrong name? That would be mortifying.

The bottom half of the blackboard now had a panoramic image of a big explosion, with a few critters running away from it and what looked like Heroes on fire in the background. It was actually pretty good.

Steffie gathered up her courage and spoke up. "You're really good at drawing," she said.

The triplets all puffed up their chests, even the one that hadn't drawn at all. "Yeah, I'm pretty great. I wanna take up graffiti."

"What?" Steffie asked. "You mean, like, with cans?"

"Yeah! I have two already."

"Two what?" Athena asked.

"Cans," one of the triplets said. "I found them." All three gasped in stereo. "We should sneak out and go tag some buildings for the Boss."

"We don't have a gang tag," Teddy said.

"We'll invent one!"

Steffie shook her head. "No, you can't do that. Graffiti is wrong."

"Yeah, but it's cool," Athena said. "You can't be wrong and cool at the same time, can you?"

Steffie shook her head. "Yes, you can. I mean, no. Crime is wrong."

"Hey, girls, let's go do crime!" Teddy cheered.

Pouting, Steffie pulled herself up so that she was sitting correctly in her chair. She knew they were just being silly, but still. "I know some graffiti is nice. There was a huge mural next to Miss Corle's ice-cream shop. It had big unicorns and all the Heroes and was really pretty."

"There's an ice-cream shop nearby?" Teddy asked.

"With lame Hero graffiti on it?" one of the girls who might have been Trinity asked.

Steffie nodded. Sometimes, if she did well on a quiz, she'd go there with her mom and they'd talk and have sundaes. "It's really nice. The owner is nice too. She gives me extra every time."

"That's it; we need to head out and go try that place," Teddy said.

"The Boss and Step-Boss are still just talking," Athena said as she poked her head out of the room. "Bet we could sneak out and they wouldn't even notice."

Steffie laughed. It was such a silly idea. "Yeah, there's a way out from Mom's room across the hall. She has Rench doors onto the patio out back. I think they unlock from the inside."

"All right, cool, let's go," Teddy said. She moved behind Steffie and pulled her chair back out from under her desk.

"H-hey, wait, where are we going?" Steffie asked.

"Ice cream," one of the triplets explained.

"We don't have money," Steffie said.

Suddenly, a pair of wallets were dropped on her lap. "I found those," one of the girls said. "They were in some people's pockets."

With trembling hands, Steffie opened one of the wallets up and stared. It had a badge. An HRF badge with some guy's driver's license and bank cards and everything. Even a few wadded bills. "This is a joke," Steffie said.

"We don't joke about ice cream," Teddy said. "Or committing casual crime. Come on, it'll be fun."

Steffie whipped her head around to the last bastion of logic and common sense. Athena had seemed nice, and smart. "You think this is a good idea?" she asked.

Athena grinned. "Don't worry. Boss will probably forgive us! Besides, it'll be a learning opportunity!"

"What are we supposed to learn from getting in trouble?" Steffie asked.

"How not to!" Athena said. And so Steffie was pushed out of the classroom, and into what she knew was going to be a heap of trouble.

CHAPTER TWENTY-FOUR

We All Scream

Trinity was having a blast.

She didn't think school and learning could be this fun.

One of her was stuffing boxes of crayons into one of her bags (she'd hidden it under her shirt) while another had snuck into Steffie's mom's room across the corridor and was going through her drawer. For a lady who wore such boring clothes, she had some weird stuff hidden away in her closet.

"Trinity!" Athena hissed.

Hissing was bad. It was too weird a sound, so it alerted people that someone was trying to be sneaky. Also, it was rude to hiss at someone. "What?" the Trinity pushing Steffie's chair asked.

Steffie was protesting about their plan to go get ice cream, but it was really a half-hearted protest, mostly muttered and whispered. She didn't actually care; otherwise, she would be protesting louder.

Athena looked down the corridor, then back. "Where are you?" she asked.

Trinity stared. "I'm right here?"

"You know what I meant," Athena said. "We can't leave one of you behind, come on."

Trinity smiled big. Slightly-Bigger-Sister Athena didn't want even a third of Trinity to be left behind. It made her feel warm on the inside, like when she ate spicy trash. "Okay, all of me's coming," she said.

Teddy pushed the door to the mom's room open, and then the rest of them followed her into the room. Trinity slipped out of the closet. She didn't find anything really fun in there. What kind of boring person didn't hide snacks in their bedroom? "How do you open that door?" Teddy muttered just above a whisper.

"I got it," Trinity said. She slipped over to the Rench door and undid the clasp over the door to open it.

Getting Steffie out proved a bit tricky. Her awesome chair with the wheels didn't quite fit through the doorway, not until all the girls got together and wiggled it past. Teddy ended up getting her fingers stuck between the chair and the door and she said a lot of the words that would have made the Boss red in the face. Finally, they got her out and into Steffie's backyard.

There wasn't a pool or anything, or even any toys. It was a boring backyard. One of Trinity went to check in their trash can, but it was one of those tall black ones, with the little wheelies at the back. Those sucked because if she tipped it back to look in, the whole thing could fall over, and if she boosted herself up to jump inside, the cover might clomp back down like some sort of giant mouth, and then she'd be stuck inside the trash can.

All in all, Trinity gave the backyard a failing grade, and the trash can an even worse one. It even had one of those discri . . . deskrimi . . .—she squinted—one of those not-nice stickers that had a racoon in a red circle with a bar across it.

"Okay, where's the ice-cream place from here?" Teddy asked.

"It's a couple of blocks down that way," Steffie said. She pointed to the right, out toward the front of the house.

"The only way out of the backyard is that path, right?" Athena asked.

There was a fence all around, with a gate on the left side of the house. "Yes," Steffie said.

"Well, we can't use that one. We'd need to cross in front of the house right after, and there are windows looking out the front," Athena said.

"Whoa," Trinity said. "That's smart. How do we get past then?"

"We'll have to go around the other way," Athena said. "Around the block, then back over to the ice-cream place."

"Awesome," Teddy said. She grabbed the handles at the back of Steffie's chair and started pushing. "Let's go already!"

Trinity ran ahead to open the gate, and then she also ran ahead to the front corner of the house, where she was able to check and see if anyone was around. "It's clear!" the her next to the others said.

"How do you know?" Steffie asked.

"Because I looked," Trinity said proudly.

Steffie frowned back at Trinity, but she didn't have time to ask many questions since they reached the sidewalk and all of them started moving along at a quick jog. "A-aren't we moving a bit fast?" Steffie asked.

"We don't wanna be around for long. What if the Boss steps out?"

"Who's the Boss?" Steffie asked.

"Uh, no one said the Boss, I said Big Sister Emily," Teddy said.

"Step-Boss could be trouble, too," Athena said.

"Who's Step-Boss?" Steffie asked next. "Those are weird names."

"No one said nothing," Teddy said. "Don't worry, we'll be fine in a bit, just as soon as we're around the corner."

Steffie squeaked as they crossed the road. "You didn't look!" she said. "You're supposed to look both ways!"

"For what?" Teddy asked.

"Cars!"

Teddy snorted. "Why would you be afraid of cars?" she asked.

Trinity shook her head and touched her bigger bear sister on the arm. "Cars are scary," she said. "More racoons die every year to cars than almost anything else. There's literally nothing you can do to stop a car from hitting you. So if you see one coming, the best thing to do is stop and stand still."

"What?" Steffie asked. "No! If you look both ways, you won't be in the car's way, so it won't hit you."

Trinity frowned. "But what if I'm crossing the road and then the car starts coming after that?"

"Then go back on the sidewalk!" Steffie said.

"That doesn't make sense. Just stand still. Cars only see you if you're moving."

Steffie huffed. "Cars don't have eyes."

The Trinity that was in front of Steffie spun around and started walking backward. She gestured to the front of a car parked on the edge of the road. There were plenty of those since all the buildings nearby were those homes that all looked nearly the same. The front of the car she was pointing to clearly had two big eyelike bits, and a big scoopy mouth part. That was the bit that thumped racoons.

"That's just . . . Uh, Mom talked about it when I was having nightmares. Sometimes the brain sees faces where there aren't any. Cars don't have eyes."

"Sure, sure," Trinity said. She knew better.

They reached the street a block down from Steffie's place, then paused at the intersection. "Which way now?" Athena asked.

Steffie pointed. "That way. Are we really doing this? If-if we go back now, we can say that we just went for a little walk."

Athena chuckled. "We *are* going for a little walk. A little walk to the ice-cream place."

"Don't worry, girl, we'll take you back home in no time!" Teddy said.

"Don't call me girl! I'm probably older than you," Steffie said.

"How would you know?" Teddy shot back.

"I'm taller than you."

"No, you're not!"

"Just because I'm sitting down."

Trinity grinned and spread her arms as she ran along the sidewalk. She liked being outside. There was sunshine, and interesting smells, and right now she was with some of her favorite people.

Maybe one of her could go back to Steffie's place and get hugs from the Boss. That would make it all perfect. But then she'd need to rotate herself out so that all of her got some ice cream.

They reached the ice-cream parlor eventually, a little shop with a bright red roof on the corner of a street. Trinity sounded out the words on the sign, which was easy for her since she had three mouths and could make all the syllable noises at the same time. *Miss Corle's*, the sign said in big swirly letters. There was a glowing cone next to them, too, and a small line of people out front.

Not too many, though! They'd get there fast!

Trinity skipped ahead so that she'd be first in line, with her sisters and Steffie filing in behind her.

"Oh, we can see the prices," Athena said. "Trinity, how many dollars do you have?"

Trinity shrugged and just handed Athena all the wallets she had, including the one from the person ahead of them in line.

Athena took all the bills out, then handed the wallets back. "Can I have one?" Trinity said, gesturing to the paper bills. She took a couple of green ones and stuffed them back into the wallet of the guy ahead of them before sneaking it back into his pocket. Everyone deserved some ice cream.

Meanwhile, another of Trinity's bodies had hit the jackpot.

She grinned from ear to ear, then looked around to make sure there wasn't any competition around. Nothing but a couple of pigeons!

An entire trash can was filled with the bottom stubs of cones and napkins with plenty of ice cream rubbed off onto them. It was like finding a tiny slice of heaven.

The girls were almost next in line when someone coughed from nearby.

All of them turned to see the Boss, her arms crossed, and her face blank. "Care to explain? she asked.

"Oh no," Steffie squeaked.

"Hey, want some ice cream?" Trinity asked. "There's enough for everyone!"

CHAPTER TWENTY-FIVE

A Bit of Quiet

Emily was slowly starting to believe that Mrs. Headerson was something of a saint.

When she returned to the house (after calling her mom to reassure both older women that everything was fine), the teacher had fetched a cloth, had helped clean off the ice-cream stains on cheeks and mouths, then had gathered all Emily's sisters and her own daughter in their little classroom and had started teaching them then and there. An impromptu lesson on math, of all things.

"I think," Emily's mom had said as they were heading out, "that Heather's actually a little glad. Her daughter's never been on an adventure of any sort, you know? A mother worries."

Emily wondered if her mother had worried about her own lack of adventures when she was younger. She had never snuck out to get ice cream before. Then again, she didn't have as many self-reinforcing bad influences as her sisters had.

When they discovered that all the girls were missing, Emily just knew it was her sisters' fault somehow. And yet, even after finding them, she still folded and bought them all ice cream. Just a small cone.

She was probably going to be a terrible parent one day, if that day ever came around.

Her mom agreed to pick up the girls at around four, which meant that for the second time in a week, Emily had a good portion of the day all to herself. Her mom dropped her off on the edge of campus, and Emily headed out to her classes. Two in a row.

She couldn't help but glance at her phone every so often, in case something went wrong with her sisters, but it stayed blessedly silent and she didn't receive any horrified texts from Heather saying that Athena had scared the postman to death or that Teddy had lit the house on fire after learning about taxes or something.

Classes ended, and Emily was a little worried that she'd only taken in about half of what she was supposed to. Fortunately, as she left the room, she noticed that a few students were half asleep even though class was over. If they were graded on a curve, she probably didn't have too much to worry about.

Nonetheless, when she arrived in her room, she pulled out her textbooks and went over the day's lessons and her sparse notes. A few things clicked, though they seemed mostly obvious in hindsight.

She went online next and looked up her courses on the school's forum and found that a few students from previous years had posted their notes on there, so she copied over a few of the better points she had missed into her own notebook.

There was this great feeling when working on something so diligently; it made her feel like she was being productive, taking control of her life in the only way that she could and— And the door to her room shuddered as someone knocked on it.

Emily's heart made a valiant attempt to burst out of her chest, but she reined it in and stood up to see who was there.

She found Sam on the other side, as well as an older woman she didn't recognize. "Uh, hello?" Emily asked.

"See," Sam said, not to Emily, but to the woman next to her. "It's just Emily in there. I don't know what you're on about."

"I received reports," the woman began.

"Yeah, sure," Sam said. "And six-oh-four has a meth lab in his bathroom."

"Pardon?!" the lady asked.

Sam shook her head. "I'm trying to make a point here, that anyone can make up anything, it doesn't mean it's true. Also, hi, Emily."

"Uh, hello," Emily said again. "Can I help you?"

Sam shook her head. "This is . . . Dorthy? She got some complaints that there were kids staying on this floor."

"Oh," Emily said. "Uh."

"I told her that the only kids around were your siblings who visited a few days ago, but they didn't stay here for long."

"R-right," Emily said. "They're in school now, I guess. Uh, with my mom. She visited, too. Is that okay?"

Dorthy sighed. "Yes, that's fine, sorry for bothering you, Miss Wright."

"It's nothing," Emily said.

Sam and Dorthy spoke a bit more while heading over to the elevator, then Sam waved the woman goodbye and rushed back to Emily. "That was something," Sam said.

"Someone made a complaint?"

"Yeah, one of the brats stole the toaster," Sam said. "Someone made a complaint about that, then someone said it was Trinity, and . . . yeah, now there's a rumor going around. But hey, no kids today, so we got lucky, right?"

"I guess," Emily said. *That could have been a disaster.*

"What're you up to?" Sam asked as she invited herself into Emily's room.

"I'm studying," Emily said, making sure to use present tense as a hint to Sam that she was busy.

Sam nodded. "Cool, cool. I won't take up too much of your time," she said as she took over Emily's chair. "Did you hear about Iron Chains?"

Emily closed the door. "No?"

"Oh, right, so, that Villain that robbed a bank a couple of days ago? They tried again, but this time they hit a jeweler's. You know the one next to that pawnshop?"

"I don't know it, but sure," Emily said. "What's that got to do with Iron Chains?"

"Right, so Iron Chains was around that area with Glamazon—"

Emily raised a hand, interrupting Sam midstory. "He's not in jail?"

"Nope," Sam said. She popped the "p" in the most obnoxious way. "He's going by a whole new name, has one of those newbie-Hero spandex costumes on, and has only gone out with an escort, but it's him. I saw the guy up close, a half mask isn't going to hide his ID from me, and besides, how many chain users can there be in a single city? Though he's using a slightly different setup now."

"How is he not in jail?" Emily asked.

Sam grinned. "Pissed?"

"I . . . no? Maybe. We arrested him."

"Yeah, but the HRF took him in, which means that he's being converted. I don't think he was actually a capital-V Villain, you know? Probably just a dude with the Hero title and too little brains for his own good. So they're rebranding and retraining him. Happens all the time."

"That's . . . that's so unfair," Emily said. She couldn't imagine the good guys ever allowing her to get away so easily, not since she was a proper Villain, at least according to her powers.

Sam nodded along. "Anyway, so he was doing a training exercise with Glamazon, right? The two of them and a pair of troopers minding them. Walk around, be seen, shake hands, do autographs, learn the ropes. Boring low-level PR stuff. Then Mister Bank Robber hits the jewelry store one road over."

"They caught him?" Emily asked.

"No, but they did fight, right out in the open. Well, it was less of a fight and more of a running battle."

Emily moved over to her bed and sat on the edge of it. "That sounds kind of scary, actually. Did they capture the robber?"

"Nope, not even close," Sam said. "Well, maybe a little bit close. I heard that they're looking for the guy at all the local hospitals. Chainboy whipped him good. There's video and everything. Glamazon tends to turn things into a whole light show, so a lot of people noticed."

"How do you know all this?" Emily asked.

"Internet."

That was a fair response.

"So Iron Chains is back out, and we might have to fight him again. He'll know more about us this time. Probably won't be caught by surprise. Might even have help."

"Yeah, but we whooped him once," Sam said with unshakable confidence. "We'll manage again. I'm more interested in the Villain."

"The bank robber?" Emily asked.

Sam nodded. "Yeah. He might be injured, which means that if some Good Samaritan happened to make him an offer, well, he wouldn't be able to refuse it, right?"

"And how do you expect to find this guy?" Emily asked.

"Protagonist powers."

"What?" Emily asked. Was there another powered person around to cause her some trouble?

"Your protagonist powers," Sam said. "You know, your ability to run into wild coincidental things that end up helping you in the long run."

"I don't have anything like that," Emily said. "I *wish* I had something like that. It would save me a lot of trouble."

Sam leaned back into Emily's chair. "Know anyone who could help then?"

"Why are you so obsessed with this guy?" Emily asked.

"He robbed a *bank*! That's, like, the quintessential Villain thing to do, and he got away with it too. I want to shake his hand, maybe give him a kiss on the cheek and a pat on the—"

"O-okay," Emily interrupted. "I might know someone who knows a lot of things. He's an information broker, but I really don't see why we need to go and find this Villain. Let the Heroes take care of him, he's not our problem."

Sam's answer was a knowing, dangerous grin.

CHAPTER TWENTY-SIX

Doing Something

Emily had two days. Two blissful, quiet days, where nothing exploded, no one ran away to get ice cream or cause Villainy, and in general, life was more or less normal and quiet.

"Big *Siiiiiis*," Athena said, stretching the last syllable out into incoherency. "We're bored."

"Yes, I noticed," Emily said. "I especially noticed the last dozen times you told me."

"So you gonna do something about it, Boss?" Teddy asked. She was currently upside down on Emily's bed, head tilted off the side so that she could see the screen of Emily's laptop. The laptop was sitting on an empty pizza box, and the low murmur of the narrator of a nature documentary was coming from the computer's speakers.

The other sisters were on the bed, too. Athena sat with her back to the wall, and Trinity was both on the floor and on the foot and head of the bed. Somehow, one of her bodies was sleeping while the other two were awake. Awake and groggy.

"I'm sorry you find this all boring," Emily said. "But I happen to really enjoy a bit of peace and quiet. Besides, you had fun at Mrs. Headerson's place, right? With Steffie?"

"Yeah, but that was ages ago," Athena whined.

It had been less than an hour since they returned.

"There's no boring school stuff tomorrow," Teddy said. "It's the weekend, and you know what those are good for. Villainy!"

Trinity perked up. "We're doing Villain stuff?"

"No," Emily said, "we're not. We're staying at home and being nice and peaceful and quiet."

Her phone chose that moment to start ringing, and Emily cursed her ill luck. It was an unknown number, but she had a feeling that if she didn't answer, she would just receive another call.

"Hello?" she asked as she pressed the call answer button.

There was a slight whimper on the other end. "Hey there, Boss," Alea Iacta said.

Emily sat up. "What's wrong?"

"I didn't say that anything was wrong. I barely said anything, actually," he said.

"You wouldn't be calling if everything was fine," Emily said. She was actually impressed with herself. There was an unforeseen amount of bite in her tone.

She heard Alea Iacta swallowing on the other end. "Well, you see, I think I've been had."

"Pardon?" Emily asked.

"The safe house you sent me to? Yeah, that's really cool and all, but, uh, it's not so safe no more. Look, I ordered delivery, and I got to talking to the delivery girl. She was kinda cute, you know? A-anyway, she mentioned that she'd been delivering to the neighborhood a lot. Even to this one van a couple of times. Thought it was weird."

Emily pinched the bridge of her nose. That had to be his luck powers kicking in to warn him. Or just plain actual luck. Or maybe it was paranoia and he had misunderstood and everything was actually okay.

She had the feeling that the last option was just her wishful thinking working overtime.

"Do you think you're safe for now? And how are you calling me?"

"I got lucky, and this guy dropped his phone, unlocked, right in front of me. Just happened to pick it up, you know? I'm at a coffee place with just about everything I care to keep in a backpack. Thought it was wise not to stick around. Uh, you wouldn't happen to have a *second* safe house? A safer house?"

"No, I don't," Emily snapped.

She calmed herself down with a couple of deep breaths. "Okay, hang tight, and give me the address of where you are."

Alea Iacta muttered an address and some rough directions, and Emily nodded along as she took note of them.

Once she hung up, she sat back and considered all the terrible things she'd done to deserve such an eventful life.

Then, once she'd moped for long enough, she stood and gestured to her sisters. "Get your costumes and your bags, we might be heading out."

There was a rush as her sisters ran around the room and packed up. They took their costumes out from their hiding place (under the bed), then shoved them into the tiny backpacks that Mrs. Headerson had given them for their school things.

A few girls walking around with schoolbags wasn't that suspicious at this time of day, Emily figured as she searched through her contacts and found Sam's number.

The girl answered on the second ring. "Heya?"

"Hey, Sam," Emily said. "Is this a, ah, bad time?"

"It's a good time if you have a distraction for me. What's up?"

"I have a little situation."

Sam laughed. "I'll be at your door in two whole minutes. Let me put some runners on."

Sam was as good as her word, knocking on Emily's door within two minutes and slipping in when Athena opened the door for her.

"Hi," Emily said. "So, you know Alea Iacta?"

"The other minion?" Sam asked.

Emily reluctantly nodded. "Yes, him."

"He hasn't actually done much to earn the title," Teddy said. She patted Sam on the side. "You're the best minion, at least according to me."

Sam grinned. "Why, thank you. Think I could manage to reach hench-woman status one of these days?"

Teddy gave her a thumbs-up. "Keep working hard. The proletariat always promotes good labor."

"Alea Iacta needs our help," Emily said, ignoring the bantering for the moment. "He's at a café downtown. He thinks that his safe house has been discovered, maybe."

"That's rough," Sam said. "What're we going to do about it?"

"I think we might be able to pick him up, and then . . . I don't know, we need another place for him."

Sam smiled, and it was a dangerous smile. "I think I know one."

"Tell me, please," Emily said. "I'd rather not wait and have you spring something on me."

"That's not my style," Sam said. "Sewer access room, near the edge of the campus. You know, next to that bus stop, the blue building."

"You want him to stay in the sewers?" Emily asked.

"Sounds nice," Trinity said.

Sam shook her head. "Nope. See, I've been busy, and that access way also accesses one of the only metro lines to actually be completed. Now they mostly use it to pass wires and stuff, but it's there."

"You can get to the metro base from there?" Emily asked.

"And all sorts of places, yeah. But here's the big idea. You can get the base to be here," Sam said.

"What?" Emily asked. "I don't understand."

Sam gestured toward the center of the city. "The base is over that way, yeah? But it's a mobile base. Get it moving, and it can be over here. Bam, easy access to your minion, and to your base at the same time. He can clean up and stuff while he stays there."

Emily milled over the idea for a bit. It wasn't the worst idea she had ever heard. It was pretty high up on the list, though. "Too risky," she said.

"Ah, come on, the base is ready, by the looks of it," Sam said. "Besides, he's a luck manipulator, right?"

"Yes, he is. He needs to charge it, though. Or steal it, rather. I'm not sure if he's full up on luck right now."

"Then maybe he'll help us get lucky. With the base, I mean. All it needs is a bit of attention."

Emily blinked. "Maybe. I mean, it's possible he can help . . . fine, we'll see. It's not like we're risking much. The base isn't useful to us, really. He might have a few ideas of his own, and this entire thing might be a trap to get us out in the open."

"Oh, I'm good for those," Trinity said.

"We'll see," Emily said, which of course got Trinity excited and she started bragging about how she was the best at being expendable. That somehow got the other two bragging about how they, too, were entirely expendable.

Emily was quite certain none of them knew what the word actually meant.

"All right, come along, brats and Boss, we've got a . . . is he a Villain?"

Emily shook her head. "No, not really. He's on that end of the spectrum, but he's more of a Mischief Maker who got in over his head than anything else. He's not a bad guy, just, he's a bit flaky."

"Oh, one of those sorts," Sam said. "Well, I'll be able to judge him poorly to his face soon enough. Shall we?"

Emily and her troupe of sisters filed out of the room, costumes tucked away, and moods suddenly much higher than they had been a few minutes ago. Emily made sure to reiterate, multiple times, that they weren't going out to do Villain stuff, but they were going to help a friend who needed them, and who she happened to have scared into subservience by accident.

CHAPTER TWENTY-SEVEN

As Subtle as a Sledgehammer to the Nose

Emily and the girls stumbled out of Sam's car like tiny overexcited clowns. The children were the clowns, not Emily. She wasn't certain where Sam fit in that analogy.

"All right, Boss, what's the plan?" Teddy asked.

The others seemed to defer to her, though Athena was also starting to take charge every so often. Emily wondered if some sort of power dynamic was at play, or if it was just her sisters being her sisters. "The plan is to meet up with Alea Iacta, then . . . I suppose we'll go from there. Trinity."

Trinity perked up, all six of her little racoon ears twitching up.

"One of you is going to make contact with Alea. Maybe with a scarf around your face? We don't want you to be too recognizable."

"Oh, I have something for that," Sam said.

She went over to the passenger side of the car, then fumbled in the glove box for a couple of minutes. She returned with a pair of shades, a neck warmer, and a baseball cap with a university's logo on the front.

"This is my inconspicuous passerby disguise," Sam said. "I have a coat in the trunk, too, but it's a bit big for Trinity."

"Why do you have that?" Emily asked.

One of Sam's eyebrows perked up. "In case I need a disguise in a hurry? The hat hides the hair, the neck warmer half your face, the glasses your eyes, and the coat's one of those poofy ones. My aunt gave it to me, but it makes me look fat, I find, so it's perfect for this."

"Right," Emily said. She added this to the tally of strange things Sam did.

A glance around revealed that they were still in the clear. Sam had parked a block over from the café where Alea Iacta was supposed to be, so Emily didn't worry too much about being spotted if he was being followed.

What worried her was leading any followers to their position.

"Sam . . ." Emily started. "You wouldn't happen to know of any places with access to the metro from here, right?"

Sam grinned, a toothy, scary kind of grin. "Why, Boss, I'm so very glad you asked." Reaching into her pocket, she pulled out her phone and tapped a few things on it. "Here, I downloaded this."

Emily took the device and looked over it. There was a map of Eauclaire, but with clear lines cutting through the city. The metro, obviously. Emily could remember seeing a more cartoony version of the same map in the train station.

"Oh," Emily said. The map didn't just have the exits where there were meant to be stations. It had accessways marked out, too.

"Yeah," Sam said as she turned the phone around. "I looked on Oogle Maps, and all those accessways are still there. They're like little huts all over the city. I'd been seeing them all my life without thinking about it. I think the city uses them to store stuff, too."

"Where's the nearest one?" Emily asked. She didn't know Eauclaire well enough to pinpoint where they were at that moment on the map.

Sam blinked at Emily, then half turned and pointed to a building about ten paces next to her.

"Oh," Emily said. It was, indeed, a bit of a shack. A small brick building wedged between two apartment buildings, with a narrow alley on either side and a sign on the front with the city's crest on it.

"Good work, Minion Sam," Teddy said. She gave Sam a thumbs-up, but Sam lowered her hand for a high-five, which prompted the others to join in, too.

Emily hummed to herself for a moment before asking an important question. "Do you have the keys?" she asked.

"Uh," Sam said. "No?"

"The building is out in the open, you know," Emily said. "We can't just pick the lock when anyone driving by could see you."

"I could smash it," Teddy said.

Emily wasn't sure she could. The door was one of those unadorned industrial doors. Even a bear would have a hard time finding the purchase to tear that off, she suspected.

"Okay, that'll be a problem for later," Emily said. "We need a way to get Trinity over to Alea Iacta, then we figure out how to leave."

"Should I go?" Trinity asked. One of her was decked out in Sam's clothes and she looked a little silly, but not terribly so. Just a girl dressed for a slightly colder day.

Emily hesitated. It probably wasn't the most responsible thing to do, sending a lone child out to meet a stranger in a café. "I'll go with you," she decided. Her current outfit didn't look anything like her Heroic one, and as far as anyone was concerned, she was probably just a local student. "You'll meet with Alea Iacta while I'm nearby. The rest of you will stay with Sam."

"Okay!" Trinity agreed.

"I don't like that you're going off on your own," Teddy said. "What if some capitalist tries to entice you away with cheap promises of pretty things? They'll come up, offer you a nice house in the suburbs, then bam! You're a wage slave paying off a mortgage for the next million years."

"I think I'll be fine," Emily said. "Don't worry so much. Besides, Trinity can tell you if anything goes wrong." She hesitated for a moment, then squatted down to be closer to Teddy's height. "I wouldn't mind a hug for good luck, though."

Hugging Teddy meant that she had to hug Athena, too, then of course Trinity wanted in. Fortunately, Sam decided not to ask for a hug because Emily wasn't sure what she would have said to that.

"Right, we're off," Emily said. She reached down and the disguised Trinity grabbed her hand. "Try to find a way into the access building that won't get us all arrested while you're here."

Sam nodded, and then Emily and Trinity were off.

The café Alea Iacta was hiding in wasn't too far off. It was on a more trendy street, with a few boutiques and clothing stores on either side of it, and a busy bus lane right in front.

"All right," Emily said as she and Trinity paused on the street across from the café. "Here's the plan: we're going to cross the road, then I'm going to order something at the counter. I'll point out which one of the people there is Alea Iacta, and you sit across from him. Tell him where to meet the others, then come back to me."

"Okay," Trinity said.

"Can you repeat everything?" Emily asked.

"We go into the food place, you get food. And while you get food, I tell the minion to go to the place where the rest of us are. Then we leave with the food."

There was more emphasis on the food than Emily had planned, but otherwise Trinity seemed to have understood. "That's right. If you do well, I'll give you two doughnuts, okay?"

Trinity's eyes sparkled, and her tail started to swish behind her.

"Ah, try to hide your tail, too; it might give us away."

Hand in hand they crossed the road—Emily made a point of teaching Trinity to look both ways again—then they slipped into the coffee shop.

It wasn't all that busy, probably owing to the hour. Too late for lunch, too early for supper, and most of the heavy after-work traffic was probably already past. Trinity sniffed at the air, and her hat wiggled until Emily patted her on the head. She glanced around and saw Alea Iacta, sitting on his own, off in a corner booth that let him have a good look at the door.

Emily lowered herself down to Trinity's height. "He's the one over there, in the blue coat. Go sit in the chair next to his booth, then tell him that the Boss wants him to go to where the rest of you are."

Trinity nodded, then with a skip, moved over to where Alea Iacta was. She scrambled up onto a seat not too far from his, then started talking to him. It looked like just an innocent girl talking to a stranger.

Emily stood in line, eyeing her sister, then when her time came she ordered a box full of mixed doughnuts—no cream-filled, they were too messy—and paid up. The moment she picked up the box, she swept around the coffee shop and told Trinity to come with her without meeting Alea Iacta's gaze.

"That went surprisingly well," Emily said once they were walking back.

"Yeah," Trinity said. "So will I get three doughnuts?"

Emily sighed. So much for feeling capable. "We'll see," she said. A glance over her shoulder as they approached the next intersection showed her Alea Iacta leaving the shop with his coat's hood pulled up.

Hopefully he wouldn't be followed, and hopefully no one had seen the exchange or thought anything of it.

CHAPTER TWENTY-EIGHT

The Lucky Boy

Jacob had to keep reminding himself that his name, at least for the moment, was Alea Iacta. It was so easy to slip up. Honestly, he wasn't sure how people living double lives did it.

He was sitting in a booth at one of his favorite coffee places, fiddling with a paper cup that was empty a while ago and contemplating the terrible turn his life had taken on Power Day.

Having powers was cool, no doubt about it. Luck powers were even cooler. Tipping the board in his favor whenever he wanted it was just so overpowered.

Being chased down by the good guys, and then maybe by shadowy organizations that wanted to do who-knows-what to Alea? Way, way less cool. In fact, he was outright not a fan of any of that. And now he was relying on some girl who looked like she was two years his junior to save his bacon . . . again.

He was stirred out of his thoughts when someone sat on the seat nearest his booth. For a moment he was worried, but then it turned out to just be a girl in a baseball cap. He considered stealing some of her luck but . . . well, she was a kid. He wasn't the nicest guy around, but he wasn't a bastard.

"Hey," the girl said.

"Hey," he replied. He wasn't sure what to say past that. The last thing he needed was for someone to think he was a creep for bothering a kid.

"The Boss said that I have to tell you stuff," the girl said.

Alea Iacta's breath caught. He swallowed, then looked at the girl again. She was . . . definitely not one of the two that he'd seen with the Boss. "Are you serious?" he asked.

She nodded. "Yeah, of course. Don't mess this up for me, okay, luck boy, there's doughnuts riding on this."

"Uh, okay," he said. "Where is the Boss?"

"You're going to meet me and the other mes and my sisters and the Boss about two roads that way." She pointed across the street, which really didn't help narrow down which direction she was talking about. "See you there," she said.

He watched her hop off her chair and run off, but lost sight of her as she went around a wall that cut off the booths from the shop's counters.

Alea Iacta looked around, saw nothing, then he leaned into his luck, just a little bit.

Still nothing.

Sighing, he pushed himself up, then walked over to the washroom. If he was going to meet the Boss, he wanted to do it without needing to use the bathroom, and washing his face might help him feel awake too. He really needed that.

He grabbed another coffee on the way out. Coffee accounted for half his diet, which was actually probably pretty common, what with the number of students living in Eauclaire.

Once outside, he pulled up the hood of his coat and eyed every car on the street. His luck sense pulled his eyes to a soccer-mom van parked just across the street. He brought his cup up close to his face and started walking. He found a spot to cross the road, then slipped into a part of the crowd that was a bit thicker. As he walked, he brushed against people, stealing little bits and pieces of luck whenever he made contact with them.

All he needed was to be close. Touching someone through their clothes was enough, but being a hair away from touching gave him nothing.

He'd tried tapping people with a length of ribbon to see if that worked, but he needed direct, physical contact. His powers were a little strange about it.

The people he touched often spun around, or exclaimed in surprise, but he was past long before they could point a finger at him. And if they did . . . what would they say? That he made them feel squeamish inside?

Following the girl's rough directions, and his own luck sense, he started down one of the roads opposite the coffee shop. He only paused along the way to pick a large scarf from where it had dropped. He draped it over his shoulders. Bright pink wasn't his color, but maybe it would distract from the outfit he was wearing.

Alea Iacta's life wasn't ideal at the moment, but his power did make it somewhat more bearable.

He reached an intersection, sang eenie-meenie-miney-mo, then took off to his right.

The Boss, along with a gaggle of children and one other woman, were waiting for him halfway down the road.

"Hey," he said as he came closer.

He recognized the girl who had met him at the shop . . . and also the same girl twice again. Triplets? The other two were the scary bear girl and the other scary girl whose powers he couldn't guess at.

Was the tall Black woman with the Boss also powered?

Just how many people did she have working for her? How strong could someone be? Maybe that was the difference between himself and a proper Villain.

"Hello, Alea Iacta," the Boss said. "We shouldn't linger out here. Did you want to talk somewhere more private?"

"Yeah, that'd be nice," he said.

She sounded, as she always did, caught between nervous and angry. He really didn't want to push her more toward the angry side.

"Now all the minions are here," the bear girl said. "Hello, Comrade Iacta."

"Uh, it's Alea Iacta, it doesn't really make sense to just cut part of it out."

The girl crossed her arms. "Sure, if you say so."

"Yeah," he said, uncertainly. "So, uh, we have a place we can talk? In private?"

The Boss nodded, then turned toward the young woman next to her. "Did you find a way to get the door open?"

"Can't exactly pick it out in the open, like you said. I looked around for some way to pry it, but I didn't bring a crowbar with me this time."

"What door?" he asked.

The Boss glanced his way, then gestured to a small maintenance building behind their group. "We need to get into there."

"Oh," Alea Iacta said. He walked over to the door and was promptly ignored. It . . . actually hurt a little, somehow. He had admitted to himself already that he perhaps craved attention a little too much, but to be dismissed so easily . . .

He reached the door. It was a solid metal thing, with a keyhole and a handle. Reaching down, he jiggled the handle, paused, then turned it. The door opened.

"Um . . . guys?"

Only the girl who had greeted him at the coffee shop turned.

"Girls?" he tried. Then, a little louder. "Boss!"

The Boss turned, saw the open door, then stared between it and him. "How?" she asked.

"It wasn't locked," he said with a shrug. "Just lucky, I guess?"

The Boss worked her jaw. "Okay then. Trinity, Athena, at the front."

Two of the girls shot off into the little building, the others following after.

"Family Menagerie: Athena," the Boss muttered. Alea wasn't sure if he was just seeing things, but he had the impression her eyes actually grew bigger. Likely just a trick of the light, he decided as he followed the group in.

The maintenance building had tools on racks and a few tanks off to the side. It stank of oil and grease and rotting lawn stuff. He didn't know what to expect. Was this where they wanted him to stay? It wasn't the worst possible option, but he had been hoping for better. Much better, even.

"There," the Boss said. She pointed to a doorway at the end of the room.

They had to move some things aside to be able to access the door. On the other side was a stairwell leading down what looked like a shaft.

Alea Iacta followed the others, but his insides were twisting up with nervous energy. Where were they heading to?

Where, it turned out, was to a doorway that opened up onto a small tunnel, which then opened up into a massive cement tunnel deep underground.

"Ah, Sam, which way?" the Boss asked. "I'm not great with directions."

Sam—so that was her name—glanced at something on her phone, then pointed. "Base is that way, Boss."

A base?

The Boss had an underground base? And some sort of massive tunnel system under the city?

"Hey, you okay?" the girl who had talked to him in the shop asked. She had removed her hat, revealing two round ears atop her head.

"I'm fine," he said. He stuffed his hands in his pockets.

The Boss, who had to be a few years younger than him, had built all this in . . . what, a couple of weeks?

Villains truly were terrifying.

CHAPTER TWENTY-NINE

Fabien the Fabulous

Things weren't going so well for William.

Ever since he was young, he had always wanted to be one of two things: either a dashing Hero, or a dashing Villain. He had practiced from the moment that he could to hone his skills.

Obviously, he wasn't a fool. He was realistic about his expectations. He aimed for a career in the Heroic Response Force, something that would allow him to work next to the Heroes he adored. Perhaps he could join one as an unpowered sidekick? But that was wishful thinking.

So he worked out, he studied, he prepared.

The day came, and as with every Power Day, he hoped.

Being a Scoundrel wasn't part of his plans, but he could work with it. Certainly it fit him perhaps a little better than some of the more Heroic options.

He leaned into it.

His powers weren't the most powerful, but they were versatile, which at times made up for much. Being flashy was nice, but staying alive was nicer.

William groaned and rested against one of the tunnel's damp walls, hand over his sides, which still smarted. Flashy powers weren't all bad, he supposed. They'd certainly smacked him around.

He knew about Glamazon before heading out, of course. He did his homework. The guy with the chains, though, wasn't in any of his studying material. He knew now—from looking it up—that he was a former . . . not-quite-Villain called Iron Chains. William hadn't even gotten the man's name.

Too many chains, combined with those explosive bursts of light—which he could now confirm had some sort of distracting component to them; all his predictions had him turning toward them even when he tried not to—had overridden his own power quite neatly.

His ability was simple. He could accurately predict an entire minute into the future. In that minute, he could choose to move with much greater ease and finesse than he did naturally. Not that he wasn't spry, but he became unnaturally so when his movements were predicted.

If he chose to follow his path, then he would, for a moment, be able to move with that same grace.

It meant that his fights were gorgeous and deadly. He acted as though he knew what was going to happen before it did, because he did know.

The problem was initiating the fight. He usually had to run through three or four iterations before he found one where he was victorious, and that meant a few seconds' hesitation before he moved.

It would get better with practice.

Practice that would be hard to get at this point. His last fight had been something of a disaster. His power was good when he was on the offensive. Less so when he was forced to duck and weave away from an aggressive foe who was willing to push against him.

Glamazon and Iron Chains had been a worst-case scenario. Now he was suffering from his incompetence.

No dwelling on it. His appearances on social media weren't all that bad. He suspected that Glamazon or one of her lackeys was posting and reposting the same GIFs of their fight to get more attention. He didn't look too bad in those, weaving around chains and darting away from Glamazon's attacks. He liked the way his rapier looked, and a few of the videos captured his good side.

He rubbed at his mouth. His skin was having a negative reaction to the tape he used for his persona's mustache. He'd need to find another way to keep that part of his disguise up.

He made a note to find some way to pad his costume a little, too. His back was bruised from having to roll across bare asphalt.

So many things to deal with.

It was better to dwell on those than on his situation in general. He couldn't go back to his dorm injured as he was. His costume didn't hide his hair well, and his injuries would be distinct if he went to a hospital.

With a sigh, he pushed himself off the wall and started walking again.

These tunnels ran across a good portion of the city. He knew more or less where the next exit was, and from there he could sneak over to his grandmother's place. She was a kindly woman, and a retired nurse.

Really, he was scraping the bottom of the barrel for ideas.

A scuffle ahead had him look up, but he had crossed paths with a few rats already. They usually saw him and skittered off to do whatever rat thing they were up to elsewhere. On the next long curve in the tunnel, he realized that it wasn't a rat he was hearing, but by then it was too late.

He met eyes with a figure standing in the dark. Its eyes glowed, glinting green in the near darkness of the tunnel, lit only by the little pocket flashlight he carried.

"Hey," a girl's voice spoke in the dark. It echoed. Really, no other voice could have been creepier at that moment. "You're probably not supposed to be here," she said.

He stood a little taller, switched his light to his other hand, then carefully gripped the hilt of his rapier. "I'm not?" he asked.

"No. I'm going to tell the Boss that you're here. Don't move, okay."

"I'd really rather you didn't tell anyone," he said.

The eyes disappeared for a moment as the child blinked. "Too late. Besides, I don't need to listen to you. Only the Boss."

Red flags. Lots of red flags.

"And where is this Boss?" he asked.

The sounds of footfalls answered that for him. Lots of footfalls, and lights farther in the tunnel that were becoming brighter as a group approached.

He considered running. That was the more intelligent thing to do.

The issue was the nearest exit was far away, and it wouldn't be hard to follow in a one-way tunnel. Also, injured as he was, he couldn't exactly run, not without making the injury substantially worse.

So his only option was to stand his ground.

He whipped off his coat, flipped it inside out, then fished a mask out from its pocket and slipped it on. It wasn't his full disguise. That would require some time, a mirror, and more of that skin glue he was beginning to suspect that he was allergic to.

He shifted over to the center of the tunnel, then stood with his back straight, one hand on the hilt of his sword.

The question was, could he defeat this bunch?

He knew how to test that.

A thought activated his power.

Fabien the Fabulous rushed forward, charging past the girl in the lead, but not without pirouetting around her and kicking her behind the knees. The girl screamed, fell back onto the track, and burst apart.

Another girl, identical, appeared next to her sibling . . . a clone power, then?

He was back in the middle of the tunnel, having not moved at all from his spot. The girl he kicked over was still before him, and the world was unchanged.

Another try, then.

He charged forward, sword rasping out of its sheath (he had it specially made to make that sound like in the movies). He smacked the hilt into the face of the first girl, spun over the tracks in the middle of the tunnel, then started to lunge toward the only man in the group.

His foot caught on something, and he tripped into his own sword.

He blinked. He had never messed up so poorly before. Usually his power made him more graceful, not less. Unless . . . a nerve-control power? Maybe something probability based or that made an adversary clumsy?

William gritted his teeth. That was two confirmed powers. Next . . . the girl in the middle of the pack, the one glaring at him in a way that was actually making him a little nervous. The ringleader?

Stepping to the side, he hopped over the tracks and onto more flat ground, then rushed forward, sword coming out of its sheath.

One of the girls stepped up into his path and promptly turned into a roaring bear, which charged right back at him.

He was, understandably, surprised, but he still spun out of the way.

It was only enough that he avoided the bear, not the three little bodies that tackled his legs and refused to let go.

He crashed to the ground and tried to roll, only to find another one of the girls standing above him. She had large eyes, and a smile like a predator seeing an injured mouse trip out of a bush.

The world darkened around the edges and—

No, that wasn't working at all.

So, another plan, then.

He placed his light down so that it shone onto him, a tiny spotlight from below, then with a flourishing bow that made every part of him hurt, he introduced himself. "I am Fabien the Fabulous, at your service," he said.

CHAPTER THIRTY

Rising Expectations

The man bent down with a flourishing bow, like something out of a period drama. "I am Fabien the Fabulous, at your service," he said.

Emily had no idea what to do with this entire situation.

Worse, she couldn't just coast along and let others handle the social niceties here. Her sisters were looking up at her for guidance, she was trying to impress Sam and Alea Iacta (though she was hesitant to admit that), and she worried that if she didn't act soon, one of her sisters might decide that they were the best choice to handle things.

That would only end in disaster.

Also, why was she attracting theater kids? She was awkward enough on her own without them around.

"Hello, Fabien the Fabulous," Emily said. She tried to keep any shake out of her voice and stood taller. It probably didn't do much, seeing as how they were all in a dimly lit tunnel. "Do you mind telling us what you're doing here?"

Fabien the Fabulous grinned, and Emily noticed that in the poor lighting, he was rather handsome. At least, for someone who was probably a threat. Hero or Villain, she wondered, and which was worse? "I'm afraid you've caught me unguarded, young miss. I was merely taking a calming midnight stroll."

"Through the abandoned metro system?" Sam asked. It was a valid question.

Fabien shrugged with an artful twirl of his sword. "It's quiet. No traffic. The people you meet are all friendly. Or so I hope."

"Are you a Mask?" Emily asked. It could just be some guy who got lost while wearing a costume. It was highly unlikely, but the possibility was there.

"I do believe I am, yes," he said.

"Wait," Sam said. She raised her phone up, the light reaching a little farther so that they could better see Fabien. "You're the bank robber!"

Fabien smiled, though it seemed a little tense. "So my exploits are known. I don't imagine that you are fans here for autographs?"

Sam's light revealed something else. Fabien's costume was roughed up pretty badly, and what Emily could see of his skin was blemished and bruised. He was injured. Even his stance showed it, now that she knew to look. He was putting a lot of weight onto one leg.

She wasn't sure what to think of the fact that they'd just run into a bank robber in the tunnels.

"You stole a bank?" Teddy asked. "That's cool. Taking from the rich is great."

"Ah, so fans indeed," Fabien said.

"Nah," Teddy said. "Never heard of you before, so there's no way I'm a fan. Besides, you're not even a proper Villain."

"Robbing banks doesn't make one a proper Villain?" Fabien asked. He seemed uncertain now.

Teddy shook her head. "That's just getting yourself rich. Proper Villainy's about having ideals. A code, you know. Integers."

"Integrity," Athena corrected.

Teddy nodded. "Yep. You don't smell like a proper Villain."

Emily sighed. "That's enough, Teddy. Let's not insult our new friend too much. Mister Fabien . . . the Fabulous, uh . . . normally I'd just say that we should walk past each other and forget that we ever even met." That was her preferred method of meeting people. "But you're hurt, aren't you?"

"I'm still able to put up a fight," he said jovially. It was dismissive, but Emily read the threat under the surface.

"Are you able to go to a hospital? Do you know any clinics that can look after you for a bit?" Emily asked.

"I'm afraid that I don't," he said.

Emily turned toward Alea Iacta. "What do you think?"

"What do I think?" he repeated, a finger pointing up to his own face. "I mean, I'm used to things happening around me that aren't likely to happen. That's just how it works, you know. It's usually good things, but that isn't always the case. But, yeah, I don't know what his powers are, but we outnumber him pretty hard right now, so I kinda doubt he'd be a real problem to handle if he tries anything. No offense, my dude."

"None taken," Fabien said. He carefully slid his sword back into its sheath. "In my experience, limited as it may be in the world of Masks, if people are talking and willing to negotiate, then violence will only occur if one side truly wants it to. This side"—he gestured to himself—"would rather avoid it."

Emily smiled. If nothing else, Fabien was rather eloquent, if in a bit of an overdone way. "Fine then, we'll stand down as well. But you still need healing. Um. I can't heal you, I'm afraid, my abilities are too specific and you wouldn't fit the, ah, criteria, but we have a base nearby. I think it has a first aid kit."

"I know my way around one of those," Sam said. At Emily's curious glance, she shrugged and explained. "Track and field for a few years. That and lots of hiking and camping. You need to know how to disinfect a cut or take care of a bruise."

"Before we go on," Fabien said. "And yes, I think I would rather like to accept your hospitality. Could you be so kind as to display your status?"

"Our status? You mean, the nameplates?" Emily asked.

Fabien the Fabulous grinned. "Just so. Here, allow me to break the ice."

Fabien the Fabulous

Level 1

Scoundrel

The words were clearly visible and easy to read, even in the gloom.

Emily hesitated a little, then shrugged her shoulders and willed her nameplate to appear above her head.

The Boss

Level 1

Villain

Soon, Teddy and Athena and Trinity had their own nameplates out. Trinity's was bizarre in that three nameplates appeared, all entirely identical.

"Uh, I'm not as impressive," Alea Iacta said. His own marked him as a Mischief Maker of the same level as everyone else here.

Fabian whistled. "So many Villains. Actual, bona fide Villains."

"Cool, huh?" Sam asked. She was staring up at the nameplate over Emily's head until Emily turned it off. It felt wrong to leave it so visible. Like . . . exposing herself or something.

"We should move on," Emily said. "And in the meantime, perhaps you could, ah, tell us about yourself, Mister Fabien the Fabulous."

"Please, ma'am, just Fabien for you." He gave another little bow, though it was obvious it hurt for him to do so.

Emily instructed Teddy to help Fabien walk, and the bear girl took to it dutifully. She didn't quite understand what Emily meant, though, and ended up grabbing Fabien's hand the same way she held on to Emily's when they walked.

Fabien didn't seem to know what to do about that. Sam, at least, seemed to think it was funny.

Emily set a slow pace, giving the injured Fabien plenty of time and room. She didn't trust him. Sure, he was handsome and well spoken—if in an overblown, theatrical way—but those were hardly reasons to trust someone.

Still, what they were about to reveal wasn't something she cared overly much about. The mobile base wasn't her creation, it was a convenience that had dropped into her lap, which could leave just as suddenly.

Sam pointed out which turns to take, not that there were many. The metro line was a rather simple route across the city.

Emily was just starting to wonder if the walk would ever end when they came upon the base. From the dark rose a wall of steel. The train's engine wasn't sleek or pretty, but instead was a boxy industrial thing, not meant for the public eye.

"Here we are," Emily said. In a lower voice, pitched so that only her sisters could hear, she said, "Athena, Trinity, can you run ahead and clean the place up? Just pick up any trash and . . . maybe start dusting?"

"No problem," Athena whispered back.

"Take care of trash, got it," Trinity said.

The two of them ran ahead, one of Trinity holding a light that bobbed in the darkness.

"What is this?" Alea Iacta asked.

"This," Sam said, "is the Boss's mobile base. It's still a work in progress. We're hoping that we can move it closer to, ah, our other base."

Emily raised an eyebrow at that. Other base? Did Sam mean their dorm?

"That is really cool," Alea Iacta said. "Is it just an old train?"

"No," Emily said. "Come on in. We'll give you a little tour. Alea, you're looking for a place to stay, right? This should be relatively safe, I think."

"And you can fix it up while we're gone," Sam said.

"I don't know how to fix trains," Alea Iacta pointed out.

Sam grinned and patted him on the back. "You're a lucky guy, right? How hard can it be?"

"Uh, I feel like you're overestimating how useful luck is," he said.

They moved over to the back of the train, Emily studiously ignoring the bangs and clangs going on inside the train while her sisters cleaned. Then they stepped into the train and Fabien let out another low whistle. "Villains are really something else," he muttered.

Emily wasn't sure if she wanted to live up to his expectations or not.

CHAPTER THIRTY-ONE

Right as Rain

"Is it going well?" Emily asked.

She didn't know Fabien well, other than through thirdhand accounts of his few exploits, but that didn't mean she couldn't be concerned about his health. The boy—no, the young man—looked entirely too injured for his own good.

"He'll be fine," Sam said. She smacked Fabien the Fabulous on the knee, then grinned over at Emily. "He's barely got a scratch on him, isn't that right, handsome?"

Fabien was partially undressed, a fact that was making Emily's cheeks warm up. There was nothing perverted to it, though. He was sitting on one of the seats in the dining area of the mobile base, shirt on the table and bandages over his biceps and arms.

Emily wasn't any sort of medical expert, but she could guess from the way he was bruised and cut that he'd crashed onto his side at some point. Some of the wounds had looked like simple scrapes. She'd seen a few of those recently, mostly on her sisters' knees.

Scrapes were nothing to worry about. A bit of disinfectant, a plaster or bandage, and a kiss on the boo-boo . . . though, maybe not for Fabien the Fabulous. In fact, she made doubly sure not to use the word *boo-boo* at all.

Better to excise it from her vocabulary for the moment than to accidentally utter the word aloud and have to dig a pit to bury herself in later.

The other wounds were more complicated. He had a lot of bruising on his side, from just under his pectoral muscle (which she made sure not to stare at when he could see her) all the way down to the waist of his pants. The bruises were ugly, mottled purple and blue, but after poking and prodding, Sam had declared that none of his ribs were misplaced.

Even if he went to a hospital, the most he'd get out of it was an order to stay in bed for a week and maybe a dose of tetanus, if he wasn't up-to-date. He assured them that he was.

"Thank you," Fabien said. He was looking right at Emily as he spoke. "Truly, thank you. I didn't know what to expect on meeting you, but it certainly wasn't this level of hospitality. Don't worry yourself over me any further, I'll repay this debt I owe you."

"Uh," Emily said. "It's nothing, really. Just some first aid stuff." Not even her own first aid stuff. It had all been tucked away in a metal case above the sink, packed there with some instructions on how to use it.

There had been some MREs and some survival equipment as well. But the girls found the MREs and were "taste testing" them in the next room over. She didn't care as long as they cleaned up the mess of crumbs they were no doubt leaving behind.

"Do you have a way to get back home?" Emily asked.

"I know how to get back from most anywhere in the city," he said.

Sam snorted. "So a local then, huh? Ah, don't worry, not prying into your secret identity. Now, take off your pants."

"Pardon?"

"What?"

Emily and Fabien spoke at the same time.

Sam rolled her eyes. "I saw you limping. Come on, off with them. Trust me, you don't have anything I haven't seen before."

Emily was quite certain he had plenty of things *she* hadn't seen before, and she wasn't sure she wanted to see them.

"It's just my ankle, I think," Fabien hurried to say. He brought his leg up and placed it on one of the free chairs, then pulled up his pants and bunched them over his calf so that Sam could better see his foot. It was pretty swollen.

Sam pulled another chair closer as she examined it. "Hmm. Tell me if it hurts," she said as she started to turn the ankle this way and that. She was being careful about it, though, and other than a wince Fabien didn't react too much.

"So, Lady . . . Boss?" he started uncertainly.

"Just Boss is fine," Emily said.

"Very well then, Boss." Fabien the Fabulous gestured around himself. "What do you need of me?"

Emily blinked. "What do you mean?"

He sighed. "I . . . I will be honest with you, as you seem to have been honest and fair with me. I have always dreamed of being someone whose name was known." He paused and hissed.

"Sorry," Sam said. "Let me go see if I can't find some ice. There's just a bit of swelling here."

"Thank you," he repeated before continuing on. "As I said, I have always dreamed of being well known. And my power allows me to take the first steps onto that path. But, well, I find myself somewhat humbled by recent experiences."

"The fight with Glamazon," Emily said. Her eyes narrowed. "And Iron Chains."

He paused before nodding. "I presume that's the Hero with the, well, iron chains."

"That's him. He was acting like a bit of a Villain for a while. We captured him."

"And now," Sam said as she returned. She didn't have ice, but she did have what looked like a lukewarm bottle of water that she poured into a little sealable bag and pressed to Fabien's ankle. "Now the good guys have decided that he's Hero material."

"I see," Fabien said. "In either case, yes, I wasn't ready to fight off either of them. Maybe if it had been just one I would have fared better. I suppose what I'm trying to say is that I am not equipped to fight on my own."

"That's easy then, just join the Boss's gang," Sam said.

"I don't have a gang," Boss said.

"Right," Sam agreed before correcting herself. "The Mafia calls it a *family*. Much classier."

Emily glared at the back of Sam's head, but no one seemed to pay attention to that.

"I-I wouldn't want to insult your hospitality, Boss, but I don't know if I'm quite ready to join your . . . ah, family," Fabien said.

Emily sighed. That was some good news, at least. For some reason, the sigh had Fabien tensing up a little. "That's fine," Emily said. "We don't need any more expanding, I don't think."

Fabien the Fabulous eyed her for a moment. "What are your goals, exactly? Just so that I don't inadvertently end up working against you. I owe you some respect, and I imagine working against your goals would be the opposite of that."

"Nothing much," Emily deflected. She was impressed and proud of herself. That deflection had come quickly and smoothly, without even a stutter. All that practice deflecting her sisters' more awkward questions was paying off.

Sam then bulldozed over her accomplishment. "We're going to take over the city, then the world."

"We are not going to take over the city," Emily said. "O-or the world."

"Ah, I see," Fabien said. He nodded. "A subtle takeover, then."

"Yeah, exactly," Sam said.

Emily shook her head. No, it was not exactly that. It was exactly not that!

Fabien's eyes grew distant for a moment. "Yes, I can imagine it now. The beautiful Boss, feared by all, with a loyal army by her side. Her boot on the neck of the greatest Heroes and the entire city in her grasp."

Emily's face warmed. She had never had a handsome shirtless man call her beautiful before.

"So, Boss, Fabulous here's all bandaged up. Do we kick him to the curb?"

Emily shook her head. "No, of course not. Fabien, you can rest here. Alea Iacta will be using the base for the next few days. He can keep you company. Ah, we'll try to bring some food down, maybe some painkillers, too." She had some in her purse, but nothing that was stronger than the anti-inflammatory that Sam had given him already.

"Yeah, we're going to have to restock the place. The brats have done a number on the MREs. And we just used up some of the medical stuff. I think it'd be wise to keep those supplies topped up. Just in case, you know?" Sam said.

Sam had the gift to switch from foolish and silly to serious in such a way that it left Emily reeling. "R-right, uh, that's a good idea." She cleared her throat. "I'm going to go check on the sisters. Fabien, I hope you heal well."

"Thank you," he said, and it sounded entirely earnest.

She stepped out of the room and made her way to the next train car up. She found her sisters sitting around the big table in the center of the room, eyes narrowed and cards held close to their faces as they watched one another suspiciously.

"Got a nine?" Teddy asked Trinity.

All three of Trinity grinned. "Go fish," she said.

Teddy mumbled something that Emily suspected was on her list of "words not to use," but she couldn't quite hear it well enough to tell.

"Hey, girls," she said.

"Hey, Boss, want us to deal you in?" Teddy asked. She had a lot of cards in hand and seemed eager to reset the game.

"Ah, I'm good," Emily said. She took note of the MREs whose contents were divided up between the girls. "Wait, are you gambling . . . with crackers?"

Trinity raised a brown pack from her pile. "And omelets too!"

CHAPTER THIRTY-TWO

Next Steps

And then what?" Emily's mom asked.

Emily swirled her cup around. It was her second; and to think that it wasn't college that had set her on the path of becoming a caffeine addict. Villainy and babysitting had done that instead. "And then we left," she said. "I've been keeping in contact with Lucky; he found a spot in the train where he gets some signal, so we've been texting back and forth."

They were in a coffee shop, because that was where Emily spent her free time now, she supposed. Emily and her mom had found seats in the corner across from each other while the girls crowded around a nearby table and watched videos on Emily's phone. The little device was a blessing. Anything that could distract the kids was.

"I see, I see. And what does *Lucky* think of all this?" she asked. The emphasis on Alea Iacta's newest alias (they didn't want to be caught saying his name aloud, just in case) was probably unnecessary.

Emily suspected that her mom was enjoying all the secretive and clandestine parts of Emily's life. More than Emily did, certainly. "I don't know what he thinks," Emily said.

"You know, a mother worries when her daughter spends the day texting boys."

"I text Sam a lot, too," Emily said.

"Well, this mother doesn't care whether her daughter likes texting boys or girls."

Emily rolled her eyes. "It's all business, trust me."

There was a snort as her mom sat back. "I know, sweetie. I suppose I can stop teasing you for a little bit. Besides, most mothers just want grand-babies and you've provided more than anyone could hope for."

"Mom," Emily said with the barest hint of warning in her tone.

Her mom grinned back at her and took a long sip from her coffee. "So, what's your next step?"

"I don't know. Sam has ideas about Eauclaire. I think she wants me to take . . . to go into, uh, politics. Maybe business. Really, I just need to make enough to take care of my sisters."

"Your father and I will help, at least where we can." A warm hand touched Emily's and she smiled. "I don't know if we can support everyone, at least not long term, but we'll do what we can."

"Thanks, Mom," Emily said. "I'm trying too. I don't like the . . . business model that I'm taking over, but it's the only reliable source of income I have. Even that's not too much. We only have, uh, contacts in a couple of little businesses. I don't know if I have the reputation I'd need to contact the rest."

"Honestly, as long as you're giving back more to the community than you're taking, I don't really mind it that much, from a moral point of view, I mean. It's like taxes."

"Doesn't dad say that taxation is theft?" Emily asked.

Her mom smiled. "Never mind that. What about that handsome boy, the one who stole your attention?"

Emily lowered her eyes as she blushed. "He didn't steal my attention."

"Just a bank, then," her mom said before giggling at her own joke.

Emily crossed her arms. "I think he's healing up well enough. I don't know what he'll do about our hospitality. Sam wants him to become another . . . business partner, but I don't know him well enough. Being handsome isn't enough to make me trust him."

"How very wise."

Emily was about to chastise her mom for poking fun at her again when her purse buzzed. She reached in, took out her phone, then frowned at the screen. "It's Alea—" She cleared her throat. "Our lucky friend."

Just another text in a long list of them. She might have been worried that any communications were dangerous, but so far they'd very carefully been replying back and forth as though talking about school.

Lucky: Hey!
Lucky: Found something cool.
Lucky: At the back of a geology classroom. There's another geology classroom. Maybe. Haven't explored it.

Emily narrowed her eyes.

"Bad news?" her mom asked.

"No, not bad, just strange," she replied absently. Geology class was the metro lines. It was underground, and the term seemed to fit. She wasn't sure if the school even had geology, but that was a minor concern. Another geology room . . . did he find another set of tunnels?

That seemed unlikely. One metro line built and abandoned was one thing, but for a city to build two? She didn't think that Eauclaire had anywhere near that kind of budget. "I think I might need to go and investigate this one."

"Always so busy," her mom said.

"I'm sorry. I wish I wasn't. There's just so much to do."

She stood and they hugged. Her mom left soon after saying goodbye to all Emily's sisters. There were a few hugs traded, and headpats, of course. The sisters were sad to see the Step-Boss go, but Emily wasn't sure if it was genuine affection, or if they just liked the candy her mom snuck over to them.

Her mom left to a chorus of "Bye, Step-Boss" farewells, then her sisters turned to her, five sets of inquisitive, curious eyes demanding to know what she wanted from them.

Emily tried on a smile and found that it fit. "We might need to do a bit of exploring," she said.

"Awesome," Teddy said. "What kind?"

"I don't know quite yet. But the sooner we go, the sooner we'll find out."

They had to call Sam, of course. The minion (Emily had to catch herself—it wasn't kind to call people a minion, no matter how much they claimed to like the title) was always willing to head out and help, at least as long as it involved something Hero or Villain related.

"What's the sitch?" Sam asked over the phone.

"I got a text, it looks like someone found an abandoned classroom, next to geology class?" Emily said. She was a bit more awkward over the phone than over text. "I was thinking we could explore that?"

"Oh, heck yeah," Sam said. "I'll be at the dorm in like, twenty?"

"Sure," Emily said. The coffee shop was just across campus, so the walk wouldn't be too long. And it would give her sisters some time to work off their excess energy. Going to school with Mrs. Headerson (who was a saint as far as Emily was concerned) left them full of energy.

As they took off, the girls regaled her with stories about their day and the stuff they'd learned.

A brisk walk later, and the group was standing before the dorms where Sam awaited, arms crossed and back leaning against the building's front. She had shades on, and they made her look far cooler than Emily could ever hope to achieve. "Hey, Boss," she said.

"Hello, Sam," Emily replied.

"What's up, comrade minion?" Teddy asked.

Sam ruffled the bear girl's hair while ignoring her vocal complaints.

"Alea texted me," Emily started. "Said he might have found a base hidden next to the base? I'm not entirely sure I understood. He did send me a meeting spot. I thought we could check it out. Maybe look first, to make sure it's not a trap, then check it out for real."

"Wow, you're a bit paranoid, you know?" Sam asked.

"It's not paranoia," Emily defended herself. "Not when you know that some of the conspiracies are entirely too real for comfort."

"Fair enough. So where's the meeting spot?"

Emily checked her phone. "It's not an address. He mentioned an overpass between the fire station and . . . this soccer field?"

"Oh," Sam said. "I know the one. That's, like, right off the edge of campus. It's probably faster to walk over than to drive, really. By the time we get to the car we'd be halfway there on foot."

Emily shrugged. "Okay, then let's check it out on foot. I don't really mind either way." And on foot she could send Trinity out ahead, to see if there was anything suspicious going on.

Her gaggle of sisters roamed around herself and Sam as they started to skirt the edge of campus. A few students jogged by, and others were profiting from the unusually warm weather by sitting together in little groups at benches and park tables. A few glanced at her sisters, but other than a few "awws" there wasn't much attention shot their way. Probably for the best.

Once they were nearer to the overpass (which allowed a four-lane highway to pass overhead) Emily sent Trinity to scout, with repeated and clear instructions not to cross the road.

Trinity's report was a bit meandering and not terribly precise, commenting on the quality of trash found under the roadway, but she didn't see anyone weird except for Alea Iacta, who was sitting on a bench in civilian clothes.

"Hey, Boss," the boy said as they approached as a group. "I just found the weirdest thing, you're going to love this."

"Let's see about that."

CHAPTER THIRTY-THREE

Cement's Legacy

"Okay," Alea Iacta said. He moved ahead of the group, a bit of a skip to his steps. He seemed to be in a good mood, Emily noted idly. "This is it," he said with a grandiose gesture to a graffiti-covered wall.

"That's one of the words that Big Sister gets mad when we say," Athena pointed out.

It was, in fact, a swear word, though one that was stylized enough that it was hard to read it. "Why are you showing this to us?" Emily asked.

"Oh, not the painting, this." He reached to the wall and pressed his hand against it. There was a small panel there, just a metal box with some wires running down it. It was probably some sort of maintenance panel. She wasn't an expert on city infrastructure. Alea Iacta popped the box open and then twisted a handle within it. "See, it's locked."

"Okay?" Emily asked.

"You're wasting the Boss's time," Teddy said.

He rolled his eyes, then fished out a key from his pocket. "You slip this in here, and then . . . pop." The handle turned completely, then a section of the wall slid in. A doorway. Emily hadn't noticed the edges until the door was pushed in. "Come on!"

Emily hesitated, then gestured Trinity ahead. Her other sisters, not wanting to be last, jammed themselves through next, then Emily and Sam followed.

Alea Iacta stood pressed up against the wall to let them in, then he pulled the key out of the box and pressed the door closed.

The hallway was lit by some neon tubes above. "It's not much to see, to be honest."

"What is it?" Emily asked. The corridor was clean. A bit dusty, but there was no detritus or trash laying around. The corridor forked at the end.

"A base!" Alea Iacta said. "So I was on the train, right? And I got to thinking, 'Why is this here?' It would make a lot more sense to park it in front of that little station, or if not there, then deeper into the tunnels so it would be harder to reach. But no, it was just kind of close but not too close to the station. Weird spot, right? Started looking around, and bam! Found a hidden doorway with one of these."

He squeezed past the group so that he was at the front, then he jogged over to a plain metal door. Opening it revealed a staircase. Cement steps leading down, with a light at every landing.

"Just like this," he said. "All the way from the ground, and out above. The other one, near the mobile base, opens up into an alleyway next to an off-ramp. I got a map of the metro tunnels and a map of the city, then matched any places where there were lots of big city-built things that intersect with the tunnels. This is the only other spot I've found though."

"That's incredible," Sam said. "A whole network of secret entrances."

"Well, two of them," Alea Iacta said.

Emily nodded. "She's right. This is incredible. It might make traveling to the base a lot easier. This one is even close to the campus."

"And it's not in a busy spot," Sam said. "Barely any traffic at all. Yeah, this is pretty nice."

Alea Iacta grinned like a kid about to pull off some prank they thought was immensely clever. Emily knew the look well. "It gets better," he said.

They followed him down the other end of the corridor, to a dead end. It had another panel on it, which when opened, revealed a handle just like the one on the door leading into the small base.

On the other side was an open space, with pillars reaching to the ceiling and rooms tucked into the sides. "I think it's supposed to be a dormitory," Alea Iacta said. A faint rumble made the lights hanging from the ceiling shake a little. "We're right under the highway here."

Everything was cement. The walls, doors, even the two long tables and benches in the center of the room. A wraparound sofa was in the middle of the room, facing a pillar that looked like it had attachments for a TV. The wires for it dangled out of the wall.

"What are all the doors to the side?" Emily asked.

"Bedrooms," Alea Iacta said. "And two of them lead into bathrooms." He had the group follow him around. Each bedroom had a pair of beds in holes bored out of the cement wall. A small desk was tucked in next to the door and a cheap chair was slid into place under the desk.

"Five rooms to a side, two bunks per room, that's enough sleeping space for twenty," Sam said.

"Cement could have built this," Emily said. "That was his power, to manipulate concrete. I don't know how much work it would have been for him to make this, but with a power . . ."

"So he built a bunch of bases across the city," Sam said. "Did the papers you got from him talk about this at all?"

Emily shook her head. "No. Not at all."

"Hey! There's a kitchen back here!" Trinity said from the end of the room opposite where they'd come in. Emily frowned. She'd lost track of one of Trinity. Her other sisters were poking around too, but they were staying closer.

The kitchen was long and narrow, with a couple of fridges and some stoves. They were entirely empty. The cupboards, too, except for some paper plates and past-date granola bars in a box that Emily swiped out of Trinity's hands.

"Why would he need a place like this?" she asked.

"Isn't that obvious?" Sam asked. "If you're going to take over the city, you need troops. And if you have troops, they need to sleep somewhere."

"If he was planning on being subtle about it, then having a bunch of bases that are hard to spot just makes sense," Alea Iacta said. "This one's right next to the school. I bet if anyone was going to resist a Villain taking over the city, then a bunch of students would be the first in line to protest."

"Unless it was a popular Villain," Sam said. She glanced at Emily meaningfully, but Emily chose to pretend she had no idea what the woman meant with that look. "So, Boss, we going to use this place?"

"What for?" Emily asked.

"You were looking for a spot to stay other than the dorms, right? This is close to the school, has access to the underground, and there's plenty of room for the brats."

"Hey! We're not brats," Teddy said. "I looked up what that word means and I think it's not nice of you to use it for us."

Sam snorted, then tussled Teddy's hair. "Sorry, bear brat."

Teddy pouted up at Sam.

"I guess," Emily said. "It's not a terrible idea. Though this place isn't exactly, ah, homey."

"It's got a bathroom and bedrooms, a roof above and power. A bit humid, but a couple of electric heaters and you'll be able to burn off the worst of that." Sam nodded as she inspected the room. "It's going to be garage-sale season soon. We can pick a few things up while doing more extortion-racket runs."

"We're not going to do more of those," Emily said.

"Come on, Boss. Think of your reputation!" Sam said.

"Yeah, Boss," Teddy said. "Just got to go around and teach people how to share . . . from their pockets to ours. We've been learning numbers in school with Steffie, bet we're great at counting money now."

"I can count the best," Trinity said. That was true; while Athena was the most gifted academically, Trinity had mastered her multiplication and division tables with ease.

Emily shook her head. "We're not going to rob people," she said.

"Okay," Sam agreed far too easily.

Emily turned to Sam, but the words froze in her throat before she could ask them. Sam was definitely planning something, but maybe it wouldn't be that bad? She hoped it wouldn't, at least.

"This isn't a terrible place to stay in, I guess," Emily said. Her sisters cheered and started running around. Fortunately it was empty enough that they couldn't really make a mess of the place. "We can bring in blankets and pillows and maybe fill the fridges a little."

"We were planning on bringing the train base closer, anyway," Sam said.

"That's true," Emily said. "But we don't know how to move the base yet. Besides, it might be expensive. I don't know what you need to run a train, but I'm sure it doesn't use the same kind of gas your car does."

"Yeah, that's fair," Sam said. "We'll figure it out, no worries, Boss. The only sad part in all of this is with Cement's network still intact, you won't get to build your own Super Villain base under the city. It's not as cool to take over another Villain's base."

Emily's eyes squinted. "Yes, I'm sure the coolness of it is a big and important factor," she said.

Both Sam and Alea Iacta stiffened and Emily realized she'd said that aloud.

"A-anyway," she continued, cheeks warming up. "Thanks for showing this to us, Alea, it's pretty wonderful."

"I was just lucky," he said. "After my good looks, it's my best asset, you know?"

CHAPTER THIRTY-FOUR

Confrontational Meetings

Things were going . . . pretty well, actually.

Emily picked up her things from her desk, heaviest binders on the bottom, laptop stuffed into her bookbag with the rest of her school things. The teacher's assistant called out over the din of students packing up. "Don't forget! That assignment is due next Friday! No extensions unless someone dies or a Villain shows up and asks nicely."

There were a few laughs across the classroom auditorium.

Emily didn't feel like laughing, but she smiled all the same. She was in a good mood.

Her sisters were taking to lessons . . . well enough. Lots of pouting still, but they seemed to actually like learning things, and once Mrs. Headerson figured them out, they were somewhat well-behaved. It helped that all three were actually pretty clever, in their own way. The teacher just had to leverage that to her advantage.

Most of the questions and assignments Mrs. Headerson gave the girls involved things like beating Heroes and counting stolen money. It kept their attention fixed on the lesson. Emily couldn't imagine getting that kind of tailored attention in any public school.

She slung her bag over her shoulder. Time to head back home. She had come upon the ingenious idea of just teleporting her sisters back home one at a time every evening. There was a long cooldown between each teleport, though.

Emily considered putting every upgrade point she had into Sisterportation. It would make the skill a little more responsive, and she could get her sisters back to the dorm faster that way.

Stepping out of the class, she looked around herself. Plenty of students tended to linger around once their class was over. Mostly in little groups or cliques. There was laughter and some jockeying around, a few were crowded around a phone sharing something.

Emily squeezed past those groups. Before, when she wasn't a Villain trying to be a Hero, she had often wondered what it would be like to be more sociable, to have more friends. Now she . . . well, she didn't exactly have friends, but minions and siblings were a close second, she imagined.

It wasn't that bad.

As she headed to the exit, a group of girls came to stand between her and the exit. She started to walk around them, but they shifted.

It wasn't exactly subtle.

Emily felt herself tensing a little. Maybe it was a coincidence? She glanced over her shoulder. There was only one person heading her way. Just one person, but a person who could mean plenty of trouble for her.

Short, brown hair, bright big eyes, made a bit bigger with an expert application of makeup. The girl was grinning as she came up to Emily. "Hey, we should talk," she said casually.

Emily swallowed. Jezebelle Winthrop. At least, when she was out of costume. "What?" Emily asked.

Jezebelle touched her elbow. "Come on, somewhere a little more quiet, yeah?"

Emily didn't resist, not for the first couple of steps. Then she stopped, rooted to the spot, and Jezebelle stopped with her. "Where?" Emily asked. It was the best she could manage without her nerves turning her voice to a warble.

Jezebelle smiled. Emily wondered if she practiced that look for the cameras. With her Glamazon costume covering her upper face, all people could see of her in costume was her mouth. "Nothing to worry about. Just don't want to make a scene, you know?"

Emily checked over her shoulder. The exit was still being covered by a gaggle of young women.

"Don't worry about them. Just some friends. They won't snoop. Besides, I haven't told them why we need to talk. I can spin some yarn about how I helped you with something the other day and just wanted to check up on you."

Emily held back a frown. That was a rather condescending story. And one that wasn't worth much. But she didn't know what else to do. Summon Teddy to deck Jezebelle? That was very tempting, actually.

Probably not a great idea, though; she was still trying to pass herself off as a Hero, and knocking out a very public Hero in a very public place wasn't a great image for that.

She hesitated for too long. Jezebelle gave her a winning grin, then tugged Emily after her.

They went around a corner, and for a moment Emily imagined she'd come face-to-face with the likes of Quantum Mothman and a few of the other iconic (and powerful) Heroes that she'd been hearing about for years, but the corridor was mostly empty.

Then Jezebelle moved over to a bathroom whose entrance was blocked off by a strip of tape and a sign that read OUT OF ORDER and shifted the sign aside so they could pass. "Come on, it's not like we'll actually need the washroom," she said.

Emily checked the bathroom, but it was empty. Two of the stalls had tape across them, and some plumbing tools sat on one of the counters as if someone had been working there just minutes ago.

"The school has its own plumber," Jezebelle explained. "But he leaves at four. Union reqs, you know? So we won't be bothered. I just wanted to chat."

"About what?" Emily asked.

"Look, I know who you are, and you know who I am," Jezebelle said.

"What do you mean?" Emily asked too quickly.

The woman rolled her eyes. "While I'm going around being glamorous, you're *bossing* people around. Mostly that little bear girl." She crossed her arms. "Really curious to know if she's related to you or not, but I'm not here to pry into your life, just chat."

Emily took a deep breath. This was probably bad. But if Glamazon, Jezebelle, didn't want to get into a fight, then maybe it wasn't so bad? She wasn't sure, and really she wouldn't know for a bit. She could still run for it, but maybe Jezebelle had friends waiting just outside the bathroom. "What do you want?" Emily asked, defeated.

"Nothing much," Jezebelle said. "You're making a name for yourself. That's fine. I'm trying to do the same thing, and . . . we're butting heads, aren't we? Competing for the same thing?"

"What?" Emily asked.

Jezebelle rubbed her lips, then turned toward the mirror and reached into her purse. She came back with a tube of lipstick and started to touch up her makeup. "We're both Heroes, yeah? I'm thinking that maybe you're a bit more on the . . . Rogue side of things. But Heroes are Heroes. Problem is, there aren't many of us in Eauclaire."

"Okay?" Emily said.

"You know how many Heroes appeared here last Power Day? One. Just one! And they moved to a bigger city. One the year before, none the year before that. Two the year before that. This is a pretty big city, but it's basically a ghost town when it comes to Heroics."

"Is it?" Emily asked.

"It is," Jezebelle said. "We have Quantum Mothman who hangs around because of the university. Silver Fox, who's just here *because* it's quiet. And Melaton, who's pretty much here because the HRF doesn't want her anywhere near trouble. She's called out to problem places all the time. Otherwise there's, like, three others who sometimes stick around. We have three guest Heroes over, but they won't be here for long."

"Why are you telling me all this?" Emily asked.

"Because this town's basically one of the most backwater places in Anada when it comes to Heroics, until this year. We had a huge surge this last Power Day."

"Is that normal?" Emily asked. She was a little curious. It sounded strange.

Jezebelle shrugged. "No. But it's not unheard of. Random places will get a big uptick in new Masks. Usually they'll be on both sides of the fence. Eauclaire just got lucky. Or unlucky. Maybe the next Endgame will be here. There's usually more people chosen to have powers before that, too."

Emily suppressed the shiver that wanted to run down her spine. An Endgame? Here? No, she decided not to think on it. "So it's busy."

"Busyish," Jezebelle said. She turned, lips freshly painted, and stared right at Emily. "What's your goal?"

"Pardon?"

"Your goal. Do you want to be a big-shot Hero? A big name? A celebrity?"

"No, no, I don't want any of that," Emily said.

"Then you're looking for Villains and the like because . . . what, you believe in love and justice and all that?"

Emily shook her head. "I'm not looking for trouble."

"You're certainly finding it," Jezebelle shot back. "Look, I have goals. Dreams. Things that are bigger than this little barely-a-city. I want to get my start here, though, start building a rep so that when I move on, it's going to be with a name that the right people know. Eauclaire might be good for that. If you're looking for something else, then maybe don't stand in my way again."

"I won't," Emily said.

"I'm not the only one, you know? Hindsight, Slaymaker. We want bigger things. Tonight we'll be taking out the last of this city's Villains, and that'll be that. Unless we can find that lucky bastard, but . . . well, he's lucky, so I doubt it." She walked past Emily, then paused next to her. "I don't want you to get in my way anymore, okay? If you want to be friends, then we'll help each other. I'm not so competitive that I'd refuse help. But I want allies, not rivals. Okay?"

"All right," Emily said.

Jezebelle flicked her hair like someone in a poorly scripted movie from the turn of the century, then slipped out of the bathroom.

Emily stared at her wide-eyed reflection for a moment. She looked like someone who was very lost and confused.

Then Jezebelle's words came to her lips as a whisper. "'Tonight we'll be taking out the last of this city's Villains.' . . . Oh no."

CHAPTER THIRTY-FIVE

Hasty Plans

It could all be a bluff," Sam offered.

Teddy turned her head toward the Boss, to see her reaction.

The Boss stomped by, brows drawn up and face set in a scary look, like when she caught Trinity rifling through the trash right after telling her not to. "Do we really want to take that risk? Did he say anything?" she asked.

Sam shook her head and wiggled her phone around, as if to show that she really hadn't gotten any replies. "Nothing. Sorry," she said.

Teddy looked back to the Boss.

The Boss had been pretty testy all day, ever since that meeting with the Glamazon girl. Teddy wasn't sure what they could do about it. If Glamazon were here, in their dorm, then all the sisters would gladly join in and kick her butt. But she wasn't, so Teddy was kind of out of ideas.

"Do you think he'd talk?" the Boss asked.

They were talking about that guy with the little sword and the strange airs about him. Fabien the Fabulous. His Villain name needed . . . a lot of work. Who would be scared of someone called Fabien the Fabulous?

Teddy got the measure of him, and she didn't think he was all that strong. He didn't even join the Boss as a minion. "Why're we worried about this guy anyway?" Teddy asked. "He's barely even a Villain at all."

The Boss sighed. "Because he knows about us, and about our base under the city. If they capture him and he talks, we might be in a terrible situation."

"Oh," Teddy said. So he'd betray the Boss? Or maybe the Heroes would have some sort of Goody Two-shoes way of convincing him to spill everything he knows. Then the Boss's plans would all be ruined.

The Boss had been working hard to take over the city since . . . for-ever, basically. Teddy understood why she'd be annoyed at losing all that progress. It was like being in bed and just about to take a nice nap, then someone came around and shoved you out of bed and forced you to wake up.

"Boss, we've got to do something about this," Teddy said.

"Yeah!" Trinity agreed.

"I suppose so," Athena said, too.

Teddy nodded, glad that her sisters were on her side with this. "We should stop the Heroes from taking out that Villain guy by beating up all the Heroes before they can do anything."

"Yeah!" Trinity agreed again.

"I'm not sure if that'll work out," Athena said. "But I'm willing to try."

The Boss shook her head while minion Sam chuckled. "I don't . . . wait . . . actually, that's not . . . well, it is a terrible idea, but I think it might be workable."

"Wait, seriously?" Sam asked.

"Attacking the Heroes would be stupid," the Boss said. "Sorry, Teddy, but I don't think we're that strong, and we don't want to look like Villains, remember?"

She gave Teddy some conciliatory headpats, so Teddy didn't feel too bad about having her idea dismissed.

"But we can interfere. What if we try to steal the spotlight?" the Boss asked.

"Oh!" Sam said. She grinned. "I see. You want us to head on over to wherever Fabien is, then take him out ourselves?"

"Or we can fail to take him out," the Boss said. "Let him get away. If we're subtle about it, no one will know that we purposefully let him win. Though I'd rather just call Fabien and tell him to cancel his plans for tonight."

Sam checked her phone again. "He still hasn't answered."

The Boss took a deep breath. "Okay. Do you have any idea what he's going to be doing tonight?"

"None," Sam said. "I don't know how much he made hitting that bank, but I imagine it was a few thousand, at least. They don't exactly keep huge piles of cash around anymore, you know? Could try to hit another bank, or another jewelry place."

"And those are all over the city," the Boss muttered. She reached her desk and pulled her phone off its charger. "I'm calling Alea Iacta. He spent more time with Fabien. He might know. In the meantime . . . girls, pack your costumes."

Teddy grinned and bounced to her feet. That was an order she was more than happy to obey. Packing up their costumes meant that there was going to be some Villainy to do that night.

She found her sundress tucked under the bed where it would be safe, then she handed her teddy-bear mask to Trinity. Another Trinity was dumping all her school stuff out of a bag and onto the floor; pencils rolled around and books flopped open. Then she started shoving all her own costumes into the bag.

Teddy was already wearing her shorts, so she changed into a T-shirt that she could wear under her sundress.

Athena's costume was a bit hard to fit into the bag—the leather jacket didn't fold so easily—so she ended up putting it into its own bag.

While they worked, the Boss prowled across the room, talking in low tones to someone on her phone. Eventually, she lowered the phone and ended the call. "I think I might know where he's going," she said.

"Oh?" Sam asked as she looked up from her own phone. "I've been checking one of the Capewatch sites. No sightings of him yet." She tilted her phone back, revealing an online forum where people were posting candid images of heroes in public.

The Boss nodded. "The last place he hit was just before closing. He might do the same thing tonight. At least, I hope so. That'll give us more time to try to reach him."

"So where is he going?" Sam asked.

"Alea Iacta said that he and Fabien spent a lot of time talking about games. He said that Fabien might try to rob an electronics store. I don't know which one, though."

"There's only one worth robbing," Sam said. "The Aim Stop. Just downtown. There's a few other places, but they're old. You wouldn't get much from robbing them. I bet the registers are filled with cobwebs."

"If he's not robbing the place, can we rob it instead?" Teddy asked.

The Boss shook her head. "No. Let me grab my costume. Actually . . . you guys go wait outside. I'm going to change into it now and toss a coat on top." Everyone was ushered out into the corridor and the Boss closed the door behind them.

Sam rubbed her chin, then looked down at where Teddy and her sisters were looking up to her. "So, uh, you guys have everything?" she asked.

"Yeah," Teddy said.

"You sure? Because once we're gone, we won't be able to get back, and it'd suck if you had to sit things out because you forgot your mask or something," Sam said. "Uh . . . what about the washroom?"

"What about it?" Teddy asked.

"Do you need to use it?" Sam asked.

Teddy scoffed. "No."

Her sisters shook their heads too.

"Are you sure?" Sam asked. "Like, one hundred percent certain? Because the moment one of you complains about needing the bathroom while out in costume, I'm going to convince the Boss to leave you at home next time."

"We're not five," Teddy said. She crossed her arms and looked away. "But I guess . . . maybe I could use the washroom, a bit."

Sam rolled her eyes and unlocked the door to her room before using some appropriately Villainous threats on them if they touched any of her things. Teddy got to go first in line because she was the fastest and the best.

By the time they were all done, the Boss was waiting for them out in the corridor. She had a coat on, with something that Teddy suspected was her costume's hat stuffed into a pocket. "Is everyone ready?" she asked.

"Yup," Sam said.

"All right then, let's head out."

"Any plan past showing up?" Sam asked.

"Get there before Glamazon. Be obvious enough that Fabien backs off and does something smart, like reply to his texts," the Boss said. They filed into the elevator and Sam tapped the button to get to the ground floor. "If that doesn't work out and we arrive in the middle of a fight, then . . . then we get involved. Trinity, Athena, you'll be important if that's the case. I need the Heroes confused."

"I can do that," Trinity said. "Sometimes I even confuse me."

Athena nodded. "No worries, Boss."

"What about me?" Teddy asked.

"You'll be fighting Fabien directly, I think. I'll need you to be extra-careful to not actually hurt him. Do you think you can do that?"

"Yeah!" Teddy said. "Don't worry. I'm great at being sneaky."

The elevator dinged and they stepped out as one big group, ready to head out and kick Hero butt.

Teddy couldn't wait.

CHAPTER THIRTY-SIX

Wherein Everything Goes Terribly Wrong

Nearly everything was going terribly wrong, but at least some things were working out in Emily's favor.

First among those was the distance they had to travel. The Aim Stop that they suspected Fabien was going to attack was only a few minutes' walk away from the campus. It was in a busier part of the city, with a four-lane road in front of it and shops lining either side of the street.

There were plenty of parking lots and open spaces all around, and, of course, alleyways.

Emily peeked out to see if anything was happening, but other than a few customers slipping in and out of the store, not much was going on.

"All right," she said as she backed up. "Girls, I'm really hoping this won't require us to do anything, but just in case. Masks on. Don't show your labels no matter what. No using your normal names."

"Got it, Boss," Teddy said. "The rest of you can call me Ursa Minor, 'cause I'm a bear as big as those star things."

"That doesn't actually make sense," Athena said. She looked to Emily. "What about Trinity and me? We don't have Hero names, just our normal names."

Emily winced. Those were meant to be their Heroic names, but at some point that had just become what they were called. She eyed her two sisters. Athena was rocking something of a punk look, with her leather jacket and some ketchup-stained jeans that had a few tears in them. Her big glasses sat on the end of her nose and made her eyes look even bigger as she stared back.

Trinity was in her burglar outfit, big bag with a money sign hooked to her side. She grinned back, and there was no missing the . . . racoon-ness of her. "Can I be Trash Panda?" Trinity asked.

"Pardon?" Emily asked.

"Yeah, it'll confuse people. They'll think I'm a panda."

"You're nothing like a bear," Teddy said.

Sam snorted. "How about the Holy Ones?"

"I don't have holes," Trinity said. "Not unless I'm dying or something."

"No, holy as in . . . you know, the Holy Trinity?" Sam asked.

Emily shook her head. "A bit too . . . meta, I think. And Trinity is many things, but holy isn't one of them. Besides, isn't that too big of a hint as to her real name?"

"Yeah, fair," Sam said. "What about, ah, what's that dog with the three heads? No, never mind. Maybe when you get a dog-themed sister. What about Bandit?"

"That's rather Villainous," Emily pointed out.

"It fits the costume, and she can play up the whole anti-Hero angle of things. Besides, she can take refuge in cuteness," Sam said.

Emily frowned. "I'm pretty sure that's not a thing."

"I like Bandit," Trinity said, which pretty much sealed the deal. She high-fived herself.

"What about you, Athena?" Emily asked.

Athena pursed her lips. "If we were being proper Villains instead of pretending to be Heroes, then I'd go with something like Paranoia. But since we are pretending to be Goody Two-shoes, then how about Owlwatch?"

"That works," Emily said. She leaned back and checked on the shop again. Nothing unusual. "We're going to have to wait a bit more."

"Check your quests," Sam suggested. "I mostly just want to see what that looks like, but I heard that they're the only way for a Mask to get stronger."

Emily reluctantly nodded. Sam wasn't wrong. Emily had originally hoped to avoid having to become stronger at all. But things weren't working out that way. If she had to use strength to get what she needed, then she might as well do what she could to make that strength a little more . . . more.

"Girls, can I trust you to pick out good quests for yourselves? Nothing that involves killing or seriously hurting people, or blowing our cover," she said.

She got five nods back.

Emily wasn't sure how much she should rely on her sisters' common sense, but she chose to hope that they knew what they were doing.

She leaned against the edge of the alley, rough brick pressing into her suit top. It was cool, which wasn't bad. The weather was slowly turning warmer, but there were still hints of coolness out, especially as the day turned a little late.

With a stray thought, she opened her quest menu and picked through them. A lot were immediately dismissed. Too dangerous, or far too violent, or they pushed her deeper into Villainy in a way she didn't appreciate.

In the end, she only kept two quests running.

Quest!

The Queen with the Silken Sword, Continued

Become an outstanding member of your community!

Reward: +1 Skill Upgrade point per 10 people who recognize you as "good." Scoundrel +1 per 10 people who recognize you as "good"!

Quest!

Queen Takes Bishop

Defeat, through subterfuge, manipulation, or force, a rival group of powered individuals!

Reward: +1 Skill Slot for defeating, capturing, or killing a powered adversary. + Villainy for properly securing your territory.

"You know," Sam said. "I was expecting glowing screens. I know that normies can't see anything, but still. That's how they show up in the movies and games, you know?"

"Oh, you can make others see 'em," Teddy said. She pinched her tongue between her lips and narrowed her eyes, then a small screen popped into existence over her hand. It had a quest called Being a Better Bear, which asked her to defeat someone in combat for some Skill Upgrade points.

"That is so neat," Sam said. "Can I take a picture of it?"

"Sure," Teddy said.

Emily almost stopped her. "Maybe do it with a quest that's less obviously one of yours?" she asked.

Teddy shrugged and the image changed to something that didn't mention bears, though it was certainly on the more Villainous side.

Emily stuck her head out of the alley again and jolted when she saw who was standing before the Aim Stop. Fabien the Fabulous, in a fresh costume that made him look like a cross between a Rogue and a pirate.

"Girls," Emily said. "It's time to move in. Trinity, think you can intercept him?"

Trinity nodded. One of her had a coat on over her costume and some big shades. "I'm right on it, Boss," she said.

Emily gave her head a pat as she ran by. Then she gasped as Trinity sprinted right across all four lanes of the road without even glancing to the side. She spun to face another Trinity. "What did I say about crossing roads?"

Trinity just said, "If I don't see the cars coming, it's not as scary."

"We're going to have road-crossing lessons," Emily decided. "That counts for the rest of you, too."

"Uh, Boss, there's other people there," Trinity said.

Emily whipped around and stared out across the road. Trinity was right. She was standing between the shop and Fabien, clearly talking to him. The people passing by were giving them a wide berth, and Emily could tell that some people were reaching for their phones already.

That didn't concern her as much as the unmarked van that turned into the parking lot, rumbled over the embarkment on the lot's edge, then opened up to disgorge half a dozen Heroes.

"Let's move," Emily said.

She stepped out of the alley, her sisters behind her. Sam remained behind to keep an eye on things. There wasn't much the woman could do if things turned to a fight. Then again, Emily wished she was the one staying behind.

"Let's hurry, Boss," Teddy said. "I wanna kick butts." She swung a few punches forward, bleeding off some excess energy. Her other sisters were just as hyped up.

"Oh, the Heroes are screaming things now," Trinity said.

Emily looked for a spot to cross the road, but she didn't have to look for long. The traffic was slowing down as people noticed actual Heroes on the roadside. It only took one or two people slowing to a stop to create a traffic jam.

Emily took a deep breath, then crossed the road with her sisters in tow. She walked with her back bowed for a bit, but she slowly straightened up as they came closer to the Heroes.

She wasn't Emily, she was the Boss. She couldn't *afford* to be nervous, even if she would much rather be back in her room, on her chair, in PJ's and wrapped up in a few layers of blankets.

She stepped on the sidewalk behind the Heroes and her sisters arrayed themselves out around her.

There was Glamazon, Iron Chains—or whatever name he went by now—Hindsight, Cheatah, . . . and Black Shield.

Emily's hands balled into fists. Five Heroes. One of whom might actually be pretty strong, and a rather big threat at that.

The Heroes noticed them eventually, half turning so that they could split their attention between Emily and her sisters and Fabien on the other side.

"This is going to be a problem," Emily said.

Somehow, her voice didn't tremble.

CHAPTER THIRTY-SEVEN

All Out

Emily watched as Glamazon turned away from Fabien and stared at her. "What are you doing here?" she asked.

For a second, just one irrational second, Emily felt like telling her the truth. Something like *We're here to stop you from capturing Fabien back there because he might tell you all that we're Villains, which isn't actually wrong, but really, I'm trying to be a good person and don't need the police knocking at my door, thank you.*

Fortunately, she had more self-control than her sisters, so instead of replying, she self-consciously stood a little taller and leveled a look at the Hero. Then she realized that she wasn't entirely sure what to say.

"We're here to kick your butts," Teddy rescued her.

More or less.

Emily's eyes darted across all the Heroes before her. Glamazon looked irate. Hindsight, confused. Cheatah was glancing between Emily and her sisters and Fabien, and Black Shield . . . it was hard to tell with the last. Her costume included a face-covering helmet, which left only her body language for Emily to figure out, and figuring out what someone was thinking from the set of their shoulders wasn't something Emily was good with.

There was one person left in the group, the odd one out. Iron Chains. He was dressed in a tight spandex suit, one that failed to hide that he had some love handles on him. It was bright blue and white, the same color as the chains wrapped around his middle and his arms. Those had links that were painted in the same pattern. Blue-white-blue-white.

Emily pointed to him, then to Black Shield. She had an idea, and it wasn't going to work. "The question is, Glamazon, why are you associating with two known Villains?"

There. Turn the tables around.

"What?" Cheatah asked. She glanced at Emily, then to the people around her. She was quick to take a small step away from Black Shield.

"What are you talking about?" Glamazon asked. "We're here to capture him." She pointed behind her, in the vague direction of where Fabien stood.

"He's just a bank robber," Athena said. For a moment Emily was worried that her sisters were going to ruin her admittedly awful plan, but then Athena went on. "We know what he's up to. It's just robbing places. But Iron Chains was doing Villain stuff. Like taking people's money. And beating people up."

"Yeah," Teddy agreed. "Fun stuff like that."

Athena nodded. "So the Boss put him in his place, with our help. Now he's working for you, isn't he?"

"That was a misunderstanding," Iron Chains said.

"Liar!" Athena shot back.

"Can we set his pants on fire?" Trinity asked in stereo.

Glamazon shook her head as if she couldn't believe what was happening. "Look, Wrap Up might have messed up a little, but that doesn't mean he's not a Hero. Show them, Wrap."

Iron Chains hesitated for a moment, mumbled something, then some words appeared over his head.

Wrap Up
Level 1
Hero

"See," Glamazon said. "He's a Hero."

Emily froze. From the corner of her eye she could see people on the sidewalks and the edges of the street, even in the store that Fabien was about to rob. They were watching, and they were listening. She knew why. With this many Masks in one place, one of them even proudly showing off his tag, they'd be taking pictures and filming, then bragging about it later.

A Mask fight was like a car crash, but a thousand times worse when it came to bystanders.

And now all those people were staring at Emily. She felt as if she was naked in the spotlight. This was her third-grade play all over again. Her heart clenched, and for a moment she wasn't sure if she could remember how to breathe.

Then she noticed the Trinity behind Fabien picking her nose.

She almost snapped at the girl. What was Trinity thinking? People were watching! She . . . she took a deep breath, then focused on Glamazon. All she had to do, she realized, was pretend that the Heroes here were misbehaving children. Easy. She dealt with those on the daily.

"The system might acknowledge that he's a Hero," Emily said. "But I don't. Same for Black Shield over there. I don't want to hear any excuses. Just because someone can conjure up a little glowing sign that says they're innocent doesn't mean they are."

Glamazon looked honestly stumped. It reminded Emily a little of when she explained to her sisters that no, stealing things wasn't okay, even if they didn't get caught.

"We both know what he did," Emily said. "I'm surprised you want to fight alongside him."

"Hey!" Iron Chains . . . no, Wrap Up, she supposed, said. "Look, I might not have been the greatest guy around, but don't I deserve a second chance?"

"Would you have gotten that second chance if your tag read Villain?" Emily asked.

He scoffed. "Well, no, but I'm a Hero."

"And that's why I can't trust you. You expect me to judge you based on some glowing word instead of your actions," Emily said.

"Look, can we talk about this after we catch that guy?" Glamazon pointed at Fabien.

Hindsight nodded. "Yeah. I'm interested in what you have to say, too, but this doesn't feel like the time or place for it."

"We're not just going to talk it out, are we?" Teddy asked, clearly disappointed. "Because I came here to fight."

"We don't need ten Heroes to capture a B-rated Villain wannabe," Glamazon said. "Wrap Up and I almost caught him last time, and that was just with the two of us."

"Athena," Emily muttered. "Your time to shine."

Athena nodded, then smiled angelically. If Emily didn't know much better, she might have assumed that Athena was the most innocent and sweet girl there was. "We think that there's a lot more Villains than that," Athena said. "So it's more like six on three."

"She's attacking me!" Black Shield said. The very first words out of her mouth since the two groups had met. She pointed to Athena. "Right now, she's attacking me mentally."

Cheatah looked between Black Shield and Athena. "What? What are you on about?"

"I can feel it," Black Shield said. Her arms snapped to the side and two black circles appeared with twin cracks.

Emily tensed up. Unfortunately, Cheatah and Hindsight seemed willing to listen to others, and they were both ready to de-escalate. Glamazon was more annoyed by her image, Emily suspected, and Wrap Up was just confused.

She knew that her plan relied on her adversaries being a little stupid, and now it wasn't working out.

"Iron Chains! Take out Glamazon! Black Shield, grab Cheatah. I'll take out Hindsight!" Fabien the Fabulous shouted.

The Heroes, who had partially turned toward Emily, stood looking entirely baffled as Fabien darted toward Hindsight, his sword sliding out of its sheath with a metallic rasp.

Everything went chaotic a moment later. Fabien stabbed toward Hindsight, who tripped backward, arms flailing.

Glamazon flung out a brilliant ball of light, and for a moment all Emily could do was track it with her eyes before she snapped her attention away.

It was just in time to notice Wrap Up flinging some of his two-colored chains toward Fabien.

Fabien spun, his sword reached out, and the very tip slipped into the hole of the leading chain link. With a continued spin, he flicked his sword out and the chain flew out and smacked Cheatah in the face.

Things spiraled out of control even further when Black Shield rushed toward Fabien only for Hindsight, who was still on the ground, to kick her legs out from under her.

Athena started to cackle. "It's beautiful!" she cheered.

Emily looked around. Some of the civilians were running away. Others, with less common sense, were running toward the fight.

Her distraction almost cost her as a length of chain whipped out and only Teddy's tackle prevented it from smacking her in the head. "Okay, enough," she said from the roadside. "Teddy, focus on Wrap Up. Athena, keep doing what you're doing. Trinity, get in there!"

"All right!" Teddy said.

She ran into the fray, then jumped up and turned into a grizzly with a happy roar.

"Not again!" Wrap Up shouted a moment before Teddy ran into him forehead first.

Fabien the Fabulous had turned his attention to Glamazon, who was swearing as she worked to dodge his attacks. She flung out a brace of light balls that exploded with powerful bangs that were loud enough to set off car alarms and make everyone wince.

Black Shield was screaming something at Cheatah, who was darting around so fast that all Emily could see of her was the occasional blur. Then Trinity got involved, two of her tackling Black Shield from either side and refusing to let go.

Somehow, this was all her fault, Emily knew. So she'd just have to do something about it.

CHAPTER THIRTY-EIGHT

A Perfectly Reasonable Escalation

Things didn't settle down.

The few times Emily had seen a Mask fight, it had been something like a highlight reel, or some distant shaky-cam video taken from someone with a common sense deficiency who was too close to the fighting for their own good.

Those fights usually ended quickly.

Intellectually, she knew why. Whoever struck harder first would usually take their opponent out of the fight. The exception was usually when the one striking second had a power that could negate the attack, then things could get messy.

She had never seen a fight with this many Masks in it before. She was sure it existed, but she hadn't paid all that much attention to the world of Masks and powers.

This fight wasn't ending quickly at all.

Fabien danced around the edge of the battlefield, between Wrap Up and the others. The way he moved Wrap Up's chains around with flicks of his sword and by dancing around them was nearly perfect. Emily doubted that she would have figured out they were enemies if she didn't know beforehand.

Black Shield was working hard to kick off Trinity from her legs. She kept stumbling around as Cheatah shoved her shield and darted around her to try to grapple the Hero down.

Hindsight looked around himself, jumped to his feet, then decided that being elsewhere was the better part of valor. Glamazon screamed something at him, and it didn't sound like a compliment.

Teddy, meanwhile, was fighting with Fabien. The bear roared and swiped at the Rogueish man. Emily knew Teddy was holding back a little, and at a glance, it was clear that Fabien's few strikes against her were meant to be shallow pokes. Wrap Up was causing more trouble, his chains tangling Teddy up even as he tried to bring them back around to catch Fabien.

"All right," Emily said. She had an idea of what was going on.

Glamazon was stomping away from the fight in her direction, looking pretty displeased about everything that was going on. Emily refocused on the Hero. "Family Menagerie: Teddy," she muttered.

She felt herself growing a little, her coat strained a bit at the back, and her pants felt tighter. Hopefully she wouldn't look too foolish; there were a lot of phones aimed their way, she knew.

"You!" Glamazon said.

Emily held back the urge to look over her shoulder. Glamazon was very clearly talking about her. "Glamazon," she said.

"You caused this mess," Glamazon said.

Emily wasn't about to argue that. The woman was right. The fight was her fault. Though, to give credit where it was due, Athena was probably helping. The owl girl was giggling to herself next to Emily, eyes flitting from one fight to another.

"What do you want to do about it?" Emily asked. "I'm not a frontline fighter. Nor is At— Owlwatch here."

Glamazon stopped, her mouth opened, then it closed again. She glanced back. The fight was actually winding down. Black Shield was on the ground, hands raised above her in a defensive stance while two of Trinity sat on her chest and a third one ran circles around the woman, arms raised in triumph.

Cheatah was panting nearby, still eyeing the woman on the ground.

On the other side, Teddy was stumbling toward Wrap Up while Fabien rolled out of the way. The Scoundrel stood up and looked around, and for a moment his eyes locked onto Emily's. He nodded, then saluted with his sword raised next to his forehead.

"Oh no," Glamazon said. "Wait! He's running!" She flung a trio of brilliant balls toward the running Villain.

Emily's breath caught as she saw Cheatah spin around. The woman could move faster than Fabien could, that was her entire power. He wouldn't be able to escape if she . . .

Then Glamazon's explosions went off, and Cheatah flinched back.

Fabien had managed to weave his way through the three. He darted into the crowd by the edge of the parking lot, people scrambling away from him, but not so quickly that he couldn't use the crowd as cover.

"Got you!" Wrap Up shouted.

Emily whipped around to find Teddy flopping onto the ground, caught up entirely in his chains.

She scowled. "Sisterportation, Ursa Minor." She didn't know if using Teddy's Hero name would work until a grizzly landed on the ground before her and shook itself so that her fur puffed out.

Wrap Up's smile faded as he realized that all eyes were on him. "Uh," he said. The many chains hovering around him lowered, some of them gently wrapping themselves back around his arms and torso, as if he was aware of every clink and clang they made.

"Are you done?" Emily asked him with the same tone she'd use on one of her sisters.

"Yes?" he said, rather meekly.

Emily nodded, then turned to Glamazon. "Now, the question, Glamazon, is if you'll do the right thing."

Emily had no idea what the right thing to do in this situation was, but maybe Glamazon had a better idea than her, so she didn't see any harm in throwing it back at the woman.

Glamazon glared at Emily, then her eyes twitched to the people on the sidewalks and the cars still paused in the middle of their commute to stare at what was going on. Some honking in the distance hinted that others weren't so happy with the traffic jam they were creating.

"We're waiting until backup arrives," she said.

"And then what?" Emily asked.

Glamazon crossed her arms. "Then we'll see. Cheatah, can you escort Black Shield to the middle of the parking lot? Wrap Up, you're joining her." Glamazon sniffed. "Boss, want to keep an eye on them too?"

Emily nodded. "Bandit, keep two of you close to them. Owlwatch, Ursa Minor, stay close, just in case."

"Yeah, Boss, no worries," Teddy said. Her voice in grizzly form was a terrifying, deep rumble.

"Got it, Boss," Athena said. She smiled, smug and pleased with herself. She had kind of earned it. Emily suspected that a lot of the paranoia that had gotten the others to act had been fed by Athena's power.

The two that Emily had accused of being Villains were ushered to the middle of the parking lot, with Emily's sisters forming a cordon around them. Glamazon stomped off to go find Hindsight who was hiding nearby.

In the meantime, Emily found herself with nothing to do except wait for her beating heart to calm down. That wasn't happening as quickly as she might have hoped. The HRF was on their way over, and there was still a good chance that they'd ruin all of Emily's not-so-carefully laid plans.

In the meantime, she walked over to Cheatah's side. "You, ah, you did good," Emily said.

Cheatah blinked, then smiled. "Thanks," she said. The woman was a few years Emily's senior, maybe as old as her late twenties. It added a little layer of awkwardness for Emily to work through. "So, you have a team going on?" Cheatah asked.

"Pardon?"

Cheatah gestured to her sisters. "A team? With the, ah, kids?"

"Oh," Emily said. "Yeah, I guess. We have another member, he's older. Well, my age. Not a frontline person. Um. We might have another person joining us soon."

"That's nice," Cheatah said. "It's not my place to say anything, but . . . they seem a bit young to be doing this kind of thing, you know?"

"A little, I guess," Emily said. She imagined that employing a bunch of preteens to do her work wasn't a great look. "I'm mostly trying to keep them out of trouble."

"Right," Cheatah said. "Just hope you're watching out for them. They seem like nice enough kids."

"You, ah, clearly haven't spent much time with them," Emily said.

Trinity chose that moment to start singing a song of her own devising whose entire lyrics were "We kicked your butts, your butts were kicked," repeated over and over again in an annoying singsong. At least she harmonized with herself really well.

Sirens sounded in the distance, and lights flashed. Cars that had been parked around so their occupants could stare started to move ahead, likely worried about the size of the ticket they'd get if the police found them clogging the road up while emergency services were trying to get closer.

The first vehicle to arrive was an Eep with the roof off. It was the black and green of the HRF, and the moment it bounced up onto the curb, a figure jumped out of the passenger side and landed in a crouch on the parking lot.

She stood slowly, then scanned her surroundings before swiping her hand across the bottom of her nose. "What in the goddamn is happening here?"

Emily swallowed as a very annoyed Melaton stomped onto the scene.

CHAPTER THIRTY-NINE

Melaton's Talk

Melaton wasn't all that impressive, not at first glance. She was a bit shorter than Emily, with a costume that didn't fit the usual bright spandex and neon colors of the typical Hero. She had too much leather on for that, and her costume didn't look like it followed any particular themes. The only concession to hiding her identity was a large half mask that covered her eyes and the upper half of her face.

Still, it wasn't her looks that made everyone snap to attention, it was her attitude.

Melaton was a whole lot of anger stuffed in a little package. She was ten wet cats in a paper bag, and at the moment there were enough cats for everyone to get a faceful.

Basically, she had all the confidence that Emily lacked, and she wielded it like a bat. "All right, who's in charge here?" she asked.

Emily, her sisters, and the collected Heroes glanced around at one another.

"I'm not going to ask twice," Melaton snapped.

"Um," Emily said.

That had Melaton paying her a lot more attention than she wanted.

"I am," Glamazon said. "At least, for some of us."

"All right," Melaton said. "And what's with the two on the ground?" She gestured to Wrap Up and Black Shield.

"They're bad guys!" Trinity cheered. "And we're Heroes."

"We were just arguing about that," Glamazon said. "The actual Villain left. Fabien the Fabulous. We were here to capture him. He's, ah, gone now."

Melaton half turned and motioned to the armed and armored agents pouring out of vans and SUVs. They immediately started forming a cordon around the area, but a few snapped to attention as Melaton waved them forward. "Watch those two. Nonlethals only. We might have an identity issue, or a mind-control power at play."

Troopers darted forward and knelt next to Black Shield and Wrap Up. Three for each of them, with one on one knee next to the Hero, another standing behind them ready to act, and the third a pace or two farther back with a handgun by their side.

"Boss, Glamazon, you two with me," Melaton said. She spun on a heel and walked over to one of the vans, fully expecting the two to follow them.

Emily found the nearest of her sisters, Athena, and gave her some quick instructions. "Be good girls," she said. "Heroes, remember. There's a lot of eyes on us right now."

"Don't worry, Boss, I'll keep the others from doing anything stupid."

"Right, thanks," Emily said. She shored up her bravery, used it to fill in the hole left by her panic, then jogged after Glamazon to the van Melaton was waiting by.

Melaton crossed her arms and only spared a glance at the traffic slowly flowing past not too far away. The van would hide them from the oncoming traffic, at least. "All right, let's get this mess over with. Who got here first?"

"We did," Glamazon said. "Myself, Hindsight, Cheatah, as well as Wrap Up and Black Shield."

Emily wondered at the list. Did she include the final two at the end like that to create some distance between them and herself? She wouldn't have put something like that past Glamazon.

"Okay, and why were you here?" Melaton asked.

"Hindsight knew that Fabien would be trying something today. We narrowed down the places he could be and then I got some friends, civilians, to watch over each place. When he showed up, we were already on our way over."

That was . . . actually kind of scary. Deploying a group of Heroes so quickly was impressive, even if they had someone in their group who could see into the future.

"And you?" Melaton asked Emily.

"We showed up just after," Emily said.

"How did you know to show up here?" Melaton asked.

"Um," Emily said. "We have someone who told us? Another member of my group. He doesn't do public stuff."

All technically true.

"So you showed up too," Melaton said. "It's usually considered bad form to steal another Hero's catch, you know."

"I doubt she does," Glamazon muttered.

"Anyway, tell me what happened next," Melaton said.

Glamazon recounted the events from her point of view. It wasn't a terrible recounting, but Emily noticed a few bits that were clearly biased in her own favor. Her sisters did the same thing when Emily asked them to explain why they were fighting, each delivering the same story in a way that made them out to be in the right.

"Our ambush was initially successful. Fabien was caught between the storefront and our group. Black Shield and Cheatah would keep the civilians safe while Wrap Up and I would capture him. Hindsight was there for backup, in case something unexpected showed up. Like the Boss here and her crew. They came up behind us, and we discussed things for a moment before she leveled some accusations toward Wrap Up and Black Shield."

"We'll get to that in a moment," Melaton said. "What happened next?"

Glamazon hesitated. "Fabien attacked. And . . . in the confusion, it's possible that Black Shield and Wrap Up acted in a way that might have made them seem hostile."

"Uh-huh," Melaton said. "Well, there's enough cameras around. We'll have a dozen angles up on Outube to see before the end of the day. The analysts will be earning their pay, I think. They eat this kind of thing up. Of course, they can never agree with one another." The last was muttered just low enough that Emily could understand.

"What now?" Emily asked.

"Now, *Boss*," Melaton said, the tone used for Emily's name hinting at a lack of respect that had her flinching back. "You tell me why you attacked two Heroes."

"Um, I don't think they're actually Heroes," Emily said.

"They have tags," Glamazon jumped on the opportunity to make Emily look bad.

Melaton waved that comment off. "Those don't mean Jack to me. Once you're in the business for long enough you'll see what something like 'Hero' really means, and it ain't much. I'll admit that most of the folk with 'Super' in their title earned it, but that's for another time. What's your evidence, Boss?"

"Wrap Up went by, uh, Iron Chains before," Emily said. "He was a Villain. My sisters . . . uh, my companions and I arrested him."

Glamazon blinked. "Sisters?"

"A slip of the tongue, I'm sure," Melaton said. "Don't poke at people's identities if you can avoid it. Now . . . Iron Chains, yeah, I heard about that."

"He's reformed," Glamazon said.

"It only took a week or two to reform him? Impressive," Melaton deadpanned. "I see where you were going there, Boss, but really, there's a number of good Heroes who strayed along the way. It doesn't make them Villains."

Emily shifted on the spot. "Oh."

"And Black Shield?"

Emily glanced around. She didn't have a good answer for that one. Which didn't mean to say that she didn't have an answer at all. "Black Shield is a member of the Cabal," Emily said.

"The what?" Glamazon asked.

Melaton scowled. "You shouldn't be interacting with them," she said.

"They started it," Emily said. She held back a wince, though she couldn't do anything for the pink rising in her cheeks. That sounded a bit too much like what the brats would say. "I was investigating something the other day when she attacked. She's bad news."

"But not a Villain," Melaton said.

"Well, no, but maybe worse?"

Glamazon looked between the two of them. "Care to share?"

"If you don't know, then best keep it that way," Melaton said. "Suffice to say, some groups are a lot of trouble, and messing with them only causes more headache. Which is something you should know." The last was aimed squarely at Emily.

"She made us miss out on catching Fabien," Glamazon said.

Melaton shook her head. "He's a small fry. Sure, robbing banks makes him annoying, but he hasn't hurt any civilians, and banks have insurance. You'll catch him next time. Besides, more fights with him will only help your popularity. That's what you're in this for, right?"

"What?" Glamazon blustered. "No, I'm here to help people."

"Sure thing, Sparkles."

Glamazon tightened her fists, but she didn't protest any further.

"I'm . . . I'm sorry about Fabien," Emily said. "Next time, maybe I'll help you. But this time, I had to do the right thing."

Melaton muttered something about idealistic Heroes under her breath. "I'm not sure if the right thing will end up being useful in this case. It'll shine some light on things that are best kept in the dark."

"What kinds of things?" Glamazon asked.

"Ask the Boss here, maybe she'll enlighten you. Heh. Not that you need lights, right, Sparkles?"

Glamazon glared. "You're not a very Heroic person, are you?"

"I'm not the ideal, no, but I'm good at what I do," Melaton said. "Boss, get back to your brats before they cause trouble. Glamazon, go smile for the cameras and sign some babies or whatever. I need to fix your messes. Oh, and for the love of everything good, don't talk any more than you have to where anyone can hear."

Time to Go

Emily gathered up her little sisters, feeling a bit like a farmer chasing after chickens as she did so. Trinity was all over the place, poking at things and asking the Heroes and police officers all sorts of questions. Athena was talking to an investigator, telling the attentive man a very inaccurate summary of what had happened, and Teddy . . .

"Ursa Minor, it's time to go," Emily said as she approached Teddy.

Teddy was standing off to the side of all the commotion. Not that she was alone. In fact, it was far worse than that. She had a crowd of people before her, maybe two dozen in all, with only a flimsy line of police tape between her and the crowd.

"Aww, but, Boss, I was just telling my comrades here about the glories of communal work," Teddy said. She turned back to the crowd, a big proud smile on full display. "Like I was sayin', for the world to be a better place, you need to get rid of anyone too busy owning stuff to realize that things can be better. Everyone should own a bit of everything so that no one owns anything. Like the Boss here, she's really good about sharing. The other day we got pizza."

"Uh," Emily said as the crowd's attention fell onto her. It was only through force of will that she didn't fold in on herself. Mostly they were older people, with a few who had their phones out. She had the impression, from all the smiles and poorly hidden laughter, that they thought Teddy's spiel was more cute than anything else. "We're heading back, I didn't want to leave you behind."

"Are we going home, or are we going to our secret base?" Teddy asked.

"Ursa Minor, you're not supposed to talk about the secret base!" Athena said. "It's a secret."

"Oh, yeah, I guess," Teddy said. There were some titters in the crowd.

Emily couldn't get out of there fast enough.

They crossed the street, passing through a crowd of people who were quick to ask for signatures and pictures. Trinity helped by taking all the papers people were handing them to sign and stuffing them into her dollar-sign bags without looking twice.

Once they were in the alley they'd used to spy from across the street, they found Sam waiting for them. "Heading out, Boss?" she asked.

"Yes," Emily said. "Before anyone back there changes their mind."

"Where to?" Sam asked as they started down the alley. A few curious onlookers followed to the start, but none of them stepped in.

"I-I don't know. Somewhere quiet?"

"The train, then," Sam said. She raised her phone and wiggled it around. "Got a text from our fabulous friend. He finally got around to replying. Makes a girl feel awful when a boy takes that long to reply, you know?"

"What did he say?" Emily asked.

"That he'd meet us underground," Sam replied. "And he said thanks for the level-up."

Emily winced, then checked on her quests.

Quest Complete!

The Queen with the Silken Sword, Continued

Become an outstanding member of your community!

Reward: +1 Skill Upgrade point per 10 people who recognize you as "good." Scoundrel +1 per 10 people who recognize you as "good"!

She could live with that. Her pool of Skill Upgrade points was growing. She'd have to pour them into something soon. Menagerie Family was a good skill, but so was Healpats and Sisterportation. Maybe an even split among all of them?

Quest Complete!

Queen Takes Bishop

Defeat, through subterfuge, manipulation, or force, a rival group of powered individuals!

Reward: +1 Skill Slot for defeating, capturing, or killing a powered adversary. + Villainy for properly securing your territory.

She stared at the total number of Skill Slots she had freed up now. Two.

Two new skills. That meant that if the pattern held, she was going to get a new sister with the very next skill. And then one more utility skill after that. "Did you girls get any level-ups?" Emily asked.

"No level-ups, Boss," Teddy said. "This wasn't an Endgame. But I got a heap of Skill Upgrade stuff, and I got a Skill Slot!"

"Yeah, me too," Athena said.

"Me three," Trinity added with a giggle.

Sam grinned. "Can you girls let me write down your progress while you upgrade your skills? For science, of course."

"Yeah, sure," Teddy agreed easily. Emily wasn't so sure it was a good idea, but other than the risk of that information falling into the wrong hands, she couldn't think of a reason why it would be a bad idea.

"Let's just get to the base, and let's also make sure we're not followed all the way there," Emily said.

They wandered around the city for a bit until they came upon that maintenance shed a couple of blocks over. There was a padlock over the door, but a grinning Sam pulled out a key and undid the lock.

"I popped over and added this," she said. "It'll piss off the municipal people, but in the meantime, we have access and no one else does. I also got some flashlights at the dollar store, so that we can finally see down there."

Sam had tucked a small plastic bag into the back of the maintenance room, one filled with flashlights and glow sticks that the girls immediately jumped on. In a matter of minutes her sisters looked like walking Christmas trees, they were so covered in lights.

"I was expecting that bag to last a few trips," Sam said as she wiggled the empty sack. "But okay. There goes twenty bucks, I guess."

"I'll reimburse you," Emily said, a bit embarrassed. She had her phone for light, but as they climbed down into the metro tunnels she realized she might not need it. Her sisters were splashing so much light around it would be hard not to see.

They followed along the tracks in the middle of the tunnel, her sisters spreading out a little as they played tag in the dark, but Emily called after them to get back whenever they went too far.

It took a few minutes to reach the train. Emily suspected she was getting used to spending time in the tunnels because the dark passageways didn't make her nearly as nervous now as they had a week ago. They were still scary, but having the laughter of her sisters echo back to her from the dark, and all the light splashing around, made it a little less fearsome.

They climbed into the rearmost train car and found two people waiting for them. Alea Iacta, in jeans and a T-shirt, with nothing but a hastily thrown-on domino mask to pretend to preserve his identity, and Fabien the Fabulous, who seemed fresh and clean and not at all as if he'd just stepped off a battlefield.

"Ah, hello," Emily said.

"Hey, Boss," Alea Iacta said. "Fabby here was telling me about your big fight. You guys come out of that okay?"

"Yeah!" Teddy said. "It was great. I was like, rawr, and the capitalist scumbag Heroes were like 'Oh no, it's a bear, don't eat me! I won't be able to work overtime if you eat me!' It was fun."

The other sisters nodded along at that, then they added their own versions of what happened, none of which were remotely accurate.

"You, ah, came out of it okay?" Emily asked Fabien.

The man nodded. "Indeed. I received all your messages as well . . . after the engagement. I must admit that in the moment I feared that you had betrayed me. I'm glad to see that wasn't the case. Thank you."

He extended a hand, and Emily reached for it almost on reflex, thinking they would shake. Then he brought her hand up to his mouth and gently pecked her knuckles.

Emily's brain fritzed out for a moment.

"Thank you, truly," he said before smiling a dazzling smile that had her knees weakening. "Today was . . . not what I had foreseen, but perhaps it was better than I had hoped for. I was given the opportunity to truly act like the Scoundrel I wish to be. Though I realize that I still need to become stronger."

"It's okay," Athena said. "I'm sure one day you'll be nearly as strong as one of the Boss's underlings."

Fabien chuckled. "Yes, I'm sure. I'm equally impressed by how you're playing the Heroes against one another."

Athena's chest puffed out. "That was all me," she said.

"I think maybe we should have this conversation at the table," Emily said. She felt like she needed to sit down.

Her sisters gasped, then surged into the train car and to whichever seat they could reach first. Fabien, Alea Iacta, and even Sam found seats for themselves too.

Which left a few empty seats, including the one at the head of the table.

Emily swallowed and walked over, then after flicking some nonexistent dust off her pants, she sat.

"All right," Trinity said. "Now what's the next bit of the plan, Big Sister Boss?"

CHAPTER FORTY-ONE

Perfect Plots

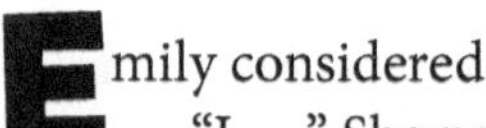**E**mily considered.

"I . . ." She paused.

Could she tell the people sitting in front of her that she had no idea what the next step of her plan was? Her sisters would take it well. They might have been little brats, but they had never been anything but supportive. A bit Villainous, and their goals for the future and her own didn't line up, but they were still unequivocally on her side.

It was the others she wasn't so sure of. Sam wanted to see chaos and turmoil; her story about writing a thesis aside, the girl was way too gleeful about being a minion. Alea Iacta was in it to keep himself safe. The Cabal scared him—for good reason—and Emily provided protection from that.

At least, he thought she did. In reality, her protection probably wasn't worth much.

Fabien the Fabulous was a little easier to work with, surprisingly. He was doing his own thing, after his own goals. She just happened to help him twice. That didn't mean he owed her anything, or that he would be in any way loyal to her.

If she was in his shoes, she'd betray herself in a blink.

Emily leaned forward, elbows on the edge of the table as she folded her hands before her chin. She needed a bit of a distraction. "Sam," she said. Sam perked up and sat straighter. "Where are we on that whole protection racket thing?"

"Oh? You want us to push that some more? I've been making a few, ah, inquiries, but I haven't been pressing anything. I'm just a minion, I don't have the gravitas to get people to spill out their valuables."

Emily felt a pressure at the front of her head. Definitely a stress headache. "I don't know if we have the option not to press that, at least a little. Maybe we can be selective? Um, only ask businesses that can afford it? Or those that wouldn't mind?"

"Wouldn't mind being extorted for cash?" Alea Iacta asked.

Emily felt her cheeks warming. She gave him a furious look, pushing the blush back as best she could. "Not extortion. Maybe . . . do we have anything we can offer?"

"Usually a protection racket offers protection," Sam said. "We could get Handsome back there to rob some places if they say no to us." She flicked a thumb to Fabien, who shifted in his seat.

"Or we could have him come to the place we're protecting, then put on a big show for the proletariat," Teddy said. "Show them how we'd protect them when the capitalist overlords inevitably turn against them."

Emily nodded slowly. "That could work, maybe. Do you think we could do advertising? With the, ah, sisters?"

Sam grinned. "Oh, I see where you're going. Have the kiddos do some advertising, then *bam*, Fabien shows up and they beat him away. Then we charge out the as— out the rear for 'advertising.'" She made little air quotes. "I bet most sensible business folk will catch on quick. Plus it could be literally good for business, which means more floating cash we can grab."

"I am not entirely unamenable to the plan," Fabien said. "It sounds vaguely like some of the ideas I had drawn up before. Not entirely the same, but similar."

Emily nodded. "We'll talk about it more. Sam, can I leave you in charge of finding places that we could work this idea on?"

Sam gave her a thumbs-up. "I'm on it, Boss. Give me like, two, three days."

That was way, way faster than Emily expected, but she worked to keep her surprise tucked away. Maybe that was just what it was like when someone was as extroverted as Sam. If Emily had to phone a shop to set up something like they were talking about, it would take an afternoon to build up the courage to pick up the phone.

"Okay. That's one thing down. Long-term income is good. What else?"

"The Cabal," Alea Iacta said.

She winced. "I don't know how to handle them," she said.

"Beat 'em up," Teddy suggested.

"Make them go insane," Athena added.

"Steal their underthings," Trinity suggested.

Emily shook her head. "I think we need to be a bit more subtle."

"I can be subtle," Trinity said.

"I . . . yes, I'm sure you can be," Emily said. "I think we're going to have to give the Cabal reasons to take the initiative here. Maybe they'll just leave the city. We put Black Shield in a bad spot today. If we can keep doing that kind of thing, maybe they'll leave us alone."

"Beat them at the PR game," Sam said. "Yeah, I can see that annoying them."

Emily nodded. It was, she thought, a terrible idea, more meant to placate Alea Iacta because she had no idea of what to really do.

"How many of them are there, anyway?" Teddy asked. "We can take them on, I bet."

"I don't know, exactly," Emily said. "I have some notes on a few members who moved to Eauclaire recently. I'll have to look at them again. I think there are at least three all-out Cabal members in the city. Some of the other Heroes might be working for them, or with them."

"What does this Cabal do?" Fabien asked.

"Oh, they're a supercool secret organization that empowers Villains," Sam said. "They give them gear, and costumes, and help them set up heists and stuff. Then they hit them with their own Heroes and take them out."

"You know a lot about them," Fabien said.

Sam nodded. "Just got to look into the right forums. The Boss knowing a bunch of actual facts about them helped narrow things down. Remove the lies and false leads, you know?"

"I see," he said.

"I think their entire gimmick is merchandising."

"What?" Emily asked.

Sam made a vague gesture in the air before her. "They make some Heroes more popular. Those Heroes owe them. They sign on to some program or some legal thing. The Cabal then sell their image out to make the big bucks. Advertising deals, their Heroic logo on panties, cereal boxes, toys, the whole schtick."

Emily didn't know what to say about that, so she just moved right on. "Okay. So we'll keep an eye out for opportunities to foil the Cabal if we can find any. It might not be easy, though. We need better information. I think I know someone for that, but he's annoying to deal with."

"Oh, an informant," Sam said. "Nice!"

"Something like that," Emily said.

She didn't want to visit Handshake. The man was skeevy. But he was also afraid of Teddy, and now Emily had even more sisters by her side.

"Okay, what else?" Emily asked. She was pretty proud of the discussion so far.

"Skill Upgrades," Teddy said. "We all got some, yeah? I bet mine will make me even tougher."

"Make your skull thicker, maybe," Athena said.

"Yeah, and the rest of me, too," Teddy enthused.

Emily knew she had two Skill Slots to work with. She didn't dare use them now. "I think we should save using those for when we're back home. Just in case," she said.

Her sisters agreed easily enough.

"In that case, I think that's it for today's meeting. Unless anyone has any-thing to add?" She glanced around the table, feeling a bit like a CEO in a movie. No one spoke up, so she continued, "Good, meeting, uh, adjourned."

Everyone got up, and Emily found herself the odd one out as the oth-ers, sisters included, started to mingle and talk. Athena chatted with Alea Iacta, Trinity went to bother Fabien, and Teddy preached to a smiling Sam about the glorious things she'd read in her little red book.

That was fine. Being alone suited Emily just fine. She took the time to decompress a little and to work out what she'd say to her mom later. She'd have to at least send a text, hopefully before her mom saw her on the evening news.

After half an hour, Emily stood up, put her phone away, and started to gather up her sisters. "We need to head home, before it gets dark," she explained.

They had a decently long walk ahead of them. Maybe getting the train to work and parking it next to the campus wouldn't be a bad idea. It would save her some time, at least.

By the time they got back to the dorms, the day was over, the sun was on its way to setting, and Emily was weary to the bone.

"So now we can get our skills up?" Teddy asked.

Emily chewed on her lip. "Fine," she said. "But one at a time. And then it'll be my turn. We . . . we might end up with another sister."

Her sisters were a lot more enthusiastic about the idea than she was. She just hoped that whomever was summoned, they wouldn't add to the chaos.

Based on past experience, her hopes weren't very high.

CHAPTER FORTY-TWO

Mad Skills

All right," Emily said. She needed to set some ground rules now, or else everything would fall apart into some chaotic mess. "Who wants to go first?"

The sisters looked at one another, then they all insisted that they would go first. It was exactly as chaotic and loud as Emily didn't want it to be.

"No, no, stop," Emily said. "We're going to do this one at a time. Last time . . . last time I think we did Teddy first? How about this time we go Trinity first, then Teddy last?"

"But that'll mean that I'm in the middle twice," Athena said.

Emily nodded. "Okay then. Athena first, then Trinity, then Teddy." She pointed to Teddy who looked ready to complain. "You went first last time, Teddy, it's only fair."

Athena grinned and moved over to Emily. Emily didn't know what to expect until Athena jumped up and sat on her lap. "Okay," she said. "I'm going to unlock my new skill now."

Emily didn't know what to do with her hands for a moment, so she settled on patting Athena on the head, which seemed to make the owl girl perfectly happy. "Do your best," Emily said.

With her tongue pinched between her lips, Athena focused ahead on nothing, then she grinned. "Got it!" she said. Then, much to Emily's mounting concern, Athena started to cackle. "Oh, this is perfect. Here, want to see?" She raised a hand and summoned a bluish square in the air with the details of her newest skill written on it.

Parliamental
Owl Seeing Eye
Level 1
Allows the user to read the surface thoughts of anyone they have eye contact with.
Activation: Visual
No Cooldown

Emily read the skill description with mounting worry and horror. She loved her sisters, she really did, but giving any one of them the ability to read minds was . . . a plainly horrific idea. Still, of all her sisters, Athena was the most responsible and mature.

There was a gasp, and she glanced at Athena, who was smiling. "You think I'm more mature than the others?" she asked. "Hear that? I'm better than you!"

"What's the power?" Teddy asked.

"I can read minds now!" Athena said.

Teddy nodded. "Cool. What am I thinking?"

Athena hopped off Emily's lap and stared intently at Teddy. "Nothing. Your mind's empty."

Teddy puffed out her chest. "My thinking is too confusing for someone so stupid to understand."

"That's not what I said."

"Girls," Emily said, cutting off that argument before it could start. She knew it was just delaying a fight that was going to happen no matter what, but putting off the inevitable was worth getting a few more minutes of peace.

"I'm next!" Trinity cheered. All three of her bodies tried to sit on Emily's lap, but there was too much Trinity and not enough lap. One of them ended up on the floor while Emily dealt with two of Trinity using her as a chair. "All right, lemme get my new awesome skill!"

"Let's see what you get," Emily said.

Trinity nodded all her heads, then she concentrated. "Got it!" she said. She raised her hand, the same sort of blue box appearing before her.

Trinventory
Eternal Racoon Hurricane
Level 1

The user can exchange objects from one body to another as long as the object is placed within a shared, similar container.
Cooldown: One Hour

Emily read over the skill message and tried to understand it. "Does it mean that you can . . . teleport things between yourself?"

"Yeah," Trinity said. "Wanna see?"

Glancing around, Emily looked for something she wouldn't mind losing. She found a pen on her desk and gave it to Trinity.

One of the Trinity on her lap bounced up while the one on the floor stood. "Okay, look, sis," the Trinity with the pen said. She put the pen into her pocket. The Trinity next to her reached into her pocket and pulled it out.

The pen had definitely moved from one Trinity to another, without any flashes or obvious signs that it had changed places. "That's something," Emily said.

She could imagine a few ways that could be useful. Combined with her Sisterportation, she could summon a Trinity while another picked something up for her and teleported it over. Or Trinity could use it to steal something and transport the thing to another Trinity in a secured location. It could also be used to hide evidence, if one Trinity was in a safe location.

"I'm going to teleport bread!" Trinity cheered.

Or, Emily reasoned, Trinity could burn her cooldown teleporting useless things around.

"My turn!" Teddy said. She ran up to Emily and hopped onto her lap, feet kicking out. "This is going to be easy."

Teddy only blinked twice before she had a new screen open.

She frowned at it. "This doesn't mean I don't get headpats though, all right?"

"Okay?" Emily asked as she read the skill.

Hibearnation
WereBear
Level 1
The user heals at a much accelerated rate. This rate doubles when the user is sleeping or has just awakened from a long rest.

Passive Ability
No Cooldown

A self-healing ability. One that seemed to rely a bit on Teddy's own natural healing. That was still impressive, and useful, too. Teddy was their frontline fighter, when there was fighting to be had. It was nice to see that she wouldn't ever be hurt for long.

Still, Emily wondered what accelerated *meant* exactly. If an injury would take a normal person a month to heal, would Teddy be back on her feet in only two weeks? Or was it faster than that?

She wasn't sure she really wanted to test the ability.

"That seems very strong," Emily said.

Teddy grinned. "Yeah! Now summon another sister so that I can go to bed sooner! I wanna use my new skill already."

"Uh," Emily said. Teddy wasn't entirely wrong though.

Do you wish to spend a Skill Slot point on the Power: Sister Summoning?

"Yes," Emily said, for once without too much hesitation.

New Skill unlocked!

Quadruple Quirkiness has been added to your Power's Skills!

Quadruple Quirkiness
Sister Summoning
Level Max
Allows you to summon a fourth sister with Create Sister. Instant use.
Activation: Vocal Command
No Cooldown
Max New Sisters: One

"I have the skill," Emily said.

Her sisters cheered. "Yeah, Boss! Use it!" Teddy said.

Emily took a deep breath. She was pretty sure this was a terrible idea. It didn't stop her from saying the words. "Create Sister."

There was never much fanfare when her power went to work. One moment there were only three sisters in the room, and the next there were four.

The odd girl out was standing in the middle of the room, just a step ahead of Emily. She had messy brown hair, all bushy and wild, and was wearing jean overalls and a white T-shirt under an all-white lab coat.

The girl stared at Emily.

Emily stared back.

The girl's entire face went red. Starting from the tips of her ears and slowly crawling to her cheeks and across the bridge of her freckle-covered nose.

"Hey!" Teddy said.

The girl squeaked, turned, saw that she had an audience, then ran around Emily's chair as if to hide from her sisters. Or at least, she tried. Halfway around she tripped over nothing and crashed belly first onto the floor, arms and legs splayed out and her tail flopping back.

"Oh no," Emily said. She stood up and raced to the girl to kneel down next to her.

Emily's other sisters all did the same, but on seeing the way the girl was peeking at her from under the tangled mess of her hair, Emily gestured them all back.

"Let's give our new sister some space, okay?" she asked. To her new sister, she spoke in a softer, more careful tone. "Are you okay? You didn't hurt yourself, did you?"

The girl shook her head, then scrambled up to her feet. She then stepped on her own lab coat and proceeded to trip again.

The others laughed, but Emily gave them a warning look.

"It's okay," Emily said. "Take your time."

"Okay," the girl whispered. It was so quiet that Emily wasn't sure if she heard it or if it was her imagination.

"I think she's a beaver girl," Teddy said. "Look at her tail. It's all flattish."

Teddy wasn't wrong. The girl did have a tail peeking out from under her white coat. A flat, brown tail that only just reached the back of her knees.

"Is that right?" Emily asked.

The girl, her face still very red, nodded twice.

No words, though. Emily suspected she had just found her quietest sister. "Are you shy?" Emily asked.

The girl's eyes watered and she nodded, though only a little.

"That's okay," Emily said. She was shy herself, which meant . . . actually, that in no way helped. Emily knew what it was like to be cripplingly shy—though she was getting better—but she had no idea how to help someone else work through their own reluctance to talk. "We'll take things slowly, okay?"

The girl nodded again. "Okay."

"Right, so . . . we can do introductions? Don't worry, you can go last. No pressure, okay?"

CHAPTER FORTY-THREE

The Sapling

She hid behind Big Sister's leg. The others were scary.

There was the big one, with the bear ears and the big smile. The taller one, with the shrewd eyes that were scary, and then the other three, who were all over the place.

She recognized them as her sisters, which meant that they couldn't be all that bad, but . . . but she was worried that they wouldn't think the same about her.

What if they thought she was too weak? Or ugly, or not strong enough, or maybe she'd say something and they'd laugh at her.

Big Sister looked down and around, meeting her eyes for just a moment. She felt her face burning up before she buried it in Big Sister's leg. Big Sister looked so smart and confident and charismatic, there was no way someone so good at talking would understand her.

"Okay," Big Sister said. "How about we go by age . . . or at least by time of summoning. That means you go first, Teddy."

The bear girl, Teddy, puffed her chest out. "I'm Teddy, and I'm the best of the Boss's sisters. I can turn into a bear and eat people, and . . . what're we supposed to say, Boss?"

"Hmm. I guess your name, hobbies, and maybe a bit about what you want to do in the future?"

"Oh, all right," Teddy said. "My hobbies are sleeping and communism. My dream's to beat up a bunch of Heroes and to end the capitalist rat race." Teddy paused, looked to the side as if thinking, then she grinned. "Yep, that's it."

"I'm next," said her tallest sister (other than Big Sister, who was very tall). "I'm Athena. My hobbies are reading, making fun of Teddy, and driving people insane. My dream is to make Big Sister proud."

She nodded against Big Sister's leg. That did sound like a nice dream.

Athena and Teddy started fighting, and she found herself pulling back a little. They were both so loud and confident.

"I'm Trinity!" the three others said. "My hobbies is eating trash and steal— not stealing things because that makes Big Sis annoyed. My dream's to own a garbage truck company."

Big Sister seemed surprised at the last. "You want to own a garbage truck company? I . . . okay, that's interesting, I didn't know that about you."

"Yeah, I get to live in the landfill with the other garbage truck people!" Trinity cheered.

"I see," Big Sister said. She sighed, then looked down. "It's your turn. Don't be afraid; your sisters will pay attention and they won't laugh, right, Teddy, Athena?"

The two who were named snapped to attention and stepped away from each other.

The new sister slid away from Big Sister and regretted it immediately, there were so many eyes on her. What if she messed up? What if she said something, and they'd remember that she said something embarrassing for the rest of forever? Her breathing became a bit ragged and she felt her hair sticking to her forehead. "Ah," she squeaked.

Big Sister dropped to her knees next to her. "It's okay," she said. Carefully, Big Sister reached out and placed her hand on her head and it was very nice. "You don't need to worry, okay? We're all family here. Your sisters might be a bit loud, but they're not mean, not really. And if anyone makes you too nervous, you just need to tell me, okay?"

Her cheeks warmed up.

She truly was the luckiest little sister ever, to have a Big Sister who was so confident and cool.

"My name is . . . I don't have a name yet. Um. I don't . . . I guess my hobby might be making things? My dream." She stopped, swallowed, then closed her fists and closed her eyes to make saying the next part easier to say. "My dream is to be as confident as Big Sister!"

"That's a . . . very nice dream," Big Sister said. "One that I'm sure you'll be able to achieve . . . in no time."

She sniffed, the emotions getting to her a little, but she wasn't going to cry in front of all her sisters after just meeting them. Big Sister believed in her!

"So what's your gimmick?" Teddy asked. "Mine's turning into a bear."

"Ah," she said. "I, um, can fix and make things."

"Wow," Big Sister said. "Can you make new things, or, well, what's your limitation?"

She smiled, though she couldn't quite meet Big Sister's eyes. "As long as I have things, I can make just about anything, I think." It was true, she had so many ideas! She was actually itching to get to work, but the room didn't seem like the right kind of place for that and . . . and what if she never had an opportunity to show Big Sister what she could do? That would be terrible!

"I can't wait to see what you can do," Big Sister said.

"Can you make a supertoaster?" Trinity asked.

She blinked. "I guess. I'd need a toaster, and some tools."

"I got the toaster!" one of Trinity said. She ran to the bathroom and came back a moment later with a toaster held up above her head. "This is Mister Toaster, he makes toast. Can you make him waterproof?"

Mister Toaster was a toaster. He had googly eyes.

"Oh, okay," she said.

"Before any of that," Big Sister said. She was eyeing Mister Toaster, then the bathroom door, "we should probably come up with a name for you."

"Bearverly," Teddy suggested.

"That's a stupid name," Athena said. "Besides, she's a beaver, not a bear."

"It ain't stupid, you are. If you're not, then come up with something better?" Teddy said.

Big Sister sighed. "Girls, no arguing. And I don't think Bearverly . . . fits."

She shook her head. She'd rather not be called that.

"I got some names," Trinity said. She snuck under the bed until only her butt was sticking out. Her tail wiggled, then she crawled back out with an armful of wallets. One flopped to the ground, and Trinity picked it up and read something inside it. "How would you like to be called Richard Green?"

"Um," she said.

"Trinity," Big Sister said.

"What about . . . Aster Card?" She tossed the wallet and picked up another. "Or you could be Kendrick Westerfeil. See, he's got an ugly nose, so you can take his place. Your nose is a lot nicer."

"Oh god, I'm going to have to call so many people," Big Sister muttered.

Athena huffed. "What about a name like the thing on her shirt?"

Everyone turned toward her, and she felt her ears warming up again with all the attention. She glanced down. Her lab coat was open at the front because she wasn't working with dangerous chemicals, and under that were her jean overalls and a T-shirt. She pulled the T-shirt up a little, revealing a drawing of a maple leaf sticking off a log. "Th-this?"

"Maple," Big Sister said. "That is a cute name."

She flushed even harder. "I-I wouldn't mind that. Having a cute name."

Big Sister clapped. "Well then, if you like the name, then why not? Maple Wright. It has a nice ring to it."

She—Maple—nodded. "Okay. Thank you," she said.

"Welcome to the family," Big Sister said. "We're a bit loud, and some of us are questionably sane, but all in all, I think we're doing pretty okay for ourselves."

"Heck yeah," Teddy said. "Bear hug time!"

Maple squeaked as Teddy jumped up and pulled her into a tight-tight hug. Athena, not to be outdone, stomped over and hugged her from the other side. Then Trinity laughed and piled on, too, until Maple was afraid she might suffocate.

Finally, Big Sister gave a long-suffering sigh and came closer. She wrapped them all up in a big hug, too, her longer arms letting her grab all of them at once.

Maple wasn't sure what to feel. Her ears and cheeks were burning, and it was really embarrassing, but it was also warm and nice, even if Teddy had lots of knee and Athena was very bony.

"Th-thank you, everyone," Maple said. She wasn't sure if the others could hear her, so she went on. "I hope I'll fit in nicely."

"Yeah, sure thing," Teddy said. "Can you make me a gun?"

"No," Big Sister said. The hug ended, and she waggled a finger at Teddy. "No asking for guns. Or anything that's a weapon for that matter. Maple, I . . . we'll see how your power works later, but if your sisters ask for weapons, you tell them no, okay?"

"O-okay," Maple said. "No weapons, I can do that." There went an entire avenue of inventions that could impress her Big Sister. She had been hoping to be able to build some giant mecha, but those were definitely weapons.

"Thank you," Big Sister said. She patted Maple on the head, which was very nice. "Now, let's catch you up, shall we?"

CHAPTER FORTY-FOUR

No One Special

Emily was nervous about heading to class the morning after summoning Maple. Mostly because she didn't know how Mrs. Headerson would react to a fourth—or technically sixth—new student in her class. Fortunately, Maple was quiet as a mouse most of the time and seemed outright anxious about anything social.

Finally, a sister who was as averse to conflict as Emily herself. Maybe Maple would rub off on her other sisters and they'd all calm down a little.

Her own classes passed by slowly. She couldn't help but look over her shoulder the entire time, and when she saw a pair of students a few rows down ignoring the lecture to watch some videos on one of those Mask news sites—videos of her and her sisters fighting with and against Heroes the day before—she almost gave in to the urge to run out of the room.

How had no one recognized her? Her costume had only masked the upper half of her face. Just narrowing down the population of Eauclaire based on her hair color, gender, and profile—too-thin girl with no muscle—would be enough to point the finger right at her.

But nothing happened, and it was with a relieved sigh that she left the campus and headed over to pick up her sisters.

She gave profuse thanks to Mrs. Headerson, who said that her sisters were unusually well-behaved, then after gathering up the gaggle of brats, they headed back home.

"Did you learn a lot today?" she asked.

"Yeah!" Trinity said. "We did numbers again. It was fun. Then we did history, which wasn't fun, so I didn't pay any attention to that part."

Emily shook her head. "You should pay attention to the entire thing, at least if you can. You'll need some of the things you'll be learning. What about you, Maple, did you enjoy your first day at school?"

Maple nodded. "It was nice," she said. "Steffie was scary at first, but she was okay."

Emily couldn't imagine Steffie scaring anyone, but then, she was old enough now that she wasn't afraid of what children thought of her. At least, that's what she told herself. "Steffie seems like a nice friend to have, so I'm glad you're all getting along." Not to mention Steffie was sane, which her sisters could definitely emulate.

From what Emily could tell, Athena was the sister who was doing the best academically. She had a sharp mind on her. Teddy was doing the worst. She wasn't unintelligent, but she was rather uninterested in anything but history. Trinity was doing worse than Teddy in some subjects, but was much better in others, mostly math, where she excelled even past Athena, and she was a decent artist. Emily would have to see with Maple, but from the first hints she got, Maple was a quick learner, she was just terrible with group work.

They continued to talk about nothing much until they neared the dorms. There they found a familiar face sitting on the ground next to the entrance, looking at her phone. Sam glanced up to them and bounced to her feet. "Heya, Bo— Emily," she said.

"Hi," Emily said. "Is something wrong?"

Sam grinned. "Yes. We can't go in there. Let's take a walk?"

Emily weighed the possibility that Sam was lying to her, then dismissed it. Sam had proven trustworthy so far, and Emily had all her sisters with her. She was about as ready for trouble as she could be, on such short notice. "What's going on?" Emily asked as she followed along next to Sam.

"You have people loitering around your dorm room," Sam said.

Emily felt an electric jolt coursing through her. "People?"

"Yeah. A couple of girls, mostly. Our age. They didn't care to explain why they were around when I asked."

"Do you think they're working with the Heroes?" Emily asked.

"Maybe, but I don't know," Sam said. "Bet they'd ping that something weird was going on if you showed up with the brat brigade here. You could pass as someone other than the Boss, but these six . . . Emily?"

"Yes?" Emily asked.

Sam kept staring at her sisters. "Did some random kid join your group by accident?"

Emily blinked, then held back a chuckle. "Right, I should introduce you. Maple, come here, please." Emily extended a hand back for Maple to grab. The girl did, but she seemed reluctant to get any closer to Sam. "Maple, this is Sam, she's . . ."

Emily tried to think of a way to introduce Sam that wouldn't scare Maple. Telling the truth—that Sam was an overly confident extrovert who didn't understand boundaries and who lacked common sense—would just scare Maple more. In the end, she settled on something a little less complicated.

"Sam is my minion." Maple's shoulders relaxed. "Sam, this is Maple, my newest little sister."

"You just pop them out, don't you," Sam said. She either ignored or missed the way Emily's cheeks flushed. "Hi there, Maple, I'm Sam. Pleased to meet you."

"Hi," Maple said.

"So what does Maple do?" Sam asked.

It was an innocent enough question. "We haven't tested her powers yet," Emily said. "For that matter, we haven't tested Menagerie Family with her yet, either. But Maple's a gadgeteer. She can tinker things up for us, I think."

"Oh!" Sam said. "Gadgeteers are, like, the ideal force multiplier. Give them enough time and junk and they can become powerhouses, too. I bet you're going to be a great addition to the team, Maple."

Maple blushed and held on to Emily's hand even tighter.

"So where are we headed to?" Emily asked.

"Well, I was thinking, we could draw suspicion away from you by making it obvious that you're not the Boss," Sam said.

"But . . . I am?"

"Well, yes, you are, and if you're spotted with this bunch, it'll be obvious that you are. I was thinking more something along the lines of disguising you in a way so that you look less like your Heroic self. A reverse costume, I guess. Think of Lark Ent's glasses in that one comic book."

Emily considered it for a moment, then nodded. "Fine, I guess that could work. What do we do with my sisters?"

"Barracks? The one that Alea found?" Sam asked. "That's where I'm heading now. I have my makeup kit with me, and a few other essentials." She patted her purse, which did seem quite full.

"How're you going to hide the Boss with just makeup?" Teddy asked.

"It won't be just makeup. We'll break up her figure a bit. I'm thinking a skirt, some lipstick to make her lips look more full, and a few more layers.

You're pretty thin, Emily, which looks great when you're dressed as the Boss in that suit. We can make you look bigger around the waist no problem. Can't do much about the hair, but you wear that hat as the Boss anyway."

"Okay?" Emily said. She was suddenly a lot less certain about things.

"In the meantime . . ." Sam started. "Did you get into contact with that information broker yet?"

"Oh, not yet," Emily said. "I wanted to call him earlier but—" But she had entirely forgotten. "But we all had class and I had to put that on the back burner. I'll call him later, if there's time."

"Cool," Sam said. "I've started making a list of all the places we can hit up for protection money. There's a decent number of them, you know. We'll have to organize some time to start hitting up places soon. Our little gadget maker here's going to need a working budget, right, Maple?"

"Um?" Maple asked. She looked up to Sam, then right back down to the ground. "I-I don't know how much things cost."

Emily felt a bit bad for the girl. "It's fine. We'll figure things out as we go. Sam, maybe you can take . . . um . . ."

"I'll go," Athena said. "I'm good at reading people. And I need to practice my new skill anyway."

Emily had almost forgotten that. Athena's ability to read minds was going to be useful. "That's a good idea. Maybe you can take Alea Iacta along, too?" More adults, or adultish people in Alea Iacta's case, would only help.

They reached the overpass soon enough, and they all filed into the cement bunker hidden behind a wall covered in graffiti. The sisters, once free, immediately started running around with various levels of enthusiasm.

Sam, meanwhile, pulled Emily to the bunker's bathroom and had the mortified Emily change into something else right there. Emily was most comfortable in her loose jeans, but Sam had her in a knee-length skirt to "break up her form" and then she had Emily put on a loose knit sweater over a blouse. "We should buy one of those wraps actors use to make themselves look bigger," Sam said.

"I don't think I need that," Emily said. The sweater, once stuffed with a few socks underneath, already gave her belly something of a pouch. She was one of those people who lost weight when stressed or anxious, and since she was always both, she tended to just naturally keep the weight off.

"All right!" Sam said before giving Emily's back a smack. "Let's go see what's what, and convince the world that you're no one special, shall we?"

CHAPTER FORTY-FIVE

Toaster

Maple stared up at her Big Sister from the seat she'd found in the corner of the bunker. It was far enough from everything else that she was left more or less alone. It was nice to be quiet sometimes.

"Okay, girls," Big Sister said. "Sam and I will be heading out. In a minute or two, Alea Iacta will be coming around to pick you up and bab— I mean . . . watch over you. You'll probably be heading back to the train. So please behave and try to stay out of trouble. If you do, then I'll pick up something nice to eat on the way back."

"Burgers!" Teddy cheered.

"Burgers! Burgers!" Trinity joined in. Soon, Teddy and all of Trinity were dancing in a circle in the middle of the room, singing about burgers. Or just singing the word *burger* over and over again.

Maple sat back and hoped her sisters didn't notice her not joining in on the dance. She'd never had a burger before, and now she wasn't sure she wanted to. Would it make her dance like that? It was embarrassing!

"Don't worry," Athena murmured as she came to stand next to Maple. "Big Sis will tell the idiots off soon enough."

Maple nodded. Athena was probably right. From what Maple could tell, Athena was one of her smartest sisters. And she was quiet, too. Or at least quieter.

"All right, all right," Big Sister said. "Enough with the chanting. It's actually kind of creepy. You'll get your burgers"—she paused to let the cheering die down—"*if* you behave."

Big Sister and minion Sam left shortly afterward. For some reason that

Maple couldn't understand, Big Sister had a sweater on with some cloth stuffed under it and Sam had put some makeup on her face that made her look a little weird.

After they left, Maple's other sisters milled around the bunker for a bit. Trinity ran all over the place all at once to see what she could find, and Teddy went to one of the bunk rooms for a nap.

Maple hesitated, hands gripping each other because she didn't know what else to do with them.

"Hey," Athena said. "Want to walk around? Just check things out?"

Maple glanced up and met Athena's big eyes for just a moment. "Okay," she said.

Athena grinned and grabbed Maple's hand. Maple was dragged across the bunker and got to explore every room. It was nice. She wanted to explore, too, but doing it all on her own while in a place that wasn't home felt a little strange.

Eventually the door to the stairwell leading down clunked open and a man stumbled through. A tall boy with lanky features and a bit of patchy stubble on his cheeks and jaw, he was about as old as Big Sister. "Hey girls," he said. "Sorry for being late. I left, forgot to bring a flashlight, then tripped over something in the tunnels." He raised a light. "Turns out someone lost theirs, though, so it wasn't a big deal. Anyway, the Boss said I had to babysit and . . . wait, are there more of you?"

He stared right at Maple, who froze up at the sudden attention. Her tail flap-flapped against the back of her legs with nervous energy. "Hi?"

"Where is she finding all these preteen disasters?" the boy muttered.

"Don't be mean, Alea Iacta," Athena said. "This is my sister Maple, and I like her more than I like you. If you hurt her feelings, I'll make your brain melt out of your nose."

"What does brain taste like?" Trinity asked.

"Bet his doesn't taste all that smart," Teddy added.

Maple blushed. Her sisters were coming to her defense. It made her tummy feel warm and fuzzy.

Alea Iacta backed off. "All right, all right. And here I thought I was lucky. Come on, let's head back over to the train. I bet you bunch are hungry."

"How'd you know?" Trinity asked.

"Because you're children, and children are always hungry. Come on, I've got a few family-size bags of chips on the train."

"Do you have candy?" Athena asked.

Alea Iacta shook his head. "No, sorry?"

"Good," Athena said. "Big Sis told us to run from anyone who offered us free candy."

Maple's other sisters nodded. She made note of that fact. She had a lot of catching up to do. Speaking of which . . . she jogged to catch up to her sisters who filed after the strange young man and out of the bunker.

They entered a big, dark tunnel. Maple felt like maybe she should have been worried, but in reality she felt rather comfortable in the tunnel. It was underground and made of thick walls and dirt. It felt safe and right to be down there.

Eventually, after a long walk that was only lit up by the few flashlights Trinity had on her, they made it to a big train that was just sitting in the middle of the tunnel.

Everyone filed to the rear, then climbed aboard the rearmost train car. Maple took a while to climb in, because her eyes were wide and she was taking everything in. There was so much stuff! It was clear that Alea Iacta had been living in the train car for a while. Some bunks had been folded up, and a TV was set against one wall with a video-game console under it. "Found this in the trash," Alea Iacta said. "Only have a few games for it, but they all work. Any of you know how to play?"

Trinity and Teddy fought over the second controller, then Athena swooped in and stole it. They arranged a schedule of sorts to see who would play while another Trinity ran to the front to get the goods. When that Trinity returned, arms full with three whole family-size chip bags, she stopped by Maple. "Hey, did you want to play, too?"

"Um, no, I can just watch," Maple said.

Trinity tilted her head to the side, her little ears wiggling. "Well, if you want something to do, there's a toaster in the kitchen that don't work good."

Maple cheered up. She could do something about that. "Oh, okay!"

It took a bit to build up the bravery to leave her sisters, but eventually she made her way to the front of the train and stopped by a small kitchen area. There were a few appliances around, including a toaster that was unplugged.

Maple picked it up and turned it this way and that. The wire was frayed near the base, and after popping the side open, she noticed that one of the elements wasn't plugged in properly. Had the weld holding it in place snapped with the change in temperature?

She looked around for tools and found a few odds and ends in some of the cupboards. Then she ended up near the front of the train, where there was a big table she could work on. It was perfect!

She started to scrounge for parts. The coffee machine had an element. And there was a clock in one of the bedrooms. That could come in handy. She found some springs in one of the mattresses, big bouncy ones. Yes, those were nice.

Maple smiled and hummed a happy tune to herself as she fixed the toaster.

The heating elements from the coffee maker weren't enough. She needed more oomph. Maybe . . . Yes, the lights were incandescent.

But then, where would the toaster get power? She found some batteries, big D-cell ones, but they weren't enough, even when loaded in sequence. Having to plug it into the wall was too much.

Fortunately, there was a generator at the back of the train. But her sisters were using that . . . no, she needed something else.

In the end, she found some copper and started wrapping it around the batteries, then she found a hand crank that had a handy handle on it.

Maple was floating along in a happy haze as she fixed the toaster.

Then Big Sister returned. "I'm back!" she said over the sound of people exploding in the game the others were playing.

Maple blinked, snapping back to the moment.

On the table was the toaster, as well as a dozen other appliances she'd taken apart.

She could barely hear her sisters cheering as what she'd done dawned on her.

The toaster now had a hand crank on the side that would charge a solenoid with just a few spins. That, in turn, would feed the rail-gun barrel set next to the bread-toasting elements. There wasn't a trigger, but the little clamp that had been on the front of the toaster was there. The digital clock now worked as a timer to tell the person using the toaster how long they had before the toast fired.

How quickly would the toast move? Mach one? Two?

"Maple?" Big Sister asked as she entered the room.

Maple grabbed the toaster and tried to hide it, but it was longer than she was tall.

Her eyes watered. "Big . . . Big Sister. I'm sorry. I made a mistake," she said.

CHAPTER FORTY-SIX

Rail Gun
(Technically more of a coil gun, but it fires toast, so your semantics don't matter here)

Emily couldn't decide what to stare at more. Her newest sister, who was standing to one side, lips trembling, eyes filled with unshed tears, and little hands shaking, or the very large, very dangerous-looking thing sitting on the table just in front of her.

A tiny sniffle made her mind up and she swooped in to hug Maple. "Hey, hey, it's okay, it's okay," she said. "No crying, you're fine. You are fine, right? You're not hurt anywhere?"

Maple shook her head into Emily's shoulder.

"Hey, Boss, what's going on?" Teddy asked as she stomped into the room.

"Give us a minute, Teddy," Emily said. For most of her sisters, having more sisters around would probably be a comfort, but she suspected that wasn't the case for Maple.

"Oh, all right, Boss," Teddy said.

Emily waited a bit, gave Maple a squeeze, then held her out in front of her. "Are you okay?" she asked.

Maple wiped her nose with the sleeve of her lab coat. "I'm okay," she said before snorting. "B-but you're going to be angry at me?" It was a question, somehow.

"No, I'm not," Emily said. "Probably not. Did you do anything to hurt your sisters? Did you hurt yourself? Did you hurt anyone else? No? Okay, then I'm officially not angry at you."

Maple tried on a smile, but her lips were too wobbly. Emily reached into the back pocket of her jeans and pulled out some napkins. She'd learned recently that she could never have enough napkins on her. She used it to rub at Maple's face. There was some grease there, somehow, and not the edible sort.

"Okay, so why don't you tell me what happened?"

Maple swallowed. "Sister Trinity said that the toaster here was broken, and it was. They were playing games, and I wanted to be a bit alone, so I decided to fix the toaster, and then I wanted to make it better and then, I don't know, I just started adding things to it."

"And this is the end result?" Emily asked.

Maple nodded. "You're not mad?" she asked, as if to make sure.

"I promise I'm not," Emily said.

Emily walked closer to the table, then pulled the "toaster" off it. The toaster had a stock made of bent tin from . . . cans? The actual toaster part was near the back, with the little handle on the side. Coat hangers formed a rudimentary handle beneath, and the entire thing had a long barrel made of cans bent into a rough oval shape with copper wires wrapped around them. There was a crank on the left side of the toaster, and some gearing inside of it whose purpose Emily could only guess at.

She tried to figure it out. It couldn't be that complex, but it almost felt as if her eyes were sliding off the mechanical parts, or maybe she just couldn't focus.

Which had a bit of a cold sweat forming on her back. "Maple. Can you do me a favor and show me your skills?"

"I only have one," Maple said. But she obliged, a familiar box appearing before her.

Builder of the Dammed
Sticks and Stones
Rank 1
Sticks and stones will allow you to break many bones.
No Cooldown

"And, um, this is my main stats page," Maple said. A second box appeared next to the first.

Name: Maple Wright		
Alignment: Villain, Little Sister		
Alias: None		
Level: 1		
Powers		
Builder of the Dammed		
Sticks and Stones	Rank 1	
Points		
Power Slots: 0	Skill Upgrades: 0	Skill Slots: 0

"That seems . . . like a very useful skill ,Maple. I'm sure that you'll be able to help us all a ton. That is, if that's what you want to do," Emily said. She knew she'd hit the nail on the head when Maple's eyes lit up and she smiled big and proud. Personally, Emily was a little horrified. That was a very open-ended gadgeteering skill.

She needed advice, and at the moment the only expert she had was—

"Hey, Boss, what's going— Oh, that's neat," Sam said as she stepped into the room.

"Sam. Just who I was thinking of." Emily stood up straighter. "What do you know about gadgeteers?"

Sam wasn't a fool. Far from it. She glanced at Emily, then Maple with her very large . . . whatever it was. "Not as much as I should," Sam said. "Hey, Maple, is that a bomb?"

Maple shook her head and focused on the floor. "It's a toaster," she said.

"That's an awful complex-looking toaster. How does it work?"

Maple lit up again. "It's easy! You put the bread here, in these slots, then you pull back on this handle." Maple pulled back on the little handle next to the toaster. It took a few tries to catch. "Then you spin this to charge the toaster." Maple started to spin the crank, as fast as she could. A display—from a clock?—popped up, numbers rising until they hit one hundred. The entire toaster was humming by then, a very dangerous, low hum. The interior glowed, illuminating Maple's excited face. "Then you point the end at the person you want to toast, and you wait for it to pop out!"

She aimed at the far end of the room, and they all waited with bated breath.

Just as Emily was about to speak up, the toaster fired.

Ding!

Emily jumped as a burst of warm air filled the room. It smelled like warm bread. A few of the things on the table shifted back from the pressure, but that was it.

"All right," Sam said. "That was interesting. How does it make the toast . . . uh, go?"

"There's coils," Maple said. She pointed with one hand at the copper wires around the barrel. "It makes the toast go."

"But toast isn't magnetic," Sam said.

Maple blinked. "It's not?" She looked at her toaster gun. "But then why does it land butter-side down?"

Emily decided that she had more pressing issues than worrying about toast. "Sam, what do we do?"

"Well, obviously we test it with some toast in it."

"Sam," Emily said.

Sam shrugged. "She's a gadgeteer. If I had to guess, she can make stuff from scrap. That seems pretty good. Better than if she needed something really specific to work with."

"What are the limits here?"

Sam frowned. "I don't know. You'd need to ask an expert. But I think the gadgeteer either has a material limit, which then allows them to make anything out of that material, or nearly anything, or there's a product limit. Like they can only make one thing, or one kind of thing, but they can use anything to make that. There was this one guy who could make laser pistols with soda bottles and a few double-A batteries."

"Oh, I could do that," Maple said. "But I'd need some glass, and maybe a few coat hangers. Oh, and chewing gum and glue and some cardboard. Crayons to make it pretty."

Emily nodded slowly. "Right, we're testing the toaster first." She needed to see if the thing actually worked, then she'd decide what to do after that. "Sam, can you find some rope and a few bits of something to hold that up? I don't want Maple holding it while it fires, just in case."

"Safety is important," Maple agreed.

"Yes, it is," Emily said.

She grabbed the toaster—which was still quite hot, a fact that disturbed her—then carried it out of the back of the train. Somehow, along the way, she gained a trail of little sisters and one Alea Iacta, all of whom were curious about what was going on and what the big machine in her hands was.

Trinity was sent on a bread-finding mission, which she did with alacrity, and Sam sat up a few chairs on the tracks before the train so that they could put the toaster down and angle it along the length of the tunnel.

It was about as good a testing space as they could manage on short notice.

Maple was the one to set the experiment up. She shyly took two pieces of bread from Trinity and placed them into the slits at the top of the toaster. Then she pressed down the handle and spun the crank on the side.

"It's going to fire!" Maple said before rushing back to hide behind Emily.

Everyone watched as the machine hummed and rattled atop the chair holding it in place.

Ding!

Emily stumbled back, her ears popping as a burst of air whumped its way through the tunnel.

In the far, far distance, she heard something crack. Then she noticed the twin trails left in the air. They were vaguely toast-shaped.

"Well, it works," Sam said.

"Thank you," Maple replied.

"Hey, there's a problem," Trinity said.

Everyone turned to her.

"How do you eat the toast if it's all the way over there?"

CHAPTER FORTY-SEVEN

Pay Phone

So how'd it go? Whatever it was?"

Emily glanced over to Alea Iacta. The young man had retaken his place on one of the couches stuffed into the living space aboard the train base. He had a controller in hand and the game on the TV was unpaused. At least he'd had the decency to lower the volume before he resumed trouncing Teddy at the fighting game they were playing.

"*It*," Emily began, "was a trio of nosy girls who showed up at the dorms and refused to leave until I talked to them."

The entire experience had been bizarre, but, perhaps not so bizarre that she would have found it suspicious.

A few weeks ago, before she gained her powers and her gaggle of sisters, having a few women her age show up at her dorms would have turned her into an anxious mess.

Now the entire thing had just felt surreal. The three girls—whose names she instantly forgot—were apparently in her class, and they wanted to form a study group. They were friendly and chatty and perfectly nice.

Exactly the wrong kind of person to send to Emily.

She didn't recognize any of them. Usually she'd have dismissed that since her classes were quite full and she hardly made a point of memorizing every face, but, no, these three were definitely not normal students.

They were about the right age, though, and they were probably local students.

Emily had talked to them for a little bit while doing her best to act nothing like the Boss—some advice given to her by Sam.

The idea was to dissuade any suspicions that she had a Heroic (or Villainous) persona.

The problem was that Emily didn't know if she really acted differently as the Boss than she did normally. She supposed that maybe she was growing a little more confident? So she did the opposite, stuttering and acting like a socially anxious mess, which came quite naturally to her.

"I'm guessing that's not normal girl stuff?" Alea Iacta asked. The character he was controlling on-screen blocked a powerful move from Teddy's character. Teddy only used power moves. Alea Iacta's character grappled Teddy's, then flung them off the edge of the stage.

Teddy started to mutter a string of bad words until she caught Emily looking, then the bear girl meekly handed the controller over to Athena.

"No," Emily said. "It wasn't normal girl stuff. Or, okay, yes, it looked a bit like a normal thing. I guess study groups aren't too uncommon, but no one would invite someone like me to one of those." You needed a modicum of socializing skill to join that kind of group.

"Why not? You get bad grades?" Alea Iacta asked.

Emily crossed her arms. Her grades were fine. She had a lot on her plate, but she still made sure to get all her assignments done and handed in on time. She was cramming hard in whatever spare moments she had.

She didn't have a choice. Some of her classes had presentations near the end of the year that she knew she was going to flub. She had to have good grades before those came around, otherwise her year-end average was going to be awful.

"My grades are fine," Emily said. She watched for a moment as Athena and Alea Iacta picked a pair of Heroes. There were Heroes from all over the world to pick from, mostly big-name, popular ones. She noted Quantum Mothman in a corner as an option, though he wasn't picked. The game looked to be about five years out of date.

The two started to fight, Alea Iacta going on the offensive while Athena backed off and tried to tag him with ranged abilities. It wasn't working out for her.

"Yeah, that's a little suspicious," Alea Iacta said. "You think it's the Cabal?"

"Or something else," Emily said. "I don't know. I'm not sure those girls knew, either."

The door at the back of the train opened and Sam stepped in. She had Maple's toaster slung under one arm, and a pair of Trinity right behind her. "We're back," she said before she dumped the toaster-gun onto a table. "We found the toast, too."

Trinity raised a piece of bread up. It was a black square, almost shiny. "This one's still in one piece. The other exploded. Maple, your toaster's no good."

Emily glanced over to Maple, who was sitting on one of the bunk beds next to another Trinity. The girl blinked. "It isn't?" she asked worriedly.

"Nope. Burnt the toast too much. I like them kinda brown, not all burnt like this," Trinity said.

"Oh. But if they're not cooked well enough, they won't fly well," Maple said.

"Yeah, but then you can't eat them," Trinity rebutted.

Maple considered it for a moment. "I can fix that. Maybe I can project a containment shield around the toast as it flies; I can even make it aerodynamic so that it flies faster."

"Let's not make the toaster any more lethal than it is," Emily said. "In fact, Maple, I think your power might well be incredible, but please try to tell me if you're going to use it. I'm worried that you might make something too dangerous, okay?"

"Okay, Big Sister," Maple said. "Um . . . what's too dangerous, though?"

Emily closed her eyes to ward off a headache. "We'll come up with some rules later," she said.

"Don't stifle Maple too much," Sam said. "She needs to be able to create some stuff. Powers need to be used, right?"

"Giving her limitations won't stifle her, I don't think," Emily said. "And it will prevent her from making a nuke and giving it to Trinity to play with."

"Are nukes fun?" Trinity asked.

Emily gestured, her point clearly made. "Today's been a bit of a roller coaster. I wish I could get some more time off from the whole Heroing thing, but I feel like our time's running short."

Not just her time, she knew; her funds, too.

"So you want to get more serious?" Sam asked, perking up at the idea.

"A little," Emily admitted. "We're running out of time if we want to use the good press from the Hero fight to get that protection racket started. And now we need to consider the three girls today. If we don't act, someone else will, and I'd rather not be forced to act. Any news from Fabien, by the way?"

"Nope," Alea Iacta said.

"You've been talking to him again?" Emily asked. She had been asking Sam about Fabien, not Alea Iacta, but he was too busy focusing on his beatdown of Trinity on the TV to notice.

"Huh? Oh yeah, we text. We tried to do a poker night, but, yeah, it kinda blows but my powers make that a no-go, but skill-based games are more fair. Fabien cheats with his power, I cheat with mine, it all works out."

Emily nodded slowly. One of her minions was having guy time with a local Villain. Sure, why not? "Well, tell us if he plans on doing something like last time again."

"Will do, Boss," he said.

"I can start the protection racket whenever," Sam said.

"We'll start soon," Emily said. "Before that, I want to talk to Handshake."

"The information broker?" Sam asked.

Emily nodded. "Yes. He might know something about the Cabal. And connected as he is, knowing what others want to know might be helpful, too."

"Then call him up," Sam said.

Emily didn't want to admit that the reason she hadn't called him yet was because she was still working up the courage to do so. She really didn't like calling people she didn't know. She didn't like calling people she did know, either. "Fine," she said, giving up on holding back. "I can't use my normal phone, though."

"There's a phone booth in the metro," Alea Iacta said. "It's plugged in and everything."

"You mean in the station?" Emily asked.

"Yeah. You need quarters for it."

"Who carries quarters with them?" Sam asked.

Alea Iacta shrugged. "I tend to find a few whenever I'm going to go use it."

"Why are you using the phone booth, exactly?" Emily asked.

"To order food. Reception down here is trash."

"What's a reception?" Trinity asked.

Emily opted not to explain that. "I guess it's not a terrible idea. Anyone who traces the call will probably assume that we're not actually using the station's phone booth." She nodded. "Anyone want to come with me?"

She got a pile of volunteers.

"We won't actually be doing anything fun," she said. "Although . . . Athena, could you come with me? I think you're going to be instrumental in dealing with Handshake."

Athena's chest puffed out. "Sure thing, Big Sis," she said.

Emily almost felt bad for Handshake, but then, if he had a mind-reading minion, she bet he'd use them on her.

CHAPTER FORTY-EIGHT

Reading the Room

Emily scoured her purse for change. She had a little pouch where she'd put her small change, but she wanted to be sure she had enough to make the call.

Before her, pressed up against a tiled wall, was a pay phone. It was very nineties, with yellowing plastic sides and a coiled cord attached to the phone itself. At least it wasn't rotary or anything like that.

"Ah," Emily said as she found another quarter.

No wonder cell phones had become so popular; just getting the money out to use the pay phone was a hassle.

Emily checked the number she had on her phone, then slid a few coins into the coin slot before dialing. She tucked the phone against her shoulder, head tilted to the side to keep it in place while she put her cell phone away.

It rang twice before someone picked up. "How can I assist you?" a smooth, familiar voice asked.

"Um, hello, Handshake," Emily said.

"Ah, if it isn't the Boss," Handshake replied. He sounded jovial enough, though Emily wouldn't call herself an expert at reading people's moods from their voices. "How can I help you today? And I hope you're not calling from your own phone. You never know who might be listening in."

"I'm not," Emily said. She considered what to say next. She wanted to know several things, and Handshake's entire business was about giving people the information they wanted. "Can we set up an exchange?"

"Oh, of what sort?" he asked.

"There are a few things I'd like to know. About, ah, clowns and Cement and the city in general, I guess."

"Eauclaire has been growing interesting as of late, hasn't it? I think I have a few questions for you, too. Do you remember the place where we first met?"

Emily could recall that well enough. A bar beneath a coffee shop. It wasn't too far from where she was now, actually. "Yes, I do."

"Will you be available in, say, an hour and a half? At around two thirty?"

"You want to meet?" Emily asked. "Um. Yes, okay, I can do that."

"Wonderful!" Handshake said. "I'll see you there. Ah, will you be bringing your furry little friend?"

He was probably talking about Teddy. "No. She's going to stay at home," Emily said. She didn't say anything about Athena, or Trinity. Emily would be foolish to leave the base without any of her sisters with her. "Is that all?"

"Seems so. I'll be seeing you soon."

The line went dead and Emily hooked the phone back onto its cradle. She placed her extra quarters onto the old phonebook at the base of the booth, just in case.

"What's going on, Boss?" Athena asked.

"We're going to visit Handshake at the coffee shop and bar he hangs out at," Emily said. "He said not to bring any furry friends, but I think you should come. One of Trinity, too."

Athena grinned. "Oh, you're smart!" she said.

"I am?"

"Yeah. I've got feathers, not fur, and most of Trinity won't be there at all, so it doesn't count as though you actually brought her, right?"

"Um, sure," Emily said.

Athena nodded solemnly. "I'm going to be just as good as you when it comes to picking what's true or not one day, don't worry!"

That was terrifying. "Take your time, please," Emily said. "And remember not to use Villainous tricks on your sisters, okay?"

"Okay, Big Sis," Athena agreed.

If Emily couldn't stop her sisters from being themselves, maybe she could at least convince them to behave around her. It was a small, faint hope. "Trinity?" Emily asked. She looked around the platform before letting out a sigh. "Trinity, stop poking at the trash."

"Okay!" Trinity said with a cheer as she ran over. "Wasn't anything there anyway."

"No one's ever really used this station; it's not surprising that there isn't much here," Emily said. "Okay, we're going to head over to meet Handshake right away. Trinity, can your other yous tell Sam that we're heading out to meet him?"

"I can do that!" Trinity said. She smiled and bobbed her head from side to side. "But can it wait? It's my turn to play against Alea Iacta, and my other me's pooping."

Emily sighed. "I think this might be more important."

Trinity frowned. "Okay, but you told us that wiping's important."

"I meant this is more important than the game. Just . . . tell Teddy that I said so, and that you can take the next round, too, okay?"

"All right!" Trinity cheered.

Emily took her feelings, balled them up, then shoved them into a deep dark hole where they wouldn't bother her for a while. "Okay, let's head on out." With that said, Emily led her two sisters toward the upper sections of the station and finally out of the side door that dropped them off into a familiar alleyway.

At some point, Sam had found the keys to the side entrances and had also found the time to make copies. Emily was pretty sure both of those things were illegal, but she also found that she didn't care too much.

The coffee shop wasn't too far away. At a brisk walk, all it took was twenty or so minutes before she was standing before it. Twenty easy minutes. Corralling only two sisters was a lot easier than three. It was almost as if having more of them made it exponentially harder to keep track of them.

The shop hadn't changed much; it was still a cozy little hipster joint, with soft jazz playing from cheap speakers and a few customers at round tables, some with laptops, others just focusing on their meals alone.

"All right," Emily said. "Trinity, your job is to smile and be yourself."

"I'm good at that," Trinity said.

Emily patted her on the head. "I'm sure you are. Athena, you have a more important job. Handshake is . . . clever. He knows a lot, and he's only somewhat of an ally."

"He's one of their neutrals, right? Not a Villain, not a Hero, all boring?" Athena asked.

"I guess so, yeah."

"Can't trust those. They don't pick a side," Athena said with a mournful shake of her head. "You want me to put the fear of Boss into him?"

"Only if you think it's absolutely necessary. We want what he knows, so we don't want to anger him. Also, he's not an enemy. Just maybe try out your new mind-reading powers on him?"

Athena nodded. "Will do, Boss. I've been practicing hard."

Emily didn't want to know on *whom* she'd been practicing. "Okay, we're going to cross the street now," Emily said.

Athena and Trinity gave her their hands and Emily made a show of looking both ways, then waiting for traffic to clear up before she crossed with her sisters in tow.

On arriving at the café, she made a beeline for the rear. The barista behind the counter looked up, obviously curious. "Uh, just heading down," Emily said.

The woman nodded and followed them with her eyes until Emily slipped into the back corridors of the shop.

"She was thinking that we're suspicious," Athena said. "Also, she thought you might be a Mask."

"Oh," Emily said. So much for her disguise if random waitresses could figure out that she had powers. She climbed down the stairs leading into the basement, then pushed the door open.

The basement smelled like cigar smoke and alcohol. It was the same dreary place she remembered. Columns broke up the room, and a few booths lined the sides. The bar was empty, as it had been the last time she visited.

Or almost empty.

Sitting at the same spot as last time was Handshake. He looked better than she remembered. His arm, at least, wasn't in a sling anymore. He had a laptop on the table before him, the light from the screen illuminating his face.

Not too far from him, leaning against one of the columns, was another man. He had a coat on, with a hood draped over his head, and with the bar's light behind him, Emily couldn't make out his features. She only assumed he was a man from the set of his shoulders and the plain clothes he was wearing.

"Ah, the Boss!" Handshake said. He stood up and tied the front buttons of his suit jacket together. "A pleasure to see you again. And you brought some friends."

"I did," Emily said. "This is Owlwatch and Bandit," she introduced her sisters by their code names.

"Hello, I hope we all have an agreeable time, and I hope that this meeting doesn't come to blows," he said while extending a hand toward her.

Emily, on reflex, reached out to shake.

Then Athena grabbed her by the wrist and pulled her arm down. "No," she said. "He's trying something tricky."

Emily froze up, then she glared at Handshake. That had been stupid of her. His power was in his name, wasn't it? What had he asked for? That she'd have an agreeable time and that she didn't attack him?

"Let's not," she said.

Handshake swallowed and lowered his hand. "As you wish," he said. "Shall we talk, then? What do you want to know?"

CHAPTER FORTY-NINE

Owl of Her Attention

Athena, being the good sister she was, kept her attention focused on Handshake and his guard. The guard wasn't much of a problem. Sure, he was all dark and brooding, with his arms crossed and the whole "leaning coolly against a pillar" look, but she caught a glimpse of his eyes and his thoughts made her relax.

Mostly, he was thinking *oh poop, oh poop* over and over again. But he was using the kind of words that the Boss didn't like. Athena didn't think that *thinking* that kind of word was against the rules, or else Big Sister would be very angry at Athena for some of the things Athena thought.

So she dismissed the guard. He had a knife and a baton, according to his own surface thoughts of grabbing either. He didn't have any powers, which meant he was just a boring normal person, and while he was bigger and probably physically stronger than Athena, she wasn't worried. The Boss would smack him around if he tried anything.

Handshake, on the other hand, had plenty of power. His thoughts were hard to read, going at a million miles an hour. It was hard for Athena to get anything from him, and his eyes didn't linger on her for long enough that she could untangle the web of his thoughts.

She had the impression that he wanted stuff from the Boss, and that he was worried about Trinity and Athena and the Boss. Athena grinned. He wasn't all that worried, but she could work on that.

Handshake gestured to the table he'd been sitting at when they'd entered the room. "Shall we sit?" he asked.

"Sure," Big Sister said. She moved to the table, pulled out a seat, and sat.

Athena took her place on Big Sister's right, and Trinity her left, neither of them sitting. Handshake glanced at both of them and smiled. It wasn't a very real smile, and it didn't take Athena's mind-reading powers to figure that out.

"So I imagine you're here because you have questions," Handshake said rather smoothly. "Of course, as per usual, I'm willing to answer what I can and discover what I cannot, for a price."

Big Sister frowned. "Would that price change now? What did you try to do earlier, with that handshake?"

Handshake raised his hands. "I was merely trying to ensure that nothing untoward would happen during our meeting, that's all. You know how my power works?"

"I don't!" Trinity cheered.

Handshake blinked, then glanced at Trinity. "I can make deals and seal them with a handshake. All parties will then be compelled—though not forced—to carry out their part of the bargain. I have a few other abilities, of course, but they all center around that core concept."

Athena nodded a little. That was a pretty strong power. Not in a fight or anything, but under the right circumstances she could see it being useful. Her power was way better though.

Big Sister Emily stared at Handshake for a long time, her brow knit together in a mean scowl. Athena was happy she wasn't the one being pressed by that stare. "You will not try that again," Emily said.

"As you say," Handshake said. He was smiling still.

The Boss's look went even darker. "You don't seem to understand. You *will not* try that again. There will be consequences if you do."

Athena gulped. That sounded serious. Like, going-to-bed-without-snacks serious.

She glanced at Handshake, looking the man in the eyes, then she blinked and turned to look at the Boss. Big Sister Emily didn't *look* like she was too warm; why did Handshake think she was hot when she was angry?

Handshake shifted in his seat. "Shall we continue on to business then? I'm certain you have plenty of questions."

"I do," Big Sister said. "First, let's talk price?"

"If you wish." Handshake rubbed at his chin. "The difficulty here is that different questions are worth different amounts. How are you in terms of liquid assets? Can you afford the answer to your own questions?"

Big Sister pursed her lips. It wasn't quite a pout. "All right then. Maybe we can trade for some things. I'll ask a question, you tell me the price, and we go from there?"

"Certainly."

"Fine then. In that case, the Cabal. How are they involved in Eauclaire?"

Handshake shrugged. "I know little, but I can, perhaps, illuminate some things for you there. Usually it's bad for business to talk about them, but lately the winds seem to be turning."

"In what way?"

Handshake shook his head. "That answer has a price too."

"Fine. What's the cost?"

"How about instead of money, I ask a question and you answer it honestly. You'll be happy to know that a lot of people are asking about you and yours. Don't look so surprised. You've been on the news twice in as many weeks."

"I . . . guess I could answer some questions," Big Sister said. "Who will decide on which question is worth more?"

"I suppose that'll be up to both of us to decide. I can shake on making this a fair trade, if you want. My powers do work on myself," Handshake offered. As far as Athena could tell, he was being honest.

"Boss," Athena said in a stage whisper, "I'll tell you if he thinks he's cheating you."

"Oh, thank you, Owlwatch, that's helpful."

Athena preened while pointedly ignoring Handshake's momentary look of confusion. He didn't know what her powers were, and that made him nervous. Good.

"So, for knowledge about the Cabal's involvement in Eauclaire, can you tell me about your team? Just the names of all the members and maybe a few tidbits about them?"

"I suppose I can do that," Big Sister said. "We have Owlwatch and Bandit here. They're owl and raccoon themed, as you can tell. You've met Ursa Minor as well and I imagine she's left an impression."

"Indeed," he said, his smile going just a bit wooden. "What are everyone's powers?"

"I don't know if I should say that," the Boss said.

Handshake nodded. "Fair enough, I won't push."

"So what can you tell me about the Cabal?"

Handshake squinted. "I'll tell you what I can, but I think my information is worth a few more questions. I don't mind if you pay afterward, of course."

"Okay," Big Sister Emily said.

"The Cabal sent three of their heroes to Eauclaire. Black Shield—whom you've met—Thunder Clot, and Spin to Win. Spin to Win is currently working with the local HRF to weed out some corruption. I suspect that he's actually working to install more Cabal members in Eauclaire's HRF. Thunder Clot, on the other hand, seems to have caused some trouble elsewhere and was sent to Eauclaire, which is a bit of a backwater in terms of Heroics, to cool their heels."

"And what are the Cabal's goals here?" Emily asked.

"Eauclaire had a surprising number of new Masks during the last Power Day. Including yourself and your young companions here, Miss Ursa Minor, and your lucky friend, there are nearly a dozen more Masks. Last year Eauclaire had four."

"That's a significant increase," Big Sister Emily said.

"It is! The Cabal will have an interest in recruiting, of course, but also in ensuring that they can get their claws into new Heroes before they make a splash or move to other cities and disrupt their operations there. I still believe that most of the Cabal's money comes from advertising."

Athena blinked. How could Villains make money from advertising? That was just weird. Didn't they have time to rob banks like proper Villains?

"Thank you," Big Sister Emily said. "I guess it's your turn to ask questions."

Handshake nodded. "Are you single?"

"W-what?"

The man across from them shrugged. His smile was still in place, but Athena knew that it was more genuine now. "It's a simple enough question."

"But why?"

"Because half the questions people have fielded me about you have lingered around that sort of gossip. It's not world-shaking news, but it's the sort of thing that people love to talk about. There are a lot of rumors out there, you know? I personally suspect that you're too young for the girls in your . . . employ to be your children, but a lot of people claim otherwise."

"What? No, they're my sisters," Big Sister protested.

"That answers another question I had, thank you. How many people are part of your group, exactly? Bandit here was quite the surprise."

"We have a couple more people," Big Sister admitted.

"I could use more accurate answers," Handshake said.

Big Sister didn't look amused by that comment. She stared hard at Handshake. "I need to prioritize the safety of my team. I can't let people know things that might hurt us."

"I understand. How about some more innocent questions then? Tabloid stuff to feed the rumor mill. What diet are you on to stay so thin? Exercise regimes? Who made your costume, your siblings? Are any of them sidekicks? Are there any rumors you really dislike? Any celebrities you have a beef with? Hero crushes? Any internal strife between the siblings? What do your parents think? Is it true that you had a fling with Glamazon?"

Athena glanced at her Big Sister and marveled at how her face remained placid while in her mind she was screaming. Truly, Big Sister Emily was incredible.

CHAPTER FIFTY

Discreet as Usual

Emily's head was spinning when she left Handshake's hidden bar. The man had a *lot* of questions. Even choosing to skip quite a number of them—people didn't need to know a lot of the things he'd asked about; why had there been so many questions about her love life?—she still had to scramble for answers for the less . . . embarrassing questions.

She imagined that to the right gossip, the answers might be worth a lot. In fact, she knew as much because Handshake had asked her if she would be willing to be interviewed by a national gossip rag.

He meant the kind of terrible magazines she'd seen next to the chocolate and candy racks at more stores than she could count. She had never imagined herself featuring in one of those. She didn't *want* to feature in one of those, but Handshake had offhandedly pointed out a few reasons why it might not be a bad idea.

As it was, an interview with a Mask of any caliber was a pretty hot item for that kind of magazine, especially if that Mask was currently on the evening news, which she unfortunately was—if only as a B story.

For her, that would mean a favorable story because the magazine wouldn't want to burn any bridges. It would also mean more money. Not a ton, but Emily could really use a few hundred dollars just for food and other expenses.

That, and it played into her protection racket plans.

Not that she was going to call them that aloud.

That evening, she returned to the dorm with her gaggle of sisters and put her problems out of her mind while she tackled some good old homework. It was nice and easy and mind-numbing, which is exactly what she needed.

The next day would be more complicated, at least in the afternoon.

In the morning, Emily had Ethics. She appreciated the irony of the class as she found a seat in the back and listened to a poorly delivered lecture on the meaning of morality and the history of various traditions and beliefs.

They even touched on Heroics and Villainy. Emily squirmed in her seat, feeling a strange new sort of anxiety. Usually she was just afraid of being picked to talk, but now she was afraid the room would turn to her, point, and accuse her of being a Hero. Or a Villain. Either was bad.

As soon as the class was over she rushed back to the dorms. She had a busy day ahead of her.

"Hey, Ems," Sam said as she caught up with Emily on the path to their dorm. "Oh . . . no, Ems doesn't work at all. You don't look like an Ems. Sorry, Emily."

"Um, it's fine," Emily said. She tried not to wilt under Sam's enthusiastic babbling. "Are you ready for today?" she asked.

"Oh yeah. It's going to be great, don't worry. What's our time frame here?"

"We have our meeting at four thirty," Emily said. "It'll just be me and the interviewer."

"Don't want to bring any of the brats?" Sam asked.

Emily gave her a *look*. "No. I don't think I will. Can you think of any sister who would be useful in that kind of meeting? Athena might, maybe. She can be discreet sometimes. But she might also decide to make the interviewer paranoid or bark out something she read in their mind."

"Yeah, she is a bit creepy, that one. Like, I shouldn't judge a kid for their looks, because that's the kind of judgmental stuff you should only reserve for adults, but Athena's got weird eyes, especially when she's just staring at you without blinking."

Emily felt a little insulted on Athena's behalf. Sam wasn't wrong, but still, on principle she felt indignant. Not enough to comment, though.

"The others would be . . . well, Teddy would use any platform to talk about communism."

"Which the gossip rags would love, if in the wrong way."

"And Trinity would definitely say *something* and then steal from the interviewer." Emily considered her newest sister for a moment. "Maple would be okay, I think. She's shy unless you get her babbling about one of her inventions, but that's mostly just cute, honestly."

Sam nodded along. "Your sisters are all cute. It's a big advantage."

"Didn't you just say that Athena was creepy?"

"Creepy can be cute if you try hard enough," Sam said. "Anything can be cute if you're willing to put some elbow grease into it."

Emily eyed her . . . maybe-friend. "I'll take your word for it," she said.

"So we have a few hours, and I have a few targets. The first one's our best bet, I think. You've heard of the Yeast Feast, yeah?"

"I'm sorry, the what?" Emily asked.

Sam snorted. "Proving again you're not a local. It's this old bakery that's, like, right next to the campus. You've walked by it, guaranteed. Anyway, the place was run by this nice old guy and his dog. Well, the dog didn't run the place, he just slept out by the door and gave people puppy eyes for food. Anyway, that was a while ago. The old man passed on a few years ago."

"What happened to the dog?" Emily asked.

"You know, I have no idea. It was an old dog, though. Big fat bread-filled mutt. Anyway, the place closed down for a year or so, then this nice gay couple bought it. Now they sell pastries and bread and cakes and stuff. It's pretty popular, at least with the richer students. They've been robbed a few times, though."

"A few times?" Emily asked. "Where is this, exactly?"

"Like I said, right next to the campus. Next to this hardware place and some apartments. It's kind of weird that people rob the place, but I guess they deal with a lot of cash. So yeah, a good place to continue our protection racket, I think. And if you want to do advertising stuff, it's probably a good place for it."

Emily nodded. Somewhere open would be somewhat safe, probably. Or it should have been in any case.

"Have you spoken to the owners?" she asked.

Sam nodded. "I did. Set up a meeting and everything. Don't worry, it'll be fine. Just get Teddy to sit out front and charge by the hour."

"Teddy?"

"In her bear form, yeah. Maybe they can make her a plus-plus-size apron or a chef's hat."

"I thought it was a bakery?" Emily asked.

Sam snorted. "Same difference. Come on, let's grab the brats, Boss!"

Emily followed Sam into the dorms, then rode the elevator up with her. When she arrived in her room and finished hugging everyone and ensuring that nothing had been set on fire, they packed up their costumes into their go bags and headed out. She was glad to see that Maple hadn't turned her computer into a laser rifle or Mister Toaster into another rail gun. Still, she made note to grab some random junk for Maple to play with.

Everything she read about gadgeteers said that they had a strong compulsion to make stuff. In fact, few powered individuals could sit on their laurels. Emily wasn't sure if that was some mental part of having a power, or if it was just plain temptation at work.

If you could fly around or turn into a bear or build neat things from junk, why wouldn't you?

"All right, girls," Emily said. "We'll be doing some . . . some Villain stuff today."

She paused while the girls cheered.

"But I still want all of you on your best behavior, okay? We might be extorting people for their money but we need to be polite and look Heroic while doing it." Sometimes Emily couldn't believe the things she was saying.

"No problem, Boss," Teddy said with a thumbs-up. "By the way, what're we gonna do about Maple?"

Maple shifted to the side where she'd be partially hidden from everyone's attention.

"Oh, right," Emily said. "We need a costume for you, don't we?"

Maple gulped. "Do I need one?"

"I . . . guess. Unless you'd rather just not be seen?"

Maple's head bobbed up and down at that.

"Well, then, maybe we can arrange something like that for you," Emily said. "We'll have to make a quick stop to drop you off at the metro tunnels. Maybe a Trinity can stay with you?"

"It's a good idea. She's not a front liner, anyway. She can tinker away in the tunnels, maybe make some cool gizmos for the others," Sam said.

Maple was still clearly a bit nervous about the attention, but Emily had the impression she was enjoying the idea.

"Well, why not," Emily said. She couldn't see the worst that could happen there.

CHAPTER FIFTY-ONE

Racket-Making

Emily occasionally, okay, frequently, thought that Sam was a bit much. The girl was an extrovert's extrovert, and Emily suspected that Sam had some issues that would take a very good psychologist to untangle. Still, for all that Sam was insane, she was insane in Emily's favor, so Emily kept her reservations close and didn't complain—aloud—about Sam's quirkier habits.

Sam was talking to one of the owners of the Yeast Feast, combining a quick, nonstop rattle of sales pitches with gestures deeper into the alleyway where they were standing.

The owner was weathering the storm better than Emily could have managed, with frequent peeks at Emily and her sisters, who were farther back in the alley. At the moment, Teddy was in her bear form, with Trinity and Athena riding on her back. One of Trinity was using the added height to look into a dumpster.

Emily glanced at Trinity, met her eyes, then shook her head slowly. The Trinity standing up on Teddy's back sat back down.

"Well, there's no doubting they're the real thing," the owner said. He gestured vaguely in the girls' direction. "But what I don't understand is what you want from us."

"Oh, it's simple," Sam said. "See, the city is growing really dangerous. There are Villains aplenty, and worse! Minions! You're a clever business owner, you know the risks you take just to keep everything afloat. Now, imagine how much safer your shop would be if the girls patrolled it. And even better, think of how many people would visit your place. *The* bakery with the Super Heroic customers. No, the Super Heroic mascots!"

The man rubbed his chin. "I guess I can see the temptation there, but it all depends on how much you're asking for."

"It's really inexpensive," Sam said. "We have three packages we're offering to local businesses. We approached you first because we know you have a good rapport with the others in the area, and we thought we could use you as a bridge. Of course, we'll offer a steep discount for that."

"Uh-huh," he said. Not rudely, Emily didn't think, just as a sort of *I'm listening* sound.

"Our base package only costs two hundred a month and includes once-a-month visits from the entire group. They'll pop in and buy some bread or croissants or whatever, maybe smile for the cameras, then scamper off to do what we do best."

"That's half of what I pay for my security systems now," he said.

Sam grinned. "Only half! Think of how much you'll be saving! Our next package up includes two monthly visits, including eating at your establishment once a month. We'll use our prime detective skills to track down anyone who tries to rob or intimidate you. All that for only four hundred dollars a month."

"That's twice as much as the previous tier."

Sam nodded. "Yes, it is. That's after your discount, of course."

"That's getting expensive."

"Our prime tier is a thousand dollars a month," Sam said. "But for you, nine fifty. That's a five percent discount!"

"That's insane," he said. Emily didn't nod, but she had to agree with him.

Sam shook her head. "No, it really isn't. For that price, we'll pop by once a month and spend at least four hours at your shop advertising it for passersby. Taking pictures, signing posters, kissing babies, the whole nine yards!"

"Four hours for a grand?" he asked.

"Four hours with several Heroes," Sam pointed out. "Do you have any idea how much it costs to get a Hero to work for you for even just one hour? Look at how many are here right now and tell me that we're not worth that much and more! Just the sheer social media presence you'll get from it should be worth ten times as much."

Emily was amazed to see the man actually thinking about it. If they could secure a deal here . . . well, she was pretty sure that was enough per month to cover food and essentials . . . probably. Just from one place.

"Would all of them show up?" he asked.

"We're busy people you know. At least two of them each time. We can rotate them around so that the crowds don't get tired. You'll get repeat customers just from people trying to get every signature."

He rubbed his hands together. "We could do special pastries. Bear paws and . . . well, I'll think of something owl and racoon themed."

"Of course," Sam said. "We will, obviously, need a cut of any merchandising sales."

"Pardon?"

"We can start at eighty percent," Sam replied.

"That's excessive."

Sam snorted. "Look me in the eyes and tell me that people wouldn't buy twenty-dollar posters if it meant getting a chance to have them signed. They'll cost you a dollar each and I bet you'll sell out every time."

"Fifty percent."

Sam shot her hand out to shake. "Seventy-five, we'll show up next Wednesday in costume at . . . fourish?"

"Make it the day after. Do you have official marketing images for posters and the like?"

"We haven't pushed our racket onto the local printers yet," Sam said, "but we'll be heading there soon enough."

They shook, and Emily had to keep herself from gawking.

"All right, do you have a number I can text to arrange all this stuff?" Sam asked. They traded numbers, with Sam handing an extra business card over to Emily, who took it gingerly and then wondered what to do with it while in costume.

Sam and the bakery owner talked for another minute or two, then he headed back inside. "That . . . was honestly kind of incredible," Emily said.

"Yeah. Poor dude just got swindled hard. But, hey, the allure of Heroes will do that to people, I guess."

Emily shook her head. "Where to next?"

"I wasn't joking about the printers. We probably can't set up as good a racket there, but we'll still need to set something up. Merchandising stuff is probably worth a whole lot, and let's face it, the brats are photogenic as heck. I swear, take any ten-second clip of them doing whatever and it'll go viral."

Emily glanced over to her sisters, then frowned. "Teddy! Trinity! What are you doing to that dumpster?"

It was weird that she could now read the facial expressions of grizzly bears, Emily thought as she watched Teddy carefully step back from the dumpster. The top clanged down and Trinity jumped down and back onto the ground.

"I have to go to that interview," Emily said. "Are you going to be okay watching over the kids?" She didn't use the word *babysit*, mostly because it insulted the girls who admittedly weren't babies. They were worse.

"I'll be fine," Sam said. "Keep your phone on, just in case, but I'm sure things will be okay. We'll take it slow."

"All right," Emily said. She actually trusted Sam. The girl had too much invested not to earn that trust by then. Also, her sisters could take care of themselves, a little, when supervised. If someone tried to hurt them, then they'd probably make that person's life a nightmare.

Teddy would turn into a bear, Athena would do horrific things to their mind, and Trinity was as hardheaded as she was immortal.

Emily probably didn't have anything to worry about.

Which made it annoying when she realized that she had a pit of worry in her gut anyway.

Emily gave her sisters a quick speech, telling them to behave and listen to Sam, and then she was off.

The bakery wasn't too far from where her interview would take place, in a nicer restaurant just a block down, the sort with a greeter by the door and where tables had to be reserved in advance, even during the middle of the day.

Emily adjusted her costume, made sure her mask was on straight, then she made an effort not to slouch as she walked along the sidewalk to the restaurant.

Two customers were ahead of her, but they slid to the side and stared at her, so she just walked up to the waiter's podium and tried to smile. "Ah, reservation for the *Cowl*?" she asked.

The waiter nodded. "R-right this way," she said.

Was the woman . . . starstruck? Or could it be that she was intimidated?

No, that was silly. Emily pushed the thought aside. People didn't feel that way about her.

She followed the waitress through the restaurant to the back where a few booths were tucked away. They had tall walls around them that enclosed the entire booth enough that it was hard to see the people sitting within. With some low classical music playing above, it would be hard for someone to accidentally overhear anyone in one of those booths.

That's where Emily found the journalist she'd be working with, a gaunt young man in a sweater who looked like he was a shade too warm for his own good and who jumped when she sat across from him.

"Hello," Emily said. "I'm the Boss. You're here for the interview?"

CHAPTER FIFTY-TWO

The Interview

Michel was fairly new to being a reporter. Personally, he preferred the term *journalist*, but, well, he could admit that where he currently worked wasn't exactly the kind of place that did journalism.

The *Cowl* was a classic gossip rag, with all the reputation that that entailed. It was a weekly magazine that mostly repeated what others had said before it and didn't bother with fact-checking. It wasn't the most glamorous job, but he had only graduated two years ago with an English degree (which was proving rather useless) and this job was the closest he could get to his dream job.

To be fair, he'd grown up on comics about mild-mannered reporters who had secret identities as Super Heroic Masks, and while he couldn't do the Heroic part, he could almost do the reporter part. Or that had been the plan.

Until today, it hadn't worked out so well. He'd been stuck in the offices, editing articles and learning the ropes, for the past six months.

Today was his big opportunity to make a name for himself, one that he only got because one of the more senior reporters had a stomach flu and no one else felt like traveling all the way to Eauclaire.

It was, in his less-than-humble-opinion, about time he caught a lucky break.

The *Cowl* had a few popular features. There was the copy-pasted gossip section, which kept some people coming, but most of the eye-catching articles were direct interviews with B-lister Heroes (they were too small-fry to ever catch a big fish) and their monthly "Under the Cowl" column, which was really just an excuse to show off images of certain Heroic figures in bathing suits and spandex outfits so tight they were basically painted on. That part of the magazine was very popular with a certain—disgusting—segment of the population.

What he was aiming for today was more on the interview side of things.

Nabbing a Hero's first interview was a big deal in the rather small world of reporters and journalists, exactly what he needed to get his name out there.

But first, he had to get the boring questions out of the way.

His leg bounced under the table with nervous energy and he fiddled with the cup of ice water the waitress had brought him earlier. He hadn't touched the complimentary garlic bread yet. The last thing he needed was to have bread crumbs down the front of his suit.

He'd picked this restaurant to give off the impression that this was more than just an interview for the seventh- (out of nine) best-selling tabloid in the region.

Someone sat across from him and he jumped. It was a young woman, one he recognized easily enough. The Boss was dressed in a pressed pin-striped suit and a small fedora. She had the standard domino mask across her upper face, which did nothing to hide her eyes that locked onto him.

"Hello," she said. "I'm the Boss. You're here for the interview?"

Michel swallowed, then smiled and tried to remember how to be personable. "Yes, that's me. I'm Michel from the *Cowl*. It's a pleasure to meet you." He extended a hand across the table.

The Boss stared at his hand for a few long seconds, then looked back up at him. "Would you mind if we don't?" she asked.

She didn't want to do the interview? His heart sank, and he pulled his arm back. "Oh? We're willing to pay, of course, and if you want to order a meal, feel free. I don't want you to be uncomfortable."

"Thank you," she said. Then, after too long a pause, she continued. "That's acceptable."

Now he was even more confused. He was about to laugh it off, maybe make some joke, but the woman across from him was staring, her expression entirely flat, and he decided that maybe his charisma wasn't as great as he thought it was.

Also, he was kind of hoping she wouldn't order anything to eat. He was footing that particular bill himself and this place was a little rich for his blood. As it was, he was planning on grabbing a few appetizers and nothing else.

"So, ah, well, usually with this kind of interview . . . actually, how much experience do you have with interviews? Not that I mean to pry into your unmasked life," Michel said.

"Not very much," the Boss replied.

Michel smiled and nodded and tried to ignore the bead of sweat slipping its way down his back. He knew he'd be interviewing all sorts of people—ideally—but he didn't expect a young woman to be so damned intimidating.

"Then that's fine," he said after recentering himself with a sip from his water. He knew what was coming next was going to be a whole lot of made-up stuff. "Usually, what we want from an interview is just a glimpse into the life. Tell us about your goals, maybe recount a nice moment of triumph. The more you give me, the more we can work on it. Your opinions matter."

One of her eyebrows perked up. "Do they?"

"Um. Yes? I mean, yes. Definitely. The people out there want to know about Heroes, and new Heroes are interesting and, well, new. So let me softball a few questions your way, just to get a taste of things. Ah, I'll be recording this, since I can't rely on my memory, is that fine?"

"Yes, go ahead," she said.

He nodded and pulled out his phone. He had an app for recording interviews, of course, and he turned that on and pressed record, then—thanks to a tip he'd gotten from another journalist before—he introduced himself, then stopped the recording and listened to it. That worked to check that the phone's microphone was working and the software worked, too.

"All right then. My name is Michel, and today I'm interviewing the new Hero called the Boss for the *Cowl*. Is that your Hero name?"

"The Boss? Ah, yes, I suppose it is now."

Names were a nice safe topic. "Can you tell us how you came upon that name? Is there a story behind it?"

"Oh, well, Ursa Minor named me, actually. She called me the boss when I took charge, I guess. And the name just sort of stuck."

"Ursa Minor is your companion who can turn into a bear, correct?" he asked. This was big. If he could get her to spill the beans on the others, well, maybe he could get more interviews, make a whole series about it.

The Boss nodded. "That's her, yes. But I'd rather not divulge too much about my sis— about my companions."

"Of course, don't worry," he said. Siblings! Siblings with powers! That was uncommon, weird, and interesting all at once. He couldn't write it outright, but he *could* imply the heck out of it later. "So, the Boss, the leader of your team, right?"

She nodded, then he gestured to the phone and she spoke aloud. "Yes, I am."

"How did that happen?" he asked.

"The other members are all preteens."

Michel smiled. "Ah, right. So, um, I guess that means asking about the dating scene in your group is right out?" he chuckled.

The chuckles died out as she just continued to stare at him. Her brows furrowed, though, and he had the impression she was very much not amused.

"Sorry. Anyway, uh. So, what are your goals as a Hero? You've only been out for a couple of weeks and you already have quite the reputation!" At least she did locally. A couple of little fights didn't make national news. "What are your goals in the short and long term?"

The Boss smiled. "Take over the city."

Michel swallowed, then the girl chuckled, darkly.

"That was a joke," she said, her smile disappearing instantly. "We plan on helping make Eauclaire a safer place to live. We are also working with a few local businesses to earn a little bit of money. The others need college tuitions and it turns out that being Heroes is expensive."

"What kind of business?"

"Mostly advertising for now. We're trying to grow our team out more, too, so we might eventually be able to explore other avenues of profit. Fighting is nice, but it doesn't pay well. Eauclaire is already a fairly safe city. There aren't any real Villains here."

"Well, there's that Fabien the Fabulous man," he said. "And I heard a rumor about a luck manipulator, too."

She stared at him. "We'll take care of them," she said.

Michel swallowed. That didn't sound very Heroic. On paper it might not look so bad, but something about her tone, the finality of it, just set alarm bells ringing in his head. "Yeah, okay. So, what do you do for fun, as a group, I mean?"

"We . . . mostly just do work, really. The others all have their own hobbies. Ursa Minor loves watching nature documentaries and hibernating, and Owlwatch likes reading. Bandit . . . likes cooking. Toast. We all like . . . eating."

"Ah, yeah, that's nice," he said.

Michel had no idea how he was going to turn this into an interesting article. "Girls Like Eating" wasn't exactly a Ulitzer headline.

CHAPTER FIFTY-THREE

Generic Desires for the Future

The interview was going great so far, Emily thought.

Michel seemed like a friendly enough man, and at least his questions weren't as probing as Handshake's had been. So far, most of the questions were kind of silly.

What sort of hobbies did they have? What did the girls do for fun? Any embarrassing stories? He asked her opinion on a few topics, but they were mostly safe topics, never touching politics or things that people had strong opinions on.

Emily answered what she could and politely asked Michel to ask another question when they came to something whose answer would be problematic. The journalist seemed to catch on quickly to what was and wasn't acceptable to ask.

"So, if you don't mind, we can move onto more . . . I guess you could call them generic questions," Michel said.

Emily nodded then took a sip from her drink. She'd only ordered a soda and Michel had ordered some cheese sticks and more garlic bread. She wasn't sure if she would even be hungry for anything else after nibbling on a few. "I don't mind generic questions," she said.

"Wonderful. In that case, do you have any goals as a Hero? Any big ambitions? Eauclaire is a small city, I can't imagine anyone wanting to stay here if they intend to build a big Heroic career." He chuckled.

Emily considered the question, then decided to answer honestly. For the most part. "I think that Eauclaire being a quiet place is fine. I wouldn't want it to be any more active than it is, really. I . . . you know how there are lots of cartoons and movies about Heroes?"

"Of course."

"I never understood the Heroes in those. They were always so flashy and . . . public. I guess I don't have the temperament or the willingness to be the center of attention that way."

"You're more quiet," Michel said.

Emily nodded. "Exactly. I guess being that loud makes sense when you have overwhelming power on your side, but I always thought that you could get a lot more done by being quiet. Sure, taking out a Villain in a big brawl in the streets is impressive, but there's a lot less collateral damage if you knock them out while they're going to the bathroom at three in the morning on a weekend. Um. For example, I mean."

"Yes, of course," he said. He gave her a quick smile, then cleared his throat. "So, how does that reflect on your goals then?"

"Oh," she said, a bit embarrassed by the tangent. "Well, I mostly plan on making Eauclaire my city. To make it a place where my companions and I can stay safe. If it was up to me, there wouldn't be any big flashy fights in the streets. Any Villain or Hero who isn't good at Heroics would learn that Eauclaire isn't a place where they can get away with their usual antics."

"Because you'd stop them," he filled in.

She shook her head. "Not necessarily me," she said, meaning that she hoped that other Heroes would take up that same attitude. "I think there are a few cities like that."

"Oh, I can think of a few, yes. But those are generally the cities where either a single very powerful Hero lives, or where the headquarters of a Heroic organization is based."

"Yes, a place like that," Emily said. "Peaceful and quiet and safe."

"Which you intend to enforce with your army of preteen Super Heroes."

Emily blinked. "No, of course not. That would be . . . awful. At most we'd just use the threat that having so many Heroes on our side brings, but not, you know, actually putting the girls in danger."

"Right, of course," he said. "Um, onto the next question then?"

"Sure, I don't mind—" Emily paused as something vibrated against her side. She slapped her hand down on her phone, then squeezed it out of her pocket. She had a call from Sam. "I'm sorry, give me a moment?"

"Sure, sure," he said.

Emily stood up and answered the call right away. "Hello?" Sam wouldn't call her for no reason. If she wanted to let Emily know about something that wasn't urgent, she'd probably just text. Emily had spoken to Sam about how much she disliked talking over the phone already, and Sam was surprisingly respectful about it.

"Heya, Boss," Sam said. "How's the interview going?"

"Fine. What's wrong?"

"Well, we have a bit of a situation developing here, and I think you might want to come over to address this yourself. Only if you can leave your interview. It's not urgent-urgent, it's just kind of very inconvenient."

"What's going on?" Emily asked.

"I was going around with the girls, doing our thing." Which meant setting up the protection racket. "And then Glamazon showed up out of nowhere and started trailing after us."

"Does she know what you were doing? Is she causing trouble? How are my sisters?"

"Fine, fine," Sam said quickly. "Uh, and no, I don't think so. This is my first chance to get away from her to call. Trinity is keeping her distracted. We gave up on the mission and have just been patrolling around."

Emily nodded. That was smart. Heroic patrols were a pretty normal, if boring, part of being a hero. "All right, where are you now?"

"We're heading north, I think closer to where you are now." Sam rattled off a street name.

"That's not too far," Emily agreed. Five, maybe six blocks away. "All right, I'm going to join you. Make sure the girls don't say anything Glamazon doesn't need to know."

"I'm working on that, yeah. Thanks, Boss. See you soon."

The line went dead and Emily walked back to the booth she was sharing with Michel. "I'm sorry, Michel, something has come up and, well, I'm needed."

"Oh, that's fine," he said. "We were drawing to a close, anyway. Did you want to take any of this with you?" He gestured to the table and the leftovers. She almost said no, then reconsidered and nodded. Michel said, "Okay, I'll get everything into a baggie. Is it urgent? A Villain, maybe?"

"It's nothing like that," she said. "Just some problems while on patrol."

"Oh, the rest of your team was out?" he asked.

"Just a normal, routine patrol around the safer parts of the city. They're with a friend and can call for help. But they've run across something that I need to help with."

"All right then, I hope that works out for you."

Emily nodded, then stepped back as a waiter appeared and efficiently shoved the garlic bread and cheese sticks into a brown paper bag. Emily accepted it with a nod and a smile. "Thank you for the interview. I hope you have enough for a good article."

"Oh, I'm sure I do. Thank you! Maybe next time I can convince you to let me interview one of your companions?"

"Possibly!" Emily said. She thanked the journalist a few more times, then walked out of the restaurant with some urgency. She was even able to ignore all the looks she was getting from the customers. They probably didn't see that many Masks moving past with a doggie bag tucked to their side.

Emily took a minute to get her bearings, then took off down the street at a quick walk. Didn't want to jog and arrive out of breath and sweaty at whatever scene her sisters had created.

Then again, maybe being a bit disheveled would be worth arriving a minute or two earlier, she thought as she picked up the pace.

The few people she crossed looked at her either startled or with something close to panic. A Mask running down the street was usually a pretty bad sign. The only problem was they didn't know if they should be running away from where she was going or toward it.

Emily slowed her jog down half a block later, a hand pressed into her side where she'd developed a nasty stitch. Gritting her teeth, she focused on just walking quickly instead.

A block passed, then another, and then, finally, she saw her sisters up ahead.

Teddy was leading the way, with a Trinity just behind her. Behind them, Athena was walking along next to a familiar figure. Glamazon, in her bright costume with all the sparkling gems fitted into it. Sam was bringing up the rear with another Trinity.

"Boss!" Teddy shouted. She jogged ahead and crashed into Emily with a crushing hug. "You're back! We found a Hero and she won't stop following us. Can we beat her up?"

Fortunately, they were far enough that Emily doubted Glamazon could hear that comment. "Not yet," she said. That earned her a worrisome smile from Teddy.

"Hey, Boss," Glamazon said with a small wave after Emily's other sisters came and said hi. "Been a while."

"Yes, it has, hasn't it?" Emily asked.

She smiled, but it was mostly just a show of teeth. It was time to figure out what Glamazon wanted.

CHAPTER FIFTY-FOUR

Chaotic Evil Children

Jezebelle was, in her mother's own words, a very ambitious young woman who would either go far, or burn herself trying. She had a somewhat rocky relationship with her mother.

That ambition was partly born from that. She wanted to get away from home. Her life at home wasn't terrible, but it wasn't idyllic, and she always thought that she deserved better. At some point that had crystallized into her growing up into a hardworking, determined student who went to school knowing that she'd pull every string and befriend anyone who stood in her path to greatness.

And then she'd gotten a superpower.

It was almost a joke. So much practice socializing, so much hard work, and then she'd just been handed the greatest boon anyone could ask for short of being born the heir of some great fortune.

Now she spent every waking moment aware of a sort of pressure in the back of her mind. Not painful, just always *there*. And whenever she felt like it, she could fling forward a ball of glittering light that would explode on command, to dazzle and surprise.

Honestly, it was kind of a lame power. Her light balls were barely strong enough to crack a window when thrown and the explosion they let out couldn't even ruffle her hair from sixteen feet away.

She had bought fireworks at a gas station and played with those for a bit, just to confirm that they were, in fact, stronger than her own light balls. The only advantage she had was the strange focus-stealing effect of her power.

Well, that and a few little tweaks. She had the impression she was a little bit stronger now, physically. No more than if she'd been working out more regularly, though. She could also stare into the sun without any harm, and her vision adapted to light and darkness much faster than before.

All in all, not as impressive as flight or laser eyes or superstrength, but she'd work with it.

She had plans. Meet the local Heroes. Make a name for herself as an up-and-comer, make friends with people who might be stronger but who weren't as socially adept. Then ride that gravy train into the bright future.

Then the Boss and her army of brats happened.

Jezebelle was a mature enough woman to understand that blaming one woman and a bunch of preteens for all her troubles was immature. But she could trace most of her recent ills to the Boss's presence.

So she was going to do what any mature, self-confident young lady would do. She would politely confront the Boss and figure out just what in the heck was going on.

That required that she actually *find* the Boss though.

She could track down Emily easily enough, but the last time she'd talked to Emily the girl had messed up her plans terribly right after. It was possible that she didn't appreciate anyone interfering in her civilian life, which Jezebelle supposed was fair.

Jezebelle and Glamazon weren't even two sides of the same coin, they were the same person with a slight wardrobe change.

Emily kept her identity as the Boss a bit further apart. It was probably not a terrible idea. Emily had managed to insert herself as the leader of a whole team. Jezebelle had done a little digging and she couldn't find anything on any of the brats who followed the Boss around. For that matter, she knew the HRF didn't have anything on them either. It had gotten to the point where if they wanted to find out, they'd have to start *actively* looking and that was usually a move only reserved for particularly violent Villains.

As long as everyone could take off the mask and go back home, then both the Heroes and the Villains had good reason to pull their punches.

Long story short, when she heard that the brats—sans Boss—were patrolling, she went out to meet them.

And that had been something of a mistake.

"Oh hey, it's sparkly lady," the bear-themed girl said while pointing right at her. The bear girl rubbed at her nose while giving Jezebelle the stink eye. "What'ch'a doing out here? Huh? Trying to be all Heroic?"

"Hello," Jezebelle said. She put on her most winning customer-service smile. She hadn't been able to go to college straight from high school so she had spent two years working reception. It was awful, but also decent experience when it came to dealing with people.

The brats weren't alone. There was the bear girl, Ursa Minor; Owlwatch in her leather coat and "I'm a little punk" outfit; two of the three bandit girls; and . . . another Hero? The woman was about Jezebelle's own age. Taller, dark skin, fashionable enough jeans, and a top with a coat on, and she had a half mask on. Something about the way she dressed suggested that she wasn't a Mask but more of a . . . minion?

Maybe it was the baseball bat. That wasn't a terribly Heroic kind of weapon.

It didn't take a genius to figure out why a troupe of children would have someone a little older along with them. This girl was either the Boss's newest Hero teammate, or a babysitter.

"Hey, girls," Jezebelle said. She smiled and gave them a little wave. "I was just passing through and thought I'd see how you were doing. Are you out on patrol?"

The punk girl, Owlwatch, narrowed her eyes. "Bullpoop," she said. "I bet you're here to spy on us."

Jezebelle rolled her eyes. She wasn't here to spy on the kids, she was here to spy on the Boss. Or something close to spying, at least. The Boss had interfered with her plans a few times already. Jezebelle was old enough to know that things rarely, if ever, went according to plan, but still, the multiple interferences were starting to bother her. Worse, they were making her look bad.

If there was one thing she couldn't afford at the moment, it was looking bad, or worse, incompetent. She needed to find out what the Boss was planning so that she could work her way around that.

She could observe the Boss, chart her actions, create something of a profile of how she acted, then determine what her goals were from that. Or she could just ask.

She was a *Hero*, after all, and asking politely seemed like the Heroic thing to do.

"I'm not here to spy on you," she said. "But, well, do you mind if I accompany you on your patrol? I'm sure if something comes up, one more set of hands won't hurt, will it?"

The girls looked at each other, clearly weighing their options. They wanted to say no, that much was easy to read in their body language, but *could* they?

"No. Go home," Bandit said.

Jezebelle blinked.

She had been operating under the assumption that the kids would act . . . well, like adults did when shoved into an awkward situation. If you cut in line in front of most people, they'd grumble and glare at your back, but they wouldn't tell you off.

Kids didn't have an awkwardness filter. "Uh . . . well, what if you need help?" she asked.

All four children snorted at the same time. Then the bear girl pointed to her. "If we need more glitter, we'll call you."

"Yeah, if we're throwing a birthday party and we need fireworks, we'll let you know," Owlwatch said.

Jezebelle felt herself flushing. These kids were just . . . mean.

"We'll let you work with us if you give us your wallet," one of the Bandit girls said.

Jezebelle didn't know what to say to that. The others were nodding along. "What would you even do with my wallet?"

"Buy ice cream and steal your identity," Bandit said. She opened her dollar-sign bag and held the opening out toward Jezebelle, as if she fully expected her to just toss in her stuff.

"I'm not giving you my wallet."

"Hey, you're Glamazon, yeah?" the possible babysitter asked.

"Yes, yes I am," Jezebelle said. She stood a little taller, hands going to her hips in the standard Heroic pose. "Did you want an autograph?"

The girl shrugged. "Maybe later."

"Hey!" Owlwatch said. "No consorting with the enemy . . . unless you're trying to seduce them into a nefarious scheme, in which case it's okay to consort with them a little."

"Or if you're consorting with their sidekicks to steal them," the other Bandit pointed out.

Jezebelle felt the stirrings of a headache starting.

"Okay," the minion said. "So, see that corner store right there?" She pointed past Jezebelle's shoulder to a store on the corner. It was a gas-station convenience stop. "Watch the brats while they terrorize the place. I need to make a phone call. Thanks!" And with that, the young woman walked off and into an alley.

"What?" Jezebelle asked.

She looked at the four girls staring back at her.

"How much candy money do you have?" Ursa Minor asked.

"None!" Jezebelle said. She had cash, of course, but it wasn't—

"She's lying! She has plenty. Come on!" Owlwatch said.

With a scream, the girls charged toward the shop, leaving Jezebelle planted right there by her lonesome.

"Wait, I'm not actually responsible for you, right?" she called after the children before she sprinted after them. "I said wait!"

What kind of ragtag mess of a team did the Boss operate?!

CHAPTER FIFTY-FIVE

Paying the Price

Emily continued to smile at Glamazon, at least until a few things became clearer.

First, the girl was disheveled. It wasn't fair to say that Jezebelle was one of those women too concerned about fashion for her own good, but Emily would be lying if she hadn't fit the girl into that neat little box already.

Second, her sisters had dirty faces. All of them. That mostly included bright neon-colored stains around their lips and on their hands, and now that she was paying attention, Teddy and Trinity were making crunching sounds as they walked, and their pockets were very full.

"One moment," Emily said with a finger raised toward Glamazon. She turned toward Athena, who Emily trusted to know what would happen if she lied. The owl girl blanched, then glanced at her sisters before refocusing on Emily.

"It was Glamazon," she said before Emily could ask anything. The girl pointed to the young Hero's back, entirely willing and able to toss her under the bus.

"What?" Glamazon asked. "What was me?"

"Why do the kids have what I hope are some sort of food-related stains all over their faces?"

Glamazon straightened. "That's not my fault! She"—she turned and pointed at Sam—"left me with the kids and they ran to the corner store, then I had to run after them and they kept opening things and eating them *right there*. Without even paying! The cashier thought it was cute for, like, a minute, then this one started going through their trash, that one started to ask about buying lottery tickets, and that one just lay down in the middle of the beer fridge!"

Emily blinked. "Did she drink anything?" she asked.

"Like, two sodas," Teddy said.

Emily stared at the bear girl, who shuffled on the spot.

"Okay, six."

Emily took a deep breath and was about to ask a few pertinent questions, but it seemed that Glamazon wasn't done. In fact, her rant had only just begun. "By the time I got her up, the other three had made a mess of the place. They raided the freezer and were trying one of every kind of Popsicle. Each! The cashier screamed at me, then their manager showed up and they screamed at me some more, then I had to pay for everything. Do you have any idea how overpriced convenience-store junk food is?"

"But it's so tasty," Trinity said.

"No, it's not! It's terrible for your health, and your teeth!" Glamazon said.

"Well . . ." Emily began. She thought about it for a moment, then nodded and continued, "We appreciate your donation to our cause. I'm sure the girls have all said thank you, right?"

The girls froze up for a second, then they smiled at Glamazon with teeth painted in different candy shades. There was a chorus of "thank yous" that all sounded both very sweet, and utterly perfunctory.

"Seriously?" Glamazon asked. She crossed her arms, looking entirely unamused. "I'm out sixty bucks from all that."

"Sixty bucks?!" Emily exclaimed. That was . . . well, actually she wasn't too surprised. Her brats could rack up a huge bill in no time. "Wow. I'm sorry."

"So . . . you're not going to pay me back?" Glamazon asked.

Emily winced.

Glamazon closed her eyes and sighed. "Wow. You know what, fine. It's only, like, my entire week's food budget."

"Oh, look, we got some snacks for Map— er, the other girl, too!" Trinity said. She opened her bag revealing a couple of candy bars and bags of chips stuffed in the bottom.

"Oh my god, they— We didn't pay for those," Glamazon said. She sounded more exasperated than anything else. Emily calmed her down before she could lose her cool any more than she had.

"Don't worry about it," she said. "I'll, uh, take care of it." And by that she meant do nothing. The place was probably one of Sam's targets for her protection racket anyway. Which, now that she thought about it, was kind of messed up and the fact that she was thinking that way wasn't exactly painting things in the most Heroic light. "So I imagine you wanted to talk about something? Or did you just want to have the single-mom experience for an afternoon?"

Glamazon snorted. "No, no, I think I've gotten my fill. Like, wow, I might need to call my mom after this and, like, apologize. Although I don't think I was as bad as, uh, anyway, yeah, I wanted to chat."

Emily nodded along, then gestured down the road. "Let's walk at the same time? I don't like sitting still." And people were staring. At least if Emily and her sisters and Glamazon moved, it would make the job of any eavesdropper that much harder. And maybe it would keep Glamazon off balance while giving Emily more time to think between replies.

"Yeah, sure," Glamazon said. They started walking at a sedate pace and Emily didn't fail to notice that her sisters were basically surrounding the Hero on all sides, with Teddy between herself and the costumed woman. If something went wrong, Teddy would probably go bear right away. "So I wanted to talk."

"Yes," Emily said.

She let the awkwardness roll over and past her. She was born in the awkward, molded by it. Glamazon was clearly not. The woman squirmed and looked a little pinched.

"Right, well, I just want to know what's going on."

Emily scowled at nothing, then turned toward Glamazon. "With regard to what?" she asked.

"With regard to . . . well, you. Look, I was under the impression you weren't playing the game, but then every time I turn around you're there. I'm not saying you're not allowed or whatever, but I feel like we're working at cross-purposes even though we should be on the same side."

Glamazon, Emily realized, really didn't know that Emily wasn't a Hero at all. That was probably for the best. "I know," Emily said. "And I guess I'm sorry. I've just been doing what I think is best. For me and my sis— my team."

"That includes making a spectacle of taking out other Heroes?" Glamazon asked. "You know, Black Shield was released without anything happening. Wrap Up, too. Though he ended up spending the night at the headquarters. None of your accusations panned out."

"That's strange," Emily said. "No one did or said anything to me about it."

"I . . . actually, yeah, that is strange."

Emily nodded. "Probably because they know the accusation is not entirely baseless. Glamazon, I think we don't see the world the same way. You trust the people in charge a lot more than I do, the institutions that regulate Heroes and punish Villains."

"Yeah, of course I trust them, they're the good guys," Glamazon said.

"Wow," Athena said. "Talk about simple."

"All glitter, no brains," Teddy said.

Glamazon puffed up, but she took control of herself. Emily imagined it would take more than a few insults to get her to insult her sisters back, which was actually a pretty good indicator of Glamazon's personality.

"I'm sorry about them," Emily said. She eyed her sisters. "They're going to apologize. Right?"

Teddy and Athena delivered a pair of unfelt apologies with all the charm and poise of a receptionist calling out someone's number at the license bureau near the end of a twelve-hour shift.

"You're forgiven," Glamazon replied, her voice entirely flat.

"Setting all that aside," Emily said. "Look, Glamazon, I don't think we need to work against each other at all. We just had different goals and happened to clash. Or I guess that's what happened. What are your goals?"

"I want to become a good Hero," Glamazon said. "And I suppose I'd like a bit of recognition, too. Not unearned recognition, though. What about you? It's only fair that you tell me if I told you, right?"

"All right," Emily said. "Well, my goal . . . I guess it's to make the city safe. Make a place for my family in it where no one will bother us."

"And that involves getting Heroes arrested?" Glamazon asked.

"It might involve rooting out corruption," Emily said. She didn't add that she wanted to root that corruption out to install her own weird brand in its place. "Removing any Villains from this city." Villains who weren't her or her sisters. "And helping the city prosper." So that the businesses in the city didn't feel so bad paying her protection money.

Glamazon eyed Emily from the corner of her vision, then she stopped walking and faced Emily head-on. "You really believe in all that conspiracy stuff, don't you?"

"Weren't you approached by them?" Emily asked.

Glamazon worked her jaw. "Maybe. I don't actually know. It was all . . . vague, I guess. But it didn't sound like bad business at the time."

"Sometimes, Villainy can be very subtle. You might be looking right at it and not know," Emily said.

Sam snorted in the background, but Glamazon didn't seem to notice.

"Right, okay. In that case, do you want to work together? I've got some plans, and I guess we could use an army of brats. Think of it as paying me back for the Popsicles."

CHAPTER FIFTY-SIX

Unflippable, Unflappable

It's a stupid idea, Boss," Teddy said.

Emily stared across the desk at her first little sister. The bear girl was sitting, but she was leaning forward with her arms crossed and her face set in a big pout.

"There's some risk," Emily admitted. "But I don't think it's dangerous enough to call it stupid."

"That's because that stupid Hero caught you with her stupid evil ways," Teddy said. "Did she try to entice you with capitalism while I wasn't paying attention? Maybe she offered insurance, or private health care?"

"No," Emily said. "She only offered to work with us for a day. Not much more than a patrol really. I don't think it's a terrible idea."

Emily, her sisters, Sam, and Alea Iacta were all gathered in the planning room segment of the train. Emily was in her place at the head of the table while the other seats were occupied by her sisters and minions.

She realized that maybe the whole Villain thing was getting ahead of her and she had no idea how to stop it. Working with Glamazon wasn't going to help with that, but it might help provide some form of basic cover. And an alibi of sorts, if only a relatively weak one.

"Did you give Sparkles a hard yes?" Sam asked. She had been a little ways back when that part of the conversation had gone down. Not so far that she didn't hear the sisters' nickname for Glamazon.

"I didn't," Emily said. "But we did trade numbers."

Sam's eyebrows shot up. "All right. That's a bold move."

"Yeah, I never get digits and I'm unnaturally lucky," Alea Iacta said.

"It's not like that," Emily said.

Sam grinned at her. "Oh, don't worry, I know you're not like that."

Emily had no idea what that was supposed to mean and she was certain she didn't want to find out. "Anyway," she pressed on. "I gave Glamazon the number for this phone." She reached into a pocket and pulled out a flip phone, one that had clearly seen better days a decade ago.

"That's not your normal phone," Sam noted.

"Um."

Everyone paused and looked to Maple, who sank into her seat at the sudden attention. "It's all right," Emily said. "Did you have a question?"

Maple nodded, then took a moment to muster up her bravery. "Is that a special Villain phone?"

Emily smiled. "No. It's a cheap old thing with a prepaid card in it. Just something to use if I don't want my real number to be out there."

"I hear the HRF give out special phones to Heroes who ask for them. Even if you're not a member of the organization. You know, for emergencies," Sam said. "They claim that they're untrackable. You know, so that Heroes can keep their IDs separate."

"I'm certain that they wouldn't extend that courtesy to a Villain, though. This is easier," Emily said while wiggling the phone around.

"I could make the phone better, if you want," Maple said.

"Oh?"

Maple nodded slowly, but she seemed a little more confident. "I could turn it into a Taser, or a mini flamethrower. Or I could make it really, really loud. Oh! I can make it unflippable."

"Unflippable?" Sam asked.

Maple nodded. "You wouldn't be able to flip it anymore."

Emily blinked at the phone, then slid it back into her pocket. "I'll keep those options in mind," she said. She made a mental note to find some things for Maple to use her powers on. She didn't want her newest little sister to feel unwanted, and it seemed important to Maple that she could make things to help them.

"I got some stuff for Maple," Trinity said just as Emily was thinking on it. The girl tipped her bag up onto the table and a bunch of junk spilled out of it. There were a few empty cans, a hair straightener, some candy wrappers, some actual candy—though less than Trinity had earlier, Emily noted—a few pebbles, some cut tie-wraps, and some earbuds with a heavily frayed wire.

It was all trash, and Emily wasn't sure she wanted it on her table. That is, until Maple let out a heartfelt gasp that had Emily's heart squeezing tight. "For me?" she asked.

"Yeah," Trinity said. She was obviously quite proud of her hard work. "Make me a gun so that I can rob people with it."

"No," Emily jumped in.

Maple shook her head. "Big Sister said no weapons. But, um, I'm sure I can make other stuff with all this." She carefully pawed through the junk, as if looking for something she could do with it.

Emily rubbed at the bridge of her nose. "Okay. Maple, we're going to go to a pawnshop. I'm sure we can pick up a few things you can use there. We don't need anything specific right now, so we'll just get you some things for you to play with, all right?"

Maple turned to her, wide-eyed. "Oh, really? Yes, okay, thank you." It looked like she couldn't decide between being excited and being quiet, so everything came out as a suppressed squeak.

"Sam, how are our financials?" Emily asked. Half the goal of the meeting was to make sure everything was in order.

"Not bad," Sam said. "Actually, pretty good. Here." Sam reached into her purse and pulled out a crumpled envelope, which she tossed onto the table. It was stuffed full of cash.

"H-how much is that?" Emily asked.

"Oh, less than it looks. That's mostly fives and tens. At least a grand?"

Alea Iacta hummed as he nodded. "I mean, for one day's work, that's not bad."

"And we were promised monthly payments, too," Sam said. She started rooting around in her purse again and came out with a piece of paper she unfolded. "More for all the advertising stuff. I've drawn up a schedule. Can you confirm the free days the brats have? I don't want to promise they'll show up on a day they can't."

Emily took the paper and discovered a very orderly calendar, with each day split into thirds for morning, afternoon, and evening shifts. A few spots were penciled in already, mostly for the bakery they'd visited. "Well, the kids have school," Emily started.

"None of us mind missing school for doing Villain stuff," Teddy said.

"I don't wanna miss math, but the rest is boring," Trinity said.

Emily shook her head. She wasn't going to allow the kids to let their education fall behind too much. She might exploit them for work, but she wasn't entirely evil. "No, we'll keep the time you spend in school marked. It's important. Um. We also need to make sure you have regular breaks."

"Yeah, don't want this to be one of those capitalist things where you end up spending every waking moment working," Teddy said. She made a disgusted face. "Overtime. Ew."

"Don't worry," Emily said. "No overtime, not unless there's a serious emergency." Mostly that was because she could barely handle her sisters as it was. Overtime would lead to her early demise. "How about we rotate days off? You don't have school on Saturday and Sunday, so we can switch between those as break days."

"Might want more than just one a week," Sam said. "Kids need playtime and such."

"We really do," Teddy agreed.

"Yeah, lots of that." Trinity bounced in her seat.

Athena made an affirmative sound. "I agree."

Emily refrained from rolling her eyes. "Fine, let's mark out Tuesday and Thursday, maybe, as days where there's only school and nothing else. I need time to catch up on my homework, too, so it makes sense."

"Gotta keep those grades up, huh?" Sam asked.

"I don't want to fail out of my classes," Emily replied. "All right, other than that . . . Alea, how's Fabien doing?"

"Huh? Oh, he's all right. Mostly lying low, I think. We've been playing a lot of . . . anyway, never mind that. Did you have a job for him or anything?"

"No, but when Glamazon and I go out on that joint patrol, I think he might want to stay home that day," Emily said.

"Yeah. We need him to act as a sort of decoy. Attack a business the kids are protecting to make a big show of how much our protection racket is worth," Sam said.

Emily shifted in her seat. Sometimes it just hit her how much she'd spiraled into Villainy without really thinking about it. Then again, no one would be hurt by that kind of thing. It was all a show. She wondered if the Cabal thought the same way.

"So the only other worry we have is the Cabal. If they're actually a worry at all." Emily hadn't had any run-ins with any of them in a while. Maybe their interests wouldn't interfere with each other and they could happily coexist?

She doubted it.

CHAPTER FIFTY-SEVEN

The Wrong Sort of Nap

Maple tried to look on the bright side of things.

It wasn't easy for her to do that, but with a bit of effort, she could manage. Big Sister Emily was very important and very busy. She couldn't be there with Maple every day, after all, and it was normal that Maple would have to take care of some things without Big Sister's help. If she wanted to be a big girl, then she'd need to learn how to take care of herself.

The thing was, Maple didn't want to be a big girl, she wanted to be a small one that Big Sister Emily could grab and hug, and one who could cuddle with her sisters.

She shook her head and put on a brave face. No. She was Maple. A brave Villain working with the best Super Villain ever. She wasn't about to get teary-eyed just because Big Sister didn't have time for her.

"Hey, kiddo, you ready to go?" Alea Iacta asked.

Maple glanced up, then nodded. "Yes, I'm ready," she said.

Today, she and Alea and Trinity were heading out to buy some stuff! That was going to be fun. Maple had so many projects swimming in her mind all the time. Every time she looked at something she could think of a dozen ways to break it apart and make something new with it. So far she'd been careful not to have a repeat of the toaster gun, but she still made a few small and useful items.

The toilet paper dispenser in the train's bathroom was now automatic and rolled out a number of squares based on the amount of sound generated while in the bathroom (she was still fine-tuning it). And it could change toilet paper rolls itself, like the way shells were loaded into a battleship's main gun.

The kitchen's sink used to only produce lukewarm water. Now it could make everything from ice to water-based plasma! (They'd been learning about the different states of matter in school.) Also, instead of having a big tank that needed to be refilled, the train now had a big tank that filled itself up by pulling water out of the air.

Mostly, her new gizmos were little things. Stuff that Big Sister probably wouldn't even notice, but that Maple thought could make their lives better. She didn't have much to work with, but that would change after their trip.

Big Sister had given Alea Iacta a big stack of bills and told him to buy whatever Maple wanted until they ran out.

Maple was practically shaking. She was so excited. They were going to the dollar store! She could build so many things from the stuff there!

"All right," Alea Iacta said. He slipped on a coat and then put on a baseball cap with the name of the school Emily went to on the front. "If anyone asks, I'm, like, your uncle or something."

Trinity grinned. "You could be our big bro," she said.

"No, I'd really rather not," Alea replied.

Maple tilted her head to the side as she thought about it. Why wouldn't he want to suddenly have five new sisters? She'd been born with four, and it was fantastic. "You could be our daddy," she said, offering up another option.

Alea recoiled. "No! No, just . . . absolutely not. Please never even suggest anything of the sort. In fact, scrub the word from your vocabulary."

Maple didn't know how to do that, but she was sure she could make something for it. Almost instantly she had plans in her mind for a massive machine that would erase everyone on Earth's knowledge of the word *daddy*. It would be tricky to make, though; she needed a lot of stuff for that, like at least three dollar stores' worth of stuff.

It wasn't a weapon, though, so she'd be allowed to make it if she wanted.

"All right, are you two ready to go?" he asked before grinning. "Or is it more like you one and one-third?"

Trinity eyed him suspiciously. "That's a dad joke," she said.

"Okay, first of all, not all wordplay is a dad joke. Second, no, just no." He glanced at Maple and Trinity. "Are you coming dressed like that?"

Maple didn't know if there was anything wrong with her outfit. She had a nice pastel pink skirt and a paler pink blouse, and of course her trusty lab coat. "Yes?" she asked.

"All right. Well, at least it hides the tail. Here." Alea opened a closet near the train's exit and found a pale blue beret. He placed it onto Maple's head. "To hide your ears," he said.

"Oh, I found a hat in the trash I can wear!" Trinity said. She reached into her dollar-sign bag—which she was going to leave behind because it was part of her Villain/Hero persona—and pulled out a ratty baseball cap.

"What about your tail?" Alea asked.

"What about it?" Trinity asked. She had jeans on, with a hole at the back for her bushy black-and-white tail.

"Never mind. All right, let's head out." Alea Iacta said. He helped Maple down from the final step out of the train, but Trinity just jumped down the gap with a big *oof* on landing. She instantly bounced back to her feet with a cheer. "What did I do to deserve this?" Alea muttered.

They headed out of the underground through one of the hidden shafts that Alea Iacta had found. The moment they were out, they started to walk along the sidewalk on their way toward the nearest shopping area. They came to the first intersection they had to cross and waited while the little stick figure went from red to green.

"Um," Maple said. She fidgeted with her hands.

"Yeah?" Alea asked.

"Uh, Mister Alea? I mean, Uncle? I think we're supposed to hold hands when crossing the street?" Maybe if she phrased it as a question it wouldn't be so bad?

Alea looked at her, then frowned. "Seriously?" he asked.

"Yeah, old man, don't you know anything?" Trinity asked. "Now hand over those digits."

"Digits? You mean my fingers? That's not how . . . never mind." He let his hands drop and Maple carefully held on to his index and middle finger as they crossed the road. Alea's attitude improved when they crossed some girls who were about Big Sister's age and they made cooing sounds while looking at Maple and Trinity. "All right, maybe this isn't the worst thing in the world," he said. "Like having a dog, but more annoying."

Their first stop was the dollar store. Alea Iacta kept a firm hold on Trinity, which prevented Maple's sister from darting around and making a mess of things. Maple, in the meantime, asked how much money she had to work with and then very carefully picked a few things from the shelves.

Sometimes she had to shyly point to something that was too high for her to grab and Alea would pick it up and toss it into their cart.

She didn't get nearly as much stuff as she wanted to, but by the time they'd gone through every aisle, the cart was halfway full of all sorts of stuff.

"Don't," Alea said at some point when he caught Trinity reaching for a candy bar. "I'm basically running on fumes here. Half the reason I agreed to come was to steal a bit of luck from people out here. So don't push it, all right?"

They paid for the stuff, and soon they left the store with big bags full of all sorts of neat things. Universal remotes, a few of those crack-back cars, some water guns, and plenty of arts and crafts supplies.

Maple could build so many things with what she had already, and she still had a third of her spending money left!

The hardware store seemed like an obvious place to check out, but it turned out to be a bust. It contained tons of good things, but mostly they were big things. Although Maple really wanted to buy some generators, and she could do a lot with plumbing stuff, it was all a bit much for her budget.

The hobbyist shop was a better bet, though. It was down on a quieter street and had plenty of things on sale that she picked up. Little tools and paints and glues.

"Happy?" Alea asked as they left. Her budget was down to the single digits. Maple was going to spend it on candy for herself and Trinity and Alea, as thanks for helping her so much.

"Yes!" she said as she exited the shop.

Maple didn't know what happened, but there was a swishing sound. Rough hands grabbed her from behind, and she heard Trinity use one of the forbidden words very loudly before someone grunted and said, "She bit me!"

Then the world went dark.

CHAPTER FIFTY-EIGHT

I'm Not Locked in Here with You

"Oh-oh," Trinity said. She said it from every available body, which was just two of them at the moment. The third was currently sleeping, which was a very strange feeling to be feeling.

It was like having an arm be asleep, but it was the entire body, and it was only one-third asleep. Trinity had to suppress a yawn to fight off the strange feeling.

Big Sister Emily looked up from her laptop where she was trying to do homework. "What is it?" she asked.

"There's a problem," Trinity said.

Big Sister sighed. "What happened?" she asked. "Did you go over budget? Were you caught stealing? I told you not to."

Trinity shook her head. "No no, nothing like that."

"Well, then it can't be that bad," Emily said. "What happened? Will I have to call Alea?"

Trinity considered it for a moment. What had happened before that guy in the black jumpsuit grabbed her and made her smell that stinky rag? She recalled seeing Maple go to sleep, too, and . . . yeah, Alea Iacta was definitely grabbed, too. He'd made a groaning sound and Trinity was pretty sure someone had punched him in the kidney. "I don't think he could answer."

Emily shook her head, her attention straying back to her laptop.

"I don't think the kidnappers would let him use his phone."

Big Sister's head whipped around so hard Trinity was worried she might hurt herself. "The *what*?"

"Oh, I guess they're not kidnappers if they took Alea Iacta, because he's not a kid, right?" Trinity asked. She looked to her other sisters for confirmation.

Teddy tapped her chin, then nodded. "Adultnappers," she suggested.

"I'm pretty sure it's still kidnapping even if you're an adult," Athena said.

"That's stupid," Teddy said, and Trinity couldn't help but agree.

"Can we please go back to the part where Alea Iacta was kidnapped?" Emily asked. Her volume had risen a lot, it was almost at "outdoor" voice levels. Trinity wondered if Big Sister would have to punish herself with no prebedtime candy if she raised her own voice?

"Okay, so Maple and Alea Iacta and one of me were doing shopping stuff for Maple," Trinity said. "Then we left a shop and a few guys in these black suits grabbed us and made us sniff these bits of cloth, and then Maple and I fell asleep," Trinity said.

Emily bounced to her feet. "No," she said.

"Uh," Trinity said. She didn't want to contradict Big Sister, but that was pretty much what happened.

"Sounds like a normal kidnapping to me," Teddy said. "Can we eat them? We're the Villains here, we're the ones who kidnap."

"Where are they taking you?" Emily asked.

"I don't know, I'm asleep," Trinity said.

Emily cursed, then she brushed her hair back. "Cabal, or HRF. HRF are more official, they'd arrest Alea first. No, this has to be the Cabal, or someone else." She started pacing. "I can . . . I can teleport one of you back here. Not Alea Iacta, though."

"Oh, leave me," Trinity said. "I can just bash my head open or something and then revive here. Maybe they'll have toasters and bathtubs in whatever Villain prison they have."

Emily hesitated, then nodded. "Athena, go get Sam, tell her it's an emergency. Teddy, Trinity, get dressed, we're going to the base, in case they've tagged Maple with a tracker or something. I swear if they hurt a hair on one of my sisters' heads I will burn them," Big Sister growled.

Trinity felt a cold shiver run down her spine. A cool one, because Big Sister sounded awesome. "What about me?" Trinity asked.

"We'll teleport you out as soon as the skill has finished its cooldown," Emily said.

Trinity nodded. She wasn't in any sort of danger. Or only a third of her was, which was an acceptable risk as far as she was concerned.

They grabbed their things. Villain costumes and some gear and, of course, snacks for the road and warmer coats, then they tumbled out of their rooms to find Sam waiting for them. "What's going on?" Sam asked.

"Maple, Alea, and Trinity were kidnapped," Emily explained.

"Oh," Sam said. "Let me get my minion gear then."

It only took a few minutes for them to leave the dorm and head out to the nearest entrance into the metro system. Trinity knew that everyone was taking things seriously because no one had asked for a pee break halfway out of the house and the mood had changed. Usually there was lots of bouncing around and fun and Teddy would argue with Athena while Sam chatted. Now they were all quiet and very focused; angry, almost.

Emily stomped forward. The few times they encountered people they scampered away at a single glance from Big Sister who was clearly channeling all her Villainy and scariness to be as intimidating as possible.

They slid into one of the entrances to the underground under an overpass and Emily immediately went to one of the rooms with a cot in it. She raised her hands over the bed and muttered something.

A blink later, Maple appeared then came bouncing down onto the little bed. Emily was on her almost immediately, checking her for wounds while patting her head. Maple had come with one of her bags from the dollar store. Her mouth was taped shut, and she had a sort of balaclava on her face, but without holes for the eyes.

"Sam, can you check online for what to do if someone breathes in too much chloroform?" Emily asked.

"Not even the weirdest search on my history this week," Sam muttered as she took out her phone.

Emily sent Teddy to get some scissors—without running—then laid Maple down so that the gadgeteer was more comfortable on the bed. "Come on, wake up, sweetie." She carefully peeled the tape off Maple's face.

Athena came in the room with a small bucket with a rag and some soap, which earned her some thanks from Big Sister Emily, who used it to wash some of the tape residue away.

Maple groaned and turned away from the ministrations, then she blinked and looked around, obviously confused. "Huh?" she asked.

"Oh, thank goodness," Emily said. She pulled Maple up into a big, tight-tight hug. "You're okay, you're okay, right?"

"Uh? Wait, Big Sister? Where am I? My head hurts." That got her some more Healpats, then more hugs as everyone joined in. No one was going to say no to group hugs. They were hardened Villains, not morons.

"This is touching and all," Sam said. "But we need to ask Maple what she knows, then we need to figure out what to do from here."

"Right," Emily said. "They still have one of Trinity, and Alea Iacta, too."

"I can save myself," Trinity said.

Emily nodded. "And you'll do just that. If they start to hurt you, you tell me right away and we'll get you out of there."

"In the meantime, though," Sam said. "Can't Trinity teleport stuff between herself?"

"I can!" Trinity said.

"Cool. So if we give her a tracking device of some sort, and she gives it to her . . . other self, then we'll know where they're taking her, right?"

"I don't exactly have that kind of thing lying around," Emily said.

Maple squirmed. "Oh, uh, I can make something like that."

Everyone glanced at her, then back to one another. "Okay, that's a plan," Emily said. "Maple, are you sure? You've been through a lot."

Maple nodded. "Yes. I want to help . . . please?"

That clinched it, and soon they took Maple to the minibase's dining room where Maple got to work. The tracker needed to be small enough to fit into one of Trinity's pockets, or maybe her mouth, so Maple looked for small stuff to work with. "I need an old phone, one of those with a little antenna, oh, maybe a flippy one, and I need a garage door remote, or a TV remote. I also need some blinky lights, and some socks."

"I've got socks!" Teddy said as she undid her boots.

"I'll go to the corner store," Sam said. "They sell prepaid phones, I'll grab a couple."

"Oh, um, if you see a map, that would be nice, too," Maple said.

Sam nodded, then ran off. In the meantime, Maple started to take apart an alarm clock and some pens and other stuff that they'd found around the base.

When Sam returned, Maple got to work right away. Within a few minutes, her hands were moving so smoothly it was hard to keep track of what she was doing, Maple created a trio of small devices. One had a rubber keypad over glowy numbers next to a ring that she placed on a map of the city, and the other two were smaller gizmos with batteries and antenna and some blinky lights.

"This one is for you," Maple said.

Trinity took it, then put it into her pocket. A moment later, it was in her cheek, on her other body, the one that was still sleeping.

"Got it!" Maple cheered. She placed the ring atop the map, and the glowing numbers glowed more toward one side than the other. They continued to blink on one side until the circle was atop a specific street, but Maple had to keep moving the circle along the road. "So, um, that's where the tracker is," she said.

"Well, then," Sam said. "That's a location. Now what?"

CHAPTER FIFTY-NINE

You're Locked in Here with Me

Jacob woke up with a pounding headache, a dry mouth, and a squirming gut.

He was a college student, so most of that wasn't entirely unusual.

What did make the situation a little more precarious was the way his hands were currently duct-taped to the arms of a rather uncomfortable chair. He tried to move his legs. Those were secured, too.

He also noted with dawning horror that he was stripped down to his tighty-whities and was currently in a rather plain, windowless room with a table set right in front of him and his clothes were nowhere to be found. He licked his lips and noticed a distinct lack of alcohol breath. So this wasn't the morning after a party.

Stretching his mind back, he tried to think of what had happened to him last. He had been babysitting two of the Boss's brats. The raccoon one (or one of its bodies? He wasn't entirely sure how that girl's power worked. He might have been with the original, or one of her clones, unless they weren't clones at all. Really, he tried not to think about it too much) and the new girl with the buckteeth and the big flat tail.

Beaver girl had a little budget and was using it all on random odds and ends. He didn't pretend to understand how gadget makers worked, but he imagined that she was going to turn some of those things into weapons of mass destruction, or just toys, because that was how the Boss and her crew of misfits operated.

He often questioned his luck-based powers, especially after they landed him right in the Boss's lap.

Speaking of which . . . he blinked a few times and looked around the room. The smart thing to do would probably have been to play dead, but it was a bit too late for that. "Hello!" he screamed.

"Hi!"

Jacob jumped in his seat and turned around. There were two more chairs behind him, smaller ones. One was empty, but the other had a familiar girl sitting in it. "Oh," he said. "You're here. Wait, where's Maple?"

Trinity wiggled a hand out from the duct tape holding it in place, then pressed a finger over her lips in a "shhh" gesture. "We don't talk about what happened to Maple," she said.

He noted that she was still in her clothes, which, actually, that was for the best. He already disliked his captors on principle, but at least they had some morals. "Do you know who captured us?"

"Nope! But maybe you'd know if you didn't spend so much time sleeping. You snored while they took your pants."

Maybe the captors could have spared some tape for the girl's mouth.

"Thanks, I'm glad to know," he said a bit sourly. He knew that most people treated kids with a bit of respect and care, but most people didn't have to deal with the Boss's terrifying brats all the time. "Any, uh, word from . . . yeah, never mind. Did you get a look at who captured us?"

"B-rated minions," Trinity said with confidence. "Not even proper minions, really, mere mooks, I think. One or two of them look like they might be goons."

"I don't know what any of that means," he said.

"Minions are people who work for a Villain, it kind of covers all of them, like, there's kinds of cans, yeah? But if they're empty then they're all trash. Mooks are minions that are hired to do something. They're trained but it's, like, a job for them. And goons are like mooks but they're gooder at fighting. There's also henchpeople, hirelings, mercenaries, scrubs, drones, small fry, pawns, grunts, cannon fodder, and a bunch of others, but they're all just flavors of minion."

"Uh-huh," he said. He was used to the brats being a bit dumb, so it always took him off guard when they had a lot of very specific knowledge into a specific subject. That fact that it was all Villainy-related should probably have bothered him more than it did. "Any plan to get out of here?"

"Yeah, don't worry," Trinity said.

"And where's Maple?" he asked with a glance to the other seat. Were they . . . no, he didn't want to imagine someone torturing one of the kids. That was too evil by half.

The door opened up and he spun back around to face it. "That's what we would like to know," a gruff voice asked.

A shorter, stocky man stepped into the room. He was wearing a suit and tie, a teal one, like a wedding singer from the late eighties, but there were little fireballs and lightning bolts patterned on the suit. His shirt, at least, was plain and white.

"You look weird," Trinity said.

The two behind the man were what Jacob assumed Trinity would call mooks. Two bigger guys in black jumpsuits with full-face masks that hugged their faces and didn't let any part of their expressions through. They had guns strapped to their hips and a few other things in their belts besides. What concerned him were the knuckle dusters they were fixing on.

"I look weird, do I?" the man asked.

"Yeah," Trinity said. "Like, if I saw what you were wearing in the trash, I wouldn't even take it."

The man sniffed. "Do you often root around in the trash?"

"Yes," Trinity said without even a hint of hesitation.

"She's weird like that," Jacob said. He felt at his reserves of luck and held back a wince. He was bottomed out. With the amount of luck he had, he would be worried about crossing a road without getting hit. Even eating was going to be a high-risk activity. He had good odds of choking on every other bite.

His reserves hadn't been that low earlier on. Half the reason he agreed to accompany Maple (and where was she, anyway?) was to steal a bit of luck here and there to replenish his reserves. The morning hadn't been superproductive, but he'd grabbed a bit.

A few strands from a lady who didn't pick up her dog's droppings, a smidge from a guy who tossed trash out of his car window, some more from a guy who was rude to a cashier. Little bits that wouldn't be easily noticed. Taking someone's luck felt like intestinal cramping, but most people who felt a little of that would pass it off as passing gas and would make a point not to react.

His tank was empty. The rest had probably been used up while he was out of it.

"So, where's the girl?" the man before him asked.

"Uh, you're not going to do introductions first?" Jacob asked.

Then the man slapped him across the face and Jacob reeled back.

Trinity laughed. "Wow, that was weak," she said. "Where's your monologue? Where's the scariness?"

Jacob worked his jaw. "I think I'm a bit scared, to be honest," he said. It was true, too.

"That's because you're lame," Trinity said. "If it was the Boss, she'd have you so scared you'd be peeing yourself. I bet she'd find a way to get sharks and, like, a big vat of acid and, like, chains so that you're hanging upside down over the acid with the sharks in it. Oh, and then she'd ask questions, but they'd only be for fun because she already read your mind and knows all your deep dark secrets so you're just hanging there and learning that there's nothing you can do while still covered in pee and about to be dropping in the acid shark tank."

The mooks and the guy with the weird suit were all looking at Trinity now. He couldn't read their expressions, but he had the impression they were worried.

"Anyway. She's coming here soon, so don't worry."

"I doubt that," suit guy said.

Trinity grinned, then spat something out that landed on the table in a pool of saliva. It was a small device, with a few twisted wires and some flashing lights.

"What is that?" the man asked. "Didn't anyone frisk her?"

"We did, sir," one of the mooks said.

"Then where was that?" he snapped.

Trinity laughed. "It wasn't made yet! Maple made it, and now she's coming here with the toaster gun!" She grinned. "The Boss is coming, too, and she's going to smack the heck out of you."

The man swiped the device off the table then gave it to one of the mooks. "Go find out what this is. Hurry."

"Yessir," the mook said before darting away.

Suitguy turned and pointed to Trinity. "Where did the other girl go?"

"Home."

"And where's that?" he asked.

She stuck her tongue out at him. "I'm not telling you."

He slammed a hand against the table, then leaned forward. "Do you think I'm beyond squeezing the information out of you?"

"What are you gonna do, kill me? I'm more afraid of disappointing the Boss than I'll ever be of dying. There's nothing you can do to me that'll make me fear you more than that." She cackled. "Can you feel it? Can you feel the Boss coming? She's going to teach you all about Villainy, and there's nothing you can do about it."

He slammed the desk again, but doing it twice only made him look petulant. "Do you have no respect for your situation?"

Trinity giggled in his face. "You can't hurt me in a way that matters, trash suit man, so run away and hide, but even that won't matter, because we'll find you, and when we do, you'll only wish you could die without consequences."

Jacob swallowed and desperately wished he wasn't in the room with the insane guy and the more insane girl.

The Frustration of Falling Apart

Spin to Win was, understandably, frustrated.

The mission was meant to be simplicity itself. Or . . . as simple as this particular kind of mission could go.

Capturing a Rogue or a Villain or even just a Hero with not-so-Heroic inclinations was *always* a risk. Even if they thought they knew a person's powers, it was possible they were hiding something away or had purposefully obfuscated their abilities.

Worse were people like himself, whose powers allowed them to literally have new powers at the drop of a hat (or the spin of a wheel, as it were). Unaccountable variabilities were *dangerous*.

It was why the interrogation was going to take place in a prepared location that wasn't entirely fortified but entirely disposable, with only one member of the Cabal's powered forces and a couple of dozen unpowered men.

The capture had been textbook. He hadn't been there, of course. His power today turned him into a man in his midthirties with one pained knee and the ability to turn anything he touched into salt, as well as a minor electrokinesis power based on the amount of power stored into nearby salt. It was a middling ability at best, and not one he wanted to take out into the field.

The problems started when his men reported that they'd kidnapped not one person, but three.

That the two others were children was also an issue. It wasn't that he minded grabbing children (hints suggested they were both powered as well), but he knew that many in the organization, including the men protecting and working at the temporary base, wouldn't appreciate them tying a pair of young girls to some chairs and duct-taping their mouths shut.

It was a headache, but he could figure a way around it, *after* the girls woke up.

Of course, just as they were starting to come around, one of them vanished.

He had reviewed the recordings of the room. One moment there was an unidentified powered girl in a chair, held in place at an angle so that her flat tail could flop down the side of the chair. She likely didn't have any sort of power that made her tougher, but they couldn't guess beyond that.

Then, the next moment, she was gone. The ropes holding her in place flopped down, proving that she hadn't just gone invisible—which would have been its own sort of nightmare. The alarm was sounded, and they scrambled to search every room and secure every exit.

No sign of the girl.

Questioning the two remaining subjects a few minutes later had proved equally fruitless. The luck manipulator was either stupid or so smart that he played stupid convincingly. That was actually great for their plans. An idiot was easier to convince than someone clever, and fools didn't hold grudges as long as the smart.

The other's questioning had . . . well, Spin to Win had seen some nasty stuff in his day; he'd faced some real Villains, and not just jumped-up Rogues or people with a darker-gray morality who decided to take on robbery and murder as hobbies, but actual, go-see-a-therapist-about-it, capital-V, Villains.

The girl scared him more than some of those had. The way she smiled, her entire lack of care about her own mortality. It was deeply, disconcertingly wrong.

They'd left the girl and the luck manipulator to stew while Spin to Win considered his options.

Obviously, everything they'd gotten so far would be transmitted to the Cabal's nearest headquarters, but he wasn't going to send anything without putting his own spin on it, as it were.

He requisitioned a desk in the base's main office area, a long room with four workstations where agents were poring over security feeds and plugging away at the endless paperwork that came with operating a clandestine black site, even one as temporary as this one.

"Anything?" he asked as he walked over to one of the stations. There was a woman there, though the only noticeable difference in her uniform was in the chest area of her top. The uniforms were meant to hide details about a person, and that included obfuscating gender where they could.

He knew how uncomfortable the uniforms could be. He'd worn them before, as a man and as a woman, and neither version sat well.

"Sorry, sir," the technician said with a shake of her head. She tapped the opened case where a small compactable laboratory was aiming most of its systems at the tiny device the girl had spat onto the interview room table. "This . . . shouldn't work."

"Gadgeteer tech?" he asked.

She shook her head, then nodded. "I . . . well, yes, but it's more than that. There's a battery to power it, but it's out of juice, but the device hasn't stopped transmitting. It's a high-frequency radio signal. I've managed to isolate and decode it, at least." She gestured to a nearby laptop.

"Impressive," he said. What kind of encryption had they been using to—he looked on the screen. The radio message was in Morse, and it merely spelled out the word *HERE*. "Not entirely subtle," he said.

"The amount of power to boost a signal that strong would drain the average phone battery in a few minutes. This is running off a single empty double-A battery," the technician said. "The antenna is a twisted-up piece of aluminum foil, and the lights are all linked serially. They shouldn't be blinking. Electricity doesn't work that way."

"Definitely a gadgeteer then," he said. "Or someone with a power close enough that it doesn't matter."

To say that this complicated things would be a gross understatement. Spin to Win rubbed at the bridge of his nose. "We're going to need to report this. And mark this location as compromised." He raised his voice. "All right, everyone, get ready to pack up and move out, we can't be sticking around here for long. I want everything stowed away for later retrieval. Start setting drives aside and get me a prisoner movement detail ready. We'll knock the two out again to move them, so get the anesthesiologist. I want—"

"Sir!"

He turned. To interrupt him like that meant something important was going on. They were professionals. That didn't mean they didn't act like children over the comms sometimes, but for the most part he didn't expect needless buffoonery.

"Sir, caught a group moving toward the main entrance. Um, one of them is standing out in the middle of the road. Mask."

He ran over to the security station and stared. They didn't rely on grimy, low-res cameras for their security. They could count the freckles on someone's nose at lowlight from a hundred yards.

So he got a perfect, high-definition view of the girl who was currently in the interrogation room standing in the middle of the little side road leading to their base. No one should have been out. It was an industrial area after most places shut down for the day.

She hefted a large object up onto her shoulder and grinned the same smile she'd given him when telling him that she would rather die than play any games with the Cabal.

"Volume?" Spin to Win asked.

The technician tugged off his earphones and brought the volume up. The rest of the room was quiet.

"All righty," the girl said. She pulled out two pieces of . . . bread? Why did she have bread, and why was she loading it into her device?

There was a familiar *crunk*, like a toaster's handle being pulled back.

"What is she— Check the interrogation room," he ordered.

The technician brought that feed up.

The girl was in her seat, leaning forward to undo the binding on her legs with . . . where did she get a knife?

"Guards to the interrogation room," he snapped. "You, back on the one outside."

The girl outside was fidgeting, shifting side to side while still holding on to her large . . . whatever it was she was wielding. "Aw, man, now I'm hungry," she said just loud enough to be picked up.

Ding!

Spin to Win winced as the base shook. The camera pointing at the other side of the door was obscured as a cloud of smoke filled the entrance hall just beyond the main door. The door itself, which was a heavy metal thing meant to take a battering ram, was folded in half and shoved into the wall hard enough to crack it.

"Oh," Spin to Win said. Then he jerked upright, adrenaline pumping into him.

"Sir! More Masks are showing up!"

There were. He didn't recognize them offhand, some locals, no doubt. The problem was the number of them currently storming his base's front door.

Spin to Win jumped to his desk and pressed a plain button on his laptop, which had every agent in the room wincing as their earbuds buzzed the alert tone. "All agents to battle stations! We're being attacked," he shouted.

He was going to have to fill out so much paperwork once this was all done.

CHAPTER SIXTY-ONE

An Invitation for Heroism

When Jezebelle got a call from the Boss, she expected . . . well, something like an invitation to patrol, or maybe just an opportunity to chat.

What she wasn't expecting was to have the Boss seethe through the phone, sounding like Jezebelle's own mother that one time she found out that Jezebelle had skipped a day of school to spend time with her then-boyfriend.

The Boss was *angry* in a way that filled Jezebelle with more than a little bit of trepidation.

Once she explained what was going on, though, Jezebelle couldn't help but understand.

Someone had literally kidnapped one of the girls and was holding them in a creepy warehouse. Worse, the girl wasn't the only one who'd been kidnapped. "So, let me get this straight," Jezebelle, now Glamazon since she'd obviously shown up in costume, said. "You've been . . . reforming this Villain?"

"He's not a *Villain*," Owlwatch said. The little owl-themed Hero looked utterly disgusted at the idea. "He wishes he was that scary. No, he's a slightly dark Rascal at best. Nothing scary about him."

"Uh-huh," Glamazon said. "So, you've been reforming him?" she asked again.

The Boss sighed. They'd decided to meet at a bus stop a block over from the location that the Boss knew—somehow—her little companion was in. "He's not a bad sort. A bit lazy, and sometimes a little . . . well, he's a boy. But I don't think he deserves to be raked through the dirt just for being somewhat on the Villainous side."

"Aren't you the one who raked Wrap Up through the coals?" Glamazon asked.

"That was different," the Boss said, without answering to the obvious hypocrisy. Glamazon sniffed, but it really wasn't the time for that. She would have loved to have that debate with her fellow Hero, but it was obvious at a glance that the Boss was just barely holding it together. Her costume looked like she'd dressed in a hurry, and she was fidgeting nervously.

When Glamazon arrived a couple of minutes before, it was to find the Boss pacing with a gaggle of her brats sitting around in the bus stop. There were two of the racoon pests, the bear pest, the owl pest, and one other who hadn't been around last time Glamazon had run into the group. Judging by the lab coat and the (admittedly quite cute) ears, she was another one of the Boss's group of strange animal-themed Masks.

Something was up with that. Maybe one of them had a power that allowed others to gain animal traits? It was the only thing that made sense to Glamazon as an explanation for why so many of them had those characteristics.

It wasn't unheard of for a Mask to have something animalish about them, but this many on one theme was stretching credibility to its limit.

She bet it was the bear girl who had a secondary ability that let others get in touch with their inner animal or something in exchange for a boost to some skills. Or maybe it was the Boss's own power that let her do that? That would make her a powerful force multiplier on any battlefield.

"Okay," the Boss said. "This is the plan. Bandit, you have the gun?"

"We're using guns?" Glamazon asked.

Then Bandit—who Glamazon was certain was a clone maker—pulled out a large gun from one of her dollar-sign bags. It looked like it weighed half as much as the girl and lying barrel down reached up to her waist.

"What the heck is that?" Glamazon asked.

The little racoon-themed bandit raised the gun up and grinned. "It's a toaster!"

"We'll be using it to breach the base," the Boss said. "That's the first step. We break in."

"What's the second step?" Glamazon asked.

The bear girl replied with a vicious grin. "We stomp in and eat them all for being inferior Villains," she said. Her childlike roar would probably have been cute if Glamazon wasn't aware that she could turn into a giant bear without a moment's notice.

"We don't have much of a plan," the Boss admitted. "We're going for shock and awe, I think. Break in, secure Bandit and our . . . friend, then leave. Not all of us are going in, though, not at the start."

"Okay?" Glamazon asked.

The Boss nodded. "Ursa Minor will be going in first after Bandit blows open the entrance. Glamazon, do you think you could send in some of your sparkles, too? I think they're meant to be distracting, right?"

Glamazon nodded. "Then I head in?"

"No, you stay behind," the Boss said. Glamazon bristled. She knew she wasn't as tough as the bear, but come on. "One of Bandit will be going in as well. The rest of us will stay out here until the entrance is cleared out and made safe. Maple here, who is new enough that she doesn't have a Heroic identity, will be providing us with equipment."

"She's a gadgeteer?" Glamazon asked.

The girl, Maple, nodded. She was half hidden behind the Boss's legs, only peeking at Glamazon with one eye. "I, um, can make bombs and stuff."

Any amount of cute sympathy Glamazon had for the obviously shy girl evaporated.

"I think we should have you focus a little more on utility items for now," the Boss said.

Maple nodded. "I made these," she said as she reached into her pockets. She pulled out a set of devices that all looked more or less the same, with an earphone in the middle and some wires around it. It looked like a kid's arts and crafts project gone wrong. "They're quantum-entanglement communicators."

"Quantum entanglement?" Glamazon asked. "As in, they each have a set of linked tunnels going between them? As in, unbreakable communication?"

The girl blinked. "The wires are all tangled up, so yes?"

The Boss picked one of the communicators and shoved it into her ear. Owlwatch did the same. "Hello? Hello!" the Boss said.

"I can hear you even without one of those," Ursa Minor said.

The Boss rolled her eyes. "They seem to be working. Good job, Maple." She patted the girl on the head, which had all the others looking momentarily quite jealous. "All right, we should head out. Bandit, you know your part. We'll hide nearby. Once the door's down, Glamazon, blow up the interior, then Ursa Minor can clear it. Bandit, you go in with her while another you stays with us."

"Got it, Boss!"

A couple of minutes later Glamazon found herself half hidden around a corner, wondering where she'd gone wrong in life, while a pint-size bandit-dressed kid fired supersonic toast at an armored door.

"It's open!" the girl called out, her voice clearly relayed through the device jammed into her ear.

Glamazon stepped out of hiding and flung a brace of her glowing spheres into and through the doorway. Some bounced, others rolled, and a few others simply detonated right away, filling the entrance area with sparkling lights that would disorient and distract.

Then Ursa Minor charged across the space, her sprint turning into a weird four-legged gait a moment before she slipped into the door and turned into a roaring grizzly bear.

"Bandit, what's going on in there?" the Boss asked.

Glamazon actually envied the girl's calm. For someone running such a shoddy operation, the Boss was cool as a cucumber, with the resting face of someone she'd rather not pick a fight with.

"It's full of mooks and goons!" Bandit shouted unnecessarily from right next to them. So the clones shared senses? That made some sort of sense, Glamazon supposed. "Oh, they have guns."

There was a clatter of gunfire, and the girl huffed. Then another Bandit appeared next to her. "Wait, let me try again," a new Bandit said before she took off sprinting into the base.

"This might be a bit beyond us," Glamazon said.

Heroes were strong, sure, but guns were a whole other level of scary. Judging by the ugly look on the Boss's face, she thought so, too. "Maple, do you think you can make anything to help?"

Maple gasped, then started to pull things out of the pockets of her lab coat. In under a minute, she had a small device that was humming ominously. "It's a jammer!" she said proudly.

"For their communications? That's useful," the Boss said.

"Huh? No, it jams their guns."

There was suddenly a distinct lack of gunfire, Glamazon noticed.

"Well, okay then," the Boss said, entirely unphased by how not-possible that was.

"Boss! The big dumb bear's done making a mess of everything, and I'm out of tape!" Bandit called out.

The Boss and Glamazon shared a look, then both of them jogged over to the entrance. Within, they found a panting grizzly bear in an open room, standing atop a shivering pile of men and women in distinctly mooklike uniforms with their arms raised, and Bandit's clone was there, lamenting over an empty roll of duct tape. "We might need to call someone about this," the Boss said as she took in the bullet-hole-covered walls.

CHAPTER SIXTY-TWO

Healpats for All!

Emily rushed to Teddy's side, hands reaching up to her sister's matted fur before she stopped. "You're hurt!" she accused.

Somehow, she managed to read the pout in Teddy's expression. "Just a little bit, Boss, I'm still good to go."

"You were shot, you can't just be good to go," Emily insisted. There was some blood on Teddy's fur, and she was pretty sure it didn't belong to any of the masked people Teddy and Trinity had tossed around. "Where are you hurt? How bad is it?"

Teddy grumbled something about how she was fine, but she didn't protest as Emily checked her over. Emily winced as she plucked a bullet right out of a wound. It was still hot to the touch. It hadn't gone deep, not once it cut past Teddy's thick fur, but it must still have hurt.

"Right, give me a moment," Emily said. "Bandit, I need the first aid kit. Ma— Uh." She paused, aware of the unfriendly ears in the room.

"I'm here," Maple said, saving her the trouble. Maple did have a mask on, but her costume at the moment was composed of her normal clothes and her lab coat.

"Do you have tweezers or something?" Emily asked.

"Hey, now, no one said anything about tweezers," Teddy said.

Emily ignored her. "Tell me where it hurts," she ordered instead. Teddy grumbled, but did her best to point to the spots where she'd been hit. It was difficult, being that she was still a bear, and those weren't exactly as flexible when it came to pointing to themselves.

Emily was mostly worried about what would happen if the wounds closed with the bullets still there, or what would happen if Teddy reverted to her girl form without removing the shells. Fortunately, most seemed to not be deep at all.

"I turned on my Iron Skin skill," Teddy explained.

"That was good thinking," Emily said, proud that her sister had done the smart thing. She tossed the last bullet out, then reached out toward Teddy's head before hesitating. "Six points to Healpats," she said.

She noticed Glamazon's head twitching up, but the other young woman didn't say anything as Emily allocated every one of her Skill Upgrade points into her only healing skill.

Healpats has reached Level 5!
Cooldown reduced to 360 seconds!
Healpats has reached Level 6!
Healing quality improved!
Healpats has reached Level 7!
Cooldown reduced to 300 seconds!
Healpats has reached Level 8!
Cooldown reduced to 240 seconds!
Healpats has reached Level 9!
Cooldown reduced to 180 seconds!
Healpats has reached Level Max!
Healpats' cooldown is now individual among sisters!

Emily stared at the prompt. Level Max already? Then again, the cooldown had dropped to a mere three minutes, and the split cooldowns would be worth a ton for her. She didn't have to hesitate about using the skill anymore.

She rubbed Teddy's head, and a level of tension she hadn't noticed until it was gone melted off the grizzly bear's shoulders. "There, there," Emily said. "All better, right? Does it still hurt anywhere?"

"It's better," Teddy rumbled. "Could use more pats though, yeah, right there, uh-huh, behind the ear, yeah." Teddy's back leg thumped the ground hard enough that Emily could feel the vibrations in her soles.

"Um, Boss," Glamazon said. Emily refocused. "What did you want to do now?"

Emily looked over at their prisoners. She saw half a dozen people in what had to be some sort of minion uniform, all of them looking kind of pitiful while two Trinities fussed over them. The racoon girl had found zip ties and was going around linking hands and feet together like a drunken shibari expert on a power trip. Her youthful cackling didn't help.

"Owlwatch, get in their heads, I need to know what's going on. Ursa Minor, Glamazon, watch the exits." Emily reached over and patted Maple on the head. "I need to know where the tracker is in relation to where we are, and . . . do you think you could do anything about that?" She pointed to the ceiling where a small, fist-sized camera was pointing their way.

"I'll do what I can, Boss," Maple said. "Um. I'm going to need a ladder, though."

"Right, Ursa Minor, give her a hand up if she needs it. Glamazon, can you keep an eye on the door yourself?"

"I'll do what I can," Glamazon said.

Emily left that in her capable hands and turned back around. There was so much to do, and being in the thick of it herself wasn't helping when it came to making it easier to understand what was going on. She walked over to Athena and started to pat the girl's head. It wasn't to comfort Athena, it was to ground herself.

It had been a long time since Emily had had an anxiety attack, but invading what was obviously some sort of Villain base with no backup and less of a plan was certainly not helping with her stress levels.

"Ah, yeah, so," Athena said. She kicked out and thumped one of the guard's shins. The man hissed and glared up at them, but he didn't say anything. "They're not talking. They have orders not to. But that doesn't mean they're not thinking. What do you need to know, boss?"

"Who they are, why they kidnapped my sisters, who's in charge, how many people they have, how long they've been here," Emily said. She paused, then nodded. Those were enough questions for now, she presumed.

"Okay then," Athena said. She squatted down and smiled at the guards. "Time to tell me all your secrets!"

Emily watched as her sister manipulated the shadows, but she was distracted as she noticed Trinity holding up a gun and pointing it at her other self. "Bandit, no!"

"Aww, but, Big Sis, it's broken, so it's trash, so it's ours," Trinity said.

"No, it's just jammed, which— Just put all the guns down in the corner over there," Emily ordered.

She added "gun safety" to the long, *long* list of things she'd have to go over with her sisters one day. The list was frankly kind of daunting, and some of the things on it gave her shivers just to think about.

"Hey, Boss," Athena said. She was holding on to one of the guard's chins. "I know a bunch of things." The men at her feet were shivering and staring out into the corners of the room. Emily kinda felt bad for them, even if they were evil kidnapping minions.

"What do you have for me?" she asked.

"These guys are definitely Cabal," Athena confirmed. "They're, like, paid by the hour. Is thirty-five an hour good?"

"That's, actually, that's not too terrible," Emily said. She was happy that Sam had been left behind to keep their getaway hatchback warm. Emily certainly couldn't afford to pay her that well.

"They get dental, too," Athena continued. "Anyway, they don't know why they kidnapped Bandit and Alea Iacta, but they don't ask a lot of questions. Also, there's a guy called Spin to Win here? Only sometimes he's a girl. I dunno how that works."

Emily cursed, if only mentally. That confirmed that this really was a Cabal operation. The Cabal had apparently sent three of their powered members to Eauclaire. Black Shield, Spin to Win, and one other whose name she couldn't remember without looking at her notes.

"We might have to fight them. Do you know where Bandit and Alea are being kept?"

Athena nodded. "Yup! This place is kind of confusing, but I think I can lead you around with my superior owl senses."

Emily nodded. "Ursa Minor, you take the lead; Bandit, sides; Glamazon and I will take the rear; you, too," she said, patting Maple's head on the way over to the door leading deeper into the base. "We're heading straight for Alea Iacta and Bandit's other body. If we can avoid fighting Spin to Win, then that's for the best."

"Wait, who?" Glamazon asked.

"He's a Mask. I think his power is that he gets new powers whenever he wants, but he can't pick them," Emily said. She could barely remember the things she'd read. Then again, she tended to forget half the stuff she studied when she sat down for a test, and this had a similar mood to it.

"Great," Glamazon said. "Should we be calling the authorities?"

"Camera's down!" Maple said from her spot atop Teddy's back. She let herself drop and slid down Teddy's furry side to land with a clack next to Emily. "I think I broke the entire security system, maybe."

"Good work," Emily said. "Right, let's head out." But before they charged into trouble, Emily muttered a quick, "Family Menagerie, Teddy," under her breath and tried not to make the shift in weight too obvious as she directed her sisters.

Better safe than sorry, she figured.

CHAPTER SIXTY-THREE

Pride Begets Fear

Athena was proud.

Not just of herself, though there was a lot of that, too. She was helping her big sister and her other sisters break into the base of some competing Villains where they beat them up and tied them down. There was nothing quite so Villainous as what they were doing.

She was also really proud of the Boss. Emily had come a long way since Athena was born. Back then, Athena couldn't read people's minds, but she was as smart and observant as any owl ought to be, and she could tell—even if her less intelligent sisters couldn't—that Emily didn't always feel like being a Villain.

Sometimes she came a bit closer, hatching plans and bossing her minions around as a proper Villain should, but other times Emily was too worried about silly, unimportant things, like caring about the law or wanting to send her sisters to school.

Still, today was a big day for Emily, and Athena was proud of her big sister.

"Ursa Minor, push in," the Boss said. She was standing among them, back straight and hat tipped back. She looked like a proper Villain, though maybe not one who should be on the front lines. Athena made sure to stay close, just in case.

"Got it, Boss," Teddy rumbled as she pushed into the next corridor. Trinity followed next, one of her holding a sock that she'd filled with rocks and the other had the toaster rifle up on her shoulders, a piece of bread in her free hand and another between her lips.

"Glamazon, when we reach the next room, Bandit will breach; can you light it up?" the Boss asked.

"I can do that," Glamazon said.

Athena wasn't sure how wise it was to bring the Hero along. She was such an attention-seeking weirdo. Maybe if they were fighting paparazzi they could use Glamazon as a distraction, but they were working against proper Villains here, and having a Hero would just be a distraction.

The Boss wanted her along for a few reasons, though. Like to give their operation some legitimacy when they pretended that it was very Heroic of them to attack another Villain's base. Athena understood, but she felt it would have been better to leave Glamazon behind.

All it took was a glance at Glamazon's eyes to tell that the girl was both afraid and a bit amazed. Afraid of the place they were in (which was just sad; Athena wasn't afraid at all, and she didn't have any exploding-light-balls power to keep her safe) and amazed at how cool the Boss was being.

As they reached a door at the end of the corridor and everyone got into place, Athena spoke up. "This next room is a big one," she said. She hadn't had a lot of time to poke around inside the heads of the mooks they'd captured, but she did have an idea of what the base's layout was.

"How big?" the Boss asked.

"Uh, it's pretty big? There's stairs at the end going up and down. Up is where the control center is, and the cells with Alea Iacta are below. The rest of this level is, like, bathrooms and break rooms and stuff like that. There should be lots of cover and boxes and stuff in this room. I think they have trucks, too?" Athena said.

"How does she know all that?" Glamazon asked with a gesture toward Athena.

Athena sniffed. "I know more things than you could ever imagine knowing, Sparkles."

Glamazon recoiled a bit at that, and Athena grinned. She loved it when people thought she was scary. It made her feel nice and cozy and warm in her chest, like when the Boss was rubbing her head or when she woke up snuggled with all her sisters.

"If they have cars . . . Is there an exit in this room?" the Boss asked.

Athena thought back. It wasn't easy. People didn't *think* the same way as one another. Some people thought in images, others in sounds, and most people had a weird mix of all their senses. She'd read some minds that skipped around all over, and even that wasn't the same from person to person.

Trinity's mind was hard to read because it was constantly filled with so many sensations and feelings and images all at once. Teddy's mind was much simpler. She saw something, she made a conclusion about it, she moved on.

The Boss, on the other hand, looked at everything a million times from a thousand angles, as if every little option she had was superimportant and everything was in danger if she didn't do the right things—and every choice was as important as the last.

Athena imagined that with practice she'd get better at reading minds, but for the moment it was still kind of tricky. "Um, I think there's a big door?"

One of the mooks they'd tied up had had a weird mind, filled with maps and room layouts. Everything in his head was really clear when it came to where things were, but at the same time, each room he imagined was also filled with memories that happened in that space. He had never used the big door, so it was a faint memory, and she wasn't reading his mind at the moment, so it was more like the memory of a memory, which only made things a whole bunch harder.

"Right, so a loading area of some sort. Maybe we can use that as our exit point," the Boss said.

"We're not leaving from the same place we came in?" Glamazon asked.

"I don't see why we should."

"Because we have prisoners there. They could be untied and get away," Glamazon said.

Athena could feel the million and one nervous ideas running through Emily's mind before she made a choice. "It doesn't matter. Our priority is saving our allies first, and capturing Villains second. Is everyone ready?"

"Wait," Athena said. The Boss turned to her. "I think there's traps."

"Traps?" the Boss asked.

Athena nodded. "In, uh, the corridor we need to go down. There's like . . . a turret thing? There's one in the corridor above."

"How are they wired?" Maple asked.

Athena shrugged. She had no idea, and she said so to Maple without meeting her sister's eyes. Maple's mind was scary. Not that Maple herself was scary. She was probably the nicest of Athena's sisters, it's just she had *so many* ideas going on, all the time, and so many of them didn't make sense.

If a normal person's mind was like a billboard in the distance on a rainy day, then Maple's mind was like being pressed right up against the billboard with a pair of spinning kaleidoscopes over her eyes.

"I don't know," Athena said at last. "They're like, big boxes, with a gun in them, that unfolds and stuff."

"That's . . . really not good," the Boss said. "Maple, will your jammer have worked on those?"

"It depends on if they're guns that can jam," Maple said.

"I can just keep running at them until they run out of bullets," Trinity suggested.

"That's so messed up," Glamazon muttered.

"We'll clear the next room first," the Boss said. "Then we'll see what we can do. Ursa Minor, you're up, Bandit, get in there fast, too. Focus on anyone who looks dangerous. Glamazon, are your balls ready?"

"Please don't— Yes, I'm ready," Glamazon said.

They reached the door and everyone tensed up, then Trinity slammed the door open and Glamazon tossed three of her sparkly glitter balls into the room in quick succession. They exploded, and for a moment all Athena could do was stare at the bright, flashy lights before she shook her head and refocused.

Sometimes, Athena wished she was more of a brute like Teddy, so she could run in and beat people up and help that way, instead of being stuck in the back.

Teddy roared into the room, followed by one of Trinity, who also roared, but a lot less impressively.

"Oh, there's people here!" Trinity cheered. She hefted up the toaster, and before anyone could tell her not to, ran into the room while putting some bread into the toaster slots.

"Oh no," the Boss said.

The rest of them rushed in to find the room utterly chaotic. There were some mooks hidden behind a cement barricade who were whacking on Teddy with pieces of wood, and more of them were off in the far end of the room, obviously caught in the middle of loading things onto a van.

That entire operation got disrupted by a very clear *Ding!* followed by the loud bang of the toast gun going off. The toast flew between the mooks and punched a hole through the van and out the front. Trinity cackled.

Glamazon tossed more of her balls around, and then Athena saw one mook rushing at them with a long baton. She laughed as she ran over and dove forehead-first into his gut.

He crumpled and she jumped on top of him and locked eyes with him. He was worried. "I'm going to eat your secrets!" she shouted. And now he was *afraid*.

This, this is what Athena lived for!

CHAPTER SIXTY-FOUR

Spinning But Still Losing

Spin to Win winced as the entire security station went on the fritz.

The computer didn't just stop working, it spat and hissed, sparks flying out of its sides, and then the screen outright burst apart, filling the room with the strangely sweet tang of burning electronics.

"Uh," the agent at the station said.

A moment ago Spin to Win was looking at a rather concerning number of Masks entering his building. Six Masks . . . and a bear. The brutality they employed in taking his people out was concerning.

Seeing what was obviously a gadgeteer at work was even more disturbing. Their guns had all ceased to work at the same moment, and now their security system was well and truly broken.

"Comms are down, too, sir," one of the agents said.

"Dammit," he swore. "Evac. Use the rear exit, they're too close to the front. Someone get to the basement and . . . no belay that. Wipe everything here, then leave. You"—he pointed to one agent–"get out of here, see if you can't contact the HRF. Stall them."

"Yessir," the agent said. They picked up a cell phone and ran out of the room.

He had his own priorities. This attack wouldn't look good on his record, but his superiors were mostly sensible. What was a single Mask supposed to do against such overwhelming odds?

With a disgusted grunt, he stomped out of the control room and into the connected washroom. He locked the door, then hung on to the edge of the sink as he closed his eyes. He spun.

It was more of a metaphorical thing than a literal one. In his mind's eye, everything twisted about, the world spun, and he weathered the sudden vertigo by holding on to the solid sink. His power wasn't the most gentle to use, but it had its advantages.

When he opened his eyes and looked into the mirror, he had a new face.

He stood up straighter, then jumped on the spot a couple of times to unlimber this new body. A woman, with brown hair and pale green eyes. Midthirties, if he was to guess. He was good at that.

He adjusted his new chest, then reached under his coat and pulled his pants up a bit and tightened his belt a notch. One of his secondary abilities made it so that any clothes he wore would change to fit him after a spin. It was why he wore tailored suits all the time as part of his costume. They were more or less unisex while remaining proper for a Mask.

Also, the gadgeteer-made bulletproof vest under his jacket was a bit thick. It was also padded to support some of the changes he went through.

He was well used to changing bodies, what took more getting used to were the powers. He closed his fist and a burst of flame appeared around it. It licked around his skin but didn't feel any warmer than the water he'd use to wash his hands. He felt a little stronger, too, maybe a little more agile.

So a minor physical boost combined with pyromancy. He could work with that.

Spin to Win stepped out of the washroom while tying his now-longer hair back so that it wouldn't whip across his face. "I'm going to the basement," he said. His voice was far different from what he had grown used to, but that was just another change he had to accommodate.

A few of the more green agents gave him some looks, but they'd been informed of his abilities already. Those eyeing him in more leery ways he ignored. It wasn't time for that.

"Do you need an escort, sir?" the head of security asked.

"Come with me, you and whomever you can spare. The rest of you, get moving, we need to evacuate sooner than later. Hurry up now."

The agents moved. Some equipment would no doubt have to be left behind. There wasn't anything to do for it. They at least wiped the drives of the computers. Most of those were equipped with tiny explosive charges that would leave nothing but cinders behind. One agent was moving around and spraying everything with a pump-fed disinfectant sprayer that made the room stink of antiseptics. It would clean off fingerprints and even make stray hairs and skin follicles melt.

Spin to Win didn't want to stay in the room. His lungs were technically brand-new to him, and he didn't want the smell to linger on his costume.

They rushed down the corridor, then down a stairwell that led straight to the basement. The automated defenses down there would . . . actually, he wasn't certain they'd be working at all. Once they reached the bottom floor, he stepped aside and away from the door, then tapped one of the agents on the shoulder. "You go in first," he said.

If the automated turrets had been turned against them, he didn't want to be the one to find out first.

The door opened and the agent wasn't blown off his feet, so they filed in after him. "We're taking the prisoners and leaving," he said.

A partial prize was still better than none.

He almost missed a step as his mind made a sudden and obvious connection. The team of Masks attacking them were local. The Boss and . . . he couldn't remember all the details of the rest. But the two children they'd grabbed had to be part of their team.

They weren't here for Alea Iacta. They were here for the remaining girl, the one who might have planted a nightmare or two.

"Focus on the male prisoner. Leave the girl behind," he said.

No point in forcing the Mask team to turn this rescue of theirs into a chase. Most of Spin to Win's escape vehicles were in the garage right next to the entrance the Masks had used. That meant Spin to Win and his people would have to rely on some of the vans they had parked around the base.

His planning was interrupted as he heard some banging at the end of the corridor. The prison cells were in the center, which meant the Masks were about to be right on top of him.

"Quick!" he snapped before taking off at a sprint down the corridor.

The head of security reached the cells first, fished out a key from his pocket, and unlocked the door, all the while the other agents held their batons and stared at the doorway at the end of the room. It led into the other stairwell, where he was certain the Masks were coming from.

The door to the cell opened, and the head of security grunted as a tiny fist rocketed out of the room and slammed him between the legs.

Spin to Win winced, even if he wasn't currently equipped that way.

"Get trashed, sucker!" the girl who was supposed to be imprisoned said.

He had specifically sent people down to ensure she wasn't freed. Had they been distracted? Did that mean she still had a knife?

The girl tried to run out, but she was tackled by two of his agents. It really took two to keep the pest down. She squirmed and kicked and even headbutted one of his agents in the nose hard enough that the man screamed and his nose bent.

"Get her!" he shouted before stomping into the cell. The boy, Alea Iacta, was halfway out of his bindings when Spin to Win pointed at Alea's face. His hand lit up with orange flames and Alea stopped moving to stare. "You're coming with us," Spin to Win said.

Then, of course, the door at the end of the hallway crashed to the ground with a resounding clang and a bear started to squeeze itself through.

By some lucky miracle, it stayed stuck, its hips too wide to let it pass.

The girl currently being grappled on the floor started to cackle. "Your butt's too big!" she shouted at the bear, who roared back.

Spin to Win wasn't going to waste any time. He grabbed the prisoner by the arm, then touched the bindings holding him to his chair and burned them off. "Move," he said.

The head of security fell into step behind him. He was walking a little crooked, but the worst of the pain had likely passed. "We should evacuate, sir," he said.

"Yes, we shou—" he began to agree, then he felt a strange sensation, like a pulling from somewhere behind his navel that slipped through his body and toward the man he was holding. It felt like the strangest indigestion he'd ever felt.

He let go of Alea Iacta, then smacked the man behind the head.

"Sir?" the head of security asked.

"He tried stealing my luck," he said.

"I think I'll need it more than you," Alea Iacta said. "Trust me, you'd want all the luck you could get, too, if you had to deal with the Boss. I've never even seen her angry and she scares me, man. Now I'm going to owe her so much, and I'm just getting a free rescue. You kidnapped two of her brats."

"Shut up," Spin to Win snapped. He did push him down the corridor faster. The bear was ripping the doorframe apart at the other end, and he didn't want to wait to see what would happen when it got free.

"Oh man, you're a dead man walking . . . wait, weren't you a guy? Why are you hot now?"

Spin to Win glared. This day couldn't get any worse.

CHAPTER SIXTY-FIVE

Toast and Ice Cream

Is it clear?" Emily asked.

Maple nodded. Emily couldn't see her eyes with her mask on, but the way her lips were pursed suggested that the little gadgeteer was taking things very seriously indeed. "It's down now, I promise."

Emily nodded, then gestured to Trinity. "Bandit, want to go in first?"

"You got it, Boss," Trinity said. She gave Emily a sloppy salute, then ran up the final few stairs and into the room beyond.

They were stuck in the staircase just past the prison cells. Earlier, they'd turned a corner and come face-to-face with a large mounted turret that click-clicked ominously as it tried to shoot at them. Since then Emily had been taking things a bit more slowly.

The consequences of that were behind her. An interrogation cell where they'd found two chairs with the remains of ropes left hanging around them. No Alea Iacta. Trinity and Teddy both confirmed what happened, though. He'd been taken by a group of enemy minions and a woman that was probably-definitely a Mask of some sort. She had the domino mask and the strange costume for it.

Had she been faster, they would have saved Alea already. Had she been slower, they might not have any idea of where he went.

Emily set aside the self-recriminations. She had the rest of her life to remember all the embarrassing mistakes she made in full, glaring detail. At the moment she had a job to do.

"It's safe!" Trinity said. There was a clang, and Emily followed Trinity into the room, the rest of her sisters and Glamazon tagging along.

Trinity had tipped the turret over, so it pointed off to the corner. Maple ran over to it, the little device she'd made to turn the turrets off (which she'd cobbled together from two walkie-talkies, some tinfoil, a paper towel roll, and some chewing gum) held close to her chest. Reaching down, Maple patted the turret. "I'm sorry," she muttered.

Emily had the disturbing impression that in the near future they'd be finding all sorts of similar turrets around their base and home.

The room wasn't all that large. There was a staircase leading up to the right, and a door at the end of the room. "Which way?" she asked.

Maple jumped up and looked at her tracker, then she pointed mutely to the door ahead of them.

"Okay. Ursa Minor, get ready to burst through and go full-bear mode. Bandit, one of you on each flank, one stays behind. Glamazon, explosions above, get them looking the wrong way. Owlwatch, if there's someone there, hit them with the full fear blast."

With her instructions handed out, the group moved. Teddy—who was still a little embarrassed about the incident with the doorway earlier—barged through the exit as a normal girl, then immediately turned into a grizzly.

Glamazon was quick to flick a few of her distraction balls through the gap above Teddy, where they exploded and filled the area beyond with scintillating lights.

An alleyway?

Emily waited for Trinity to be through before she followed out, Glamazon right on her heels.

They were definitely in an alley, one just wide enough a car could drive through without too much difficulty.

At the end of the alley was a van with the address and logo of a plumbing company on its side. It was currently crushed into the side of a familiar hatchback. Sam, in a rather normal outfit and without her minion mask, was shouting at one of the mooks from across the roof of her car.

"What do you mean, why was I there? I'm allowed to park here! You were going like fifty out of this alley, that can't be legal! Why're you wearing that stupid hat anyway, huh? Maybe you hit me because you couldn't see?" Sam was shouting to a mook who was shouting at her to get her car out of the way. "I'm not moving until the police show up! I need a report for my insurance!"

Emily pieced things together in a single moment. The Villains had Alea in the van. They'd likely tried to book it out of the alley. Then Sam parked her car at the entrance and the Cabal mooks and Mask had rammed right into it.

From the looks of things . . . well, Emily wasn't an expert of any sort when it came to cars, but usually when the airbags were popped and the car's doors were squished in that badly, the whole thing was a write-off.

The van's side door opened and five mooks stumbled out of it. Then, from the passenger side, came the Cabal's Mask.

Emily's sisters fanned out a little until they blocked off the entire alleyway, with Teddy in the center, Trinity around her, and the rest a little farther back.

"Welp, I'm out of here," Sam said before she ran off.

Emily looked at the group before her, then she locked eyes with the Cabal Mask. If she had to guess, this was Spin to Win . . . maybe. She wasn't certain of that yet.

"So you're the ones causing all this mess?" Spin to Win asked. The Mask stepped up and came to stand next to her mooks. The mooks pulled out simple weapons. Batons and combat knives. No guns, surprisingly. Was Maple's jammer still functioning? "Barely more than a gaggle of children."

"Hey!" Athena said. "We're not a gaggle of anything, ugly."

Spin to Win perked an eyebrow at that. "I'm sorry, child, but you'll find me rather immune to insults aimed at my physicality."

Athena huffed. "He's some sort of shape-shifter. Also, he's actually a guy. Even if he has, like, boobs."

"That's so weird," Teddy, who was currently a bear, grumbled.

"And now that one has become very interesting," Spin to Win said. She—he?—was eyeing Athena in a way that Emily did not like.

So she stepped up and instantly became the center of everyone's attention. Which happened at about the same time as she realized that she didn't know what it was she intended to say. "G-give us back Alea Iacta," she decided on.

It was a nice, fairly neutral statement of intent. They were here for their sorta-friend and her sorta-minion. The Cabal had him, so they demanded him back. Nice and simple as far as social interactions went. Even the implied violence if Spin to Win didn't comply wasn't all that complex as far as subtext went.

"We've lost a fair deal today already, don't push us any more than you have, or you might find your luck turning," Spin to Win said. They snapped their fingers and with a whoosh, both hands were covered in flames.

"Cool," Bandit said. "I want fire hands."

"I could make something that does that," Maple muttered.

Emily would have to absolutely nix that idea later. The last thing she needed was Trinity running around setting dumpsters on fire. Her life was enough of a burning dumpster already.

"We don't want to fight," Emily said. "But if it comes to that, we will win."

The Villain was outnumbered quite spectacularly already.

"Oh, we don't need victory. We just need to escape."

Then things grew really complicated in a matter of seconds.

A pair of fireballs raced across the darkened alley on a course to hit Emily and Glamazon. Glamazon ducked, but Emily was too slow. That was, until Athena shoved her out of the way and she gasped as the warm ball of roiling flames licked past her side.

She stumbled, then glanced toward the Cabal folk just in time to see one of the mooks underhand something in their direction.

It clinked on the ground, a small metal ball that was immediately recognizable thanks to countless movies and games. A grenade.

"Awesome!" Bandit shouted.

She ran forward and scooped up the explosive, then with a wild grin on her face, she ran toward the mooks.

"Toast for the toast god! Death brings glory! I have a bomb!" she cackled as she sprinted all-out toward the mooks, who panicked and turned tail.

Emily gasped and hugged the nearest of her sisters close. She was bowled over a moment later as Teddy brought her down and covered her in smothering fur.

The grenade went off with a teeth-rattling loud bang.

"Oh, I died," Trinity muttered.

Emily blinked and took in the scene. She was hugging Maple, Athena, and one of Trinity close while Teddy stood protectively over them.

"Aww, it wasn't a bomb grenade, just one of those flashy ones," Trinity complained.

"Hey, could use your help here!" Glamazon shouted.

She was flinging her balls of light forward, some of which were expertly intercepting fireballs out of the air and creating those familiar, and very distracting, bursts of light.

The mooks were stunned behind Spin to Win, who was . . . flinging fire out blindly?

"Bandit, get him!" Emily snapped.

Trinity ran ahead with a gleeful yell and launched herself forehead-first into the Villain's gut.

There was a bright flash of flame, and Trinity "popped" away.

The Villain stood, spun, and with a grunt, started to run away.

"Wait!" Emily called out. "Leave him. It's not worth it."

They'd won here. Capturing Spin to Win would just lead to them having to answer a lot more questions.

"Good call," Glamazon said.

"Thanks. Let's tie these guys up, then free Alea. I think we need a break, too."

"Ice cream?" Teddy growled.

That perked all the others right up.

CHAPTER SIXTY-SIX

Yet Another Call

Melanie was almost getting used to being called by the Heroic Response Force to deal with Boss-related issues.

Most new Heroes, or Hero-adjacents, got into a bit of trouble every month or so. In the bigger, busier cities, with an actual Villain presence, there would be more frequent issues, but even then, it was rarely the same person every time.

The Boss and her brats were trying to turn the norm into an exception. Melanie pulled her mask up to rub at her eyes, then tugged it back down. The troopers in the armored van with her made a point of not looking.

Who could blame her for being a little tired? It was nearing supper-time. She should have been in her little flat, eating canned spaghetti, not being shuttled over to some supercrime scene.

The van rolled to a stop, the back doors opened, and the troopers leapt out of the vehicle. Of the six, four carried nonlethals, guns that fired elec-trified nets or large-bore guns that fired beanbag rounds. They had Tasers and pepper-spray cans on their hips. The last two had proper assault rifles, loaded with a mix of tracer, armor-piercing, and hollow-point rounds.

The HRF met violence with violence in kind. A Rogue playing around and landing softened blows while avoiding civilians would get a beanbag to the face. A Villain on a murder spree would be put down like a rabid dog.

That was the price of civilization in an era of Heroes and Villains.

Melanie jumped out last, then she straightened her back and took on the guise of Melaton. She wasn't all that keen on acting the Hero. It took too much energy, and all the other Heroes got from it was some better PR.

She didn't care if her action figures didn't sell well or if her Witter didn't have the most followers. She cared more about getting stuff done. Which had somehow translated into a style of its own that the damned HRF PR reps adored. It was "genuine" and "business-like" in a way that appealed to a certain demographic.

Point was, Melanie climbed out of the van as Melaton, looking like she was about to confront someone who owed her a heap of cash.

What she found was a few warehouses, some smaller factories, and a couple of empty lots nearby. This was the more active, industrial side of Eauclaire, a city that was very much not known for its industry.

A couple of police cars were parked on either end of the street, and a few more HRF vans, too, with white-green lights flashing and lighting up the area even though the sun wasn't down yet.

There weren't many gawkers out, but Melanie knew that would change. The news crews were probably already breaking speed limits to be the first on the scene.

Most of the attention was on a nondescript building in the middle of the street. Just some warehouse made of cinder blocks with a loading door at the front and not much of a yard around it.

A row of men and women were being held to one side. She counted nine of them, in all-black one-piece outfits that made it hard to make out any details about them. Chubby or thin, male or female, it was all hidden by the bagginess. The pile of helmets nearby suggested that there was more to it than just that.

"What in all the damns is that?" she muttered.

"Ma'am," a trooper said as he approached her. It was one of the legal adviser troopers. Lightly armed and armored, with a tablet computer practically fixed to his hands. "We have the, ah, Heroes of the day off to the side. If you want to address them."

"Yeah, sure," she said. He led her, but stayed close enough to talk. "What's the situation here?"

"Multiple calls from pedestrians and passersby, they heard gunshots within the warehouse. One distressed call from a young woman whose car was wrecked, just over there." He pointed to an alley next to the warehouse where a car was, indeed, a write-off. By the looks of it a van coming from the alley had rammed into its side. "We arrived on the scene to find the Boss and her, ah, brigade, as well as HRF-affiliate Hero Glamazon on the scene. They captured a number of suspects."

"I can see that," Melanie said. The Boss had a real gift for finding trouble. "Any idea of the time line yet?"

"Um, no, ma'am. There's a big gap between the call and our arrival," he said.

"Why's that?" she asked.

"Initial reports didn't suggest Mask involvement. The first responders were the police. Um, it's possible that the Heroes here left, then returned."

That was a little weird. "Hmm. Why do you think that?"

"Well, they have ice cream."

When she found the Boss, her many brats (was there another, new one?), and Glamazon, they were all grouped together next to a bus stop. The Boss was straight-backed and looked serious, with her lips in a thin line and what Melanie could see of her brows pressed together. She was holding a chocolate-vanilla swirl in one hand, partially licked.

The kids had ice cream, too, though most of theirs was spread across their cheeks and hands and some on their costumes. The bear girl, Ursa Minor, had her plastic bear mask lifted up so much to eat that Melanie was quite certain she couldn't see anything.

"So," Melanie said as she got closer. "What was it this time?"

The Boss shrugged. "They kidnapped my sis— one of my companions." She gestured to two of the girls, including the one that Melanie wasn't familiar with and who didn't seem to have much of a costume going on except for a half mask and a lab coat. "And a friend, too," the Boss added.

The legal trooper was noting things down, though she knew this was being recorded. "So they kidnapped two kids off the street or something?"

"We were at the dollar store!" Bandit . . . one of Bandit, said.

Melanie rubbed her eyes. There was a lot she wanted to say. The Boss was being something of a thorn. But, on the other hand, how could you tell a young woman not to act to save her own sister?

The fact that at least one of the Boss's brats was her sister was an open secret. Money was on two of the girls being sisters and the other being a family friend who just tagged along. Now there was yet another new girl.

It was common knowledge that Power Day tended to work out best for younger people, but that usually meant teens to young adults, with the average age being something like twenty-one. The Boss and her crew were going to skew the entire statistics on their own at this rate.

The Boss nodded, and Melanie snapped back to attention.

"They kidnapped two of them, yes. We knew where they were since . . . well, keep this between us?"

Melanie touched the trooper on the shoulder, and he paused the recording. She knew he'd start it up as soon as he could. "Go on?"

"Bandit can see through all her . . . selves," the Boss said

Melanie nodded. That wasn't too surprising. A few clone makers could see and sense through their own clones. Usually it came with a downside, like the clones only lasting a certain amount of time, or something like that. In this case, it seemed like Bandit was limited to three identical or near-identical clones of herself. That was probably for the best. The HRF got really twitchy when people had exponential powers.

"We'll keep it to ourselves," she said. "So you knew where they'd taken her. Or one of her, anyway. Why didn't you call it in?"

Glamazon looked to the Boss, then back to Melanie. There was something else, but the girl was being quiet about it. Maybe she could poke later.

"We didn't have time? They have a torture room in there," the Boss said. "We came as soon as we could."

"Right," Melanie said. What kind of mess was all this? "What'd you find in there?" she asked with a gesture over her shoulder to the warehouse.

The Boss worked her jaw while eyeing the building in question, then she turned her focus back to Melanie.

When had she gone from a shy, bumbling girl to someone Melanie wasn't sure she wanted to meet in a dark alleyway? There was something about the kid that had changed, or maybe that had become more obvious since they'd first met.

"Nothing happened that we couldn't handle," she said.

And that was that.

They asked a few more questions, got no answers, and then the girls took their leave, which left the HRF and Melanie with a whole lot more questions to ask.

CHAPTER SIXTY-SEVEN

Definitely the Best Outcome

Jacob jumped as the door to the warehouse he was hiding in opened up, but his heart settled down as voices poured in. Specifically, the excited voices of a half dozen or so girls. "And then she was all, like, 'how'd you do that?' and I was, like, 'because I'm the coolest bear ever.'"

"She didn't say that!"

"She did!"

"I was there, you dumbest bear ever!"

"I was there too!"

"We know!"

Jacob wasn't sure if being rescued by the brat brigade was the best outcome after all. Now he had to deal with the kids being . . . themselves all around him some more. They were insufferable and annoying at the best of times. Maple was all right, though; she was quiet and only wanted to build doomsday devices, which he could sympathize with.

He stepped out of the shadows behind a tall stack of crates and then raised a hand to cover his face from the light shone on him by the girls. "Hey," he said.

The warehouse Emily—or rather, the Boss—had left Alea Iacta in was just a block down from the one he'd been held at, but instead of a group of nefarious Villains this one was mostly filled with crates and rows upon rows of dusty racks.

The lights lowered, and he found himself blinking to adjust his vision to the light. Emily had her phone out, flashlight mode on, and so did Glamazon. For that matter, all three of Trinity had phones with lights on, too.

No one seemed ready to question where the racoon girl had gotten so many smartphones, so he wasn't going to poke at that.

The Boss stepped up to him, then eyed him up and down. He felt a little exposed, standing before her while she checked him out as if he was a side of beef. There was no sympathy in her eyes. "You're okay?" she asked.

"Uh, yeah, I'm fine," he said. "A bit shaken up, but overall, not too bad. How did it go with the law?"

"Well enough. I think there was enough obvious evidence that something was wrong that we won't be suspected of anything," the Boss said.

As soon as they'd scared away that Spin to Win guy (who was, at the time, a woman?—Jacob wasn't sure what was going on there) they'd pulled him from the van and the Boss had gotten her brats to tie up the remaining mooks. Then they'd gone for ice cream. On the way, they'd shoved him into the warehouse he was still currently hiding in.

They didn't even bring him a cone, but he understood well enough. Some of the mooks might talk about him, and so they had to make it seem as if he was never with the "Heroes" in the first place.

If the Boss was asked, she could claim that he got away during the confusion, which had the benefit of being somewhat partially true . . . if he squinted really hard and didn't pay attention to any pertinent details.

"That's great," he said while running a hand through his hair. "I don't know how well my luck would hold out from here on."

Emily nodded. "Right, that's good. We'll get you back home, don't worry. Then you can continue to work on reforming yourself away from a life of Villainy."

He blinked. What was she talking about? Then the Boss very pointedly glanced to the side toward Glamazon, as if trying to say *This is for her.*

He caught on well enough. "Yeah, right. Just, trying to be a good person, you know? Ha ha."

Glamazon stepped over, half her attention on the brats, who started to run around the warehouse like kids on a sugar rush, which Alea imagined they very much were. As long as they didn't start throwing things around and someone kept an eye on Maple to stop her from building anything too dangerous, then they were probably fine.

"We didn't have time to meet properly," Glamazon said. She extended a hand to him, and he jumped a bit before grabbing it for a shake. "I'm Glamazon."

"Uh, hi," he said. He tried on a smile. "I'm Alea Iacta. Um, we kind of met, once before."

"Yes, I remember chasing after you," she said. Her grip tightened and her eyes narrowed. "You were making a ruckus in the middle of the city."

"In my defense, I'd just gotten cool new powers and had to try them out," he said while giving the best "boys will be boys" kind of shrug he could manage. "It was kind of exciting. But I made sure not to hurt anyone."

"Uh-huh," Glamazon said. "And now you're on the straight and narrow?"

"Well, I'm certainly straight," he replied with a grin.

She didn't think he was very funny.

"Look, getting powers was cool and all, but it hasn't exactly made my life simpler. Right now I'm basically on the run from what I think might be a Super Villain organization, and the only one keeping me safe is the Boss. I'm just a guy who's sometimes a little lucky. I guess that luck let me meet the Boss and things have been . . . interesting since."

Glamazon sighed. "Yeah, that's fair."

Emily nodded. "Right, you two keep chatting or whatever. I need to make a call or two. I think our ride home might be scrap, so . . . yeah, it's going to be a walk. Alea, we'll try to find a way to get you back to the, uh, base."

"Cool, cool," he said while the Boss walked off. She was probably going to keep an eye on her sisters, too. "So what's it like, being a big-time Hero?"

Glamazon snorted. She was kinda cute, he noticed, now that she wasn't chasing him through the streets while flinging explosives at his heels. "I'm not a big-time anything. The more time I spend in this business, the more I feel like I'm just a small fry."

"Tell me about it," he said. "I thought my powers were kind of neat, but then, yeah, they're not all that awesome in the end."

"Luck powers seem pretty strong," she said.

"Maybe one day, but right now it feels kind of underwhelming." He'd actually gotten a Skill Upgrade from escaping, but he wasn't sure if it was going to be all that potent a change.

Glamazon nodded. "Yeah, I know what you mean." She glanced over to the Boss, who was wagging her fingers at a group of chastised brats. "Some people get really lucky, you know?"

He laughed. "Oh, please, don't look at her like that. I think she's the least lucky one here."

"Really?" Glamazon asked.

"Would you want to be responsible for all that?" He waved in the Boss's general direction.

Glamazon considered it for a second, then winced. "Okay, fair point. It's a lot of responsibility, and it's probably not all that easy to begin with."

"Yeah. I don't think I'd want to deal with it," he said. "She's not that terrible otherwise. Scary as hell, though."

"The Boss?" Glamazon asked.

"Oh yeah. She's got that, like, . . . repressed madwoman vibe going on. Like she's one bad day from burning the city down."

Glamazon laughed, just a low chuckle that didn't carry much. "You have a high opinion of the Hero who saved you."

Right, he reminded himself that Glamazon didn't know that Emily was a capital V Villain, fledgling criminal empire and all. "She's not a bad sort. Just very intense, I guess."

"Yeah, I felt that too. I thought she was a bit of a pushover at first, but I guess that was all just an act, huh?"

He nodded. That made sense. Emily was pretending to be all shy and anxious, but in reality, she was a stone-cold killer in disguise. It fit everything he knew about the woman. "So, you joining her crew, too?"

"Me? Oh, no, I'm not. This was a one-off. A favor. She needed help so I came along. I'm signed on with the HRF, you know?"

"How's that?" he asked.

"It's okay? They mostly want new Heroes to do patrols and look pretty for the media. It's not great for gaining experience. I think I earned more of that tonight than in all the previous time I spent as a Hero. It's not surprising that the Boss and her brats are so far ahead if this is what they do all the time."

"Yeah, they're a bit wild," he said. "Still, it sounds like a safer job than whatever this is."

"Oh, totally," she agreed. "I'll take my winnings and lie low for a while, I think. But tonight was fun. I'm glad we were able to save you."

"Me too," he said. Then, even though he wasn't feeling particularly lucky, Jacob did something that he usually wouldn't. "So . . . you like coffee?"

She laughed again, then stared at him for a moment. "You know, maybe I do."

"Really? Because I know this great place . . ."

CHAPTER SIXTY-EIGHT

Keeping It Up

Giving her sisters pizza only a couple of hours after feeding them ice cream was probably not the brightest idea, but Emily felt that they all deserved a reward of sorts, and really, she wanted a slice of something greasy and unhealthy for herself, too.

They brought the pizza boxes, still warm to the touch and smelling divine, down into the metro network and over to their little base where Emily set the boxes on the big planning table in the center car.

Paper plates were handed out, arguments were had about who would get how much, and then soon enough, the table was surrounded by munching and moaning sounds as everyone dug in.

"So," Emily said as she lowered her slice, then dabbed at her lips with a balled-up napkin. "Are you feeling okay?"

The question was directed to Alea Iacta, who sat in his usual seat. He shrugged. "I'm all right, I think."

"Yeah, because you wouldn't stop talking to Sparkles," Athena said.

"Ew," Trinity chorused.

"Why is it ew? What's going on?" Maple asked.

Teddy sniffed. "Alea wants to do nature documentary stuff with that Hero the Boss conned into working for us," she explained.

"And that's ew?" Maple's pizza toppings were starting to slip off the crust as she paused to ask.

"Yeah, it's disgusting. At least do that kind of thing with another Villain, come on," Teddy said. Then she stared daggers at Alea across the table. "But not with the Boss. She's too good for you."

Alea shook his head while Emily fought not to tell Teddy off. To be fair, she figured her chances with the opposite sex were slim, and that was before she inherited a gaggle of sisters and the role of sudden single mom.

"Well, I'm glad you're feeling all right," Emily said. "We'll have to figure out a way to prevent what happened today from happening again."

"Maybe he could man up and be less wimpy, then no one would try to kidnap him," Teddy said. She narrowed her eyes at Alea. "Have you ever tried communism? It'll grow out your muscles."

"How would communism make me more muscular?" Alea asked.

"Because carrying the proletariat is hard work. There's a reason that their symbol's a bear, you know, and it's not *just* because bears are the best," Teddy said.

"Is there a place that has an owl to represent them?" Athena asked.

"I don't think so," Sam said. "I know owls are used as symbolism in a lot of places, either for wisdom or evil, but I don't think there's any political group that uses an owl."

Athena sniffed. "Well, that's okay. Evil and wisdom works for me."

Sam laughed. "Maple has it easy; the country we're in uses beavers as symbols often enough."

"Oh, that's nice," Maple muttered.

"What about racoons? What's those mean?" Trinity asked.

"Uh," Sam said. She looked to Emily for help.

"No one's been brave enough to use a racoon as their symbol yet," Emily said. "I'm sure it'll happen one day, don't worry."

"Okay," Trinity said. Then she reached over for another slice and got into an argument with her sisters over who had eaten the most.

Emily turned to Sam. "How about you? Were you in your car when it was hit?"

"Huh? Oh, yeah, but it wasn't bad. Had an ambulance guy check me out. No signs of whiplash. I wasn't really moving and the van didn't have much time to accelerate, so it was more of a bump than anything."

"And your car?" Emily asked.

"A real mess," Sam said. She sighed. "Going to have to shop for something else. But the big pro is that I splurged for superinsurance last month, just in case. Cost a heap, but it should cover everything. Got some papers from the HRF and police and everything. Even got a pat on the back for kind of helping."

"That's good," Emily said.

Sam nodded. "Gonna get myself something a bit bigger. Maybe a minivan?"

That would be nice, Emily thought. A car with enough room for all her sisters to sit in would be a huge boon.

Emily nodded, then she considered what to say next. She was at the head of the table, and that came with a certain level of expectation. She settled on praising her sisters. They'd done surprisingly good work, and they could use the reinforcement. The last thing she wanted was for them to turn into actual Villains just because she didn't give them the attention they deserved.

"So," Emily said. "I wanted to congratulate you all. Alea, well done making it back; Sam, thanks for the sacrifice you made. That was some quick thinking, and it certainly helped a ton."

"No problem, Boss," Sam said.

Emily turned to Teddy, who blinked back. "Teddy, you did really well tonight."

Teddy's cheeks warmed up. "Ah, well, just doing my job?"

"I know, but you were very brave, and I'm proud of you," Emily said. She injected as much sincerity as she could into the words. It helped that they were true. "I know that protecting your smaller sisters is your 'job' but that doesn't mean I'm any less proud of you for doing it so well."

"Yeah!" Trinity cheered. "Even when your butt's too big."

"Even despite small issues, yes," Emily said.

Teddy puffed her chest out. "Yeah, I'm pretty awesome," she said. It didn't hide the redness to her cheeks though.

Emily smiled, then turned to Athena. "You too. You've been invaluable whenever we head out and do something. Not just because of your powers, but because you're a quick thinker."

Athena grinned back. "Thanks. I'll continue being the smart one, no worries, Big Sister!"

"Uh-huh," Emily said. "Trinity, you did extra good today too. You might have taken a few . . . unnecessary risks, but everything worked out in the end, and I'm happy to see that you're safe and sound."

"I'll always be fine," Trinity said.

"It wouldn't hurt to be a little more careful," Emily said. Mostly, the thing it wouldn't hurt was her own anxiety levels. "Just think about it, okay?"

"Okay!" Trinity agreed.

Emily figured the raccoon girl would spend a tenth of a second longer considering whether or not to look down both sides of the street before choosing not to next time, but it was a (tiny) step in the right direction.

"And, Maple, without your tracker, and without the tools you made, we wouldn't have been able to save Alea at all. I know you're the newest little sister here, but your help has been invaluable already!"

Maple didn't reply, except to blush up to her roots and stare at the table while waiting for the attention to leave her.

Emily was more than willing to help out her favorite introvert in that regard. "So . . . I'm thinking . . . group hug as a reward?"

"Heck yeah!" Teddy said.

"Cuddles!" Trinity cheered.

Emily coughed as she was charged into by her sisters. Even the rather shy Maple joined in, though only on the edge.

"Okay, okay," Emily said. She patted heads and rubbed backs until the hug was over.

She wouldn't admit it, because it was rather embarrassing, but she was growing rather fond of that kind of simple physical affection. It felt nice in a way she had a hard time articulating.

"You did good, too," Athena said once she was free. She half turned and slapped Trinity's hand away from her paper plate without looking. "Breaking into a Villain's lair, beating up their mooks, stealing a kidnapped ally? That's some top-grade Villain work!"

"Yeah!" Teddy added. "Plus you convinced Sparkles to work for you. That'll set up a really cool reveal later."

"Oh, we need to find a huge pit to do the reveal next to," Athena said. "Or a lava moat."

"Trash heap," Trinity suggested. "Like, the hugest one ever. And we do the reveal in a helicopter above it."

"I could build a floating platform," Maple muttered.

"Okay, girls," Emily said. Their enthusiasm was nice sometimes, but less so at other times. "I don't think we need to, ah, worry about that kind of stuff, okay?"

Athena nodded. "Yeah, we know you're, like, ten steps ahead of all of us in terms of Villainy. That's what makes you the best Big Sister."

Sam was grinning way too hard at that pronouncement.

"Right, yeah," Emily said. "Anyway, we still have a lot of work to do, including cleaning up for today. So make sure there aren't any leftovers, okay?"

That produced another cheer, and she desperately hoped that the energy her sisters had right now was a last gasp of manic energy before they all crashed, because she couldn't deal with them being this hyper once they got back to the dorms.

"What's the plan from here on out?" Sam asked.

Emily considered it for a moment. "I think . . . well, we'll continue to do what we've been doing. Earn more money, gain more influence, try not to get into too much trouble, and maybe I'll have enough time between all that to do my homework and get decent grades."

CHAPTER SIXTY-NINE

Sugar Rush Crash

They made it back home before the girls finally started to crash.

Emily was relieved; the level of energy her sisters had displayed was just a bit too much for comfort, even if they probably deserved to be a little more energetic than usual.

They arrived and Emily immediately ushered her sisters into the bathroom one at a time for showers while she set out changes of clothes for them. There wasn't even that much grumbling about it, though she did curse the lack of space in her drawers.

Emily didn't have too much, clothes-wise, but the jeans and loose hoodies she liked took up space, and they were competing with all her sisters' stuff.

Soon, very soon, they'd have to find a new place to stay. It probably wasn't healthy to have them all stuffed into this one room anyway. Maybe it would be a good idea to revisit using Cement's barrackslike dorm base that Alea had shown them.

Once everyone was showered and yawns were being shared around freely, Emily sat on her chair cross-legged, with Maple up on her lap where she could idly play with the beaver girl's still-wet hair.

"So," Emily said. "Did anyone get any improvements from that?" she asked.

Her Queen quest line had improved once after the day's fiasco, giving her a new Skill Slot point. A few other minor quests had gone off, too, earning her a whole three new Skill Upgrade points.

It didn't feel like a great reward considering the amount of risk they'd been in, but she wasn't going to complain. She had to go over her quests and pick out new ones, but at the moment she was feeling rather lazy about it.

Her sisters replied with a chorus of yeses. "Anyone feel like upgrading skills before bed?" Emily asked.

"Who goes first?" Teddy asked.

"I think last time it was Athena first?" Emily asked. She was about 50 percent sure of that. "Which means this time it should be Trinity first, right?"

"Yeah!" Trinity cheered, then all three of her paused midcheer to yawn.

Emily didn't say anything, but she thought it was kind of cute. "So, want to see what new ability you get? Then it'll be Maple's turn, then Teddy, then Athena, right?"

She got a bunch of nods and no complaints.

She loved her sisters so much more when they were tired.

"Ohhh," Trinity said. "I got two new skills and a heap of points for stuff."

"Two?" Teddy said. "I only got one."

"She was kidnapped," Athena said. "Maybe that helped?"

Teddy snorted. "Please, I could get kidnapped, like, supereasily."

"Girls, please don't get kidnapped on purpose just to earn points," Emily said. Maybe she didn't love her tired sisters more.

"Got my first one," Trinity said. "Did you wanna see both at the same time or, like, one at a time?"

"Um, one at a time is fine," Emily said.

Trinity nodded, then grinned. "It makes me more better at spying and stuff. See?" She showed off her new skill, the screen she summoned large enough for everyone to read.

Racoon-aissance
Eternal Racoon Hurricane
Level 1
The user can now triple the perceptive senses of one of their bodies as long as that body is separate from its others.
Activation: Thought
No Cooldown

"Huh," Emily said. "That actually seems really handy. Improved senses are nice." Her own sense-improving skill had come in handy already, and this one seemed better, if less flexible.

"Yeah, I can make a third of myself three times more good, which is, like, uh, that's one hundred and sixty-six percent better?"

Emily wasn't sure about that math, but she wasn't going to pull out a calculator without having to. "That's great," she said.

Trinity grinned, big and proud. "Yeah, got another one. It's like an Athena skill."

Athena's head whipped around, and she narrowed her eyes at Trinity. "Lemme see," she demanded.

Hide and Cheek
Eternal Racoon Hurricane
Level 1
The user can convince anyone who notices them that they are not attempting to hide, spy, or otherwise infiltrate the area. This does not assist in convincing a party that the user is meant to be in the location.
Activation: Vocal
Cooldown: Thirty Minutes

Emily read the skill's description, then reread it to be sure. That was . . . a very bizarre skill. "That's, um, interesting."

"Ain't it?" Trinity asked. She raised her arms in a cheer, then all three of her flopped backward onto the bed. "Okay, Maple's turn."

Maple bounced on her spot on Emily's lap. "My turn? Oh, um. I only got the one."

"That's fine," Emily said.

Maple nodded, then her brow knit together as she thought. "Okay, here," she eventually said while shyly showing Emily the results of her work.

Approximate Gnawledge
Sticks and Stones
Level Max
The user gains approximate and temporary knowledge about any subject related to an item they are building.
No Cooldown

"I, ah, have two points, too," Maple said. "For upgrading. But I can't use them yet."

"That's fine," Emily said. This was the first time she'd seen one of her sisters get a maxed skill before. It . . . probably didn't mean anything though. She'd poke around online if she had time to visit a library. The skill itself seemed useful, except for the vagueness of "approximate."

Emily wasn't an expert, but she was under the impression that approximates and careful engineering didn't mix well.

"Does it roll around to me now?" Teddy asked. "I kinda spent all my upgrade points though."

"Yeah, I guess so," Emily said.

Teddy grinned. "Yeah, awesome! Here's what I got!"

Harder Better Fatter Stronger
WereBear
Level Max
The user can, at will, manipulate their weight, mass, and musculature while transformed.
Activation: Thought
Cooldown: One Hour

"That sounds superstrong," Emily said.

"I will be superstrong!" Teddy said. She flexed her bicep, which didn't do much through her loose bear-print PJ's.

"I'm last then," Athena said. "My new skill's nothing too impressive."

Scowl
Owl Seeing Eye
Level 1
The user can make anyone who lies to them feel discomfort. The more the subject obfuscates the truth, the more the discomfort grows. Does not otherwise assist the user in sussing out the truth.
Activation: Visual
No Cooldown

"I disagree," Emily said. "This sounds pretty strong."

Athena smiled a little. "It's okay," she said.

It wouldn't let Athena know when someone was lying, but it would give her another lever from which to apply pressure on people in tense situations, which was what Athena's powers were all about.

Emily clapped. "Okay, that's everyone then? Time for bed?"

"Hey!" Teddy said. "I'm not one to avoid bedtime, but what about you, huh?"

"Ah," Emily said. She had one skill to unlock, but at the moment it was acting as a buffer between her and her next sister. "I can wait until tomorrow," she said.

Athena fixed her eyes on Emily, and she immediately felt a twist in her gut, as if she was stepping on a stage and a thousand eyes were on her.

"Athena," she warned.

"Oops," Athena said.

"But . . . fine, let's see what I got," she said. In the end, it was only fair. Besides, a bit more time with a new skill might help Emily figure out how to use it.

All it took was a thought to bring up the appropriate question.

Do you wish to spend a Skill Slot point on the Power: Sister Summoning?

"Yes," Emily muttered,

New Skill unlocked!

Center of Attention has been added to your Power's Skills!

She did not like that name, not one bit. With a quick thought, she opened her status screen, taking note of the new skill wedged at the bottom of it.

Name: Emily Wright	
Alignment: Villain	
Alias: The Boss	
Level: 1	
Powers	
Sister Summoning	
Create Sister	Rank 9
Sisterportation	Level 1
Double Trouble	Level Max
Healpats	Level Max
Triple Threat	Level Max

Menagerie Family	Level 1
Quadruple Quirkiness	Level Max
Center of Attention	Level 1
Points	
Power Slots: 0	Skill Upgrades: 0	Skill Slots: 0

She tapped the last skill on the list, which opened a new box for her to look at.

Center of Attention
Sister Summoning
Level Max
Allows the user to temporarily become the center of attention, dragging all focus onto them as long as they are delivering a stern warning or monologue.
Activation: Vocal Command
Cooldown: One Hour

"What'ch'a get?" Teddy asked. "Is it good?"

"Are we going to have another sister?" Athena asked.

Emily rubbed her face. Her powers clearly hated her. This was pretty much exactly the opposite of what she'd want as a skill. And the description . . . a warning or a monologue? That was pure Villain talk.

"Here, you can look," she said with a dejected sigh.

Her sisters were overjoyed with the skill, going on about how Big Sis would have to practice proper monologuing and how she could use it to scare Heroes.

Emily set Maple down, flicked off the lights, then went to bed. At least she wasn't cold at night, being covered by a heap of snoring brats.

Epilogue

"Trinity, fingers out of your nose. And, yes, I mean all fingers, even the ones from your other bodies. Teddy, strutting around with your chest out is cute and all, but remember to look where you're going, you almost tripped twice already. Athena, remember not to turn my parents paranoid, please. Maple . . . um, don't be afraid to say hi to Mom and Dad, okay?"

She had to scramble for that last one. It wouldn't do to tell all the other sisters off and not have anything to say to Maple.

So far, though, despite her terrifying abilities, Maple was the quietest of her sisters, and Emily was entirely appreciative of the fact.

She and her brat pack of sisters were heading to Mrs. Headerson's place. The kindly teacher had said that she didn't mind Emily using her place as a meeting point for her and her parents, and she was used to dealing with Emily's sisters.

Besides, having them come over to play instead of getting lessons would be good for them, and for Steffie, who'd taken a liking to the girls even if they tended to get her into a heap of trouble all the time.

Emily suspected that Heather was mostly just happy for the almost normalcy her sisters brought to Steffie's life. The girl's only companion was her mom, which wasn't terrible, but she did need to make proper friends, and Emily's sisters counted, even if they were the "bad influence" sort of friends.

"Okay, we're crossing the road here," Emily said. "Which means . . ."

"Look both ways," Athena said.

"Hold the Boss's hand," Teddy added. She grabbed Emily's right hand before any of the others had time to swipe for it.

"Play dead," Trinity said.

"No to that last one," Emily said. "Okay, everyone grab one of your sisters' hands, yes, that's right. No, Trinity, all three of you need to be holding on." Once that was done, she made a big show of looking both ways, then waited for a car to rumble past, even if they probably had plenty of time to cross in front of it.

It was the principle of the thing. And besides, if one of the girls tripped or something, she'd need to untangle herself, stop, pick them up, then run back to safety. She suppressed a sigh. It used to be that jaywalking was an easy crime.

Mrs. Headerson's house had a familiar car parked out front, Emily's mom's old beater as opposed to her dad's pickup.

She checked her sisters one last time, brushed some lint off her skirt, then walked over to Mrs. Headerson's front door and let Teddy ring the doorbell (but only once) since it was her turn.

The door opened, revealing the teacher and Emily's mom. "Hey," Emily said.

They filed into the house and exchanged the usual pleasantries and a few quick hugs. Once her mom gave her a hug, all her sisters insisted on getting their own; even the otherwise shy Maple walked over and quietly raised her arms.

"Come on, your dad's in the living room," her mom said.

Emily nodded and followed her. She wasn't sure why she had a tiny pit in her stomach. Her dad was one of the kindest people she knew.

He was standing in the living room, a big guy with a bit of a gut with a plate of triangle-cut sandwiches in one hand who somehow looked surprised despite all the noise they'd made on arriving. "Em," he said before setting the plate down on the coffee table. Then he smiled and raised his arms.

Emily walked into the hug and returned it as best she could, but her dad was a head and a bit taller than her and he more engulfed her than hugged her.

"So, these are my new girls, huh?" he asked.

"Hey, old man," Teddy said, making exactly the kind of first impression Emily didn't want her to make.

He laughed. "You must be Teddy, right? Come here." He got to one knee and was still taller than any of her sisters.

They got through the introductions with surprising ease. Each sister got a hug and a pat on the head, and he didn't comment when Trinity stole one of his sandwich triangles and started to nibble on it right there.

"Hey!" Steffie said as she rolled into the room. "You're here!"

"Girls, why don't you all go play in Steffie's room while the adults talk?" Heather asked. "But no leaving the house. You remember the rules, right?"

Soon enough the entire gaggle, plus Steffie, were making a mess and plenty of noise as they crossed the home toward the girl's room.

"Cute kids," her dad said with the tone of someone who had absolute certainty in what they said.

Emily felt a weight coming off her back. "Yeah, they can be when they want to."

He nodded. "You doing okay?" he asked.

"I am," she said.

He nodded again, and that was that. He always took her at her word and didn't mince his own.

"Are you certain, sweetie?" her mom asked. "You have a lot on your plate, and now with Maple, too, that just adds to your workload, doesn't it?"

"It's not so bad," Emily said. "We've been keeping a low profile, and with Sam's help we've started to earn a bit of money. We're starting this advertising thing, and I'm looking for another place to stay. The dorm isn't big enough for all of us."

"That's nice," her mom said. "You're not doing anything dangerous then?" she asked.

Emily considered what to say, then settled on a comfortable lie. "Nope."

"In that case, sweetie, why are you on the news?" her mom asked with a gesture past Emily's shoulder.

She turned and saw herself and her sisters on the TV, standing next to that warehouse she'd saved Alea from. The headline crawler at the bottom of the screen was Daring Rescue in Eauclaire Villain Hideout!

"Well, uh, I can explain."

About the Author

RavensDagger is a Canadian writer who wants to make people smile. The best way to do that, he has found, is by pecking away at the keyboard and hoping for the best.